DEEP SHELTER

ALSO BY OLIVER HARRIS

The Hollow Man

DEEP SHELTER

A Novel

OLIVER HARRIS

BOURBON
STREET
BOOKS

An Imprint of HarperCollinsPublishers
www.harpercollins.com

First published in Great Britain in 2014 by Jonathan Cape

FIRST U.S. EDITION

Library of Congress Cataloging-in-Publication Data has been
applied for.

ISBN 978-0-06-213672-5

14 15 16 17 18 OV/RRD 10 9 8 7 6 5 4 3 2 1

Everything secret degenerates.

Lord Acton

HE WAS TRYING TO GET A MOMENT'S PEACE WHEN THE car appeared. Monday 10 June, end of a hot day. The city had started drinking at lunchtime and by 3 or 4 p.m. crime seemed the only appropriate response to the beauty of the afternoon. Belsey's shift had consisted of two stabbed fourteen-year-olds and a disgruntled customer attacking his local pub with an electric drill. At quarter to five he felt his contribution to law and order had been made. He parked off the high street, sunk two shots of pure grain vodka into iced Nicaraguan espresso and put his seat back. In an hour he'd be off duty, and in a couple more he'd be on a date with an art student he'd recently arrested for drugs possession. All he had left to do, so he thought, was avoid getting any more blood on his suit.

The BMW tore into view before he'd taken a sip. There was a screech of tyres; someone screamed. Belsey watched it skid around the corner of Heath Street, almost tipping onto two wheels. Pedestrians dived off the crossing. A taxi swerved to avoid it, drove through the window of Gap Kids.

Belsey stuck his sirens on. He jammed his drink in the holder and swung back onto the high street, lifting his radio.

"Got a pursuit: silver BMW heading south on Rosslyn Hill. Possible injured up by Hampstead tube."

Still no other sirens. Belsey sighed, raised his seat and took his own car over sixty. The force owned good Skodas tweaked for high-speed driving. This wasn't one of them. He could hear the control room trying to scramble back-up, but no one was nearer than a mile away. You and me, he thought. He kept tight with the car as they approached Belsize Park. It looked like the driver was alone.

The BMW stuck to the high street. Which was odd. There were emptier roads if he wanted an escape but the driver had a plan, or liked having an audience. Or he didn't give a fuck, was high, having the time of his life; sun's up, steal a car. Belsey waved for him to pull over. It was optimistic. They crashed through a set of red lights at the junction with Pond Street and Belsey knew someone was going to get killed. He prepared to abandon the pursuit. Then the driver braked.

The BMW skidded straight over the crossing. Belsey veered to the side, clipped a minibus and swung to a stop twenty metres further down the hill. He grabbed his cuffs as the BMW's door opened and a white man in black gloves jumped out. The driver pulled up a hood, grabbed a black rucksack from the car.

"Pursuit on foot," Belsey radioed. "Belsize Park."

The man barged through pedestrians. But he was off home ground, it seemed: he sprinted into an alleyway at the side of Costa Coffee. Belsey knew it was a dead end. He took the clip off his spray and turned the corner.

Something swung towards his face. Belsey lifted his arm. Metal slammed into his elbow and then his left cheek. He turned, dropping the spray, blinded with pain. He heard the man run deeper into the cul-de-sac. Belsey made sure he was still blocking the only way out. He extended his arm. It worked. He had vision. He picked up his spray and turned back to the alleyway, face throbbing.

"Police! Come out with your hands in front of you!"

The alleyway ended at a patch of concrete behind the coffee shop. It was sometimes used for parking, with space enough to squeeze in three or four cars. But no one was parked there now. There was no suspect either, just weeds fringing cracked tarmac.

"Come out slowly. I can see where you are."

Nothing moved. The empty space was blocked at the end by a small brick building. No way in, blank metal panels blocking what must once have been a doorway; no handles on them, no lock. Belsey pushed and they were sealed shut. The building had no visible windows, nothing anyone could get through. It was flanked by high fencing, topped with rusted barbed wire. The fence wasn't climbable. It divided the parking area from junk-strewn brambles. Even if you could climb the fence, there was nowhere to go, and Belsey would have heard the chain-link rattle. The man had disappeared.

THE CAVALRY ARRIVED A minute later. Belsey went back to the main road and saw a lot of flashing blue lights and his colleagues disembarking, less brightly, wiping sweat and staring at the minor pile-up in the road.

"He's gone," Belsey said.

"You lost the guy?"

"You off the pace, Nick?"

"Get a look at him?"

"He had his hood up," Belsey said. "Pretty sure he was white. In a dark grey hoodie. He had a rucksack. And gloves, I think. Was anyone hurt, up by the station?"

"Nothing serious. You reckon he was in gloves?" They squinted at the sun. "Where did he go?"

"Down beside the coffee shop. It doesn't lead anywhere."

His colleagues wandered into the alleyway, turning their radios down. Belsey assessed the moment of drama preserved in the road: his car and the BMW each with their driver's door thrown open, black lines scarring the tarmac behind them. He thought of the sudden stop. And then the sense of purpose that led up to it. The driver knew where he was going.

Belsey reached into his own car and shoved the vodka under the passenger seat. Then he called the control room and ran a check on the BMW. It had been reported stolen three days ago, taken from outside a house in Highgate. Belsey stepped into the Costa. A barista asked for his order.

"The parking lot at the back, does that belong to you?"

"It's not ours."

"Do you know who owns it?"

"No."

His colleagues emerged back onto the high street, shrugging. Their first thought would be that he'd fucked up somehow. They would suspect him of getting it wrong: intoxication, imagination, heatstroke. He walked past them, back into that closed stub of world and searched for CCTV. There were few corners of London so unloved that no one filmed them. Sure enough, mounted high on one of the fence's struts was a fixed camera, angled to cover the bare space. It was weather-beaten but looked in working condition. *Protected by Stronghold*, a sign beneath it announced. Stronghold gave a London telephone number.

Belsey called it. No one answered. He searched for Stronghold on his phone. There were no security companies with that name.

He ran a search on the phone number itself. It didn't link to anything about Stronghold, but was offered as the maintenance contact number on a smart-looking page for an organisation called Property Services Agency. According to its website, PSA managed facilities for the UK government and armed forces.

Belsey turned towards the empty lot. He stared at the bleached cans and broken furniture in the weeds, the back of Costa, finally the building which sealed the alley shut. This structure was odd, he saw now. The ground floor was perfectly round. The floor above it formed a square tower with ventilation slats.

Belsey peered through the chain-link fence at the side. A tall brick outcrop to the building jutted into the brambles. This did have something that looked like it might once have been a window, but it was boarded up now. He stepped back and appraised the structure as a whole. It possessed an air of seriousness. Something began to play at the edges of his memory.

Belsey walked two minutes down the high street. He found an identical structure on the corner of a residential road, the same round base and a ventilation tower on top of it, only this one was painted entirely white. Years ago he had asked one of the older Hampstead CID officers what it was and promptly buried the answer. He had passed the building a thousand times since and not thought about it again. The structure sat behind tall gates. Through them, Belsey could see an entrance to the tower, sealed by black mesh with a bright yellow sign: *DANGER: DEEP SHAFT.*

MOST CID OFFICERS WERE IN THE CANTEEN WHEN he got back. Belsey checked the swelling on his face and took a paracetamol. He bought what passed for a coffee and joined the noisiest table: Detective Constable Derek Rosen, oldest on the team, was working solemnly through a plate of chips. DC Rob Trapping, twenty years less worn, had come in for an evening shift armed with Ray-Bans and a handheld electric fan. With them were Wendy Chan and Janice Crosby, civilian stalwarts who managed the front desk. They were all talking about a new detective sergeant who had apparently arrived that morning.

2

Belsey waited, wondering why he was the last to hear about these things. In a lull he said: "Up on Haverstock Hill there's a round, white building. On the corner of Downside Crescent." The group turned to him.

"The old bomb shelter," Rosen said.

"Bomb shelter?" It was coming back to him. "There's another one behind Costa," Belsey said.

Officers at an adjacent table turned, ready to be amused. They were familiar with Belsey's tangents. DC Derek Rosen, being the station's elder states-man, held up a fat hand.

"It's not another one," he said. "It's another entrance to the same shelter." He leaned back and wiped the ketchup from his mouth. Rosen liked the War. He started wearing a poppy in September. "In case one of them is hit when you're down there," he elaborated.

"That would make it about half a kilometre long," Belsey said.

"It is."

"There's one in Camden as well," Crosby added.

"Where?"

"Behind Marks & Sparks."

"How many are there?"

"There's a few about," Rosen said. "Five or six in London, maybe more."

"What are they used for now?"

"*Used* for?"

"Someone's looking after them," Belsey said. "The Belsize shelter's still got a camera on it. What's down there?"

There was silence, a few shrugs. No one knew.

"Why?" Rosen asked.

"The guy I was chasing, I think he might have gone in."

This provoked laughter alongside a more considered scepticism, but no more information. Talk turned to cold beer and evening plans.

Belsey wanted to go down.

He'd need a warrant. If he could prove his man entered, hit a police officer, was an ongoing threat . . . One problem was that, technically, Belsey was meant to be on restricted duties. He'd misbehaved last year, toying with some minor identity theft, and this was his punishment: sit back, do the grunt work, don't chase. Then he remembered the conversation he'd walked in on. If there was a new sergeant he might be able to take advantage, hustle authorisation before they caught up with his dubious credentials.

"What do we know about the new Sarge?" he asked.

"Fit," Trapping said. He aimed his fan in Belsey's face. "Chilli hot, my friend." The rest of the table shook their heads. Trapping winked. He was the kind of officer Belsey admired: untroubled. Twenty-four, six foot four, and a police detective, confident that these facts were good news for himself and society.

"She's meant to be very good," Crosby said.

"I didn't think we were getting anyone."

"We decided, if we stopped paying you, we could afford the Sergeant." Rosen dropped a chip into his mouth.

"What's her name?"

"Kirsty Craik."

"You're joking."

Belsey went up to the CID office. There was something different, and after a few seconds he realised what it was: the place *felt* like an office: an air of quiet industry, of paperwork being dutifully completed. Detective Constable Adnan Aziz winked, then nodded to the corner office. Belsey knocked on the open door. A woman with a blonde ponytail looked up and smiled coolly.

"Nick."

"Kirsty."

Kirsty Craik stood up, smoothing her skirt. She offered

her hand and seemed aware that it was an odd form of greeting after their last physical contact. Belsey tried to ignore a
pang of nostalgic lust.

"How are you doing?" he said.

"Good. I heard you might be around."

"I'm told it's expected of me. It's nice to see you."

"Yeah?"

"Of course."

Craik didn't look too fazed. Here was that law of nature
that gathers up the indiscretions you've left behind and
strews them in front of you. They did the split-second rou-
tine: checked each other's bare ring fingers, apportioned
guilt.

"So, take a seat," she said. "What are the chances?"

"Moderately high, I guess. It's a small police force."

"Smaller by the day. What happened to your face?"

"Straight in with the insults." Belsey smiled. Craik rolled
her eyes. "I was chasing someone. They didn't like it so they
hit me."

"Are you all right?"

"Never felt better." He had felt better. And he had looked
better, he realised. Craik, though, looked in good shape,
even after another few years in the force. She still had the
blue eyes, wet and bright. They could make her seem startled
when she was just thinking. He'd learned that. He'd been
assigned to mentor her during the twilight days of his posting at Borough station. She was new to CID; he was a few
weeks away from nearly being sent to jail along with half the
officers on the team. So Kirsty Craik got a slightly unusual
introduction to detective work.

"Where've you been?" Belsey asked.

"Most recently, Kent. Kent CID." She didn't expand on the journey that had brought her to Hampstead police station. Maybe his bosses saw an officious, straight-A new blood; someone they could push around. Belsey looked at Craik and didn't see that at all. He made a vow that he wouldn't try to sleep with her this time.

"I heard Hampstead was nice," she said.

"Idyllic."

She hesitated.

"I need to get my feet under the desk and all the other clichés. Are you in tomorrow?"

"Yes."

"Let's talk more then." She glanced across her paperwork, unenthusiastically.

"Want to pass some jobs my way?"

"Well, seeing as you ask . . ." Craik selected a duty sheet and handed it over. She seemed only slightly uncomfortable with this exchange of roles. "Looks like it's been sitting around for a while." Belsey skimmed it and felt disappointed.

"Break-in at St. Pancras public library?" he said.

"Third this month."

"That's the literacy drive paying off."

"It sounds like someone in the council's getting a bit upset. Maybe this is a north London thing, I don't know. Want to give it a look?"

"Of course." Belsey pocketed the sheet. He had been hoping for something more high-end. This killed the reunion a little. "Consider it done."

When he was halfway out of the door, he turned back.

"Kirsty, this is a bit of a long shot—the guy who hit me, I've been trying to figure out where he went. Near where I lost him, there's a deep-level bomb shelter, built in the Second World War." He paused to gauge her reaction. She didn't even blink. "I think he might have gone in. I want to take a look inside, eliminate it as a line of inquiry. I think it would be easy enough, I'd just need a warrant."

"A warrant on what grounds? That he disappeared close by?"

"Exactly."

"Who owns it?"

"I don't know. There's a camera there, belongs to some government firm, so I guess it used to be the government, maybe a subsidiary of the government."

"You want to get a warrant on government property but have no evidence that it's involved in a crime?"

"I'm not sure who owns it now. It looks disused."

"OK, Nick. I'll think about it. I'm not sure we're in a warrant situation here."

"I guess not."

He went back to his desk, wrote up the afternoon's events and filed them. A fan stirred the heat. Belsey watched DC Aziz wipe his large brow with a paper serviette, then his shaven head, then his neck. Adnan Aziz had been on the team six weeks and had already acquired the workmanlike pace necessary to survive the long haul. He offered a wad of KFC napkins to Belsey and Belsey politely declined.

What a strange end to a strange afternoon. Belsey straightened his paperwork. He briefly wondered what he had done to his life. It was almost six thirty pm; his date was in one and a half hours. He looked at the library break-ins then put them to the side and touched his face where he'd been hit. He saw the man in his grey hoodie, speeding out of nowhere, falling into existence and out again. Belsey typed *PSA* into his browser and stared at the website. He picked up his phone and called downstairs.

"Is the storeroom open?" he asked.

"I haven't locked it."

"I need some oil in the Skoda."

"Help yourself."

Belsey went down to the basement. He took a hand axe, bolt cutters and a twelve-inch Maglite, loaded them into his car and drove to Belsize Park.

QUARTER TO SEVEN AND THE HIGH STREET WAS packed. Belsize Park had continental pretensions and only a few weeks of sunshine a year to exercise them. Restaurants spilled furniture onto the pavement. People spoiled the effect, sitting on kerbs holding dented cans. Office workers who'd been playing truant were safe now, lost among the crowds of reinforcements outside every pub. Everyone was drunk. Everything was launching unsteadily into the night.

3

Belsey parked across from the Costa, took his tools and walked down the alleyway. He stared at the entrance tower and felt it staring back at him. No one could see him from the high street. He knocked on the metal and wondered what he expected to happen. He considered obscuring the CCTV, but if someone somewhere was monitoring this set-up then they knew him by now. He made a final attempt at calling PSA, a gesture for his own conscience. Again it rang without answer. Well, they could try getting in touch with him if they had a problem.

He cut through the wire fence. Soon there

was a gap big enough to clamber through. He took a broken chair from among the rubbish in the high weeds. It was stable enough on its side and got him to what he took to be a boarded-up window. The wood, rotted around its nails, came away easily when he wedged the axe blade in, exposing a black gap.

Belsey chucked the rotten boards into the weeds and stared through what had been a small window, no glass, some thin, rusted mesh folded down. He shone the torch. He could make out a scattering of dead leaves, curved brick walls and the grille of an ancient lift. Narrow passageways led either side of the lift. He hid the axe and bolt cutters among the brambles, then pulled himself up to the ledge and jumped in. The bare concrete made for a heavy landing. He straightened and tingled. It was dark. A lot cooler than outside. The ventilation slats afforded milky strips of light. The floor was messy with brick dust and bird feathers.

He peered through the lift's grille into the endless black shaft. He checked the inside of the front panels that blocked the entrance and saw a brass padlock fastening them, cheap but new. He looked for scratches around the lock; hardly any. He handled the cold metal. Then he walked around the lift to the back of the turret. The torch beam lit a lot of white growth like cotton wool; not cobwebs. He peeled a strand. It was a kind of mould. It stuck to his hands. Then, where the mould had been cleared, he found a wooden door. Belsey turned the handle and it opened, towards him. On the other side concrete stairs spiralled downwards between blackened brickwork.

"Hello?" he called.

He felt stupid. He stepped in and eased the door closed behind him, leaving it just ajar. The stairs twisted around the mesh cage of the lift shaft. Dust-furred suspension ropes sunk down inside the cage. Belsey descended five steps, then ten, then committed to reaching the bottom. He followed the torch beam, timing his descent. The blood-like smell of rusting iron and damp stone grew thicker. He felt he was being swallowed—that it was no longer curiosity driving him but some form of peristalsis. The shelter nourished itself on over-curious detectives. Maybe his man in the BMW procured them.

Two minutes later he paused, still on the stairs, and tried to assess his depth. The earth above him rumbled. So he was beneath the tube. The track between Hampstead and Belsize Park ran almost two hundred feet below the surface. That was a fair slice of London clay above his head. He remembered how much he liked space, being able to move, change location if he wanted. On the two occasions he'd been locked in a cell this was the revelation: he hadn't thought he was claustrophobic because he was rarely confined. After another minute Belsey reached a corrugated iron panel screwed into the walls either side, blocking the way down. A notice had been pasted over the metal a long time ago: *DANGER: NO ENTRY*. But someone had decided to ignore the notice, smashing the metal off its fixings. Belsey pushed and it toppled over with a clang.

"Police!" he said, then forced a laugh to take the edge off the silence. Here was the law: darkness behave. He stepped over the metal. No more stairs. A short corridor led to a brick wall. To his left, a cell of rusting machinery. To his right there was a heavy iron door, painted battleship grey with a handwheel in the centre. It was the sort of thing you might find in a bank vault. Belsey tried turning the wheel, then pulled hard and the door eased towards him on recently oiled hinges.

He couldn't understand what he was seeing at first: iron racks, long rows of metal shelving, which he realised, after a moment, were beds. Three-tiered bunk beds. The dormitory was low with a rounded ceiling formed by arched sections of metal. The walls glistened in the torchlight. Belsey walked in. The beds stretched endlessly down each side. To the left was a door with a tin sign: *Warden's Post*. The warden's post was a small square room with a wooden seat and a desk supporting one empty champagne bottle. Evidently the warden had been celebrating. Belsey lifted the bottle: 1970 Krug. He sniffed it and could still smell the alcohol. There were fresh fingers marks in the dust.

A porcelain sink at the back of the warden's post contained flakes of plaster. Above it was a cabinet. Belsey opened the mirrored doors and found a heap of tiny bones and a mouse skull, like parts from an assembly kit. On the top shelf were two brown pharmaceutical bottles. One was labelled "Evipan," the other "Dexedrine." They were empty. No date, no patient name. They weren't standard pharmacy labels.

He checked his watch. It was five past seven but this felt as if it related to somewhere far away. Belsey walked back into the dorm. He tested a bunk with his hand then lay down on the metal. It was comfortable enough when his weight settled. He switched the torch off. The darkness was so thick it had its own texture. It bristled. The mind rebelled and projected images, then patterns, then tried to come to terms with the total absence of sight. This is death, he thought. He could smell old blankets. There was a wave of stale fear left by the original shelterers, then boredom, then both passed. He began to feel an astonishing sense of calm, as if someone had just explained that the world above ground was an elaborate hoax.

He sat up and switched the Maglite back on. There were the curved ribs of wall, like whale bones. A faded sign: *Put out all lights before leaving at night.* Then his torchlight hit glass, low down: bottles glinting on the floor between the bunks. He stepped closer. Champagne bottles. They had been arranged like skittles. These ones were unopened. There were more cases stacked against the sides: sealed 1970 Krug, seven cases, six bottles each. Then, further in, smaller, unmarked boxes. Belsey tore them open. Taylor's Vintage Port and Hennessy cognac. It was all old: labels in styles he recognised from framed adverts on pub walls. The boxes were marked *For Dispatch: Red Lion.* Which Red Lion had lost this haul? There were also cartons of Embassy cigarettes and three plastic cases marked with a first-aid cross. Belsey opened one and whistled: eleven bottles of pills. They had the same neat, bare labels as the two he had seen in the warden's cabinet, only these were still brimming: hexobarbitone, modafinil, sodium amytal, Evipan, Pentothal, benzylpiperazine. He'd stumbled upon a treasure trove.

Belsey stuffed a couple of medication bottles into his jacket pocket, then took the foil off a Krug and popped the cork. The champagne ran over his hands and fizzed in the dirt. He swigged. It was fine champagne. Even at room temperature—subterranean temperature. There were many Red Lion pubs, many he knew and had enjoyed, few with a wine list like this. The bubbles crackled around his shoes; then all was silent with secret joy. He swigged again. It was peaceful. He tried to remember the last time he'd been out of the earshot of sirens.

7:20 P.M. AND BELSEY hauled himself out through the window, blinking at the shine of the present day. He brushed Blitz dust off his suit. It was remarkably unstained, which seemed to accentuate the ease, and therefore opportunity, of the whole thing.

He called a contact as he drove back to the station: Mr. Kostas, proprietor of Diamante's on the Seven Sisters Road. They went back years, and Belsey knew Kostas could do with some help. He'd started talking about torching the place.

"Mr. K. I've got a few crates of bubbly going cheap, if you're interested."

"How cheap?"

"Champagne at twenty. It's genuine Krug. Also cognac at ten, which is robbing myself. I'll throw in five cartons of cigarettes, maybe a bottle of port."

"How much have you got?"

"Forty bottles thereabouts."

"Saturday I've got a hen party coming, Nick. You do something that looks classy at fifteen a bottle I'd get the lot."

"I'll be in touch."

Belsey made a quick calculation: fifteen a bottle, six bottles a crate, make two or three trips up and down, plus a hundred quid for the cigarettes, then the meds—benzylpiperazine was an upper, so was Dexedrine; he didn't know modafinil; hexobarbitone was presumably a barbiturate. Say five hundred for the drugs at a very conservative estimate and he was looking at over a grand.

He got back to the station and sat at his desk. The office was empty, fan still turning. The real world felt disappointing after his adventure. He reached into his pocket and retrieved a pill bottle, studying it in the light. It was real. Belsey wondered when he could go back down. Live his Blitz fantasy. Take shelter. What did he know about London in the War? He saw the dome of St. Paul's, indomitable, surrounded by destruction. He'd been told that in Regent's Park there was rubble from bombed houses buried ten feet deep. In summer the grass died above it because the bricks couldn't hold water.

He turned his computer on, typed *Blitz* into his browser and clicked *I'm feeling lucky*. A black and white photograph appeared. It showed a group of people standing next to a fresh bomb crater. *A Crowd on Walbrook, 2 May 1941.* The caption stated that one and a half thousand people had been killed in raids the previous night. Belsey looked at the faces of the crowd, expecting numb shock. But some were smiling. They had formed an orderly queue, waiting to peer down. He read the caption fully. *Members of the public queued to see the temple of Mithras, a Roman temple forgotten beneath the City of London, revealed by the overnight bombing.* Belsey tried to see the temple in the blackened crater. He printed a copy and folded it into his jacket.

Maybe he could go down tomorrow. He should have brought up a bottle of champagne for his date. That would have been cute. And then he had a better idea.

He put the pill bottles away in his desk then took one out again. He dropped half a benzylpiperazine. If it was stale it wouldn't kill him, if it was still lively it would knock the dust off and get him bright-eyed and articulate. He stood up and checked the window. The late shift was arriving. There was some impressive sunburn; no one looked very happy. Sirens came from every direction as the evening began to curdle. London was turning edgy with undelivered promises.

Late shift, which meant it was almost 8 p.m.

Belsey shaved in the CID toilets. The swelling had gone down, which looked more appropriate for a date, if less heroic. There was no time to get home first, not that it was ever tempting. Home, currently, was the crumbling Hotel President on Caledonian Road. The arrangement had been a stop-gap while Belsey looked for a flat and had extended to six months now. It meant he could pay by the week and never had to worry about running out of soap. He didn't spend more time there than he had to. He shaved, showered, splashed on some of Trapping's Calvin Klein aftershave, found a box of condoms at the back of his desk drawer.

Halfway out of the station he saw Kirsty Craik, alone in the canteen. The canteen's shutters were all down. Belsey stopped. He felt a pang of guilt about the shelter, a pang of lingering disbelief that she should have reappeared in his life. He brushed his suit again.

"Working overtime already."

She looked up, a little weary, not ungrateful for distraction. In front of her were personnel files.

"Just pausing before home. It's cooler down here."

"Where are you living?"

"Kentish Town."

"Good area."

She nodded and studied him with an expression he remembered: contemplative, undecided.

"Do we need to talk?" Craik asked.

"We're OK, I think. As far as I'm concerned you're the new DS. I've seen you in action and you're good. Professionally, I mean. I'm looking forward to it."

She smiled, then softened her smile.

"You're on restricted duties." Belsey nodded. So she'd checked his file. What kind of journey would she imagine he'd been on, reading that? "How are you finding it?" Craik asked.

"Restrictive." He wondered what else she'd been told, pictured her face as she was warned about him: *Oh, he's trouble, is he*? "Things are fine, though. Much better. But when full duty wants me back I'm ready to serve. Restricted sometimes feels like being a Community Support Officer."

"You could visit schools, give talks." Craik smiled.

"I'd happily visit schools and give talks."

"I don't think anyone's going to be sending you to any schools, Nick."

She was watching him, calculating something. Old flame was a strange expression, Belsey thought. Maybe that was the point. It was all made more complicated by the way memory gets thick with fantasy. And they had liked each other. That had been the problem, although he couldn't put his finger on the logic of it right now.

"This must be odd for you," she said.

"Odd for both of us. But there are odder things in life. Last month I attended a scene where someone had broken into a vet's surgery and OD'd on Euthasol. They were there, stretched out on the operating table. We work well together, you know that. I said you'd rise fast."

He prepared to leave before the conversation got deeper. Then she surprised him.

"Where's good for a late bite around here? Dark rum and dry roasted peanuts—that was your dinner of choice, I seem to recall."

The late hour had turned the gleam of her eyes opaque. Good CID eyes, hard to read. But the offer was clear enough. Part of him would have loved to. There would be time, he thought. If this was how it was going to go.

"On the high street head to La Traviata. It's better than it looks. Or try Carluccio's. Skip Nights of India. Believe me." He smiled again, didn't offer to accompany her, and she cast a detective's gaze across his suit and fresh shave. He felt the reek of Calvin Klein coming off him.

"You've got a date."

"Just meeting a friend."

"OK, Nick. Don't be late for your friend." She turned back to the paperwork but not quick enough to hide her blush.

"See you tomorrow. Bright and early to catch the library robbers."

He left, amused by a faint regret. Then his phone buzzed, and all thoughts evaporated: *On way*, three kisses.

Jemma with a J, as she'd introduced herself in the custody suite. Someone who was all future. His chat-up line: "You take three grams of cocaine on a political protest? How much fun is it meant to be?" Third date, three kisses. Time to put a plan into action.

He visited the florist's by Belsize Park station and bought a bunch of carnations with cream petals and crimson edges. The Co-op only had birthday candles, but they were better than nothing. He bought a box of twenty. He bought new batteries for the Maglite, paid ten pence for an extra-large shopping bag to hide it all in. He went into the Haverstock Arms and ordered two glasses of cava, drank them, placed the glasses in the bag with the torch and flowers.

Jemma with a J was twenty-two years old: a student of art, a tequila girl and a political protestor. Three noble ways to pass the time. She'd love it. She'd get to know him a little better. And it would save him the embarrassment of explaining his current living arrangements. So far he had visited the club where she worked a couple of times, paid for one dinner together, then last weekend she invited him to some free drinks at a gallery launch. Still no bed time. She'd asked for a glimpse of his life, perhaps in that misguided belief that police detectives roll with some kind of glamour. Other than the glamour they make for themselves. He was going to show her his art.

JEMMA WAS WAITING OUTSIDE BELSIZE PARK tube station, dressed for heat: cut-off shorts, vest top and sandals, large shades pinning down long black hair. They kissed and he forgot a lot of potential complications.

"What's in the bag?" she asked.

"A surprise."

"Grab a coffee?"

They sat for a moment in the Costa with the shelter turret at its back, talked about their days, the bank robbers he'd caught, criminal empires brought down; then her work, sleazy men in the club, an art piece she was making with Lego and broken glass. She had wry mascaraed eyes and a smile that gave the lie to them, excitable, too young for him.

"Jemma, are you up for an adventure?"

"Yes."

"I want to show you something."

Belsey took her hand. They left the coffee shop and turned into the alleyway beside it. He led her towards the shelter. She looked at Belsey, puzzled.

"What is it?"

"A space ship." He directed her to the cut fence and the chair, still in place beneath the window. "Are you OK climbing through?"

"Sure." She shifted her handbag around and climbed in, making it look easy. "What the hell is this?" she asked from inside.

"This is where I live," Belsey said. He dropped down beside her.

"You're joking."

"I'm joking." He gave her the Maglite and pointed towards the stairs. "Lift's out of order."

"What's down there?"

"Monsters."

She led them down.

"Are we allowed to be in here?"

"Of course. That's why they keep it clean and well lit."

They stepped over the corrugated panel labelled *No Entry* and he directed her to the warden's post.

"Go in and close your eyes," Belsey instructed. She did as she was told. He followed. He lit three birthday candles, used their wax to stick them to the warden's table, arranged the flowers in the empty bottle and set the champagne flutes up next to a fresh one.

"OK, you can open them."

"Oh my God." She laughed. "What the fuck, Nick? Whose birthday is it?"

"Ours. We've known each other precisely forty-two days."

"Do I blow them out and make a wish?"

"You blow them out, I make a wish. You have to see if you can feel what it is."

She punched him in the chest. He sat down and poured the drinks while she explored. The benzylpiperazine was working. He felt electric.

"Is this where you take all the girls?"

"I only found it today."

"What is it?"

"It's a bomb shelter from the Second World War." He retrieved a first-aid kit from the dorm, emptied it onto the warden's table and unscrewed the bottles: reds, blues, whites. Pills to make you bigger, pills to make you small. He read the labels again: the drugs apparently belonged to Site 3. Where was Site 3 and its party?

Jemma took her drink and sat on his lap. She plucked a carnation and threaded it into her hair. She kissed him.

"We're celebrating a windfall," Belsey said. "Plan is we enjoy ourselves, then take the bottles up. I sell them and we split the profit. You could walk off a few hundred quid up."

"Just for coming down here?"

"For helping me carry them up. That's my estimation." He poured more champagne. They drank, kissed again and he slid a hand under the frayed hem of her cut-offs. She wriggled off him. Then she blew the candles out.

"Wow."

There was that velvety darkness again. They were sinking through it. Belsey found his lighter and waited. He felt a hand on his crotch. Then it went. Then a few seconds later a torch beam appeared, deep in the dorm. It was Jemma.

"Happy birthday to us," she sang.

Belsey stood up, felt his way to the dorm entrance and

watched her explore among the bunk beds and boxes of drink. She clicked the Maglite off then on again.

"Can you hear something?" she said.

"What did you hear?"

"I don't know. Where does it all lead?"

"It doesn't." He returned to the table, lit a candle, opened the rest of the first-aid boxes and began filling his jacket with their contents. He was uneasy.

"Jemma?"

"Yeah."

"Be careful."

"Why?"

"Break a leg down here and I'm not sure they'd get the ambulance down the stairs."

She giggled. He downed his champagne. Then he heard a man singing. It was very faint. Belsey told himself he was imagining things.

"Jemma?"

"Nick? Is that you?"

The birthday candle flickered. Belsey looked around. Something at the back of the dorm creaked stiffly.

"Hang on, Jemma. Stay there."

Belsey took the candle and walked into the dorm. Bunk cages danced in the wavering light. No sign of her. He waited for his date to jump out. That would be classic. She didn't.

"Are you OK?" he called, and his voice sounded like the voice of someone on their own.

Belsey made a circuit of the dorm and arrived back at the spiral stairs. But he would have heard if she went back that way. He called up them, then returned to the warden's post, pocketed the box of candles and walked through the dorm again. The candles were pathetic. He used the light from his iPhone instead. He headed past the cases of champagne. Had she been drunk enough to fall? Maybe she was pre-loaded when they met. At the end of the dorm he saw that a bunk had been pulled askew to reveal another door out. This door had been painted over at some point, forced open more recently. The wood around the lock was splintered. Belsey walked through into a narrow brick passageway. It turned sharp left after a couple of metres and you were at the start of a low, rounded tunnel. The tunnel stretched as far as Belsey could see.

"Jemma!'

He began along it, running. Thirty seconds later he saw something on the ground and the nightmare became a little more concrete. It was Jemma's bag, the strap broken at one end, a sequinned purse still inside. No phone—but he'd felt that in the back pocket of her shorts. Belsey checked the break of the strap and listened to a silence that now had a very different tenor. He headed on, still gripping the bag.

The tunnel presumably led to the other shelter entrance. It was just about tall enough to stand in. Belsey could hear his own blood pulse. He couldn't hear anyone else. He half walked, half ran as much as the narrow strip between the curved sides allowed. It was marked with tracks where something had been dragged. He followed these tracks, using the light of his phone. After ten minutes in the tunnel he knew he had gone too far to connect with the other entrance. He kept walking. He assumed for some reason he was heading south, under Haverstock Hill, under Chalk Farm. He listened for the rumble of tube trains. Nothing. Every couple of hundred metres there was a bulb behind wire mesh, none lit. No visible security of any kind.

"Jemma."

Belsey made a loop out of the bag's strap, knotted it and slung it over his shoulder. He walked for another twenty minutes. If his hunch that he was heading south was right, he would be under Camden now, passing beneath the crowded pubs and teen tourists, under the canal and the market stalls. Eventually he reached a T-junction. A passage, identical to the one he was on, veered off to the left. It added a whole new level of complexity, turning a simple tunnel into a potential maze. Belsey imagined leaving the medication in a trail. He called her name again. He searched around for any signs of which way someone might have gone. Stencilled in red paint onto the concrete of his original route were the words: *Passholders only.*

Odd. But also promising—with a sense that he was, at least, heading *somewhere.* He continued. There was strength in a straight line. After another moment he checked his phone screen and saw one bar of battery. It was 9:20 p.m. He had been walking for thirty-five minutes. He had no food or water. He had a lot of drugs. He wanted to preserve enough juice to make a call in case of emergency, pictured himself trapped behind a vent somewhere, peeking out at the world. He lit a meagre candle instead. The tunnels seemed a different thing in candlelight, less man-made, his journey one that led out of the human world altogether.

Belsey wondered about the technicalities of marching

someone along this route, dragging or forcing them. Wondered whether there were places to imprison them. He rode out a sudden blast of claustrophobia. Then he saw something on the ground ahead of him. Belsey stepped closer. It was a folding bike, a Raleigh Stowaway, paintwork scratched. Above it was a ladder. Belsey held his candle up and saw a square brick shaft.

He climbed unsteadily, candle dripping in one hand, until his head knocked the underside of a metal hatch. Belsey inspected it in the dim light. It had been propped a few inches open with the handle of a screwdriver. He pushed upwards, wedged his shoulder against the metal and clambered through, rolling out of the way as the screwdriver fell and the hatch slammed closed with an ominous clunk.

It blew the candle out. Belsey sparked his lighter. He was lying on the floor of a small office, or a studio of some kind. One table by the wall was loaded with equipment: a cabinet speaker, a cassette player, a typewriter. It had a brown swivel chair in front of it. He was alone.

The lighter got too hot. Belsey released the wheel. He lit another candle and stood up.

One door led out of the place, with a metal sign: *To Situation Room.* Belsey tried the handle. Locked. He flicked the light switch beside it and nothing happened. And then he knew what he was about to discover. He went back to the hatch in the floor. There was no handle. He tried to work a key under the edge but the hatch was fastened shut.

Belsey secured the candle to the table. He kicked the Situation Room door hard, aiming beneath the handle. It didn't budge. He swung the chair against it, then had a brief round of banging the chair against the hatch in the floor. It was pointless

He placed the chair beside the table and sat down.

As well as the Sony cassette player and the grey electric typewriter there were two silver microphones like antennae, a desk lamp and a glass ashtray resting on a hardback book. The ashtray was clean. The cabinet speaker had a corner to itself. On the wall above the equipment was what looked like a fuse box, with old-fashioned telephone receivers on either side, one black, one red. On the box itself were four switches labelled "Attack," "Flood," "Fire," "Chemical." These, it seemed, were the options.

A plain, round wall clock gave the time as quarter to four. A calendar beneath it hung at November, its square days crossed out to Friday 11. Belsey took it off its nail and turned to the front. The year was 1983. He hung it back.

He lifted the red telephone and put it to his ear. No dialling tone.

"Hello," he said. But he didn't like the sound of his voice in the small, locked room. He checked the alert switches. Attack was up. Belsey flicked it down and waited, then flicked it up again. He tried "Flood," imagined an outbreak of panic somewhere.

He moved the ashtray and picked up the book beneath it: *Guide to the Standing Stones of Wiltshire.* It was an old hardback, with black-and-white plates. Belsey imagined someone down here, sitting out a war, trying to remember what the world above was like; thinking about the puzzles mankind had posed before destroying them. So this would be his desert-island reading. He'd survive a fortnight with-

out food but only three or four days without water. Sufficient time to acquaint himself with Wiltshire's mysteries. He
found his tobacco and papers, rolled a cigarette, then he
wondered about oxygen supplies and put the rollie down.

So.

Belsey worked through the scenario that would unfold if
he failed to return. They'd find his car still at the police station. Last solid witness was Kirsty Craik: *I think he had a
date; he stank of aftershave . . .* That was unlikely to trigger
a search of local bomb shelters. Maybe they'd trace CCTV,
get Jemma and himself as they entered the alleyway. Then
someone would replicate his puzzlement: *But it doesn't lead
anywhere. What's this building?* Then that officer would de-
scend, disappear . . .

He searched Jemma's bag. A purse with cards: debit,
Oyster, uni ID, some loose change and house keys. He transferred the purse and keys to his jacket. It would have been
nice to imagine her surfacing, being able to raise the alarm.
He wondered if she too was stuck somewhere in her own
subterranean bubble of the 1980s, flicking the switches. Buried alive.

Then the rats woke up. Belsey listened to the scurry on
the other side of the ceiling. They sounded burly; his last
companions, waiting to strip the flesh from his bones. He
stood on the desk and used up some of his remaining lighter
fluid studying the ceiling. It was panelled, but one panel was
different, fringed with thin black strands where liquid had
oozed around the edges. Belsey took the desk lamp and
knocked it against the panel. It sounded dull with rot. He
flipped the lamp around, smashed the base through the

wood, and a stream of filthy water ran into his face. Belsey
stepped back and fell off the table.

He banged his shoulder but was more perturbed by the
polluted flow. A rat bolted down the wall. Belsey gagged and
waited. When the black trickle stopped he climbed back
onto the desk. The panel had crumbled. Belsey scraped splin-
ters out of the way and hauled himself up.

For a moment, he lay on the damp floor on the other
side. He'd left the lighter and candles and Jemma's bag in
the room below. He had her purse, a stash of pill bottles
stuffed in his pockets and his mobile. Its screen lit a flooded
corridor. Bulbous cascades of orange dry-rot cloaked the
walls. Plastic doorframes had folded into the passageway as
if half-melted. Belsey got to his feet. He could smell sulphur
fumes, sodden wood rotting away. He covered his nose and
mouth. Sluggish reflections lapped at his shoes. He stepped
over drooping frames, avoided low-hanging wires and an
asbestos-lagged pipe.

The doorways at the side led into rooms of smashed porcelain: stems of toilets, shower tiles. Then it all went black.
He pressed various buttons on his phone but the battery had
gone. That's it, he thought: eternal darkness. But not com-
plete. A very faint, grey light hovered a couple of yards
ahead. Belsey splashed his foot and the pale square moved.
He went towards it and looked up. Light was creeping in
somewhere above him. He felt around the walls until his
knuckles hit the clammy metal of a ladder.

Desperation opened a new reserve of strength. He climbed
for a minute to a small platform, a ledge of some kind with
railings and, at the far end, concrete steps. These twisted up

for more than ten floors but Belsey climbed them fast, propelled by the idea of ascent. He reached a heavy, wooden door. It shifted an inch when he pushed. Something was blocking it. Belsey leaned in, and both the door and the obstacle scraped far enough for him to squeeze through the gap. He found himself in a small room filled with cleaning products. Beyond it was a corridor glowing green with emergency exit lights. Belsey knelt and smelt dry carpet. It seemed, blissfully, like people had been there recently. He glanced back at the doorway from which he'd emerged. The obstacle had been a cupboard with a handwritten sign announcing: *Cleaners Only.* Where was he?

On the other side of the corridor was an office with a potted plant and a PC. Belsey walked in. He switched the computer on. Then he saw a trolley of books behind the door. He lifted a pink, laminated paperback: *Seduction of a Servant Girl.* There was a yellow borrowing slip from St. Pancras Library pasted inside.

You're joking, he thought. Belsey returned to the corridor. He followed the arrows on the Fire Exit signs to a door at the end, climbed one more flight of steps and found himself standing behind the issue desk. There were the shelves and computer terminals of the library, waiting in the gloom. Through the floor-length windows to his right St. Pancras Station rose into the sky, fairy-tale as ever, surrounded by the unenchanted hub of King's Cross. Night traffic streamed east and west. He'd spent many pleasant hours in here, admiring this grey view, browsing the sports sections or even trying to improve himself with the classics. He felt physically stretched between the familiar world and the one from which he'd emerged. It was only detail by detail that King's Cross convinced him he was in it.

His hands left smears where he touched. He crouched to see his face in a computer monitor and even his silhouette looked wrecked. He smoothed his hair down and felt it wet with sludge.

The main door out of the library was locked. He found a side door and pushed the steel emergency bar to open it. Alarms rang out. He stepped onto the pavement and the warm air felt incredibly fresh. Belsey looked up at the building from which he'd emerged. The library occupied the base of a ten-floor office block housing all the council departments, from street cleaning to pest control, a stark modern annexe to the old town hall next door. Its outmoded lead-streaked concrete struck him now as militaristic. He realised it had always appeared militaristic. It had been hiding in plain sight.

He crossed the road and watched from a bus stop as a young security guard in a yellow tabard appeared, assessing the open door, glancing up and down the street. It was 10.39 pm. Belsey had spent two hours underground. It felt three times as long. The walk back to Hampstead police station would take him a good forty-five minutes, but he didn't want to get a taxi. That instinct was itself a wake-up call, a welcome to a new and complicated situation. He didn't want a witness, someone able to say: yes, I saw him there, at that time, looking half-ruined. But witness to what?

Belsey walked. He still had energy. Benzylpiperazine lingered inappropriately in his blood. He tried to steady his mind and work one thought at a time.

Was there *any* possibility she'd surfaced, that she was safe and well among people and sky? He told himself he was covering every angle when he was looking for some shred of hope. He felt Jemma's purse in his pocket and thought of the broken bag strap. And once again Belsey saw the BMW crashing into his life, the man jumping from it, pulling his hood up.

THROUGH CAMDEN, BACK TO BELSIZE PARK. THE crowd was still out. Belsey kept to the quiet side of the street. But he was relatively incognito among the damage of closing-time London. He walked into the petrol station at the top of Haverstock Hill and found a cheap torch. His wallet contained no cash. He didn't want to use his card, didn't want to be traced. Belsey turned away from the CCTV and took a crumpled fiver from Jemma's purse and paid with that. It didn't make him feel wonderful.

5

There were no clues around either of the Belsize shelter towers, no signs that Jemma had come up, or been brought up, the way they had gone in. Belsey combed the weeds then climbed in through the window again. He walked to the top of the stairs and called.

Down the stairs again, wishing he had the Maglite rather than whatever crap BP were hawking. Even in the yellow beam he could see that the warden's post was as he'd left it: champagne bottle, glasses, carnations. He was surprised by a sudden wave of anger. Stupid girl for wandering off. Stupid him. What a ridiculous amount of trouble for the sake of touching up an art student. He walked past the bunks, through the hidden door and brick passageway into the tunnel where he'd found her bag. He got down on his knees, looking for footprints or blood. Praying in the only way detectives know how. He wasn't set up for forensics. He sat with his back against the curved tunnel wall, energy gone.

"Jemma!" he yelled. He closed his eyes. After five minutes he returned to the stairs.

He climbed out of the tower, retrieved the axe and bolt cutters. He shifted some mildewed cardboard to obscure the cut fence. Next stop was visiting her home, just in case. But that meant calling the station to request the address off criminal records. Or going in himself.

THE STATION WAS SUMMER-NIGHT busy, custody full, officers distracted. A gang of men in swimwear with towels and bloodied faces crowded the corridor, next to a line of sullen Koreans with bags of bootleg DVDs. The smell of vomit permeated the ground floor. Belsey returned the equipment to the storeroom and went up to CID.

He walked into the office and out again. The sight of Rob Trapping had taken him by surprise. It was a discomfiting splash of normality alongside his transgressions. He removed his soiled jacket. There was nothing he could do about his trousers. Belsey checked Jemma's purse was well stuffed inside it, then made his entrance again. The young detective constable looked up and gave a cautious smile.

"You OK, mate? Look a state. Where've you been?"

Belsey sat down at his desk.

"Underground," he said.

Trapping grinned. "You were at the Skinner's. You've been drinking."

Belsey stared at his grin.

"I've been drinking, that's right."

"You should have called," Trapping said.

"It was just a swift one." Belsey winked. Trapping shook his head. Belsey turned his desk light on. He plugged his phone in to charge and checked for messages. No messages. He tried Jemma's mobile and it went straight to voicemail. He hung up. He stuck her purse in his drawer while he decided what to do with it, then brought up the evening's reports. No shortage of crime. Nothing involving a young woman of Jemma's description.

What did he know about St. Pancras Library? Sitting at his desk, he sensed an uneasy coincidence close at hand. He picked up the pile of papers Kirsty Craik had given him: incident reports from St. Pancras Library. There had been three supposed "break-ins"; the most recent had been two days ago, then eight days ago and ten days ago. Someone had been setting off the emergency exit alarm as they left the building. It was unclear how they got in in the first place. Belsey thought it might be getting clearer. The man he had chased that afternoon had shown him the route down, and Belsey felt with certainty that this same man had been breaking out through the library. And that this same man had Jemma with him now. If his suspect was coming and going via the bunker there must have been an easier route up, one more straightforward than breaking through the ceiling.

Maybe via that locked door—the one marked *To Situation Room*, whatever that was.

What was any of it?

Trapping packed up.

"Going to sleep under the desk again?" Trapping asked. He held his jacket, a bag of Japanese food and a couple of bootleg DVDs.

"Saves time in the morning."

When he was gone Belsey dialled Jemma's mobile again, hesitated before leaving a message, then reasoned that if someone got to checking her phone records they'd be all over him anyway.

"Call me," he said. "Let me know if you're OK."

He emptied his pockets. The pharmacy covered his paperwork. Eleven bottles in all and some foil-wrapped packets marked *oral administration*. He split the foil. Inside was a small plastic stick, shaped like a cotton bud, with writing along the shaft: *1200 mcg fentanyl citrate*.

There was only one thing that wasn't in his pockets: his police badge.

Belsey searched them again, more urgently. He checked his desk. Did he take it out with him? Of course he took it out. It was gone. He pictured it sinking into antique slime. It wasn't his greatest problem, but it was the one that brought unavoidable consequences soonest. What other traces had he left down there? A lot of prints, champagne glasses, some flowers, a box of birthday candles, her bag.

He needed to get a grip on this.

He showered and found a spare shirt and a clean pair of trainers in his locker. He searched Trapping's desk to see if his colleague had received anything connected to Jemma or the tunnels. The paperwork was all requests from Kirsty, minor queries to which Trapping was responding with un-precedented care and attention. He'd fallen in love. Good luck to him. Belsey put the bottles in his desk drawer and ran Jemma's name through the Police National Computer. There were the details he himself had entered: Jemma Stevens, born 2/5/1991, cautioned for possession of a controlled sub-stance 1 May 2013: home address 34 Kynaston Road, N16. Arresting officer DC Nick Belsey.

He took her house keys from his jacket. It was quarter to midnight.

SHE SHARED A RAMSHACKLE END TERRACE ON THE border of Stoke Newington and Stamford Hill, between the organic cafes and the orthodox synagogues. Belsey parked outside. No lights on in the house. He walked to the front door and peered through the letter box. A shabby hallway: one pair of men's trainers and a lot of women's shoes. No sandals. He let himself in.

A corridor led through the ground floor with a living room to the left. It smelt of weed and stale beer. Belsey looked into the living room. A boy snored on the sofa. Cans covered the coffee table edge to edge. He continued down the corridor to a door at the end, opened it and watched a blonde girl sleeping. Early night for all. Must have been a big weekend. He had a very vague recollection of meeting her at Euphoria, the club where Jemma worked. Another tequila girl. Latvian. She lay diagonally across the bed, a thin arm pushing a duvet off her naked body. Belsey eased the door shut.

He went upstairs and tried the door beside a small bathroom. It led into another bedroom. Paintings and sculptures covered the floor and walls. There were photographs of Jemma with friends, a portfolio case, a lot of clothes and loose papers. Belsey stepped inside. He could smell her. Make-up lay strewn across a dresser, underwear in a pile on the floor. So he'd finally made it to her bedroom. He found a tissue and wiped his prints off the door handle and kept the tissue wrapped around his hand. It was a gesture: he'd already trailed DNA all over the place. A note on the bedside table said *Belsize Park, 8*. He took it. Above the bed was a calendar with shifts marked in. No mention of their date. She wasn't due at work until the night after next.

He walked back to the living room and crouched close to the sleeper's face. Belsey recognised him too. A guy who worked behind the bar at Euphoria. He'd served Belsey several times. Kiwi, well built, fixed a good mojito. Had clearly fixed himself a few. The reek of ashtray and stale beer triggered a sharp comedown. The surface of the world was broad and varied, but it did not contain the one thing he was looking for. He had lost someone underground. Belsey walked to the front door, let himself out and eased it shut.

HE RETURNED TO HAMPSTEAD police station with the joyrider on his mind, increasingly sure that this was his suspect. He was the only other person with a connection to the shelter and the tunnels. The dark grey hood. And someone had broken into the dormitory, oiled the hinges, made themselves at home. Found themselves a neat getaway for when police were chasing them.

The station was quieter now. Belsey turned the lights back on in the CID office and ran some checks. The BMW had been stolen from outside its owner's house in NW6, reported four p.m. on Friday 7 June. It looked like the thief got keys from just inside the front door. As car manufacturers got more ingenious at preventing hotwiring, car thieves got more ingenious at simply taking the keys. The summer's trend was a powerful magnet strung on a fishing rod and dangled through the letter box. Urban angling.

No witnesses to the car theft. The thief then had the BMW for three days before his race down Rosslyn Hill. It didn't come up in connection with any crimes in the interim.

While he had the force intelligence system up Belsey ran a search for any Red Lions that had reported loss of stock. Nothing on the system. But then the records only went back ten years.

Belsey went over to the borough map on the wall of the CID office. He traced the line a tunnel would have to follow, beneath Belsize, beneath Camden to the library in King's Cross. Just under three miles. Where else might it lead?

He found a twenty-four-hour number for emergencies relating to Camden Council facilities. A man answered with the tone of someone paid to wait for a call and not delighted to receive one.

"Do you know anything about the cold-war bunker, under St. Pancras Library?"

"About what?"

"The bunker."

"Is this a wind-up?"

"No. There's an old communications room, set up for a nuclear war or something."

"This is for emergencies with council facilities."

"This is an emergency with a council facility."

"Comedian." He hung up. As a final stab Belsey typed in *London deep shelters*. He clicked the first link that came up. *The government began construction of deep level shelters under London in 1940 . . .*

There were eight that had been used. Belsize Park, Camden and Goodge Street in north London. South of the river there were shelters at Clapham South, Clapham Common, Clapham North, Stockwell and Oval. A ninth, at Chancery Lane, was never put into operation. One at St. Paul's was started but not completed.

They'd been built in secret. Work took place between 1940 and 1942. Until then, London's population had been using tube platforms during air raids. Then bombs hit Bank and Balham tube stations killing 124 people already underground. The government decided it was time to dig deeper.

It wasn't clear how the veil of secrecy was finally lifted. Belsey imagined London waking to find these defences sprung up, overnight, like mushrooms. Originally they were used by the government. In 1944 they were opened to the general public. There was no mention of connecting tunnels between them. No suggestion of communications rooms from 1983. But one obscure reference on a trainspotter's website gave him pause:

It was originally claimed that following the conclusion of the war the deep tunnels would be joined together to constitute an express route beneath the congested Northern Line offering speedy access to the West End and City, but as Londoners are fully aware, this has never transpired.

But something had transpired.

Belsey printed out everything he could find on the shelters—articles, web pages, essays. He rescued a battered Umbro kitbag from beneath his desk, shook out some loose tobacco and replaced it with the medication bottles, the notes on the shelters and finally Jemma's purse. He needed to find her. Spending all night in the CID office wasn't going to help.

He got into the Skoda and drove around Belsize Park, down to the Camden shelter behind M&S. He drove past Euphoria on Eversholt Street, its short, desperate queue waiting for 1 a.m., when the entry fee dropped to three pounds. Then past her house again. He didn't know how this was going to help. When he almost crashed into a cyclist on Stoke Newington Road he decided to head home.

QUARTER PAST ONE, HOTEL PRESIDENT. MARTYNA, the night receptionist, nodded as he walked in.

"Long day, Nick. Busy?"

"Not really. You?"

"Busy? Here?"

He took the lift up to his room on the fifth floor. The place was empty as ever, a maze of peeling plaster and worn carpets. The current owner lived in Belarus, while he waited to convert it into something profitable. A German website confused it with a hotel of the same name and occasional families stayed for a disappointing night before leaving. Martyna worked triple-shifts and slept behind the desk. Peace reigned.

7

Belsey's room sweated above the tracks of King's Cross. He could hear the trains through the night, grinding on their rails like someone sharpening knives. If he leaned out of his window he could see the steep, brick back of Pentonville Prison. That gave him food for thought. Bringing Jemma here didn't seem like such an awful option in retrospect.

He sat on the edge of his bed. Propped beside

it was a gift that Jemma had given him the first time they met, a square of broken placard sprayed with the advice *Fuck the Feds*. He'd been asked to remove it from the CID office. Now Belsey turned it to face the wall. He tried her mobile again without success. The purse in his bag felt like a ticking bomb. He took it out and put it in a drawer, then took it out of the drawer down to the hotel basement, through the sad shadows of Disco President and wedged it in the cavity beneath a bench seat.

He returned to his room and opened his laptop, logged into Facebook and found Jemma's page. He looked for photos of himself. None that he could see. Ten minutes later he was still sifting through images of her life. He studied the other men, knowing they would deflect attention from him should any investigation arise and not certain how he should feel about this.

At 2 a.m. he put the laptop down, opened his window and checked his phone wasn't on silent. The night was cooling. He emptied his pockets, unfolded a piece of paper. There was the crowd on Walbrook, staring at the Roman temple. Belsey propped the picture on the windowsill and thought of the journey he had walked, the old communications equipment, the noxious sludge. And somewhere down there was his police badge. He would have to report it, devise some explanation for his new line manager and former lover. *Where's good for a late bite around here?* He should have gone with Kirsty. What hadn't even been a decision now appeared as a crossroads, with endless implications. The fuck-up was great.

Belsey drifted into a thin, uncertain sleep as he contemplated it. He dreamed of a room filled with 1980s furniture, brown sofas around a steel mortuary slab. Suddenly it became busy. Jemma Stevens was wheeled in, naked and very pale. A forensic pathologist lifted the skin away from her chest, prised the girl's ribcage apart and, with glee, showed Belsey her internal organs blackened by dirt, hardened like concrete.

AT 6 A.M. HE DROVE BACK TO BELSIZE PARK. THE sky was bright already, with the soft, lemon light that spelt another hot day. The shelter entrance behind Costa was as he left it. He climbed in again, called again.

He drove by Jemma's home and counted the same shoes through the letter box. He unlocked the front door and walked up the stairs, past the same snoring, to the darkness of her bedroom and back down again.

8

Into the station. The sound of hoovering filled the corridors, the chatter of the Uruguayan cleaners. Belsey ran every system check he could think of, looking for someone who might fit his tunneler: men currently wanted for sex crimes and abduction; men recently released from sentences for such crimes; men on the run, possibly in London. No leads. And no overnight reports that connected. On the plus side, no bodies had been found. Then Belsey saw the brown envelope propped against his monitor.

It was blank, A3 size. He picked it up, shook it and his police badge fell out.

Belsey stared at the badge. It rested against

his keyboard. He switched his desk lamp on and could see a layer of orange-brown sediment over the imitation leather wallet. He checked the envelope again. No markings, uncreased, nothing else inside.

Julia Coates was on the front desk, busy giving herself a manicure.

"Did someone bring this in?" Belsey asked, showing her both badge and envelope.

"Yes. A member of the public, I think. Said they found it, you lucky sod. What have you been up to?"

"Did you see them?"

"Not me. It was Patrick. Couple of hours ago."

"Can you check the book?"

She checked the duty log and read: "Badge and warrant card belonging to DC Belsey returned, 4:20 a.m. Individual declines to leave name."

"Nothing else?"

"No. Why? Were you offering a reward?"

"Could you get the tapes up?"

She frowned, then wheeled her chair over to the CCTV monitor. It took a moment. She got the shot up.

The station entrance led into what was essentially a cubicle with the front counter protected by a Perspex screen, a bench to the right beneath a noticeboard, one camera trained on the ledge in front of the screen.

What you saw was that Patrick was a liar. He wasn't on the desk—he'd left it for ten seconds to retrieve a cup of tea. Whoever handed the badge in must have been waiting and knew where the camera was. They held back, never quite stepping into view. They left the envelope on the ledge, in front of the Perspex. They wore gloves.

"Pause it."

The gloves. Belsey thought of the joyrider running. Black gloves. On the screen you could see that they had a back panel, a strap, and what looked like paler fingertips, possibly retractable.

"Those are specialist gloves."

"A biker," Coates said.

"Or a climber."

Belsey went back upstairs and checked the envelope again. He turned his computer on and saw he had mail. A message had arrived at 4:14 a.m. to his work email address. From Ferryman@tempmail.net. Subject line: *Did you get your badge?*

Belsey opened the email. It consisted of a photograph of a building, or a slice of building: concrete and windows. The side of an office block. No detail visible through the windows. The concrete was grey and stained.

Someone could find his work email easily enough on the station website. But why send this? His tunneler having an episode, perhaps, working their own violent logic, tripping on Dexedrine and hearing voices give bad instructions. He read the subject line again, then the name, Ferryman, and tried to attach it to the image of the building. The shot was pretty. In a strange way. The honeycomb pattern of the deep-set windows receding into the sky, sunshine glaring the top right corner. Was it meant to be some kind of invitation? A clue?

He looked up Tempmail. It was a service that provided you with a temporary email address, no sign-up, no password, totally anonymous; destroyed content after fourteen days. He clicked *reply*, changed the subject line to: *Curious*. He typed: *Thanks, tell me more*, then clicked *send*.

Belsey ran "Ferryman" through the national system in case the name came up in connection with any other crimes. No one had logged it. He waited ten minutes. No reply. He printed a copy of the email. It was only when he was studying the printout that he saw a line of text beneath the photograph:

Jemma says don't leave me down here.

He felt sick.

He went downstairs, got the axe again, took a head torch, gloves and a stab vest, and went to his car.

NO ATTEMPT AT BEING discreet this time. He parked by the coffee shop and marched down the alleyway, armed and equipped. His heart sunk. Two uniformed police stood in front of the shelter, Constables Andy Durham and Ravni Singh, with a man he recognised as one of the Costa baristas.

"What's going on?" Belsey said.

"Someone's been messing around with the fence here. What are you doing up this early, Nick?" They saw the equipment in his hand.

"Couldn't sleep. Messing around doing what?"

"The fence has been cut."

Belsey gave it a look.

"Got any theories?" Singh asked.

"Seems a strange place to break into," Belsey said.

HE DROVE DOWN TO St. Pancras Library. 7:10 a.m. The library was shut. He went around the back of the building. There was a delivery van with its doors open, parked beside a service entrance, someone trying to balance a vending machine on a porter's trolley. Belsey walked in alongside the new machine, then headed for the library.

He was past the issue desk, moving down the stairs when someone ran around the corner in a security uniform.

"Stop," he shouted.

The guard was young, black, with sharp sideburns and a two-way radio.

"It's OK," Belsey said.

"Stay there. I've called the police."

"I'm police. There's nothing to worry about."

A second guard appeared, seven foot, with a boxer's flat face: "That's him. That's the man on the tapes."

"I need to go down here. Someone's life may be in danger."

"You're not going anywhere."

Belsey gripped the axe a little tighter. It seemed to get their attention. He carried on down the stairs to a staff-only corridor. The guards followed him at a safe distance. The corridor ended at a small staff room he hadn't seen before. He tried a few doors to the side but they were locked. His memory of the place was fogged with adrenalin. He searched for his dirty footprints but couldn't see any.

He tried the other direction, opening a lot of small storerooms, none of which contained a cupboard marked *Cleaners Only* or a door down into a bunker. The guards kept with him.

"It was here," Belsey said. "There was a cleaners' room, a corridor, an office. Where's the cleaners' cupboard?"

"You're looking for the cleaners' cupboard?"

Finally a man with cropped hair ran around the corner, speaking into a radio handset.

"Boss," someone called. "He's got an axe."

The security boss was short and fierce. Either he didn't hear the warning or he was ready to lay down his life for his library. He placed himself between Belsey and the next set of doors. Then before Belsey knew what was going on the man had a hand up in his face and Belsey was grabbing his wrist, throwing him to the floor. He was going for his cuffs, thinking: What am I doing? He stopped. This was stupid. This was what happened: you piled mistakes on top of each other. You became conspicuous.

He lifted the security guard to his feet and walked out.

THIS WAS SMOOTH, HE THOUGHT, BLEAKLY; THIS was all going well.

Into the office again and it was still only quarter to eight, sun now burning accusations through the window. No response from Ferryman in his inbox. Belsey looked at the original email, the picture of the windows. He sifted through a list of other crimes he should be investigating: a spate of stolen mobility scooters, someone selling ecstasy to twelve-year-olds. He checked the news. Refugees. Fighters on the back of a lorry. That was as useful as it got.

9

He stepped out to the fire escape and tried to borrow some early-morning clarity. Panic was never useful. It drew attention. Attention right now meant arrest. That was one course of action, of course: come clean, take his chances. Only there were no chances. First rule of detective work: find the guy who led the girl into the abandoned tunnels from which she never returned. The phrase "slam dunk" rattled around his brain. He had never in his entire working life heard any London police officer use it and yet no other choice of words seemed appropriate. The case would be a slam dunk even if he had no previous; as it was he had a particularly lavish disciplinary record, violence and substance abuse being highlights. He'd been close to getting thrown out of the force on several occasions. He'd met the girl by arresting her, for Christ's sake. He knew what added up; that was his job.

He needed to stay un-arrested then. The abductor wanted to play. That wasn't necessarily the worst situation. Usually, if you're going to kill someone you do it quickly. His joy-rider, this Ferryman, was playing games and that worked best if Jemma remained alive. Right now it was possible Belsey was the only one willing or able to play along.

He was left with three questions: Where was she? Who was Ferryman? What did they want? To answer the last question first: he knew at least that they wanted *something*. At the very least they wanted Belsey to play detective. That was a role he had rehearsed.

Who was he? Belsey wrote down what he knew. The profile of the man he had chased down Rosslyn Hill: white male, physically able to handle himself, auto-theft skills, local knowledge, comfort zone extending two hundred feet beneath the surface of the earth. Wears gloves in a heatwave. Gloves indicated preparation and intent and forensic concern, all of which distinguished you from ninety-nine per cent of lawbreakers. And then he'd set up an untraceable email account—so add computer-literate. High intelligence.

The individual knew where to find Hampstead police station. He paid a visit. He got himself *involved* with police. Maybe he had bad history with law enforcement. A score to settle. Belsey checked the obvious databases: Registered Sex

Offenders, police harassers; he checked recent sex crimes, then all unsolved violent crimes in the borough, then abductions of young women going back ten years. He cross-checked abductions and auto theft. He didn't turn up anything useful. He looked for any references to tunnels, but nothing connected at all. Finally he phoned John Cassidy, a grass who knew the local car-thieving community as well as anyone. Cassidy hadn't heard anything about a BMW or a deep shelter or a looted Red Lion.

A skilled criminal with no apparent connections. They existed. They were a rare breed. They tended to keep themselves apart for good reasons: efficiency, distrust, penchants that were judged ill-advised even by the criminal fraternity. Like subterranean kidnapping.

Which led him back to the first question: Where was she? Belsey interrogated the wall map again, face close to it as if, by refocusing his eyes, a new pattern might appear beneath the familiar postcodes. Belsize Park to King's Cross. He walked that route last night, under Haverstock Hill, under Camden High Street. He didn't see her. She wasn't there and hadn't surfaced. The T-junction he'd seen last night, that tunnel veering off to the left began to haunt him.

He put a notice out through the all-points system, a high priority query to CID in other boroughs: Have you had any incidents involving your deep-level bomb shelters? The strangest request he'd ever sent.

He got six calls in fifteen minutes.

ON THE NIGHT OF Saturday, 1 June, the weekend before last, while the city was drunk and distracted, a white male in a stolen white Vauxhall van had driven around deep shelters in central and south London, apparently trying to get in. He'd drawn enough attention to have his own file created.

23.45, 1 June—intruder reported at Whitfield Street property to rear of Goodge Street shelter. Police attended. Retrieved a ladder suspected to have been used in attempted entry. Suspect not found.

Fifty-five minutes later three drivers reported seeing an individual with a power tool attempting to enter the Stockwell deep shelter. Individual departed before police arrived. Fled in a white van.

01.18—Clapham South deep shelter. Damage discovered to steel doors after reports by members of the public concerning an individual seen tampering with them. Suspect ID: white male, dark sports clothing, rucksack. Fled in a white van, but not before a witness wrote down the make and registration. Vauxhall Vivaro, five years old, stolen that morning. Belsey printed out the list of the incidents and found his *A-Z* in his desk drawer. It was coming apart, page by page, like every Londoner's, the result of living in a city you'd never entirely get your head around. But he needed something he could mark up. Amid the increasingly unstable surfaces of London there was something comforting in a paper map. He turned through, marked the city's eight deep shelters with a cross, then put it in the Umbro bag and took the bag to his car.

HE DROVE TO ONE shelter after the other, before rush hour clogged the roads and the present reformed itself. It seemed, in the dawn, they'd stepped forward. They were weights, holding the city in place.

All shelters were constructed identically, but each turret had acquired its own character over time. On Tottenham Court Road, the Goodge Street station bunker had an entrance that maintained the sober brown brickwork of a neighbouring church. Its sister tower, on a side street, was painted in cream and pink stripes. Belsey tried to imagine it connecting back up to Camden, to Belsize Park.

Stockwell's south tower was behind garages on Studley Road. No visible damage. The northern entrance drew all the attention, sitting multicoloured on a traffic island in the centre of Stockwell roundabout. Belsey used to drive past it, heading into Brixton from his old posting at Borough. Lambeth council had taken responsibility for its own street art, commissioning a bright mural of local war heroes to cover the tower's curved walls. Belsey walked around the base until he saw damage. The rainbow-coloured slats of a vent had been mangled, opening a small aperture to the darkness inside. He put his mouth to the hole.

"Hello?" And then, feeling as ridiculous as he did desperate: "Jemma?"

It was seven miles back under central London to Belsize Park. Long tunnel if it connected. Again, Belsey tried to see it from the abductor's perspective; he wondered about the mechanics of forcing someone through that network. But then it wasn't too hard to force all sorts of things when you've got someone alone underground.

Clapham South had one entrance tower on Balham Hill, the other rising from the dew of Clapham Common. He hadn't been in the area since the riots. You could still see faint scars where the bins had melted. But everything was sparkling again. The suspicious individual had been spotted on the common. Belsey found several small holes at chest height in the shelter's metal entrance panel. He listened, although he didn't know what he expected to hear. An officer drove by and stopped. He was small, eager, deeply tanned. Belsey showed his badge.

"I'm interested in the man who was messing around with this a couple of Saturdays ago."

"Someone really wanted to get in," the officer said. "Member of the public saw sparks. Blowtorch."

"Did he gain access?"

"I don't know. It was locked when we arrived."

"Do you know if he was caught on any cameras?"

"There's nothing. But his vehicle connects to an incident on the Central Hill Estate, Gipsy Hill. Same night. They might have more."

"What kind of incident?"

"Vandalism again."

"Is there a shelter there?"

"I don't think so."

CENTRAL HILL ESTATE CLUNG to the top of Gipsy Hill, all jagged concrete, tiered ranks of houses poised before the view as if ready to defend themselves from the rest of south-east London. A high canopy of leaves let thick light through to the dark glass and walkways. The only colour came from the red and blue flashing sign of an off-licence.

Belsey walked around the estate until one block of flats made him stop. Pear Tree House. He saw immediately that something was wrong with the building. From the front it was a four-storey block of flats, but from the back the hill fell away to expose a further four floors below. These lower floors were windowless, a solid block of concrete washed with pale blue paint. The only thing interrupting the concrete was a set of black iron doors at the base.

He radioed a request for any local officers to attend—said he was interested in the vandalism from the night of Saturday, 1 June—and a patrol car swung by five minutes later. It contained a silver-haired sergeant and his young probationer, who was sporting fresh lipstick.

"There was an incident, Saturday the first," Belsey said.

"Yes. We called it in," said the Sergeant.

"What did you see?"

He got out of the car and pointed towards the base of Pear Tree House. "Bloke was trying to break open those doors. Then, when we approached, he bombed it back to the van and tore off. Almost knocked some kid off his scooter."

"What's in there?"

"I don't know."

"There are no windows on the lower floors."

The Sergeant looked at the block as if seeing it for the first time. "No."

"Do you know why?"

"No idea."

Belsey approached the double iron doors and saw the beginnings of an attempt to cut through them with a blowtorch. He went to the front of the building and rang each flat number until someone buzzed him into the entrance hall. There was a pushchair, two bikes, no stairs down. He checked the lift. The buttons inside offered nothing beneath the ground floor. A man called down the stairway.

"Hello?"

"Hi," Belsey said. "Do you know what's beneath the flats?"

"No. What's there?"

"That's what I'm asking."

"Who are you looking for?"

Belsey walked out. He took a picture of the building on his phone and emailed it to Ferryman with a question mark.

The city was getting stranger by the minute.

HE SAT IN HIS CAR AT THE TOP OF GIPSY HILL. THE Umbro bag contained nothing on Pear Tree House. He found the meds under the papers and inspected the labels. *Site 3.*

South London stretched beneath him. He knew a lot of people down there; a lot of esoteric knowledge was archived in those brown terraces and grey estates. Someone had to have a lead.

10

THE CHEMIST ANSWERED HIS door ten floors above Lewisham Way, at the summit of one of the area's more respectable tower blocks. He wore a white bathrobe, long rust-coloured hair wet around his shoulders. A pendant hung against his chest where the robe sagged, the goddess Shiva glinting in the light of New Cross Gate.

"I know it's early," Belsey said. "I need your mind."

The chemist checked the walkway with faintly luminescent eyes. He let Belsey in. Cushions lay on the floor around a square of glass propped up on bricks. The glass supported an ashtray full of eggshells and a pint glass containing a fork and three raw eggs. Belsey took the bottles from his bag and lined them up beside the ashtray. The chemist whisked his eggs. He considered the bottles. He drank and Belsey averted his eyes. When he looked back the chemist was wiping yolk from his moustache. He turned the bottles to read the labels then unscrewed one and poured small pink pills into his palm.

"Where did you get these?"

"Underground."

"What's Site 3?"

"I don't know."

"You busted someone?"

"Not exactly. Seen anything like this before?"

The chemist rolled a pill between thumb and forefinger. He touched it to his tongue.

"How many of these can you get?"

"I'm not selling. I need to know what they are, where they're from."

"Modafinil's a pep pill. Soldiers use it on patrols to stay awake. Same with the benzyls and Dexis." He moved three bottles to the side. "These are downers: Evipan is a sedative. Amytal's similar—those are the yellow ones. Pentothal's a brand of sodium thiopental; more like an anaesthetic."

"What are these fentanyl things?"

"Fentanyl citrate. One hundred times more potent than morphine."

"Why a lollipop?"

"Emergency situations. You don't have to fuss about with fluids or needles. Just suck it and see. What you've got is a field kit."

"What do you mean?"

"Military supplies. That's where I've seen it, not on civvy street. Most of these haven't been available on script since the seventies."

"Too much fun?"

"Too much fatality. Six or seven of these barbs and it's goodbye cruel world. Like signing a prescription for a noose."

"When did they stop doing them?"

"I'd say they were phased out 1985, 1986. I used to see amobarbital and Evipan around in the early eighties, before it all went heroin."

Belsey's phone rang. It was the CID office, which felt ominous. He let it ring. The chemist contemplated an un-opened bottle.

"The pills are in good condition. Where have they been?"

"I don't know. I've got to go. I owe you one."

The chemist nodded. He watched Belsey gather up his merchandise and walk to the door.

"I'd give you twelve hundred for the lot," he said.

Belsey stopped.

"You're kidding."

"Have you tried them?"

NINE O'CLOCK AND THE CID office was getting lively. Craik's door was shut, but he could see through its small window that she had company.

"Who's with the Sarge?" Belsey asked his colleagues.

"Head of security, St. Pancras Library."

"Great."

Belsey surfed the gloom. He walked past her office again and recognised the man as his sparring partner from the library that morning. There were CCTV stills being spread on Craik's desk.

Belsey sat down at his own desk and checked his emails. No more word from Ferryman. He checked the intelligence system; no bodies had been found. He tried Jemma's phone with no more luck. Thirteen hours gone. People would be starting to wonder where she was. He got a landline for Jemma's home off his arrest report.

"Hello," a girl answered, and for a brief second his heart soared.

"Jemma?"

"No. This is Eva." Now he heard the Eastern European accent. "Who is this?"

"Does Jemma Stevens live there?"

"Yes."

"This is the police. When did you last see Jemma?"

"I haven't see her since yesterday. Is she OK?"

"We're concerned about her whereabouts. If she shows up, call me. If she doesn't, call me. OK?" He gave his direct number.

"Why? What's happened?"

"Just let me know."

He poured a coffee. He had missed calls, two messages: the chemist offering fifteen hundred for the army drugs, Mr. Kostas calling from Diamante's: "When can I collect those bottles?"

He told Kostas to forget the arrangement, then tried another reply to Ferryman: *Is she OK? What do you want?*

No action from Craik's office; they were still tight in discussion. He called the Marine Policing Unit. For reasons that had never been entirely clear MPU incorporated the Confined Space Search Team. Maybe they wanted all the adventure boys together, gazing over the Thames from their Wapping base, planning their next challenge. He asked for DI Mick Conroy, a former Olympic rower and amateur cliff diver he'd met on a stag do.

"It's Nick Belsey, from Hampstead CID."

"Nicky, you rascal."

"Got a hypothetical situation, Mick, need to pick your brains. Say there's a girl lost somewhere down in disused tunnels under London—how could I get you down there searching?"

"We'd need authorisation from a Yard unit. Chief Inspector. Something like that."

"And how would you go about finding where she is? What kit do you use?"

"Audio equipment, probably. If it stretches more than a mile. Maybe heat-detecting cameras."

"You could respond immediately?"

"We'd have to check safety first. Especially if it's disused. See if there was structural damage. See who has the latest map of the system."

"If it was a hostage situation underground?"

"Christ. I suppose we'd need negotiators with us, maybe firearms. Would be a bit of a nightmare."

"OK."

"This is hypothetical?"

"Until you hear otherwise."

A map of the system. Belsey looked at his *A-Z*, the shelters marked. He ran a check on the stolen Vauxhall Vivaro seen touring the entrance towers. The van had been taken ten days ago, from a back road in Clerkenwell, EC1. It was a face-to-face jacking. A whole new style compared to the theft of the BMW.

The Vauxhall's driver had been returning from a cash machine at 10:15 a.m. when a man stepped out from beside the van. The man threatened him with a kitchen knife, took his wallet and car keys and drove off with the van in the direction of Holborn. The hour alone made Belsey pause—a mid-morning carjacking was novel. Suspect described as white, twenty-five to thirty-five, fair, some stubble, six foot or thereabouts. An unhelpful note informed Belsey that an e-fit was yet to be completed. The officers on the case probably thought one of the usual suspects would be apprehended by now. But it was unusual every way you looked at it.

The robbery occurred on Phoenix Place. Belsey checked Phoenix Place in his *A-Z*. It was behind the Royal Mail depot. The robbed owner was Victor Patridis, a chef at the depot itself. The van contained eggs, a tin of coffee and twenty-three loaves of white bread.

What was the suspect doing behind a postal depot at 10.15 in the morning? And why steal a van? The Vauxhall was five years old, one of the old Royal Mail fleet repainted, with minor scratches and a dent on the left side. Hardly very desirable. And not discreet, either—a Vivaro was big. It seemed an odd choice for a surreptitious run-around. Good for transporting all sorts of things, though. Tools, people. It was yet to turn up.

For whatever reason, six days after his tour around the shelters he stole the BMW. New wheels, new start. The BMW theft had been reported at 4 p.m. on Friday, 7 June. It crashed into Belsey's life Monday the tenth.

Three days was plenty of time for a BMW 7 Series to draw attention. Belsey returned to the force intelligence system. The car didn't come up in connection with any crimes. But there were other lines of inquiry; this was London, it was a lot easier to kill a man than to park legally. Belsey called Camden Council Parking Enforcement. Sure enough the BMW had been ticketed the day before yesterday, 7:34 a.m. Sunday, 9 June, on double yellows and a bus route.

"Do you know if any of your officers spoke to the driver?"

"No. It says the vehicle was unattended My officers didn't see anyone return while they were there."

"Where exactly?"

"Earnshaw Street. Just behind Centre Point."

Earnshaw Street was a good result. Bang in the centre of town. The street itself was a back road off an incredibly busy junction. It was a hive of muggings and dealings. It was bound to be cameraed. He wanted the man's face.

Belsey called the council's CCTV control room and told them he needed footage relating to an urgent investigation. He gave the time and location of the parking ticket and said he was on his way. Halfway out of the door Belsey heard his name. He turned.

"Kirsty."

"Nick, could I speak to you?"

He entered her office as the security boss left. The man turned back to Craik and nodded at Belsey.

"That's the one."

Belsey shut the door. Craik gestured at the images from the library spread across her desk.

"Is this you?"

He picked up a CCTV still. He'd been caught on two cameras, two angles, both good shots, neither flattering. At the time he had been staggering around in disbelief, but he looked like he'd broken in, filthy, desperate to browse the shelves.

"It seems to be."

"You've been breaking into the library?"

"No. And the break-ins are more likely to be break-outs, someone trying to leave the building having arrived via tunnels beneath it." Craik looked bemused and slightly pained. "That's why I was there."

"Could you expand on this a little?"

"Underneath the library is an old war control centre or something—tunnels lead from it up to the deep shelter in Belsize Park. That's how I got there."

"The shelter that you wanted a warrant on and I said we weren't in a warrant situation."

"I have reason to believe someone is down there. I went in because I thought a life was in danger."

Belsey evaluated this new strategy as it came out of his mouth. He was embarking upon a course of half-truth, it seemed. A necessary risk. He had to account for his presence in the library and force some action. But it was still a door he had opened and would be unable to close.

"Someone's down there?"

"I heard cries from the shelter. There's definitely signs someone's been in. Ask Constables Andy Durham and Ravni Singh. They were there this morning."

"What kind of cries?"

"A woman. That's what I thought I heard."

Belsey wanted to tell her about the email but that would give them half an ID on the girl and place him centre stage at the same time. It was there if he needed it. He still believed he could get a team down to the tunnels without ever needing to be the object of an investigation himself.

"You threatened council staff with an axe."

"I didn't threaten them. I had an axe with me. I was trying to get to the tunnels and they were obstructing an investigation."

"And what did you find? When you turned up wielding an axe?"

"I was *carrying* it. I didn't find anything. I couldn't find the cupboard with the door behind it. The door's . . . behind a cupboard."

Craik winced.

"Nick, the security manager didn't mention anything about a bunker."

"No one knows about it. I don't think current council staff realise it's there. It's disused. But we need to move on this. We need a specialist team down there taking a look. We might not have long."

She checked his eyes.

"Calm down, Nick. OK?"

His phone rang. He thought it might be CCTV control. He picked it up without looking at the number.

"Two grand, final offer," the chemist said, loudly. "I can clear those pills in a—"

Belsey killed it. Craik stared at him. He began to leave. Then he saw the flowers.

A vase on a shelf at the back was filled with carnations. They had creamy white petals, a line of crimson encroaching on the white. Belsey stared at them. He went over and touched a petal. Black dust came off on his fingers. He turned.

"Where did you get these?" Craik studied his face to see if he was winding her up.

"I don't know," she said. "Do you?"

"They just appeared?"

"Reception gave them to me."

Belsey went downstairs. Crosby was polishing her glasses.

"The carnations," he said.

"Pretty, aren't they?"

"Where did they come from?"

"Someone left them outside. No name. So I thought—given she's just settling in, a welcoming touch."

Crosby stared at Belsey's hand and he realised he was still gripping a petal. He returned to the main office, took a sheet of paper and set the petal down on it. He tapped the petal and watched the deposit that came off. A shadow settling. Subterranean dirt. They were his flowers. Jemma's flowers. His phone rang again.

"Nick Belsey?"

"Yes."

"It's Chib, from Camden CCTV. Those tapes you wanted—can you come in?" He sounded nervous.

"Do you see him park?"

"A bit more than that."

"I'll come in now."

"I think you better."

CCTV CONTROL. THE SPACE STATION, AS IT WAS
known among police, hidden at the top of an
anonymous office block behind Great Portland
Street. It had nine rooms lit by banks of monitors, by the grey forms of oblivious individuals
going about their business.

11

He knew something was up
because they'd given him a
screening room of his own, with
a dedicated CCTV officer running the footage. The room was
dark, dominated by a desk of
switches and digital displays.
The officer on the controls, Chib
Kwesi, was good. Belsey saw him
often enough, pulling footage of
street fights, phone grabs, car crashes. Kwesi
wore a crucifix over his shirt and had a passion
for his job that belonged either to a stern moralist
or a dedicated voyeur. He had the tape lined up.
The stolen BMW was coming into shot. It was
frozen on the screen, approaching from High
Holborn into the shadows beneath Centre Point,
the tower block that dominated the intersection
of Oxford Street and Charing Cross Road.

Time stamp: 04.19 a.m. Three hours, fifteen
minutes before the parking ticket was issued.

"It's not a great angle," Kwesi said.

"Do we get his face?"

"Not well."

"What do we get?"

He hit play. The BMW parked across the road from the camera, facing towards New Oxford Street. For a moment the car just sat there. The footage was low res, black-and-white, five frames per second. The vehicle sat right at the back of the shot. It wasn't going to give a clear account of anything, let alone a face.

"Is this the only camera we get him on?"

"Yes."

A couple of early morning revellers appeared, cutting unsteadily towards Charing Cross Road. Two more minutes passed. Then the driver's door opened and a man got out. He wore a familiar grey hoodie, hood up.

"Wait," Kwesi said.

Belsey expected the suspect to turn but he didn't. He went to the rear door closest to the camera and opened it. There was someone else in the car. The driver reached in and they embraced. The passenger put an arm around his shoulder. Then, as the driver moved back, you saw that the arm was bare, his passenger naked. The passenger refused to release the driver, apparently trying to drag him back into the car. Finally the driver pushed backwards and the naked figure fell to the pavement. Kwesi hit pause.

"Corpse," Belsey said.

"That's what it looks like to me."

Belsey caught his breath. He seized implications. Firstly, whatever doubts he may have had as to the gravity of the situation, the intent of his antagonist, could be packed away. Here was someone who trafficked in dead bodies. It made Jemma's abduction part of something bigger. How did they connect? Kill someone Saturday night, abduct someone Monday evening. Was she a bargaining chip? A last hurrah? Just the latest?

More to the point, what was his suspect doing here, parked thirty seconds from Oxford Street? London wasn't short of neglected corners to dispose of unwanted dead.

They rewound and watched the extraction again—he couldn't see if the body was male or female. The driver stood above the body, obscuring it. He spent a moment staring down. Then he crouched and dragged it into the road, then out of shot beneath the camera. He couldn't have dragged it far. He came back into shot fifteen seconds later, looking around the sides of the surrounding buildings as if he planned to scale them. At 04.23 he reached into the car and retrieved something from either the glove compartment or the dashboard. He took it across the road, in the direction of the corpse, shaking it.

"A can of something," Kwesi said.

"A spray can."

Eighty seconds passed. The suspect returned without the can, checked the doors of the BMW were locked and strolled off towards New Oxford Street.

"He just leaves the car and body there?" Belsey asked.

"That's right."

Kwesi hit fast forward. At 04.44 a man and woman staggered into view; he pressed her up against a wall and she slipped a hand under his shirt as they kissed. Then she looked past him. You saw the woman recoil. The man turned, then also took a step back. You couldn't see their expressions. You saw the woman fish a phone out of her handbag and speak without taking her eyes off the corpse.

04.57. The windows of the car and the office block began to flash: an ambulance with high top lights arriving somewhere to the left. At 05.02 more bulbs began to gather in the glass: police. The concrete lit up. The BMW sat insouciant throughout it all. No one paid it any attention. By 05.20, crime scene technicians must have got there. An indistinct figure crossed into shot, non-uniform. Someone strung tape in the distance, blocking the road from Holborn. The activity went on for about an hour, building, then dispersing. Then nothing at all: 06.37.

"What happened?" Belsey said.

06.59. A man in T-shirt and shorts urinated against the wall to the right of the shot before staggering back to Tottenham Court Road.

"Go to when it was ticketed," Belsey said.

07.29. A parking attendant waddled into view. He checked his watch, circled the vehicle, bit a pen. The clock hit 07.30 and he tapped away at his machine. Nothing appeared to alert him to the fact that he was a few metres from a recent body dump. The ticket was logged at 07.34. Belsey knew wardens: he could almost believe that the man's attention to parking violations would eclipse any homicide concerns, but not quite.

"That, my friend, is one hell of a quick clean-up operation."

Earnshaw Street, he thought. Back of Centre Point. Belsey brought up the email from Ferryman. The image of the building. The side of a tower block.

"Look at this." He passed the phone over. "What do you reckon?"

"It's Centre Point." Kwesi read the subject line. "'Did you get your badge?' Who is this?"

"I think the email's from whoever's leaving the body. Go back to when he drops it. Can you enhance his face?"

"Not well."

Chib showed him. The image of the suspect's face was grained almost to the point of pixelated anonymity. Belsey could see the corpse's arm. It was thin. Still hard to tell if the flesh had belonged to a man or a woman. Belsey's instinct was leaning towards male. No long hair visible anyway. Then it dropped.

The spray can. Followed by the eighty seconds off camera. The stroll away.

"Where does he go?"

"Nowhere. That's the strangest thing. There's eight cameras within a couple of hundred metres and he's not on any of them. I've checked."

"He disappears."

"Exactly."

Belsey felt a familiar combination of emotions: awe, frustration, total perplexity.

"But he collects the BMW at some point," Belsey said. "I was chasing it thirty-six hours later."

Kwesi skipped to 09.20 a.m. The man returned alone, walking fast, checking the street. He spent a moment beside the BMW, apparently admiring the clean-up. A school party crossed in front of him, young children holding hands. Then he tore the parking ticket off the windscreen and climbed back in. He pulled out hurriedly and disappeared towards New Oxford Street. Kwesi paused the tape.

Belsey called in a check on the body. He didn't remember hearing of any corpses turning up on Sunday morning. He was right: no bodies had been discovered at that time. Not according to Local Intelligence. He tried Central Communications Command and they knew nothing either. Nor did the Met-wide emergency response system or the Yard's own call-handling centre. Belsey phoned the two squads that bordered the dump site: Camden Borough headquarters, then Westminster police at West End Central. He got flat denials.

Belsey turned back to the tapes. This wasn't right.

"Run it from when the police arrive, triple speed."

They watched the empty space, lit by the refracted light-show of an emergency. The comical high-speed blooming of the incident—the shadows of *someone*, *some* people on the concrete. Then the departure.

"See how fast they leave?" Belsey said. "Police, SOC; they just pile out of there."

They watched the whole thing from start to finish, three times. Kwesi crossed himself. Belsey crossed himself. They spent a few seconds staring at their reflections in the blank screen.

BELSEY HEADED TO CENTRE POINT WITH A CD OF THE footage in his pocket, wondering what story it contained.

He arrived as the day hit noon, parked on the corner of Oxford Street and Charing Cross Road, pushed through the mesh of pedestrians towards the tower block. What a place to leave a corpse: the spiritual centre of the West End, which was a contradiction in terms. Centre Point was thirty-four floors of bleak, latticed concrete. It marked a meeting of the ways—the retail purgatory of Oxford Street, Soho to the west: bars and clubs and strip-shows. To the south was theatreland, to the east the museums and universities of Bloomsbury. You could see the tower block for miles, stuck in the middle of all this, its name lit up across the top as if it meant something. A beacon. A lighthouse warning you away from the rocks.

12

Everything converged on Centre Point, including the traffic which knotted at its foot. The area around the base was dismal, its confusion currently exacerbated by the endless construc-

tion site for a new rail link. Heavy grey columns elevated the
first floor of the building and created a maze of dark passages, leading seamlessly into a grim subway. As a child
Belsey had associated this burrow with the sleeping homeless who filled it. As a young man, with the pool hall that led
off the same loveless underpass.

Earnshaw Street, where the body had been left, was
part of this mess, a cut-through created by the crash-land-
ing of the tower block. It was a gap, with three Korean
restaurants and a lesbian bar, all huddled together in deep
shadow, as if there was strength in numbers. He saw the
bloodstains immediately. They were on a stub of pavement
beside the stairs up to Centre Point's main entrance. They'd
been scrubbed into strange patterns: pale, interlocked circles that Belsey decoded as an attempt to clean the paving
stones with a sponge of some kind. Garters of police tape
clung to railings. Tiny silver fragments of a foil ambulance
blanket remained caught in the spikes of some dead shrubbery potted at the base. They looked like futuristic blos-
soms. He saw fingerprint dust on the glass behind it. The
place had evidently received full forensic attention at some
point.

He plucked a scrap of foil from the shrubbery. The corpse
can't have looked that old if they'd tried to wrap it. He stuck
a toe into the mulch of old carrier bags and cigarette packets
behind the plant pot and saw something wedged there. A
spray can. Belsey pulled it out and shook it. The brand was
"Hycote," colour: "Colorado Red." It was still heavy with
paint. Whoever had done the clearing must have been in a
hurry.

But not too hurried for a bit of redecoration. Belsey sniffed. He touched the wall in front of him. It was tacky with a fresh coat of grey paint. He stepped back, then crossed the road to gain a better vantage. Sprayed in upper case letters three feet high, on the concrete underbelly of Centre Point itself, was the word "CAVE." The attempt to hide the word with a rushed paint job only made it seem more significant. Letters seemed to be emerging from the concrete itself.

Belsey took the spray can to his car and threw it in. He checked with Dispatch once more. No record of a body came up. He tried three officers who might have been patrolling the area. None had heard of anything. There are clean-ups and then there are cover-ups, he thought. To wipe a record from the Emergency Response Database you needed to be sitting at or near the top.

He went and stood where the BMW had been parked and tried to trace the route the body would have been dragged. The individual would have had extra cover: Denmark Street to the south was entirely blocked by the hoardings of the Crossrail building site. The car itself would be rich with evidence. Where was it? He realised he had no idea of its fate since he'd last seen it abandoned by the deep shelter. He called Camden Borough HQ.

"There was a stolen BMW left in Belsize Park yesterday, around five p.m. Do you know what happened to it?"

"Sure. It's in Perivale."

Perivale was home to the Met's car pound. Belsey gave them a call.

"A silver BMW 7 series brought in yesterday—have you still got it?"

"Yes. We've just been told it can be released."

"OK, it's just become evidence in a murder inquiry. You need to hold it. I'm on my way over now."

IT WAS 12:30 P.M. when he got to the Vehicle and Evidence Recovery Service. Belsey turned off the A40, past the giant Tesco, to the car pound. A guard opened locked gates and directed Belsey to an office in a Portakabin. Another guard checked the records then led Belsey across the tarmac.

The place was a cross between a prison and an eccentric museum. There were distinct zones: the sculptures of destruction, the plain old uninsured, the stolen. Then, on the high-security wing, under a plastic roof, there were those awaiting forensics attention.

The BMW was at the front. Belsey put latex gloves on. He opened the doors and stepped back as the reek escaped. Clearly no one had checked it. The car had a plush interior: beige leather upholstery, chrome trim, headrest DVD screens. But it stank. You could see faint red-brown staining over the back seat. It smelt like purge fluid: blood but also stomach acid, and stomach contents. He gave the upholstery a bang. No maggots. So the corpse hadn't been more than a few hours old. He'd seen cars that had transported older corpses. They were a crawling mess.

The boot was empty. He searched the front of the car, trying not to breathe. A packet of tissues in the map pocket, aviator sunglasses, a 500ml bottle of Evian. In the footwell of the passenger seat was a magazine. Belsey lifted it out. The page it was turned to contained classified adverts:

*Write to service men and women . . . Military Memorabilia
Fair . . . Army–Navy Rugby Match.*

He turned to the front cover. *Military Heritage*, from
February 2013. The cover showed a picture of a tank. He
flicked through the pages: two separate features on D-Day,
articles on the first Gulf war, the Eastern Front, amphibious
vehicles and medal collecting. Then a lot of adverts: memorabilia for sale, regimental reunions, charities for veterans.
Nothing on shelters or tunnels.

The magazine wasn't scuffed. There were no footmarks,
suggesting it had been thrown off the passenger seat during
the chase. Belsey turned it back as he'd found it. Then he
took it to his car and placed it in an evidence bag.

ACCORDING TO THE REPORT, the BMW belonged to a Dr. Joseph Green, resident of 12 Windmill Drive, Highgate. Belsey
drove over. He felt the usual release from destitution as he
climbed Highgate Hill. London was a city of villages but
only a few of them had the high ground needed to keep the
rest of the population at bay. The doctor's house was tall,
Georgian, covered in ivy, with a melancholy space in front
where its BMW should have been. It was almost 2 p.m.
Jemma had been missing seventeen hours—seventeen hours
in the company of a man who was careless with dead bodies.
Belsey walked through a wild front garden containing several statues of the Buddha, knocked on Green's front door,
then pushed. It opened.

"Coming," a woman called.

Not only was the front door open, they kept their keys on

a rack just inside it. Why make it difficult for criminals? Maybe it was assumed that all the crime stayed at the bottom of the hill. The woman appeared, holding secateurs, in an airy blue dress and an explosion of silver-streaked hair.

"Is this always open?" Belsey asked.

"Oh, someone must have left it like that. Do you have an appointment?" she asked. Then she glanced uncertainly at the bagged magazine in his hand.

"I have a few questions about the theft of your BMW. I'm from Hampstead CID."

"Ah, police. It's Joseph you want to speak to. I'm Rebecca, his wife. The car's nothing to do with me. Come through. He's just with a patient."

She led him down a corridor sagging with bookshelves to a large room with four chairs, a lot of plants and one man already waiting. "Joseph won't be a minute." Rebecca gestured at a closed door, then excused herself. The other man shifted his weight and seemed anxious about losing his place in the queue. He wore a tweed suit, ginger goatee and glasses. Belsey checked his watch. He checked the books around the room. No evidence of military interests. Practically every other interest though: ritual, myth, dreams, childhood. It was dawning on him what kind of medicine Green practised.

"Your first time?" The man in tweed asked.

"Not really. You?"

"Me?" This amused him greatly. "I'm one of the disciples." He laughed. "I'm writing about the development of his theories."

"Are they good?"

"Are they good!" The man laughed again. The study

door opened and a patient emerged, fresh from confession and unsettled by the laughter. He straightened his tie. His navy suit looked second-hand. The disciple turned to him. "What would you say? Is Joseph any good?"

"Joseph? Yes, of course. He's . . . Joseph." The patient blinked, a little clammy, eager to please.

"Excuse me," Belsey said, and moved past him into the consultation room. The doctor was behind a desk, writing fast. He had very bright white hair and a long, clean-shaven face. He wore a blue jumper over a white shirt, a little elegantly crumpled like the room around him. The desk was large and crowded, the backs of photo frames arranged like a defensive wall. Sash windows looked onto a luxuriously unkempt garden. Beside the window were African masks, Indian puppets, Japanese prints. Everything you'd expect to find. Beneath the window was the couch.

"Detective Constable Nick Belsey," Belsey said, showing his badge. Joseph Green looked up and his eyes sparkled. He capped his pen. There was the sheen of health worn by successful seventy-year-olds in the healing professions. It was around the edges you saw he was old: the veins of the hands, the corners of the eyes. He glimpsed the "disciple" outside and seemed glad of Belsey as a delay.

"Is this yours?" Belsey handed him the magazine in the evidence bag.

Green studied it.

"No. Why?"

"It was in your car. Can you think of any way it might have got there?"

"Got there? No. It's only me who uses the BMW." The

doctor seemed simultaneously amused and appalled by the magazine, handling the evidence bag as if it contained something exotic and possibly dangerous. He read through the plastic. "Signal squadron . . . Veterans . . ."

So, Belsey thought, he had a solid lead: a rare magazine, a specialist community. His suspect was a man of certain interests.

"What is it?" Green asked.

"A magazine called *Military Heritage.* Did anyone see the man who took your car?"

"I don't think so. Does this belong to him?"

"That would be one explanation. Have police run any forensic checks on your home? The front door? The key rack?"

"No." Green handed the magazine back. "To be honest, I got the impression . . . I got the feeling they would investigate but it wasn't top priority. I know you people are busy."

There was a knock.

"Ah, Hugh," Green forced a smile. The disciple had moved his restless shifting to the doorway. Belsey thanked the doctor and left.

He moved from the Bohemian clutter of the house into the smart road and worked a hypothesis. The suspect had the magazine when he stole the car. He had it out, open at a certain page. Belsey slipped it from the bag. He glanced across the adverts for service charities and veterans' associations. Filling the lower half of the right-hand page was a black-and-white photograph of a crowd in uniform. *Were you here? Did you or any family members serve in the 2nd Signal Brigade, 81 Signal Squadron . . .*

He wondered how to edge this situation into significance, enough for door-to-door enquiries, *Military Heritage* enquiries, forensic checks, all while keeping himself out of the picture. He sensed he was almost making progress. Then his phone rang.

"Nick," Rosen said. "We've got a journalist calling for you—about a missing woman." Belsey felt a jolt. He scrambled for the meaning of this. "Said it was urgent."

"Who?"

"Tom Monroe, on the *Express*. Know him?"

"We used to drink together. What's he saying?"

"He needed to ask you about a missing woman."

"A current investigation?"

"I don't know."

"Have there been any other calls about it?"

"No."

"What woman? Is something going on?"

"Not that I know of, Nick. But it wasn't me he wanted a conversation with."

Belsey called Monroe. He caught him at his desk for once. He could hear keyboards in the background.

"Tom, what have you heard?"

"Someone gone missing yesterday. Your neck of the woods."

"Who?"

"Let's say she was twenty-something, cute, long black hair."

"How do you know about this?"

"I got an email."

"From who?"

"I don't know exactly."

"Tom, this is highly sensitive, OK? This is not out there. I'm heading over to you now. Don't do anything. Don't write anything."

"In that case I'd probably be better off in the Jamaica, Nick. Your round."

THE *EXPRESS* OFFICES WERE ON LOWER THAMES Street, by the river. The Jamaica Wine House hid around the corner on a back street and Monroe used to boast he could make it there from his desk, drink a pint and return in under three and a half minutes.

He was taking it slower today. Belsey saw the depleted pint of Guinness first, then the legs stretched out, scuffed Chelsea boots crossed. Monroe was sunk deep in an ox-blood leather booth. He had the back room to himself, lunch crowd gone, empties still on the tables. He eyed Belsey and tilted himself upright without removing his hands from his pockets. His black suit had worn to a greasy shine. He looked like an undertaker who'd just been fired.

"What have you got?" Belsey said.

Monroe found his hands, then produced a pack of Camel Blues from one pocket and his phone from the other. He balanced the phone on the cigarettes and tapped it. The email appeared:

From: Ferryman@tempmail.net
Subject: Missing 11/06/2013. NW3 area.
Can you help?

"Can you help?" Monroe asked.

Attached was a photograph. Jemma turned her head towards the camera. Her wrists were bound with duct tape, another twisted cord of tape running from the improvised restraints to a control panel in front of her. The panel was similar to the one Belsey had seen the previous night: telephone receivers, attack switches. Same equipment, but the room was larger, painted white. Her hair was tied back, a messy ponytail held in a rubber band. Her mascara was streaked but the eyes were dry now. Hostage weariness. Not someone really in the mood for photos. There was grazing on the upper arms. He couldn't see other injuries. His Maglite sat on the table beside the equipment.

"Is it for real?" Monroe asked.

"Looks real enough to me. Any idea who she is?"

"No. Do you?"

"Not yet."

Monroe looked thoughtful. But also aroused. His eyes were black and bright. There were people Belsey would prefer had this story. Monroe possessed one of the finest minds Belsey had drunk with, which hadn't made the journalist happy, rich or very often sober. They'd first met under an East London fish market, in the Ship Tavern, a basement bar that kept strange hours for the market porters. It served pints at dawn. A group of them went through a big Ship phase: journalists, police and a few nocturnal entrepreneurs. They called themselves the Breakfast Club and thought it was witty.

Monroe had been an art historian when they started drinking together, but he'd written a series of books on espionage to pay off drug debts and two of these were almost best sellers. *Britain's Most Notorious Spies* was still in print. Then someone on the *Express* killed themselves, and he was offered the defence desk and eventually news. He was good at it because he was genuinely curious but seemed indifferent and aloof. His books did well because they were about secrets. Belsey used to say he should be a detective. There was something cold at the centre of Monroe that made him good company on self-destructive nights and made you wonder what you'd told him when you woke the next morning. When Borough CID fell, he splashed the lot.

"This isn't public yet," Belsey said. "It needs to not be public. You could jeopardise an investigation and put her in real danger."

"What's she in right now?"

"It looks like she's alive, which is something."

Monroe considered this.

"I thought maybe it was off a fetish website. Technology perverts. Then something made me sit up. The machine she's taped to, it's part of HANDEL."

"What's HANDEL?"

"The old emergency communications system, for spreading word of a nuclear attack." Belsey took a closer look at the machine. "The lights come on if an impending strike is detected," Monroe explained. "Then the operator flicks the switch here and says their piece. It uses the frequency of the speaking clock. The clock was a warm-up act. It kept the line in working order, ready."

Belsey looked from the machine to Jemma's eyes again. Had she been drugged? Beaten? Monroe also met her eyes.

"Who is she, Nick? Either you've got a name for her or

you don't. If you don't then I reckon you need to publicise this picture pretty quickly and get one. If you know already, then why are you holding out on a friend? Have you sold this to someone else?"

"No. Are others on this?"

"Not that I'm aware of."

"Why did it go to you?"

"That was the other thing that made me sit up. I wrote about him."

"Who?"

"Ferryman." Monroe pointed at the email address. His face flickered with a smile, as if he'd surprised himself with this news.

"What do you mean?"

"Paraomshtik. Ferryman. He was a spy for the Soviets during the cold war. A mole. Passed intelligence on UK nuclear arrangements."

Two women came into the back room holding wine. They looked at Belsey and Monroe and walked out again.

"Tell me about Ferryman," Belsey said.

"There's nothing more to tell. He's one of the unsolved. No one knows who he was."

"Is it possible this is him?"

Monroe laughed. "Sending us mail? How can I put this, Nick: it's not standard tradecraft."

"Then someone's borrowed the name. I need to know why."

The journalist looked surprised and slightly disappointed that Belsey had chosen this detail to latch on to.

"Ferryman was a British citizen, someone involved with

the government, high up, close to very sensitive information. He must have been in a position of some influence in the late seventies and early eighties because the Russians went to great lengths to protect him. That's all anyone knows, outside of the KGB and maybe MI6. MI6 still doesn't discuss it. If he's alive, he's old. Old and no doubt very tired. Sound like your man?"

"So someone's chosen his name and got in touch with you."

"I get odd emails. The cold war does things to people. There are obsessives."

"What did you write about him?"

"Not much beyond what I've told you."

"Must have livened up the book."

Monroe shrugged. "People like a bit of mystery. They like a drink too." He finished his pint and displayed the empty glass. Belsey got two Guinnesses in, thinking through this new development as they settled. Paraomshtik. Ferryman. *The cold war does things to people.* What kind of obsessive was he dealing with? He brought the drinks over.

"You say it's still confidential."

"Details remain sensitive."

"Why?"

"I don't know. Obviously."

"So where did you get information?"

"I stole it off some better writers who'd put a lot of time and effort in. Where do you think? He's an interesting figure. Interesting enough for both sides to have allowed him to sink back into obscurity. Still, I don't think he reinvented himself along these lines. I don't think he's resurrected his old handle for the sake of abducting girls and trying to create a media commotion."

They sat in silence for a moment. Then Belsey decided to share.

"Do you know St. Pancras Library? The ugly concrete building opposite the train station?"

"Some would call it a masterpiece of the Brutalist style, but yes, go on." Monroe sipped, intrigued.

"Last night I followed a tunnel from a deep-level bomb shelter in Belsize Park to a bunker under the library. I ended up in a room with communications equipment. It was set up with this system: HANDEL."

The journalist checked Belsey's face for sincerity.

"Are you sure?"

"I'm pretty clean these days, Tom. I know when I'm stuck in a cold-war bunker and when I'm just having a bad night. I was there: it had the switches, the phones, all under the council HQ. Have you heard anything about tunnels like that? A system?"

"No. What were you *doing* down there?"

"Trying very hard to get out. The bunker beneath the library was last used in 1983, by the look of it. Does that make sense?"

"I don't see why not. There was almost a nuclear war in the eighties. It wasn't all cocaine and Duran Duran. Things were tense."

"Does Ferryman connect to that?"

"Sure. That's the period. Why?"

"Why? Because I'm trying to get something to make sense here. You can see I'm struggling."

"I can see you're struggling, but I can't see what it's about. Is there an ongoing investigation? Is there a media team I can speak to? Or are you just tunnelling around on your own. Who made *you* Spycatcher?"

Belsey drank. He wondered. He'd walked into it. Driven into it. He'd been in the wrong place at the right time—was that it? And then he'd encroached on someone's lair.

"I can't go into more details just yet."

"So I'm not meant to run any of this."

"Not a word. I can make sure you're the first to know when we've got something. You'll have it on exclusive. But I need you to help. To find out about this underground system."

"It would be more helpful running this picture."

"No. That's what he wants." Belsey picked up Monroe's phone. "Have you replied to the email?"

"Of course not."

Belsey pressed reply and typed: *I'd like to interview you. Speak to me, I think I can help.* He sent the message, then forwarded the email to himself. Then he deleted it from Monroe's phone.

"Tell me if you hear anything," he said. "Me, not anyone else."

"I might call the police next time." Monroe took his phone and cigarettes and walked out. Belsey sat for a moment in the shadows with the pint glasses. He looked at the picture of Jemma again and the HANDEL attack-warning equipment. He tried calling her mobile and it went to voicemail. Phone could be dead. She could be dead. She could be underground; phone could be underground. He had a thought.

Belsey called three mobile phone companies and ran Jemma's number by them. Jemma Stevens wasn't a customer of Talk Talk or O2. He got a result from Vodafone: she had been a contract customer for two years. Belsey gave the necessary credentials to be put through to their police liaison department.

"Hamish speaking."

"Hamish, does this phone have a locator service?" Belsey gave her number.

"No."

"Any kind of tracking set up?"

"Afraid not. There's no GPS on this make of Nokia."

"Could you tell me when it was last used?"

"No calls or texts have been made since Monday evening."

"We've got a possible kidnap situation. Can you ping it for me?"

"Hold on a minute."

Pinging a phone the old-school way meant locating it by establishing which mast was closest. 999 calls automatically got a ping location. Otherwise, without consent of the phone owner, it was slightly more complicated. Sure enough, when Hamish came back he asked if Belsey had a court order.

"I'm getting it through now. But we're looking at minutes rather than hours. Hang on." He half covered the receiver. "They matched the skin patch? OK, no. Removed while they were alive? A square of skin? Are you joking? Yes, I'm speaking to her phone company now. Hamish? Are you still there?"

"NW3, yesterday," Hamish said. "8:21 p.m. That's when the phone was last in signal." NW3 was Belsize Park. 8:21 p.m.

was Belsey taking her down. Not much help. "Then the signal cut out."

"OK."

Belsey was about to ring off when Hamish said: "Hang on. Are you still there?"

"I'm here."

"There's a weak signal now."

"Same mast?"

"No. Holborn area."

"The phone's in Holborn now?"

"It's a very weak signal, coming and going. Either the batteries are dying or there's some obstruction."

Belsey grabbed the *A-Z* from his jacket.

"Can you narrow that down at all?"

"The tower covers WC1. That's the tower she's receiving signals from. I can't tell you any more than that."

Belsey tried to remember the nearest deep shelter to Holborn. He'd marked nothing on the *A-Z* until Goodge Street, a mile away. He brought up the list of shelters on his phone. It mentioned one around Chancery Lane. According to the site it had been built but never opened to the public. Built between 1940 and 1942 and never opened. So what the hell was down there?

FIVE O'CLOCK, ELECTRICITY IN THE AIR, STORM CLOUDS imposing a heavy silver twilight. Belsey parked on Gray's Inn Road and walked to Chancery Lane tube station. The shelters never seemed to stray far from the tube. Men and women streamed past, out of the courts and legal chambers, smart, harried, scanning the sky. He searched the surrounding architecture for war. His senses were open. He looked for the tell-tale bricks and geometry, for cameras and barbed wire. He walked up and down High Holborn, gazing over the heads of the crowd, looking in the cracks between sandwich shops and newsagents.

The pavement prickled. She was under his feet. There were hatches in the ground. Once Belsey began looking he saw them everywhere: iron manhole covers, weathered, some ancient, marked with the names of companies who once had privileged access to what lay below. TWA— Thames Water Authority, long gone. LEB, London Electricity Board, that was disbanded. CATV? He had no idea. There were some with the old 1980s British Telecom logo. Belsey knelt and checked the locks. Commuters parted around him. The hatches needed special lifting tools. A pair of Community Support Officers saw him and stopped. Belsey straightened. They lifted a radio and he slipped off the main road onto a narrow side street.

Furnival Street. He sensed something about the place before he knew what it was. A security camera assessed him from the top of a pole planted on a narrow island in the centre of the road. *Images are recorded in the interests of National Security.* The City of London liked to keep itself secure but didn't camera every square inch. No banks around, nothing high risk. Then Belsey saw it, squeezed nonchalantly between the office buildings: a slab of moody brick and grey tiles. It conformed to the size and shape of the buildings either side but this structure had no windows, just black steel doors at ground level and a ventilation grille across the whole of the second floor, like a mouth. Its most striking feature, however, was an industrial-size winch mechanism swivelled to fit flush against the bricks. It looked like something you'd see on an old warehouse or a mine.

The internet on his phone was down. Belsey hesitated, then called the office. Rob Trapping picked up.

"Rob, I need you to run a search online for me."

"What is it?"

"I need you to find out what happened to the deep-level bomb shelter at Chancery Lane."

"What?"

"Just search it: Chancery Lane deep shelter."

Trapping tapped at his keyboard.

"It never opened," he said.

"I know. But it was built."

"Hang on." It took him a minute. "Nick, I've got a website that says twin tunnels were excavated under Chancery Lane during the Second World War." Trapping paused. "This is weird."

"What is it?"

"They were then used by the government."

"For what?"

"They reckon some kind of secret telephone exchange."

"Underground?"

"Yes. According to this it stretches for a mile beneath High Holborn. It says here it has its own water supply from an underground water source, food stores, oil reserves."

"Stretches for a mile in which direction?"

"Nick, this could all be bollocks. It's just some amateur's website."

Belsey was already heading back to the main road.

"It follows the length of High Holborn?"

"Supposedly. This is what the site says." Trapping read in a faltering monotone: "The spine of the exchange is a tunnel 100 feet down on the northern side of High Holborn, between Hatton Garden and Bloomsbury Square. It runs under Gray's Inn Road. Eating and sleeping facilities are situated on the Bloomsbury side. The Hatton Garden end has communications equipment and generators."

"Where's the entrance?"

"31 High Holborn, apparently."

"Hold on."

Belsey found number 31. It was a new apartment building, its salmon-pink imitation marble no more than ten years old. A passageway split the building from a tax accountant's. Belsey ran down and saw an older extension jutting out: darker bricks, windowless, with one wooden door and an old sign: *London Transport Executive*. The door didn't budge a millimetre when he pushed it. There was no handle. He thumped with his fist, and it felt solid as a wall.

"Any other entrances?"

"Furnival Street," Trapping said. "It had a goods lift for transporting machinery down to the tunnels."

"I saw that. The winch is still there but there's no way in."

"That's everything, Nick. I've got to go. Sergeant Craik's back."

Belsey circled the area a final time. He found a metal chimney rising improbably out of a pedestrianized area on Leather Lane. It looked like some piece of public art. Office workers sat on the base, checking their phones, feet dangling over the abyss. He imagined cries for help coming from the chimney, startling them from their cappuccinos.

It stretches for a mile . . .

Belsey tried to feel the shape of it beneath him. Where did it end? He went back to High Holborn and turned, looking west over what must have been the length of it. He stared towards the hubbub of Oxford Street, the junction with Charing Cross Road, the one building alone against the sky: Centre Point.

THE RECEPTION AREA AT THE BASE OF CENTRE POINT
was very white, with a list of the building's occupants on a backlit panel behind the security
desk. Belsey read through, ignoring the stare of
the guard sunk low in his swivel chair: a couple
of foreign oil companies, a talent agency, a restaurant on the top floor. Nothing
that leapt out and said nuclear-
proof telephone exchange. The
restaurant had its own lift. It
also had a sign saying "Closed
for Private Function." But he
wasn't looking to go up anyway.
He wanted to explore the lowest
floors. Belsey moved for the
stairs.

15

 "Excuse me," the guard said.
 "Hi."
 "Who are you visiting?"
Belsey glanced at the list again.
 "All-Star Talent Agency." It was a bad choice.
The guard raised an eyebrow.
 "Your name?"
 "They're not expecting me."
 "Really."
 "I'll give them a call instead."
 Belsey left the reception and walked around
the concrete struts to a bar that occupied part of

the building's ground-level sprawl. Until a few months ago it had been a cheap and cheerful dive for students, and businessmen looking to prey on them. Now it had installed a girl by the door and was calling itself a private members' club. Still his best chance of gaining access.

"I'm interested in joining," he told the young gatekeeper. The girl looked him up and down.

"Have you emailed?"

"I don't use email."

This threw her a little. He glanced past. It looked quiet inside.

"Do you have any members?" he asked.

"It's early."

"I'd like to take a look around, see if it meets my needs."

The girl was too detached for a confrontation. She squeezed a click counter and let him through "for a few minutes." The bar was as he remembered it, only they'd stripped off the wallpaper and painted the furniture white. The barmaid was a stoned Spanish girl with a tongue piercing. Belsey waited for her to finish chalking up a list of cocktails.

"Strange question," Belsey said. "Are you aware of any levels beneath the building?"

She shook her head.

"Do you have a basement?"

"Just the toilets."

"Where are the kitchens?"

The girl pointed behind the bar.

Belsey got a whisky sour. He sunk into a sofa at the back, dialled the number for Land Registry and asked when Centre Point was built. They said 1963. He asked who the first occupants were and this took them longer.

"We don't have anyone until 1973. Then several private businesses."

"1973? I need to know who was in it first, after it was built."

"It was empty. That is the first: 1973."

"There was no one in it for ten years?"

"That's right."

He turned his mobile off and on. Internet returned. He typed *Centre Point* into his phone and found articles about the West End, redevelopment, bars, tourism. Then, several scrolls down, one entitled: "Mystery of Central London Eye-Sore."

Recent weeks have seen proposals to re-landscape the notorious urban mess around the base of Centre Point. Yet what the glossy presentations fail to disclose is the mysterious past of this London landmark. The tower block has always been dogged by controversy. When it was built in 1963 it flew in the face of all planning regulations, leading members of the public to wonder why the government stepped in at the last moment to push it through. Suspicions grew when the building was subsequently left empty for the first ten years of its life.

Its special status, not only as central London's first skyscraper but also as one of the very first buildings in the UK to be fully air-conditioned, led some to speculate as to its usefulness to the government in the event of a nuclear attack. Rumours also suggest that the building's height served, at least in part, as a pretext for excavation, and that Centre Point goes down almost as far as it goes up, with at least ten floors of reinforced offices beneath the structure.

Either way, the priority appears to have been strength and security. Street-level landscaping was an after-thought, and possibly determined by the need to pro-tect whatever lies below.

Belsey found a couple more articles along the same lines. He walked out and looked up at the building, up to the storm clouds it was threatening to puncture. He walked through the struts of the building to the site of the body dump. Some-one had been back, since his visit this morning, this time with the tools to clean up properly. All traces were now gone: no ends of police tape, no debris; the graffiti had been painted over again, obscuring the letters absolutely.

He walked further round the base. A ramp at the side went down to the entrance of an underground car park. The entrance was sealed by electronic gates through which he could see the ramp continuing, lit by a single yellow light, corkscrewing down between white-painted breeze blocks. The camera watching over this had a familiar sign beneath it: *Stronghold*. It gave the same phone number as the camera beside the Belsize Park shelter.

Belsey tried the gates just in case. He pressed a buzzer on the wall beside the entrance. He waited five minutes for a car to come in or out. None did.

He returned to the bar. A few more customers had ar-rived. He picked up the whisky sour he'd been enjoying, then put it down. He touched the glass again. He lifted the drink to the light and there were no lip marks. No ice had melted. The drink was colder than he'd left it. He looked around.

He shared the bar with a thirty-something couple on an awkward date, three men loudly celebrating, two women who looked like models. Dance music pumped half-heartedly. The sky flashed.

Belsey walked out into a thunder clap loud as a bomb. It set off car alarms. There was sudden laughter, howls. Some-one slammed into him—"Sorry mate"—a gang of kids high on weather, off to steam the late-openings. Belsey checked that he still had his wallet. Clouds opened with a ripping sound. He stared up through the rain at Centre Point. Then back through the streaming windows at his drink.

He checked his jacket for the disc from Camden CCTV and it was gone.

IT WAS 7:15 P.M. BY THE TIME HE MADE IT BACK TO THE station. A crowd had gathered in the small office behind reception. It included Kirsty Craik.

"Sarge, I need to talk to you," Belsey said. It was quite a get together in the little room. People stared at him. Everyone was there, civilian staff, even custody officers. They stood around a small table as if paying their last respects.

16

"Nick," Craik said. "Look."

A package of pale blue tissue paper had been torn open. He thought at first it contained a wig. The hair was dark, long. It was in good condition, glossy beneath the neon bulb; a full head's worth. It spilled from the paper onto the white tabletop. No one touched it.

Belsey put on a pair of latex gloves from a box at the side. He picked up the paper and a small white card fell out. In neat black biro someone had written: *To DC Nick Belsey.*

"Where did it come from?" he asked.

"Left in reception, ten minutes ago," Craik said. Belsey placed the card beside the strands and crouched to the level of the tabletop. The hair had been chopped unevenly. He rubbed a couple of strands between his fingers and a familiar dark dust came off.

"Someone actually entered reception?"

"Yes."

"Who was here?"

"I was," Wendy Chan said. She was back at the reception monitor now, checking the tapes.

"What happened?"

"He walked in, said it was for you, said you'd know what it was about and left. He was white, with a hood up. I'd say thirty to forty."

"Grey hood?"

"Yes. Grey hood, and gloves, I think. We've checked the tapes and there are no clear shots. What is this, Nick? Who is he? Someone winding you up?" Her voice was weak and hopeful.

"Anyone see which way he went?"

"He was gone before we realised what had happened," Chan said.

"Have patrols been alerted?"

"Yes."

Belsey moved past the crowd, back into the rain. The street was empty. He drove to the Belsize Park shelter. No sign of any recent activity around the turret. A little further down the hill there was action, a small, soaked crowd around the tube station. Gates had been drawn across the entrance. Tempers were fraying. A couple of damp Transport Police constables loitered.

"What's going on?" Belsey asked.

"Person on the tracks, near Golders Green."

"A suicide?"

"Don't think so. In the tunnels."

BELSEY SWUNG THE SKODA around and sped to Golders Green. It had a similarly frustrated crowd, blocked by a whiteboard: *Station closed due to person on tracks.* Belsey moved past the notice and showed his badge to the staff member on duty.

"I need to speak to the Station Manager immediately." He was led into the station, along a platform. The platforms were open-air: Golders Green was where the Northern Line surfaced after fifteen miles underground. To the north, overground track ran through low-built suburbia. To the south, a tangle of rails ran into three black holes, sinking under central London. It was an obvious entry point for someone wanting to explore what lay beneath the city.

The Station Manager greeted Belsey wearily. He was tall and grey with thick-lensed glasses. He had his bicycle clips on and was holding empty Tupperware. Home time. Only one colleague remained; he wore a hi-vis jacket and was reading a paperback propped on his stomach.

"What can we do for you?"

"I need to know about the trespasser."

"Yes, I spoke to one of your lot a moment ago. Southbound tunnels. Don't know what happened."

"Did anyone see the intruder?"

"No. But they triggered an alarm." The manager didn't seem unduly fazed.

"When was this?"

"About half an hour ago. I don't know where they went. Haven't been any more alarms set off."

"Are people looking for them now?"

"No."

"Are you able to pinpoint exactly where they triggered the alarm?"

The manager put his Tupperware down and showed Belsey a metal alarm panel in a control room behind the office. It had a map of the tracks studded with small bulbs, then switches underneath for deactivating alarms at entry points and stretches of tracks while engineering or inspections took place.

"Here." The manager touched a bulb in the centre, halfway between Hampstead and Golders Green. "Around North End."

"What's North End?"

"The old station."

Belsey peered closer. He had spent half his life travelling the Northern Line. There was no station between Hampstead and Golders Green. Yet the map thought there was: North End.

"When was there a station?"

"Never." Now the man allowed himself a smile. "It never opened. Abandoned before it was half-built. Stupid idea. They thought there was going to be a development on the Heath."

"When was that?"

"About a century ago."

"What's there now?"

"Bits and pieces." He checked his watch and drummed his fingers on the Tupperware.

"What's that meant to mean?"

"I don't know what's there now."

"Is there an entrance above ground?"

"Sort of, but it's not obvious. It's on the corner of Hampstead Way and Wildwood Road—just a little white box, like a Portakabin. There's stairs down to what's left of the station."

Belsey knew Hampstead Way and Wildwood Road. Nice houses, occasional burglaries. He'd never noticed any portals leading underground.

"Could the trespasser have got in that way?"

"Not easily."

Belsey went back to the map of the track and tunnel system.

"But they triggered the alarm near the abandoned station."

"Roughly."

"And there was no sighting of them here or at Hampstead?"

"No."

"How far is North End from the stations on either side?"

"About a kilometre in each direction."

"I'd like to see it."

"North End?"

"Yes."

He stared at Belsey. An odd smile curled his upper lip.

"You've got to be joking. I couldn't authorise it anyway. North End's nothing to do with us."

"Who's it to do with?"

"It's got special security."

"What do you mean?"

The man shrugged. "I don't have authorisation. Besides, there's only the two of us on duty and I'm about to clock off." He checked his watch again and swore. "I've got to run now, in fact."

Belsey was about to explain that he was in pursuit of a murder suspect and what this meant in terms of priorities, but it seemed unlikely to win the manager over. He seemed scared by the place and Belsey wanted to know why.

"OK," Belsey said. "I just need to do some checks around here."

"For what?"

"Fingerprints."

"Fingerprints?"

"I'll see myself out." This was all the manager needed to hear. He picked up his bike helmet, bade farewell to his colleague and left. Belsey waited. The colleague settled back down on his chins. The book rose and fell as he breathed. Belsey gave it thirty seconds. He took a step towards the room with the alarm panel. He waited for his companion to look up. There was no movement. Belsey walked in. He reached for the panel, found the alarm switch for North End and eased it down. He did the same for the sections leading south from Golders Green, then slipped a torch off its hook.

He walked down the platforms to the southern end, past the sign *No Passengers Beyond This Point*, beneath the last of the security cameras. No one stopped him. The platform sloped down to the tracks. He walked on the gravel, along the sidings towards the three black mouths of the tunnels.

He didn't know if all routes passed the ghost station. The middle tunnel seemed as good as any. He stepped over the tracks towards it. The darkness looked solid. Some vague superstition made him wonder if he could just walk in. He could. The air was immediately cooler. Belsey kept the torch off for eighty metres or so, until the entrance was a small coin of world behind him. Then the tunnel curved and the world was gone.

Silence again. Belsey continued south. There'd been a trespasser half an hour ago. How far could he get in that time? Was he heading back to his captive? Belsey stepped from sleeper to sleeper. Every minute or so he'd stop and listen. If someone decided to run a train he'd feel the vibrations. He would have time to press himself against the sides. He'd be visible, though.

Ten minutes in he found North End. There was a gap in the bricks beside him. A small arched passageway led from one darkness to another. He walked through and found himself beside a platform. The platform was at shoulder height. It had been taken over for storage: sacks of loose ballast, wooden sleepers, cable reels. All had become a uniform grey, like deep-sea creatures starved of light. He lifted himself up to the platform, blackening his hands in the process, and stepped past the abandoned ballast into a central corridor. It had unpainted plaster walls but modern emergency exit signs pointing to the bottom of a concrete spiral staircase. There were bright red fire extinguishers as well, shiny as Christmas baubles. To the right of the stairs were the steel doors of a lift that hadn't been installed earlier than the 1970s. It had an up button and a down button, but the down button needed a key card to operate it. He could hear the station manager's uncertain voice: *It's got special security.* Belsey pushed the buttons. No lift came. Something scraped behind him.

The sound came from the far end of the central corridor. It was the sound of metal being dragged along the ground. His torchlight picked out a small door at the end of the corridor: *No Access to LU Staff.* Belsey walked through and almost fell to his death.

The cover of a square hatch had been removed. It opened onto a brick shaft with a ladder on one side, leading down into bottomless darkness. His stomach turned. He was standing in a dank cubicle, apparently built for the purpose of housing this hatch. There were two notices on the wall, one with health and safety regulations, one detailing the Official Secrets Act.

Belsey could hear someone at the bottom, running. He tucked the torch into his belt and started down.

When he reached the bottom he found a familiar set-up: the low, rounded tunnel in the torchlight, a subterranean fug. He smelled wax and rust and something marshy, the slow decay of metal and concrete. But this time there was company, running fast. Belsey headed in pursuit of the sound. The narrow strip between the curved walls made chasing difficult. Twice he tripped and fell. After five minutes or so Belsey stopped and could still hear the person ahead. He set off again. He ran for twenty minutes. It was impossible to tell how far ahead his target was. They sounded tantalisingly close, but then there wasn't much going on to drown them out. Belsey wondered if he was chasing echo. Then he thought of the package of hair and gathered his strength for a final sprint. The sound of steps had gone. He reached a T-junction and felt sure this was where he had been the previous night, but that now he was rejoining the tunnel he'd originally investigated. The sense of familiarity gave him hope. He headed left, towards the library bunker.

Somebody screamed. It was a woman, up ahead. A couple of seconds later there was a crash. Belsey sprinted again. He almost ran straight past the ladder he'd used twenty-four hours earlier. There was no bike today. The hatch at the top was open. He looked at the square of darkness and imagined someone ready to decapitate him as he surfaced. He could hear breathing just by the hatch. Belsey hauled himself up slowly, then reached into the space of the room and his hand brushed a leg.

Fabric. Shin bone. Calf muscle taut. He grabbed ankles and pulled hard. The individual tumbled. Belsey levered himself out and onto them. Fingers went for his eyes. He felt the Kevlar padding of a stab vest against his chest.

There was a blue glow and then he was convulsing, electricity in his teeth and fingernails, stars buzzing before his eyes. He managed to think: Taser. He waited for the stun-cycle to pass. Then the world came back. Some more stars. Then the sun. Then the sun moved out of his eyes and he could see Kirsty Craik.

"Shit," she said.

"Jesus Christ."

Craik lowered the torch. She was injured. Blood smeared her blouse.

"Are you OK?" he asked.

"I'm OK. You?"

Belsey found the Taser barb in the flesh beneath his ribs and plucked it out.

"I think you've cured my depression." He lay back, holding the barb, catching his breath. She sat beside him. He could see she'd grazed her right cheekbone and right ear. Most of the blood came from her lower lip, though. "What are you doing here?" he said.

"Hampstead Way. There's a building . . ."

"Leads down to North End."

"To something. A dead station of some kind."

"Why were you there?"

"We got a report, just after you left—someone worried about a man in their garden. Matched the description of our man at the station: grey hood, black gloves. I was taking a look, then I heard someone breaking into my car. I think it was him. When I got closer he ran into the small building— like a white cabin. I looked in there, and I think it was rigged to lock behind me. I don't know. I couldn't get out, so I went down the stairs . . ."

"And got here."

"Someone was chasing me."

"I was chasing you. I went into the tunnels at Golders Green. You pursued him on your own?"

"I didn't have much choice."

"And he attacked you?"

"Here. Yes. I didn't see him. I think he got my CS spray."

Belsey listened. He didn't like the idea of getting sprayed underground. He saw the desk of communications equipment had been knocked in the fight, amplifier toppled, *Guide to the Standing Stones of Wiltshire* on the floor. The ceiling showed broken ends of wood where he'd smashed his way out. He couldn't see Jemma's bag or the box of candles. There was one other difference: the door marked *To Situation Room* was ajar. Faint light leaked through the crack. And now there was a noise from the same direction. A splash and then what sounded like rusted hinges creaking.

Belsey and Craik exchanged a glance. Craik was at the doorway before Belsey could say anything. He followed her into a bare corridor. An arrow scrawled on the concrete wall pointed left. Craik touched the mark. Belsey did the same. It was greasy. It smelt like lipstick.

They turned the next corner. There was a line of light beneath a narrow door at the end. Both stepped closer, exchanged a nod and Craik kicked it open. Birthday candles flickered and swooned. Twelve of them lit a double-height room centred on a large, hexagonal table. Calcium bled out of the concrete ceiling, dividing the space with tapering white stalactites. Similar growths rose up beneath each strand, from the table surface and the floor, like two thin fingers trying to touch. Candles burnt among them, five on the table itself, seven up on the rail of a balcony casting a glow over old maps. They'd been lit no more than five minutes ago.

Around the edges of the room were bottle-green filing cabinets, ledges covered in papers, blackboards with painted columns headed *Reconnaissance, Rescue* and *Casualty Collection.* The place had been methodically searched. A filing cabinet stood with its drawers open. The papers spread across the hexagonal plotting table had been sorted into rough piles: maps, graphs, tables of figures. There was a yellowed *Guardian*: "US Troops Invade Grenada," "CND March Attracts Biggest Ever Crowd." Belsey picked up an exercise book from beside a mug with a head of mould. On the front, in heavy black pen, someone had written *Regional Defence Group 4, London North*. He opened it.

Wednesday, 2 November 1983
USSR has demanded Norwegian and Dutch withdrawal from NATO. Local Government Emergency Planning Officers have taken up contingency roles.
Warsaw Pact forces mobilising.

"Look," Craik said, quietly. Belsey slipped the book into his pocket. At the back of the room was a chair with silver duct tape around the legs, the tape sliced roughly to free whomever it had restrained. Craik pointed the torch beam down. Something red reflected back beneath the chair. A Costa Coffee loyalty card. Craik peeled it from the dirt.

"No ID on it," she said.

She held it by the edges and showed him. It was red, with a picture of a coffee cup. *Costa Coffee Club. Enjoy FREE Costa coffee when you collect points!*

"Don't reckon it's from the cold war," Belsey said.

"Know how these work? Would it be registered to a name?"

"Possibly."

He remembered Jemma using it. The card must have been in a pocket of her shorts. It would have recorded details of their visit—which store, what time, two coffees. Easy lead to in-store CCTV. That would look cute, the two of them at the till, just before she disappeared. If she'd registered it there would be her name and address on the system. Clever thing to drop if you wanted to notify the world of your predicament.

Craik pocketed it carefully.

"Hello?" she called. There was another door at the far end of the room. She investigated the darkness on the other side. "Nick, look here."

The doorway led into a short stub of bare, unpainted corridor that ended at a locked grille. More tunnel was visible through the bars, steel sections bolted together with rivets the size of fists. Directly in front of the grille was a wooden sentry post, not much larger than a cupboard. It contained a bench seat. Nailed above it was a sign in a slightly hysterical antique font: *Red Passholders Only!*

"You think he went through here?"

"We heard this gate closing."

Craik shook the bars. The grille was secured with a new D-lock. They took turns rattling the metal, which must have amused their suspect if he was still in earshot.

"How did you get out last night?" Craik asked.

They returned to the communications room. Belsey gave Craik a leg-up through the crumbled ceiling panel to the next floor, then pulled himself after her. They splashed their way down the fetid corridor and climbed the winding stairway up to the door that led into the library basement. The cupboard was wedged firmly in front of it again but together they pushed, hearing the cupboard shift loudly until it top-

pled over. By then the young black guard with the sideburns
was waiting.

"Good to see a familiar face," Belsey said. The guard
looked slightly horrified. He was joined a second later by his
colossal friend. They peered past Belsey and Craik at the
darkness from which they'd emerged.

"Call the police," the first guard said to his companion.
Belsey turned to Craik.

"You explain."

Craik got her badge out and persuaded him there was no
need. She was more convincing than Belsey had been. They
went upstairs. Belsey made a mental note of their route to
street level and its landmarks. He wasn't going to lose the
door again. When they were outside the library, Craik got on
her radio to Serious Crime and told them to hustle a full
SOC team. She gave directions along with a brief explanation of what they'd find. It was quarter past ten. The rain had
stopped; the city glistened.

"How are you feeling?" Belsey asked.

"Worried."

The first patrols arrived, followed by CID from local stations, then senior command. Craik directed them down.
Belsey hung back. She spent fifteen minutes giving an account to two chief superintendents from the Yard's Serious
Crime squad. Craik dispatched Jemma's loyalty card with
instructions to get owner ID and a record of recent use,
along with files on any missing women, by dawn.

And then there was a moment's peace. The two of them
swept aside by the arriving army of crime scene investigators
like people who've had their party crashed.

"Need us here?" she asked the Yard team.

They were instructed to clean themselves up and get some rest.

"Well, I need a shower," Craik said to Belsey. "I'm still shaking."

"You say he broke into your car."

"That's right."

"Was there anything in it with your address on it?"

Craik thought about this.

"Some post."

"I don't think you should go home."

"What are you suggesting?"

"Nightcap, my place."

EVEN MARTYNA'S POKER FACE WAS TESTED AS BELSEY led Kirsty Craik, bloodstained, through the reception of Hotel President. The women exchanged glances.

"Does she see this a lot?" Craik asked, when they were in the lift.

"No."

"Is this really where you live?"

"For the moment."

The lift took them unsteadily upwards. They were both silent, then silent along the corridor to his room.

17

"This is the Presidential Suite," Belsey said. He unlocked his door and scanned the room for any traces of corruption and deceit. It looked innocent enough. It looked inadequate for a man in his late thirties. Craik managed a smile. She appraised the uneven stacks of books, the well-stocked bar on an upturned grocer's crate. She sat on his bed. Belsey opted for the window seat. When they were sleeping together in Borough he had a London Bridge apartment. Not paid for out of entirely legitimate income. Maybe this new set-up looked honest, ascetic. Her presence made it feel a little absurd.

"What does he want?" Craik asked, finally.

"To show us that he can," Belsey said. "He has knowledge and power. I think these tunnels involve more than is in the public domain." He paused, choosing his words. "Kirsty, there's a possibility we're into more than we can handle, something that has confidentiality from the top, from the government, or military intelligence. That kind of scene."

"Why do you think that?"

"All sorts of reasons. I had a disc of what looked like someone disposing of a body behind Centre Point—same suspect, moving a corpse from the BMW he stole on Friday. I couldn't tell much about the corpse. On CCTV you can see police and ambulances attending. But there's no record of it happening, nothing on the system. The site has been cleaned up. I think someone stole the disc from me when I was examining the area."

Craik digested this. The night's events had opened her mind.

"You think he's connected to the government?"

"No, but I think he's possibly encroached on their secrets. I don't know how or why. I think he's holding someone hostage because he wants to draw us into whatever game he's playing. It involves revealing this system. Look." Belsey found his *A-Z* in his jacket and sat beside her. "They're deep-level tunnels. The system involves the old shelters but extends further." He took a pencil and put a cross between Hampstead and Golders Green. "We saw North End station. We know it connects to St. Pancras Library. We saw tunnels beyond that. Red Passholders Only. From the library it's just a kilometre along the Gray's Inn Road before you hit a secret telephone exchange under Chancery Lane." He placed a cross on Furnival Street.

"A telephone exchange."

"A huge exchange. All underground. There's bound to be some tunnel connecting them. If you follow that west you get to Centre Point where he decided to leave the body. He was deliberately placing it there. He sprayed the word 'CAVE' on the side of the building. Centre Point's got an interesting history. There was a dispute over planning permission: the building went against all regulations. At the last moment, the government steps in and says it has to be built. The permit's waved through. But it sits empty for ten years. Totally unoccupied."

"What are you saying?"

"The main problem with the planning permission was the height. It meant they had to excavate incredibly deep to stabilise it. Something is in that space beneath the building, and it's being watched by the same people who have their cameras trained on the deep shelters—Property Services Agency, which is a government subsidiary and doesn't like answering its phones."

Craik studied the map.

"Where else does this system go?"

"I don't know. If the Chancery Lane exchange continues east along High Holborn, you're in the City. If the Goodge Street shelter goes south, then you're approaching Trafalgar Square, then Whitehall. Obviously there are tunnels down there."

He took a handful of papers from the Umbro bag and passed them over. Craik leafed through. The online aficionados couldn't help themselves when it came to Whitehall. But amid their wilder speculation, there were recurring points of consensus. Downing Street and Parliament connected underground. Each government department had extensive tunnels beneath its own headquarters, each warren probably leading to the next. Belsey knew that for Diana's funeral they had to plant Parliament Square with flowers to deter the huge crowds that would have fallen straight through. A few streets away, under the Treasury building on Horse Guards Road, were the old War Rooms, preserved for tourists with a waxwork high command in place. And from these, logically enough, a select few could have walked the few hundred metres to the Prime Minister's residence, or passed under Whitehall itself to whatever delights lay beneath the glum colossus of the Ministry of Defence.

Less certain, but far from implausible: there had been a tunnel dug under the river connecting Westminster and Waterloo. There was a bunker retained for an unspecified purpose beneath the Queen Elizabeth II Conference Centre on Broad Sanctuary. Tunnels had been extended from the Cabinet War Rooms to a new subterranean complex under Victoria, with an emergency exit in the basement of the old Westminster Hospital.

"He's not going to get beneath Whitehall," Craik said.

"Maybe not, but I reckon he'd like to. This individual has sent threatening emails to members of the press, signing himself as Ferryman. Ferryman was the codename for a Soviet spy."

"A spy?"

"In the seventies and eighties. I've no idea what to make

of it. He's interested in cold-war history. A fantasist. But on to something."

"This is insane."

Craik sifted through the papers. Then she put them down and exhaled. Her body relaxed against his own.

"I thought I was going to die," she said. Belsey put a hand on her back and then moved it so his arm was around her shoulders.

"Me too," he said. "Someone shot me."

"Oh, God." She lifted a corner of his shirt and touched a hand to the Taser wound.

"Does it hurt?"

"Yes."

She felt where the barb had torn a neat line.

"Have you got a shower?" Craik asked.

"Through there. I'll get some towels."

She went into the bathroom. He headed to the store cupboard at the end of the corridor and took a stack of towels and a bathrobe. The shower was running when he returned. He threw the towels and robe into the bathroom along with jogging bottoms and an old T-shirt. Then he poured vodka into mugs.

"Join me in problem drinking?" he called through.

"Are you serious?"

"Medicinal. It will keep us going."

Belsey drank and the situation immediately seemed more manageable. He was getting closer. He took his shirt off and splashed some vodka on the wound, then split a hexobarbitone with his thumbnail and took a speculative half. He called the CID office. There had been no more sightings of the suspect. The forensics team was working on the package of hair; London Underground and the Transport Police were keeping an eye out for any more trespass incidents.

He emptied an ashtray into the bin and tidied some clothes away, then took a seat on the bed and listened to the water trickle off Kirsty Craik's body. It was past midnight now.

The water stopped. After another five minutes Craik appeared. She'd gone for the robe. She was pink with heat, hair under a towel. She sat beside him, then lay back across the bed. He lay beside her. He slipped the robe off her shoulder. There was the tattoo. He couldn't remember if the writing was Thai or Vietnamese, but knew it was meant to offer protection in battle.

"Checking it's me?" she asked. She rolled onto her side, away from him. He watched her neck. He had the feeling of returning to a place after years and the odd wonder that it should still be there, that things go on without you, but also that you might return.

"I should have trusted you," Craik said. "About all this."

"Not unless you're mad."

He put his arm over her. She wove her fingers into his own. A train slowed into King's Cross with an interminable hiss as if the machinery of the city itself was decompressing. Then everything was quiet. He could hear the echo of platform announcements. I can have this moment, Belsey thought. He felt he'd overcome several insurmountable laws, of time as well as morality. He inhaled the peace, dragging it deep into his lungs. This was what corrupted: peace and quiet. It was what secrets fed off, growing inside you.

"Can I ask you something?" Craik said.

"Of course."

"Why did you just vanish?"

Belsey hesitated.

"Tonight?"

"At Borough."

"I didn't vanish. You were posted away. I was almost prosecuted for all manner of offences. You didn't want me messing up your career as well."

"I was posted two miles away. It wasn't overseas."

"You were on the up."

She unlocked her hand and turned towards him, studying his face as if for later identification purposes.

"What did you really think when you saw me at Hampstead?" she asked.

"I thought about us breaking into Brockwell Lido at three in the morning. I wondered if you were going to lead me astray again."

"That was an amazing night." Craik smiled, then glanced around the hotel room. "Do you like living here?"

"Not particularly."

"What's the picture, propped against the window?"

Belsey turned to see. There was Walbrook, the well mannered crowd peering into London's fresh wound.

"It's a bomb crater from the Second World War. It revealed a Roman temple buried beneath the City."

"Why is it there?"

"I don't know." Belsey felt the pure present collapsing. The picture brought back memories of last night. He untangled himself and went over to it. He didn't need the polygraph of Craik's body against his own, monitoring his heartbeat. He opened the window and lit a cigarette. "Have you been to Rome?"

"Once, a few years ago."

"When they got rid of Nero they buried his palace. Centuries later a shepherd boy fell through a crack in the hillside and discovered it. He fell into the palace. All the treasures and artworks were still there. Everyone came and let themselves down on ropes to see it—all this art from ancient times greater than they had thought possible. There it was, buried beneath their feet."

"You were thinking about that?"

"Not exactly. I was thinking about people sleeping in shelters and tube stations during the Blitz, trying to imagine better ways of protecting themselves. Architects sleeping down there, dreaming of something that's going to keep them safe for ever, and then they surface and the bombs have cleared space for them to have a go. So they start flinging up things like Centre Point. They want concrete. Somewhere they can hide."

Craik made a noise that could have been assent or a yawn. After a moment she said:

"How far did we run?"

"Golders Green to King's Cross, four miles or so."

"Jesus. I can feel it in my legs."

Belsey looked at her. Her courage wasn't news to him. A moral kind of courage: he'd seen Kirsty Craik break up pub fights and stride into bloodstained domestics. She'd probably been missing the action.

"Sleep," he said. "We're not going anywhere for a while."

He went to shower. A moment later she called through: "Who's Jemma Stevens?"

Belsey froze, water streaming into his face. The laptop. He turned the shower off, dried himself, and made a calculation as he dressed. The loyalty card was already being analysed: he had an hour or two before her name came up. Detectives didn't do coincidences.

Craik had his laptop up on the bed. She wore a look of amused disapproval. The screen had blinked straight to Jemma's Facebook page.

"Cute," she said. "Bit young for you."

"It may be our missing person," he said. Craik's expression darkened. "Her flatmate called the station a few hours ago and said she'd gone AWOL. I had a look at her page while you were showering. It could be nothing."

Craik studied Jemma's hair in the most recent pictures. It was long and dyed black.

"Or it could be something," she said.

"It's something to check. I feel like I might have come across her before. She sounds like a wild child." The fact that he had remained calm was, Belsey suspected, testament to the soothing powers of hexobarbitone. "It's just a possibility. I called the station; there's been no developments."

"Jemma Stevens." Craik lay back. "I don't think I'm going to sleep."

"Just rest your eyes then."

He sat by the window. Next time he looked she had her eyes closed. Belsey assessed his immediate future. First thing that would happen tomorrow: they get a positive ID from the loyalty card. Next, Jemma Stevens comes up on the po-

lice database with Belsey as arresting officer. They visit the
flatmates who recognise him from visits to the club; then
they get footage from Costa matching her card and see them
together a few minutes before she goes missing. As investiga-
tions go that was pretty sweet. The whole thing would be
wrapped in less than three hours.

So he needed to be clever. He stood up and no clever
thoughts came. He lifted his jacket from the floor and something fell out. It was an exercise book. And then he remembered—the diary from the bunker. Belsey picked it up and
flicked through. Neat biro covered the pages. The entries
were initialled "S.R."—the cover signed by "Regional Con-
troller: Suzanne Riggs." Each page was divided down the
middle: on the left side was a commentary on the state of the
nation; on the right, the scene down in the bunker. This
listed officers present, alarm settings used, supply levels,
sickness. But nothing was as vivid as the reports coming in
from the outside world.

Thursday, 3 November
Military build-up along Soviet Union border with Tur-
    key.
Covert civil preparations ongoing across London. Key
    personnel meeting at relevant centres.
Wartime Broadcasting Service in place, police support
    units on standby, local authorities briefed.

Friday, 4 November
Fire Brigade moved out of London, plus all hospital
    staff within 15-mile radius of Charing Cross. Non-

critical patients sent home. Schools and libraries
given Level 2 protection; communications installed.
Protests in Camden and Southwark.
Petrol rationing.

Belsey read on. Things didn't improve. By the end of Sunday, 6 November all transport was under government control including British Airways and commercial shipping. The
Cabinet's War Measures Committee had begun moving art
treasures out of London, Edinburgh and Cardiff. Twelve
major roads had been reserved for government traffic.

At 12:30 p.m. on 7 November the Cabinet approved
Queen's Order 2. Parliament was suspended, emergency
powers activated.

That was when the panic buying became serious.
Alongside increased protests and acts of sabotage. Evening
of 7 November: terrorist bomb at Immingham destroyed
the oil refinery and fuel stocks. A bomb at Devonport
naval base killed four. The Prime Minister made three
broadcasts discouraging evacuation, promising that the
government was going to stay side by side with ordinary
Londoners.

The place to be was the bunker. Alarm setting to black,
stocks sufficient, communications 100 per cent, no sickness
reported. Standing by.

The banks closed on Tuesday 8, the same day the BBC
suspended weather forecasts and Warsaw Pact divisions entered Yugoslavia. Meanwhile, King's Cross and Paddington
stations shut down due to a mass attempt to flee the capital.

World War III began at 11 a.m.

11:05. Attack Warning sounded.

11:32. Three 20-megaton ground-bursts. Croydon, Brentford and Heathrow destroyed.

12:00. Putney Bridge and Wandsworth Bridge down, plus elevated section of the M4.

16:00. First radiation sickness reported across Essex and Cambridgeshire.

Wind NW.

Four more waves of attacks came over the next twenty-four hours. When the smoke cleared the first stats arrived: two and a half thousand dead in Barking; Southwark close second with over two thousand casualties. Camden and Westminster fared better: fifteen hundred dead between them but a lot of survivors trapped under houses.

Belsey tried to remember November 1983. He had been nine years old, living in Lewisham, preparing for life as a professional footballer while avoiding an alcoholic detective father. *Lewisham—1300 dead, 8000 injured.*

He got up to fix another drink.

What did he do in the cold war? He remembered the Soviet Union on maps, Reagan, Thatcher, a theatre group that visited his secondary school and performed a play about the bomb. CND put on an exhibition at Catford Library showing Japanese children with third-degree burns. He didn't remember half the population disappearing.

London appeared to still be there tonight, rain-soaked. It had survived, even if the peace felt fragile.

He sat down again, beside the window, leaned his head back against the wall and closed his eyes.

Ferryman.

Why take Jemma? What did he want Belsey to do? There are obsessives, Monroe warned. Cold-war obsessives. Spy obsessives. An individual alights on the mysterious figure of Ferryman. What does it mean to them? Ferryman's someone at the heart of the secret state, betraying it; he passed intelligence on and then disappeared. That was something to idolise, Belsey supposed. And everyone liked spies. They resembled us, only ever half in their own lives. But with a purpose. They survived on a familiar diet of deception and selective betrayal. Sometimes they got away. Ferryman was a myth and still perhaps in the world, in the London of 2013, abandoned on his island of secrecy.

Belsey saw the deep shelters being passed from war to war, preserved in the ice of the nuclear age. He saw the tunnels, and then Jemma bound to the HANDEL machine. When he next opened his eyes the room had turned grey with morning. Craik's phone was ringing. He found it among her clothes and gently shook her awake.

"It's the station," Belsey said. "Want it?"

Craik swung herself upright. Belsey went into the bathroom and splashed his face. He could hear the conversation.

"No, not *all* CCTV. Establish where and when the card was last used, which branch. Then, if there's footage, whether she was with anyone. It's not complicated. Have them send it directly to me."

Belsey was thinking he could do with some coffee. His muscles were stiff from the electrocution. He walked back into the room and his own phone rang. It wasn't the station; it was a local landline. Very local: same initial digits as the hotel.

"Hello?" Belsey said. No one spoke. He checked the signal; the call was connected. He walked over to the window. "Belsey speaking."

No one speaking back. No one hanging up either.

Craik said: "I'll head over now. No, I'm not at home. I'm . . . close by."

Belsey grabbed a shirt and stepped out to the corridor.

"Talk to me," he said.

"Did I disturb the two of you?"

The voice was calm, soft. Background of street—a car passing, a shutter being rolled up. Then the clunk of coin; a phone box. Belsey walked to the window at the end of the corridor and checked the slice of Caledonian Road beneath it. No one there.

The two of you. Had he followed them from St. Pancras last night?

"No. Now's good," Belsey said, heading for the stairs barefoot, shirt flapping open. Where was the nearest phone box?

"Nice hotel."

"Thanks."

"Are you on holiday?"

"I wish." There were traces of an accent. He was English but not from London. There was a softer cadence. Belsey couldn't place it. He took the steps quickly, trying to remember the rudiments of hostage negotiation. "I reckon we could both do with a holiday."

"That's true. This is a crazy situation we've got ourselves into."

"How do you see it unfolding exactly?"

"I thought you were going to impress me with your detective skills."

Belsey sighed. "You chose the wrong detective for that. I can recommend better ones. Holborn station has a good team."

"Can I speak to Sergeant Craik?"

"No."

"Should I contact her directly?"

Belsey crossed the hotel reception. He turned to Martyna, muting his phone.

"Anyone been around, looking for me?" She shook her head. He walked out into the street, the world cheery with dawn, clouds uplit, paving slabs cold. He knew there was a phone box by Market Road, usually broken, one on the corner of Huntingdon Street. He headed towards Huntingdon Street.

"Is Jemma OK?"

"Not great."

"What do you want?" Belsey asked.

"I want you to do your job."

"What job? Finding you?"

"Following the clues. Detective work. I thought maybe Sergeant Craik could help. She could be the brains."

Belsey got a stare from a street cleaner, another from a man walking his dogs. He was still slightly cocooned in hexobarbitone, but waking up fast.

"The brains. That's funny."

"Was Kentish Town too far for her to get home last night?" the voice asked. Belsey winced.

"Leave Kirsty Craik out of it."

"That's sweet. What shall I do to Jemma?"

"Let her go. It's nothing to do with her."

"Who is it to do with?"

"How about it's just us?" Belsey suggested. "What's the problem?"

"We're dead men," the caller said. "That's the problem."

"Why's that?"

"It's a good question. Maybe that can be your question for today: why are they going to kill you?"

"Who's going to kill me?"

"She's not looking in a good way, Nick. Jemma, I mean. She wishes you'd hurry up, while you can."

Belsey saw the phone box a few metres away, glass obscured by prostitute cards. They both went silent. He moved around to the front and it was empty.

He began up Caledonian Road.

"No luck?" the caller said.

"Do you think you'll get away with this?"

"I don't care."

"OK."

"I dreamed of you."

"That's nice."

"You were on fire. You said you wanted to give me a map before it burnt. You were ignoring the pain of your own skin burning. Do you think you could do that?"

"What was it a map of?"

"Site 3. You said I should take Jemma there."

"Site 3. Like on the pill bottles."

"Well spotted."

"I've been wondering where that is." Belsey arrived at the next phone box. No one. He turned and ran back past Pentonville Prison, down towards Copenhagen Street.

"I've got to go. Jemma says she wants to visit Site 3."

"Are you sure?"

"She says she doesn't want to die there, though."

Click.

He got to the phone box thirty seconds later. He knew it was the right one: the handset was gleaming. He could smell lemon and lime, see the smear of a cleaning wipe. He looked around—empty streets: no witnesses, easy escape routes into the Thornhill Estate. He had a futile look among the cagey council homes, then walked back to Hotel President. Craik was searching through her clothes, trying to construct an outfit that didn't involve dried blood.

"Where did you go?"

"That was him," Belsey said. "Our man. He was in a phone box nearby."

Craik straightened and stared at him.

"You're joking."

"He knew we were both here. He knows you live in Kentish Town."

"What did he say?"

"He asked if it was too far for you to go home last night, back to Kentish Town. What was your call about?"

"It was the office. They can't get through to anyone at Costa. He knows where I live?"

"That's right."

"Get forensics on the phone boxes."

A squad car collected Craik a few minutes later. Belsey said he'd catch her up. Then she was gone and he was still barefoot. He called forensics. He rinsed his feet. Craik's clothes lay across the bathroom floor. This was one way to handle a morning after.

HE PICKED HIS CAR UP FROM GOLDERS GREEN, RE-turned the torch to a puzzled member of staff at the tube station and thought about fleeing. He wasn't going to, but it was an ongoing area of interest. Freedom was starting to feel precious. He drove to the corner of Hampstead Way and Wildwood Road and saw Kirsty's Mondeo, its back window smashed, dutifully watched over by a bored-looking constable. A few metres away, behind a green fence, was the entrance to the tunnels: a low, white windowless structure with a sign that said: *Keep Clear. Contact Control for Access to Substation.* But the vent on it was too big for an electrical substation. Its door was padlocked.

18

Belsey drove on. He found himself at the top of the hill, where you got a view of London laid out beneath you. There it was: Centre Point, St. Pancras, Chancery Lane; the whole a facade, a cover story. He felt a lifetime's memories and associations subtly undermined. The city had betrayed him.

That can be your question for today: why are they going to kill you?

He returned to the station. Craik had produced a blouse and skirt from somewhere. She looked sharp.

"Still no ID from Costa," she said. "Trying to get someone out of bed to run the check. Head office isn't open."

Belsey sat down and slapped himself awake. He backdated a call log from Jemma's flatmate to fit the story he'd given Craik. Then he called Camden CCTV.

"Chib there?"

"No."

"I need a new copy of some footage I was looking at yesterday." Belsey gave him the details. The man said he'd check. He called back a moment later.

"The tape's wiped."

"You're kidding me."

"No."

"I thought you kept the tapes for thirty days."

"Not this one, it seems."

"When's Chib in?"

"Tomorrow. Not much Chib's going to do, though."

Craik walked over. She wore a look of anxious uncertainty. Belsey hung up.

"They've put the investigation on hold," Craik said. "The search of the bunker has been called off, pending 'official authorisation.'"

"Of course it has. I told you we were on strange territory."

"I'm going to see what I can do. Apparently I need some jabs first. You should get checked."

Jabs. He hadn't had time to contemplate the health-and-safety issues of the tunnels. Hepatitis was not chief among them. Craik went down to the duty medic. Belsey turned his computer on and typed in *Site 3*.

There was nothing online about a subterranean Site 3. He tried a search on North End Underground station and scrolled through rumours on enthusiasts' bulletin boards. North End was half built and then abandoned around 1905. Forty-five years later a lift and stairs were installed. No one knew why. The most popular explanation was that it was being set up as London Transport's emergency headquarters in the event of nuclear war. This, it seemed, would involve more than the safeguarding of your daily commute. Work carried out on North End by the government and MOD in the 1950s transformed the place. The websites thought it attained the power to seal off parts of the Underground system entirely using lock gates hidden in tunnels. It meant that some routes could remain open, even during an attack, while hermetically sealed from flooding or nuclear fallout.

One indisputable fact: the system remained classified.

Belsey called Vodafone. He jumped through the necessary security hoops, only to learn that there were no more signals reaching Jemma's phone. He tried to count how many hours sleep he'd had in the last two days and gave up. He made a coffee and crumbled a blue Dexedrine into the oily liquid. Breakfast was served. He switched on the office TV and searched for news. Then his name boomed from the doorway. The Chief had arrived.

The Borough Commander, Chief Superintendent Northwood, was in fine voice. He'd put his uniform on especially. He was a tall, broad man and everything seemed tight.

"Sir," Belsey said. Northwood towered over him.

"What's going on?"

"There's a woman down there, in deep-level tunnels. Her hair was delivered to the station yesterday evening."

"I've just had a call from the editor of the *Express*. He has a journalist friend of yours who knows a lot more about what's going on than I do."

"The suspect is sending messages to the press. Not me."

"Who are they? What do you know?"

"I know very little. Just that we need to get down there."

"Where's Sergeant Craik?"

"With the medical examiner."

The Chief was starting to look slightly unwell himself. "What happened?" he asked.

"She was attacked by the suspect. Down there. In a bunker under the library. She was in pursuit. We were in pursuit. We believed that a serious crime was underway."

"And now you've sent in half the Yard?"

"I tried. The Yard is being recalcitrant." Belsey sipped his concoction and shuddered. Chemical volts raced down his spine.

"You had no authorisation."

"Tell me who can authorise it. I'll speak to them."

"No you bloody won't," Northwood said. "This is chaos."

"We could try asking him to go about things in a more orderly fashion."

"It was my idea to send them down," Craik said. Both men turned. Craik stood in the doorway to the office, one sleeve rolled up. "I authorised it. I judged it urgent."

"She had instructed me not to go near it," Belsey said. "She was only there because I was."

"That's crap," she said.

"You are not to pursue this, either of you." Northwood turned to Craik and pointed at Belsey. "Remember what I told you about him. Liaise with Serious Crime. No more heroics." He marched off. They waited for the Chief to turn the corner.

"You were right," Craik said.

"About what?"

"Card belongs to one Jemma Stevens, twenty-two years old, lives at 34 Kynaston Road."

"Bingo," Belsey said. He played it expressionless. "What now?"

"Want to return to full duties?"

He felt a swirl of uncertainty. It would buy him time, of course. And one day could be enough to sort this out. Keep the investigation close.

"What about Northwood?"

"I'm your Sergeant, not Northwood. Prove him wrong. Run this."

"Sure."

"See when Jemma Stevens was last home. Try to find out when her bank card was last used. Take Rob with you."

"Are you sure we can spare him?"

Craik rolled her eyes. "You say flatmates called it in yesterday?"

"That's right. She was last seen Monday."

"I want to know what made them worried so quickly."

She returned to her office. Belsey finished his coffee and let it enter his bloodstream. He watched the news for a couple of minutes. He was waking up now. Then Trapping strode in with his Ray-Bans on.

"Sounds like we've got a mission," he said.

BELSEY LET HIS YOUNGER COLLEAGUE DRIVE. They entered Stoke Newington at 8:30 a.m. Trapping was quiet.

"Something going on with you and the new Sarge?" he asked, eventually.

"Why?"

19

"Just wondered." He smiled uneasily. A minute later they pulled up at Jemma's home.

"Looks like a student house," Belsey said. "Might not be used to early calls."

"Student house." Trapping nodded.

"Let me do the talking."

"What do we know?"

"Twenty-two years old, missing since Monday night. Her Costa card was down in a bunker beneath St. Pancras Library."

Trapping shook his head as they got out and approached the front door.

"What's this bunker about? Is it connected to the Chancery Lane stuff I looked up?"

"Maybe."

Belsey rang the bell. He hoped the change of context would make him less recognisable. Both flatmates had encountered him in Euphoria, neither of them more than twice. He wasn't sure if they had known he was a police officer. It took three long rings, then the Latvian girl answered. She was sleepy-eyed, in a baggy T-shirt and shorts, hair in blonde pigtails. Belsey didn't pick up any hints of recognition. He showed his badge.

"Does Jemma Stevens live here?

"Yes."

"Is she in?"

"No. We haven't seen her for a couple of days."

"Can we speak to you inside?"

"What's happened?"

"Please."

The girl led them into the living room. The cans were still on the table, torn posters on the wall. She sat down but didn't offer them a seat. They chose to stand.

"When did you last see Jemma?" Belsey asked.

"Monday afternoon."

"Do you know where she was going?"

"She was meeting someone."

"Who?"

The girl paused.

"A man. I don't know who." She looked at Belsey blankly.

"A man she was seeing?"

"Something like that."

"Could you show us her room?"

The girl led them upstairs, then went to wake the third flatmate. There had been no change to Jemma's room. Trapping admired the photos on the wall.

"She's fit. She'll be dead."

"Shut up, Rob."

"True though, isn't it. It's what you said. That's how it goes." He sat down and switched on her computer.

"Don't," Belsey said. "Might be traces."

"You think someone's been in here?"

"Look at the shoe print on the paper by the bed. It's not a woman's foot size." Trapping went and stood over the sheet. Then he turned to Belsey with a quizzical expression.

"What's going on?"

"My guess is that a man's been in here recently. Either that or she's been wearing men's shoes."

"You got a suspect? Someone in mind?"

"Not yet."

Trapping picked the sheet up by its corner. They returned to the living room. The girl was smoking a menthol cigarette.

"Anywhere else she might stay?" Belsey asked. "Parents, maybe, or friends?"

"No one's heard from her."

Out of the corner of his eye Belsey saw the boy, the barman, stretching in the doorway. He wore silk boxer shorts and a lot of thick black ink. He studied Belsey's face as if he couldn't quite place it. Alongside the tattoos were a pierced eyebrow, spiky hair and a lot of beer-softened muscle. His stare was too steady for Belsey's liking. He was a good barman. Good barmen remember customers. Especially ones chatting up their flatmate and probable fuck-buddy.

"What's happened?" he said.

"They don't know where she is," the girl explained.

"When did you last see her?" Belsey asked. The barman watched him.

"You come to the club," he said. "You were talking to her."

"That's right. Any ideas where Jemma might be?"

"No."

Trapping sensed something wasn't right and chose sides.

"What is your relationship to her exactly?" he asked the barman.

"What's that got to do with anything?"

"Answer the question," Trapping said.

"I work with her. I live with her." He turned to Belsey, forming his own next question.

"Let us know if you hear anything," Belsey said before he could ask it. "We'll be in touch." He led his colleague out and felt the barman's eyes on them all the way.

They sat in the Skoda. Trapping dropped the shoe print into an evidence bag. He put his hands on the wheel.

"You knew her?" he said, after a moment.

"So it turns out." Belsey shut his eyes. "Jemma Stevens," he said, quietly. He repeated the name a few times. "It's the same girl."

"Who is she?"

"I arrested her on a march a while back. She was carrying three grams of coke. I decided to put her under a bit of informal observation—see if she was dealing, see where she was getting the stuff. She works at Euphoria, the bar on Eversholt Street. I swung by a couple of times. That guy was there. He's a barman."

"He doesn't like you."

"He wouldn't. Probably flushed his stash when I turned up. Wouldn't be surprised if he was part of the supply chain."

Belsey shook his head in wonder. "Jemma Stevens," he muttered again.

Trapping considered all this. He found his fan but didn't
turn it on.

"I knew there was something with that guy. I could tell.
Just from his eyes."

BELSEY GOT DROPPED OFF in Hampstead Village. He
walked to Waterstones, asked for *Britain's Most Notorious
Spies* by Thomas Monroe. No copy in stock. So he crossed
the high street to the second-hand bookshop on Flask Walk.
The owner was opening up, first pipe of the day sending
smoke signals.

"You're keen," he said.

The shop was a maze burrowed through yellow paper,
leaning towers of books prevented from collapse by some
mysterious property of dust. The sections weren't exactly
alphabetical but his luck was in: he found Monroe's book
quickly enough, filed under twentieth-century history. He
turned to the page he needed:

Ferryman (dates unknown; identity unknown)
One of the cold war's most enduring mysteries . . .

It cost £3.00 according to the pencil mark on the inside
front cover. Belsey took it to the counter and counted his
change. The owner clamped the pipe between his teeth and
turned it over in his hands.

"A bargain," he said, folding it into a paper bag.

BELSEY TOOK HIS PURCHASE to the small cafe next door. He couldn't face the food. He ordered a smoothie, which promised to satisfy most of his daily nutritional needs. Then he turned to the book.

The Ferryman entry was only two pages long. Monroe didn't have much but he delivered it with style. Ferryman was privy to top-secret information about the UK's preparations for nuclear war. This was now accepted as fact. He was a central part of the KGB's intelligence drive in response to Russian fears about NATO in the early 1980s—fears that NATO was ready to launch a first-strike attack on the Soviet Union. All Soviet agents in NATO countries were told to keep an eye out for signs that war was looming: the mass slaughter of cattle, putting of food into cold storage, the stockpiling of blood, the distribution of civil defence leaflets. But the KGB also established a department specifically devoted to monitoring preparations by government and military command. This department was called Line X.

No one knew exactly what Line X was about. But Ferryman was part of it.

There was one inset box devoted to "Ferryman and Exercise Able Archer" and it achieved little other than adding some mystery to this enigma.

Soviet insecurity reached a crisis point in early November 1983. The cause of this was a NATO conflict simulation exercise codenamed ABLE ARCHER, which ran 2–11 November . . .

Belsey brought out the war diary he'd found beneath King's Cross. *Covert civil preparations ongoing across London. Key personnel meeting at relevant centres . . .* This had to be the exercise it was recording: Able Archer. According to Monroe, the Soviets were thrown by a new level of secrecy surrounding the exercise. They knew the UK government was hiding something . . . And then the rest of the entry descended into speculation. Exercise Able Archer was rumoured to have been called off midway through. Was Ferryman somehow responsible for this premature conclusion? Maybe because Britain's military chiefs realised their security had been compromised? As no one seemed to know what exactly the exercise involved it was hard to say. Monroe did manage to turn up a "Foreign Office insider" who claimed: "There is more to this than any government will feel comfortable revealing for at least a hundred years." Monroe added, with a swirl of the cape: "By that time the true identity of Ferryman may be lost forever."

Belsey turned through the diary again. Able Archer 1983. He had an actual relic. And a name. He knew one person who had been involved: the dutiful S.R., Suzanne Riggs. The diary ended abruptly.

11 November 1983: thirty-eight fires reported across north-west London, retaliatory strikes on Omsk and Samara; another Soviet attack predicted. Awaiting further instructions.

Then nothing. The bunker must have been hit. Suzanne Riggs had become a victim of the war she imagined. Unless she was as fictional as it was.

He typed the name into his phone's browser. According to the Internet, not only did a Suzanne Riggs exist, she was now MP for Camberwell and Peckham. She had entered Parliament in 1987. Before that she was Leader of Camden Council.

That put her in the right place at the right time. Belsey found the number for her constituency office and dialled.

"Can I speak to Suzanne Riggs?"

"Not this morning, I'm afraid," a young man said.

"It's urgent."

"She's out of the office."

"Can I call her?"

"She's at a funeral," the man said. Then added, "Sir Douglas Argyle's," with a stretch on the vowels as if this might scare Belsey off.

"When does it finish?"

"She'll be going straight to another appointment. But you can try again on Thursday."

"It's urgent."

"Nothing I can do about that, I'm afraid."

Belsey hung up. He called Diplomatic Protection.

"Are you covering Sir Douglas Argyle's funeral today?"

"Yes."

"Where is it?"

"St. Mary's in Kensington. It's on now."

KENSINGTON, 11 A.M. A SOFT, SUNLIT RAIN HUNG IN front of the church like confetti. The church itself looked as smart and well preserved as the houses around it. Mourners had begun to spill out, grief offset by the satisfaction of being on the guest list. He checked the latest pictures of Riggs on his phone and scanned the women in their funeral dresses until he saw her.

20

Riggs was wearing pearls and a large black hat. She was a little bigger than in her publicity shots, less groomed than some of the aristocratic company around her. She said goodbye to a handful of people then headed to the roadside to look for a taxi, trying to hold a BlackBerry, a handbag and the order of service while putting up an umbrella. Belsey found his badge and cut her off.

"Suzanne Riggs?"

"Yes."

"I need to speak to you concerning a police investigation."

Riggs's expression faltered.

"What's happened?"

"A woman is missing. I think she may be being held in deep-level tunnels under London."

There was a double beat, as Riggs processed these words and then the fact that she had been singled out to receive this news. She didn't offer to share her umbrella.

"And why exactly do you want to speak to me?" she asked.

Belsey took the diary from his pocket and handed it to her. Riggs studied the front, then opened it carefully, turned a few pages and gave a bemused smile.

"Where on earth did you get this?"

"Beneath St. Pancras Library."

She nodded slowly. Belsey watched a reunion with old knowledge and its implications.

"What do you want to know?"

"I want to know what's down there, where the tunnels lead."

She paused again, turning the question over with bomb-disposal caution.

"I have to be at a TV studio in fifty minutes. I need to go home first. Can we do this tomorrow?"

"No."

"Who did you say you were?"

"Detective Constable Nick Belsey, Hampstead CID."

The whole thing was puzzling her.

"Can I ask, with all due respect, why there is not a more senior officer investigating? I'd like to speak to whoever's in charge before answering any questions."

"I'm in charge. We don't have time to waste. It's going to be a lot easier talking about it now than to some journalist after she's found dead."

Riggs widened her eyes. They were starting to draw attention. The rain picked up.

"Do you understand the Official Secrets Act?" she asked.

"Not as well as I need to, it seems." Belsey steered her to his Skoda and opened the passenger door. "Perhaps you can explain while I drive. I'll give you a discount on the fare."

Riggs climbed in, still clutching the diary, muttering displeasure. She removed her hat and smoothed down business-like brown hair.

"Where to?" Belsey asked.

"Pimlico."

He drove. She turned through the diary again. "I've no idea how much of this has been declassified. That's why I'm being cautious. We were a small part of a very big thing."

"What did your part involve?"

"I was head of the north London Regional Defence Group. Not a role I was sorry to pass on."

"That was your full-time job?"

"No." She laughed. "I ran the council. Chief Regional Defence Officer in my spare time."

"And this log?"

"I was told to record our experience of the exercise: the course of events, how we held up in the bunker, how it all functioned. I assume everyone in an equivalent position kept one."

"What happened?"

"What do you mean?"

"The war? How did it end?"

"You mean who won?" She laughed again. "I don't know. It just ended. Suddenly. No reasons given. I know *when* it ended because I remember observing the two minutes' silence down there. Very surreal. It ended on the eleventh of November, Remembrance Day."

"Then you just came back up."

"Yes, thank God. I believe there were cyanide capsules available as an alternative. To spare us the radiation-crazed hordes. But we thought we'd risk it."

"Why is everything still down there?"

"Why wouldn't it be, I suppose? No one ever turned round and said, 'The cold war's over, clear up.' No one tidies a decommissioned nuclear bunker. How did you get in?"

"The first time, I came from the deep shelter in Belsize Park, then from Golders Green tube station via a place called North End. Know about that?"

Again a look crossed her face as she divided what she knew from what was public knowledge. "North End. Well . . ." She was saved by the ringing of her mobile. "Hello? Yes, speaking . . . A quote? I barely knew the man. Yes. Well, the funeral was fine. Douglas Argyle himself was a cornerstone of the nation that won't be replaced. Will that do? No, I can't say I even knew him personally, and I'm not going to peddle gossip. Goodbye." She shook her head. They passed Sloane Square.

"What's the gossip?" Belsey asked.

Riggs laughed, hesitated. "Well," she said, "in what slightly awkward situation do ageing Lotharios have heart attacks?"

Belsey liked Sir Douglas a little more.

"Out jogging?"

"Not quite."

She directed Belsey to a house on Warwick Square, freshly painted white with a shiny black door.

"Hello?" Riggs called as they stepped inside. Belsey followed her into a large kitchen. Radio 4 was on, a kettle already bubbling. A silver-haired man in expensive glasses sat in a paved garden behind the kitchen with an *FT* on his lap.

"Richard," the MP said, "this is Detective Constable . . ."

"Belsey."

"Belsey."

"What have you done now?" the man asked, folding the paper.

"He wants to know about my experiences in the nuclear bunker."

"Really?" Her husband looked amused. "That's an awfully long time ago."

They sat down at a kitchen table crowded with letters and headed House of Commons paper. Riggs spilled her bag and belongings onto the surface and glanced at the clock on the microwave. "You've got ten minutes." She shrugged her jacket off and took her earrings out.

"That bunker is part of a bigger tunnel system. I need to know what it is, where it goes."

"I don't know much about any 'system.' I know each borough had its own control centre."

"So there are more like this?"

"One in every borough. Most are beneath town halls. I know there's a large one under Commercial Road for Tower Hamlets staff. And I always remember the one in Southall because it's under a primary school."

"Were they all involved in the 1983 exercise?"

"I believe so. That's what I'm saying—we were a small

cog, and the whole point was we did our thing and didn't have to know about the rest."

"Do you know of any underground connections to other bunkers?"

"No."

"Did you move about underground at all? Beyond the shelter itself?"

"Nothing like that."

"There was a sign down there that said 'Red Passholders Only.' What does that mean?"

"I don't know."

"Would the security services know?"

"Look, I don't have any more privileged access to the security services than you do. Thirty years ago I was involved in this exercise. I've barely thought about it since."

"There's something still being kept secret."

"There's a lot being kept secret. There are institutions that do not like to think the public will ever get their grubby hands on certain kinds of material."

Belsey produced his phone and brought up the picture of Jemma taped to the HANDEL machine.

"Recognise this equipment?"

"It's the Attack Warning System," she said quietly, but she was looking at the girl, as he'd hoped. Riggs took a deep breath, an intake of humanity. "Wait there."

She went upstairs. He could hear searching, opening cupboards, dragging furniture. She came back a few moments later with a tattered cardboard folder and dropped it on the table. It was filled with memorabilia: papers, clippings and photographs. The photos weren't of the exercise, he was dis-

appointed to see: they were protests. There was Riggs—
Belsey only just recognised her—long hair and a jumper,
serious glasses, the diligent diary keeper, more earnest than
she appeared today.

"This is everything I've got." She checked her watch.
"Four minutes."

There were several newspaper clippings: *Civil Defence a
"cruel deception" says Lambeth Council. Government in-
ducing "war psychosis"—Cook MP*. There were photographs of bearded men marching beneath hand-painted
signs. In one photograph a small group gathered with CND
placards around a four-storey block of flats. It took Belsey
a moment to recognise it: Pear Tree House. The block
floated on its windowless concrete. The surrounding trees
were saplings, the concrete newer, but the building was unmistakable.

"This is in Gipsy Hill," Belsey said. "My suspect tried to
break into it."

"Yes. Pear Tree House. It became the site of a lot of protests."

"What is it?"

"Headquarters of the South-East London Regional Seat
of Government. That's in the basement, beneath the flats.
Pear Tree," she said softly. "I haven't thought about any of
this for years."

Belsey leafed through fast, searching for clues to the underground network. Riggs, meanwhile, had become wistful.

"What did I keep all this for? I must have been saving it
for my memoir. For after I became Prime Minister." She
sifted the pages. As she did, Belsey saw a map of Britain

covered in small triangles, similar to one he'd seen beneath the library.

"What's the map of?"

"It shows Warning and Monitoring Posts. Two- or three-man bunkers. There are more than a thousand of them across the country."

"What about these?" He lifted another set of maps.

"Civil defence boundaries, the regions into which we'd be divided, the Regional Seats of Government that would rule us, dividing up hell. The grid is so we can chart details of nuclear bursts." She shook her head in wonder. "Croydon, Kingston—it's hard to imagine them sounding as forbidding as Nagasaki and Hiroshima. I guess the residents of Nagasaki didn't feel they were living anywhere special."

He sifted through the various maps but there were none of the London tunnel system.

"Who'd know if there *was* a way of moving between bunkers underground?"

"Possibly no one. Departments become extinct, knowledge expires. Maybe, when they're declassified, the files themselves will make it into an archive. Until then I guess they're in limbo, neither alive nor dead. I remember, when I was in the cabinet, hearing that one of the secret government bunkers had flooded. Turns out it had been built on top of the buried stream of the Tyburn. For three weeks nothing was done. No one could remember who was responsible, you see; no department accepted responsibility." She laughed. "Most of these contingency arrangements were secret from MPs themselves."

"Where was this top-secret bunker?"

"I don't know. Once again, you've reached my limits."
She checked the clock.

"So who knew about the shelters back in the day?"

"That group of people who don't get voted in and out.
Government is a frail, transitory thing. You'd need to dig
down into the heart of the intelligence service for the people
who ran this. These things are passed on, generation to generation, among a very small handful of individuals."

Belsey was starting to give up. Riggs was enjoying a last
moment of nostalgia. She picked up another document.

"Here you go: public sector workers, the roles we'd be
assigned after the bomb. The bin man or park keeper turns
up for work to be told his new duties are those of a gravedig-
ger; a director of social services becomes responsible for
sorting out refugee camps. Here's you." She waved a pam-
phlet entitled *Police Manual of Home Defence*. "Controll-
ing the movement of subversive or potentially subversive
persons," the MP read. "What do you think that would involve, Detective Constable? Round up the communists, the
socialists. No courts necessary; police commanders enforce
the law in whatever way they see fit. On the spot if need be.
This is war, remember."

Her phone rang. She got up and spoke briefly to someone,
then hung up.

"I've got to go. I hope that helped." Riggs took a hair-
brush from her bag. The nostalgia evaporated and she fixed
Belsey with a professional stare. "I'm talking to you because
you're a police officer and you've told me someone's in danger. I'd be very uneasy if I thought any of this was going to
appear anywhere. As I say, I was a small cog in the machine
but I am, like all of us, subject to the Official Secrets Act."

"Where is Site 3?" Belsey asked.

"I don't know anywhere called Site 3," Riggs said.

"Heard of Ferryman?" Belsey tried.

"Ferryman? No."

"Codename for a spy, someone who leaked information to the Soviets. Maybe about this exercise."

"You may have misunderstood which part of government I worked in. I don't know about spies."

"Who could I speak to?"

Riggs looked at the picture of Jemma. Then she reached into her handbag and took out a pen. She found the order of service from the funeral and hesitated. It was a plush job, more like a brochure for a reputation. Sir Douglas Argyle stared accusingly from a portrait reproduced on the front. She apologised to the dead man, then scribbled a number in the margin.

"This is someone who probably won't talk to you. But it's the best I can do. Get a senior officer to call him and don't, whatever you do, tell anyone where you got it."

There was a number. No name. Belsey thanked her and left.

He walked to a pub on Vauxhall Bridge Road, innocuous for the passing tourists and businessmen, drank half a coffee while trying to decide what to say, then he stepped outside and dialled the number. A man answered.

"Yes?"

"This is Detective Constable Nick Belsey. I need information about deep-level tunnels beneath London. I was told someone might be able to help."

There was a second's pause.

"I see," the man said, evenly. "Tunnels. Let me get someone to call you back." He sounded urbane, affable. Someone on leather seating. Belsey gave his number.

"Soon as possible, thanks."

He took a seat outside the pub and rolled a cigarette. Someone called back in two minutes. Belsey couldn't tell if it was the same man. He didn't introduce himself.

"These shelters. I wouldn't worry about them," he said.

"Wouldn't worry about them?" This cheerful rejection threw Belsey. "I kind of need to worry about them. A young woman is in danger down there now."

"Forget it happened. You asked me for advice, that's it."

"I asked you for information."

"The information is that it's a good idea to leave it."

Belsey paused, holding his phone, order of service in hand. What could he say? Sir Douglas looked unimpressed. He sat before his map of Europe and a flag. Belsey stared at the flag, pinned across the wall. It bore the image of a dagger emerging from a cloud of smoke. Beneath the smoke was a scrolled banner containing the word: CAVE.

"Sorry I can't be of more help," the man said.

Belsey put the phone down.

CAVE. The graffiti on the side of Centre Point. He thought of the body being dropped and he looked at the Order of Service again.

He went back in and sipped his coffee. Then he ran a search for obituaries of Douglas Argyle. There was nothing substantial yet, just a death announcement in the *Telegraph*: *Air Chief Marshal Sir Douglas Argyle, Former Chief of the Defence Staff, died peacefully on Saturday night surrounded by his family.* Belsey called the Metropolitan Police control room and asked for a search on the police log for the night of his supposed death. It didn't record any bodies identified as Douglas Argyle or Sir Douglas. No emergency services attended the Lord's home. No hospitals reported him dead.

Belsey tried to remember the timing of the corpse dump on the vanished CCTV. Around four thirty Sunday morning. Then something that Riggs had said came back to him.

I'm not going to peddle gossip . . .

In what situation do ageing Lotharios have heart attacks?

Belsey decided to risk a call to Monroe, to see what Fleet Street knew about the gossip. His phone vibrated before he could dial. A Hampstead landline. Belsey answered.

"Hey."

"There's a gun trained on you."

Belsey cast an eye over the nearby windows.

"Is that right?"

"I don't know. It's the sort of thing they do. Now that we're working together there will always be a gun trained on you. Like an eye."

"Are we working together?"

"So it seems."

"As colleagues, shall we lay down a few ground rules about abducting each other's dates?"

"It's too late for that."

"Did you kill Douglas Argyle?"

"Apparently not. What would happen if I killed you? Maybe they'd sweep it up. Then would you be dead?"

"What do you want?"

"What do they want? It's a predicament, Nick. She's started complaining—doesn't like the restraints. I've got to go back, check she's OK. Think outside the box."

"Is that what you called to say?"

"London is a jigsaw puzzle."

"Give me a clue. What am I meant to be doing exactly?" The caller laughed.

"You can't give a clue to a jigsaw puzzle, Nick. You just put the pieces together." Then he was gone.

Belsey finished his coffee and walked to the river. Vauxhall Bridge rose up as it left the north bank, so that it looked like it was heading into clear blue sky. Then you saw the buildings on the other side: glass apartment blocks, MI6.

He looked at his phone, at the call. He could trace it. But there was no point. The forensic caution—the wiped receiver at the phone box this morning—suggested his target was already on the system. Or suspected he might be. *Where has he had contact?* He was being careful, but no one's careful all the time. People leave prints when they're off guard, in situations where it's difficult to use gloves. Fiddly things.

Like turning pages.

Belsey took the diary out and angled it in a square of sunlight. It was covered in fingerprints. They didn't look thirty years old.

HE WALKED INTO THE ANODYNE HOME OF PGC Forensic Services on Hammersmith Road, ready to hustle. Since the government closed down its own Forensic Science Service, work had been outsourced to innumerable companies cashing in on Britain's contact traces. PGC did most of the jobs for Camden Borough. They had access to the relevant databases. They were also the easiest to squeeze for prompt results. And they'd headhunted his favourite scientist, Isha Sharvani.

21

The front desk liked to make him wait. The building was cold, fierce air-con obliterating any whiff of the unsterile life going on outside. Belsey sat in reception, studying the diary in the light of the halogen bulbs. The paper itself was speckled with blue spots of damp but the prints overlaid the damp. They were made with what looked like the same residue of dirt and grease that coated the tunnels. But it wasn't Belsey's print. After ten years in CID he knew his own whorls. Someone else had been leafing through, past the commencement of war and the destruction of London, trying to find out how it ends.

After five minutes he was sent up. He knew the lab would tell him it would take a couple of hours to process. He didn't have that time. The more he looked at the print the more confident he felt that it was his man. At the third floor he put on the regulation overalls, then found Sharvani's lab. She was alone. Up on a large screen was what looked like a tree that had been struck by lightning: a blackened, exploded stump. Belsey checked the microscope beneath it and saw a hair. Isha Sharvani was using tweezers to portion the rest of the strands into small bags marked *Hampstead Station*. If she knew about the hair, Belsey reasoned, she knew why the hairdresser's print might require fast-track attention.

"Was she alive when it was cut?" Belsey asked.

Sharvani turned.

"Jesus, Nick. How did you get in?"

"I told them I was a detective."

"You're a nuisance." She straightened and took her mask down. Then she saw he was serious. "Was she alive? I don't know. You're not the first to ask."

"Who was first?"

"We've had press calling."

"What press?"

"Press press."

"When?"

"The last couple of hours."

"What did you tell them?"

"Nothing, of course." Sharvani put the tweezers down and adjusted the microscope. "If she'd been dead for a while you'd see death rings: decomposition in the follicle. We don't have many follicles and no banding on the ones we do have. It doesn't mean she was alive, just not dead for ages."

"Any good news?"

"Depends what cheers you up. The hair was hacked off with a knife. But it looks like the victim struggled because at least a few strands have come out at the root. You can see the root is stretched and has broken with some tissue attached. It's going to take a while to do full DNA."

"What about the dirt on it?"

"The black deposit is actually particles of metal and carbon. You see it where there's been machinery wearing down over a long period of time. Friction."

"Brake pads."

"Yes."

"Brake pads for tube trains."

Sharvani was hesitant, but conceded: "Sure. There are other traces you'd expect from tube tunnels: dense skin particles, rat urine. But I'm not sure what kind of tunnel this is. There are flakes of paint that contain lead."

"And lead paint's banned."

"Exactly."

"When did we ban it?"

"1958, I just checked. So go on, fill me in. What is this?"

"She was abducted on Monday night. I think she's being kept underground somewhere. It might be in tunnels that haven't been used for a long while. She's being held there and we're receiving threats that she's going to be killed soon."

"Have you got a suspect?"

"I'm glad you asked." Belsey brought the diary out. "These might be his prints." He handed it over. She inspected the marks.

"Not bad."

"I need them processed."

"I can tell the print team to do it this afternoon."

"We have minutes rather than hours."

Sharvani looked at the diary again. She walked him down the corridor to Fingerprints. The lab was a similar set up to Photographic, same white worktops, same smell of cleaning products and new technology. It had more stations, more computers, fewer empty mugs lying about.

"Jack," Sharvani said. The print technician came over. He wore several earrings and traces of eyeliner. She explained the situation and he seemed open to helping. He placed the page under a lens of the IDENT1 machine and it appeared on his monitor. Belsey looked up and saw the words large across the screen: *Croydon fatalities: 130,000.*

"What is this?" the technician asked, looking impressed.

"Someone's diary."

"They had a worse week than me."

He adjusted the page—*Kingston forty percent destruction. Fallout high*—then the fingerprint loops appeared, white on a black background. The technician isolated a print. He clicked a mouse, leaving a trail of crosses along the various ridges. A few more keystrokes and it was connecting to the national database. With a print that clear, if he was logged with a criminal record, results could be almost instantaneous. If he was on the rest of the system—people who've been printed as part of an inquiry but who have no record—it could take hours.

Belsey grabbed a seat at the side. Argyle, he thought. He looked at the portrait again. CAVE. Was it a motto? He got his phone out and typed in *Cave military motto.* No "Cave," a lot of others; they were all in Latin.

"Does 'cave' mean something in Latin?" Belsey asked.

" 'Beware,'" Jack said, without looking up from the print scanner. "Why?"

"It means 'beware'?"

"Like in 'caveat.'"

"You're wasted here, Jack," Belsey said.

"Never during office hours."

Beware. A dagger and smoke clouds. Belsey found what he could about Argyle's career. Chief of the Defence Staff 1951–66. Permanent secretary at the Ministry of Defence in 1970. He oversaw Britain's civil defence arrangements in the cold-war period.

Civil defence was Riggs's Saturday job. He opened another browser and typed in *local authority defence bunkers.* There was a list compiled by a group of enthusiasts: thirty-seven bunkers across the UK, stashed beneath innocent neighbourhoods, waiting. Hardened civil defence control for the Corporation of London could be found beneath the Guildhall, for the middle classes under Stoke Newington Town Hall. Salt-of-the-earth Bermondsey placed its council's nuclear bunker under a garage adjoining the council offices, Dagenham beneath the grounds of a civic centre.

The same site also listed UK radar stations, NATO bases, the anonymous depots where emergency food and medical supplies were kept; finally, the Warning and Monitoring posts Riggs had mentioned. There were more than a thousand scattered about, operated by an army of volunteers until 1995. Belsey had to read the year twice. The posts consisted of an underground room big enough for three, equipment for them to monitor the surrounding landscape for bombs, fallout, chemical or biological attack, and riots. According to the site, the government had replaced all the old computers in these posts in the early nineties before someone somewhere pointed out the insanity.

So much effort. So much fear still down there, unspent. No one cleans up. He was starting to understand: something that never happens has a strange relationship to time. It can't become the past. It gets lodged. And this was his suspect's obsession—all the breaking into shelters, the rifled drawers beneath St. Pancras Library, trying to gather up abandoned paperwork . . .

"You're a lucky man, Nick. You should take up gambling. Again."

Sharvani and the print technician were staring at the computer.

"What have you got?" he said.

"Eighty-seven percent match."

"He's on the system?"

"Duncan Powell, West London, forty years old."

Belsey went over.

"What's it on for?"

"Dangerous driving—arrested, not charged, twenty-third of January this year. He was in a blue Volkswagen Passat. Taken to Kilburn police station."

"What's the address?"

"12 Viners Road, Willesden Junction."

BELSEY SLOWED DOWN ONCE HE WAS IN WILLES-
den. Viners Road was a short street of red-brick
houses blocked at one end by the chain-link of a
school playground. Belsey tried to match the
placid scene with his image of the man torment-
ing him. Why not? Suburbs lent themselves to
sadism and espionage. There
was number 12, there was the
blue Volkswagen owned by a
man whose prints were all over
Riggs's diary. It was the last
house on the row. Belsey parked,
blocking the Volkswagen in, just
in case Mr. Powell made a run
for it. He grabbed his cuffs.

22

   The house was well kept,
unlit, recycling boxes stacked and empty, front
curtains drawn. No lights visible inside. The
Volkswagen's bonnet was ice cold. Belsey rang
the doorbell and braced himself. No one answered. He went down a side path to bins and a
second door. A window beside the door showed
plates in a drying rack. The centre of the door
itself was frosted glass. Belsey put his eye to the
lock, saw it had a key on the inside. It didn't feel
bolted. He stepped along the path until he found
a loose paving slab, levered it up and smashed

the door's glass panel. He waited for any response, then reached in, unlocked it and stepped inside.

It was a nice kitchen. Not hi-tech but not neglected. Cookbooks, casserole dishes, a handbag on the kitchen table. He walked through a beaded curtain to a living room with an upright piano and a lot of books. The home of a middle-class couple. Or not a couple any more.

He smelt the grief before he saw it. There was a bed made up on the sofa littered with tissues; toast and soup on the table beside it, a greeting card lying on its back. *Sorry for your loss*. Belsey picked it up. "I knew Duncan well," it began. It amounted to a small, earnest letter. The whole thing was "tragic," "cruel," "senseless"; signed Gillian, dated yesterday.

There were more unopened on the mat by the front door addressed to an Andrea Powell.

Death is a fairly solid alibi. 87 percent was a pretty solid print match. Belsey tore an envelope open and read another card. "His talent will be missed as well as his warmth." He looked around, trying to identify the nature of Duncan Powell's talent. A key turned in the front door. He was standing there with the condolence card in his hand as Powell's widow walked in and screamed. She dropped a carrier bag and lifted a hand to her mouth. She had a friend behind her, ready to fight. Belsey took his badge out.

"Police," he said, as an alternative to "surprise" or "sorry" and sounding halfway between the two. "Don't worry." He didn't convince himself.

"What's going on? How did you get in?" She was a tall woman, black hair clipped back, large dark eyes reddened.

Her friend was blonder, smaller, with a lot of bangles and outraged eyes.

"Come in. Sit down," Belsey said. She came in and sat on the sofa, shaking. The friend watched from the doorway, arms folded. "Andrea?"

"Yes."

"I'm Nick Belsey, a detective. I need to ask you a few questions about Duncan. Is that OK?" She nodded. "When did he pass away?"

"Two days ago. Monday." She spoke with the traces of a Spanish or Italian accent but London had flattened the vowels and the skin tone.

"How?"

"I thought you were police," the friend said.

"I'm on a separate investigation. Duncan's name came up in possible connection with it." Andrea was hesitant. He couldn't blame her. "What happened?" he asked.

"He was hit by a car," the blonde friend said.

Belsey kept his focus on the widow.

"Do they know who was driving?"

"No," Andrea said.

"Where was he?"

"Around Golders Hill Park."

That was getting close to Belsey's neck of the woods.

"When exactly on Monday?"

"Around quarter to five."

"Description of the car?"

"Silver," she said. "That's all."

Quarter to five, Monday. Where was he around that time? He knew exactly where he was. Sitting parked up off

Hampstead High Street, waiting for a silver BMW to tear his world apart. Now he had an idea what it was speeding from—a man's death.

Andrea started to cry. She pulled a tissue from her sleeve. Her friend sat behind her and stared daggers at Belsey.

"What did Duncan do, professionally?" Belsey asked.

"He was a writer."

"What did he write?"

"Excuse me, what's going on?" The friend asked. "You're upsetting her."

Andrea pointed to a shelf beside the piano. Belsey stood up and went over. Hardbacks from the last ten years on an eclectic range of subjects: political scandal, organised crime, censorship, the cold war. But mostly the cold war. *Counter-intelligence after Brezhnev*, *The New Spy Chiefs*, *Soviet Special Operations 1956–75*. Propped against the books was a photograph of Powell in regulation overcoat and Cossack hat in Red Square, next to the McDonald's. He was tall, with a thin, clean-shaven face, wire-rimmed glasses and an ironic smile. In another photograph he was sitting in the living room beside his wife, playing an acoustic guitar.

"Andrea, was Duncan working on the day he died?"

"Yes. Someone had said they wanted to meet him."

"About what?"

"Work."

"What was he working on?"

"I don't know."

"But this person wanted to help."

"Yes. I think so. Duncan seemed . . . anxious."

"Why anxious, do you think?"

"He said we should maybe think about getting away soon. He never used to talk about holidays. He said he'd leave his work and we would get away for a few months." She gestured at a bereft pile of library books on the floor. Books on sailing, hiking, bird watching; birds of Southern Europe, the Adriatic, other places far from London and its secrets.

"Did Duncan ever mention underground tunnels?"

Both women stared at Belsey with renewed suspicion. The friend got up in disgust and went to the kitchen.

"Underground?" Andrea said. "No. I don't understand. I don't understand why you're here." Then the friend gasped melodramatically from behind the beaded curtain.

"What have you done to the door?"

"I'll call a glazier," Belsey said.

"Andrea, he's smashed the side door."

"Could you leave?" Andrea pleaded, weakly.

"Did you see any equipment he might have been using? Torches? Maybe dirty clothes?"

"Please."

The friend returned to the living room.

"You need to leave now."

"Look," Belsey began, then saw another careless and conspicuous incident developing. Slow down, he thought. Keep calm. The friend's expression said: What are you doing, you heartless bastard? Belsey wondered. He'd added a lot of confusion to the sorrow, like someone trying to improve a bad meal by covering it in paint. He gave Andrea Powell one of his cards and told her he may need to be in touch again, more as a final gesture of validation than in any hope she'd speak to him.

THE STORY WAS BREAKING ON THE TWO O'CLOCK NEWS
when he got back in the car. "Concern is mount-
ing for missing art student, Jemma Stevens. The
twenty-two-year-old from Stoke Newington
failed to return home after going out on Monday . . ." No last sighting was mentioned. No
mention of the hair parcel either,
although word of it must have
spread—he had no doubt this
was driving the media interest.

23

Hampstead station leaked like a
sieve. Journalists knew it was
going to be box office. But they
were acting well behaved for
now and holding back on details. They gave Northwood's
name as senior investigator.

Belsey turned the radio off, called a trusted
glazier, then drove back towards the station. He
stopped for coffee at a place with vintage furniture and china teacups, ate a croissant and
thought. Duncan Powell's published works had
made him conscious of quite how large a world
he had entered, swept into a current of unfin-
ished history that nineteen years of criminal investigation had not prepared him for. Powell
never made it home. Nor had Argyle. Argyle, a

former chief of the defence staff. Killed on Saturday night. Then Powell approximately twenty-four hours later, a cold-war historian. And now the suspect had another to hand. An art student.

Belsey pondered this, watching mothers with buggies and men hunched over iPads. He thought: London is a jigsaw puzzle. Because it fits together? Because it breaks apart? Because there's a piece missing?

THERE WAS A FURIOUS message from Tom Monroe waiting for him on his office answering machine.

"I had this story. I was sitting around on your instructions and every other journalist in the city is having a big fucking laugh and wondering why I'm so slow."

No sign of Rob Trapping or Kirsty Craik. Rosen was trying to outstare a crossword.

"Any word from the Sarge?" Belsey asked.

"She was called in by the brass about last night."

"Where's Rob?"

"Interview Room 3."

Belsey felt a flicker of concern.

"Doing what?"

"Interviewing someone, I imagine."

"Who?"

"The guy who lives with the missing girl." Rosen tossed the crossword aside. Belsey shut his eyes. He went to the interview room and threw the door open. There was the Kiwi barman, leaning back, arms folded. He saw Belsey and got to his feet.

"Sit down," Belsey said. "Rob, corridor, word."

Trapping bounded out.

"He's got previous, Nick: assault and possession. They were seeing each other. She broke it off. I've left a message for Sergeant Craik."

"What's he saying?"

"A lot of bullshit about you, of course."

"Like?"

"That you know something, you're responsible, you were shagging her. Were you?" Trapping smiled.

"What's his name?"

"Jayden Culler."

"Give me a moment."

Belsey walked in and shut the door. He stopped the tape recorder. The barman glowered.

"Jayden, relax."

"What the fuck is this? What am I doing here?"

"Leaving. You're on your way out, my friend. I'm working hard to find out what's happened to Jemma. I've got nothing to do with her disappearance. Do you understand? I know it's not to do with you either. It doesn't help anyone if you go on talking crap about me."

"How do you know it's not to do with me then?"

"I can *not* know it pretty fast if that's how you want it to go."

"Don't threaten me. Where is she?"

Belsey marched him out of the room, past Trapping, out of the station.

"Nick, what the fuck . . ."

"He's alibied."

Belsey ignored Trapping's pained stare. He watched Jayden walk away. A few seconds later he watched Trapping march off towards the pub. Then he returned to the CID office and searched the Local Intelligence system for Duncan Powell's death.

Knocked down on North End Way, 4:46 p.m. Monday. Logged as a fail-to-stop collision. The car hit Powell from behind before continuing south towards Hampstead. The body had been thrown ten metres. One witness saw it. The witness was called Colin Thorpe. He had stopped his Land Rover on the far side of North End Road to take a call. He described Powell running "as if being chased." He had been running when he was hit. Powell wasn't dressed for a jog: jeans, jumper, walking boots. He'd been running from Hampstead Way, onto North End Road—running from the entrance to the abandoned North End Station? This sounded slightly more complicated than a fail-to-stop.

It was a silver car that hit him—"probably a BMW," according to Thorpe. Duncan Powell was pronounced dead at the scene at 5.11 pm. The pathologist logged cause of death as "blunt-force trauma."

Belsey called the witness, Thorpe, and left a message on a BT voicemail to get in touch with him urgently.

He looked for who was leading the investigation. Technically the accident happened in the borough of Barnet, just over the border from Camden, beyond Belsey's jurisdiction. So while the crash occurred less than a mile from Hampstead it had gone to an entirely different team. Not a team covering themselves in glory. They'd obviously smelt something slightly odd, interviewed Powell's friends and family to try to establish what he'd been up to. But it had all become a bit much for them. The effort must have seemed unrewarding and, on Tuesday morning, they chalked it up as a straight hit-and-run. Who wants an unsolved murder on your books when you can have a road-traffic accident?

Belsey checked his own report of the car chase. It was there on the system: Silver BMW 7 Series, driving dangerously down Rosslyn Hill, 4:48 p.m. That was two minutes after Powell was hit, one mile away, by the same make of car.

How hard was it to connect those incidents?

Belsey tried calling the officer named as main point of contact for Powell's investigation, DI Gary Finch. He spent five minutes being bounced around extensions before someone told him that Finch was out of the office at a birthday party. "Call back tomorrow."

Belsey slammed the phone down. He emailed Ferryman@tempmail.net: *Why did you kill Duncan Powell?*

He spent ten minutes typing up a detailed account of all this and left it on Craik's desk. She could try her luck with the elusive Gary Finch. It would give her something to chew on, at least.

By the time he got back to his computer there was a block of ten emails from Ferryman. Subject line: *Memorials.* He opened the most recent. It contained a link. He clicked the link and a video appeared. But the video was just a still black-and-white photograph, a modern concrete building: ugly, bare, with small dark windows.

He turned the sound on and screams filled the office. His colleagues turned. Belsey hit mute. He stole the headphones off Rob Trapping's desk and plugged them in.

Ten emails, ten concrete buildings, ten soundtracks involving a young woman who wanted to go home. Belsey shut his eyes and forced himself to listen, just in case he could extract any useful information—in the voice, the acoustics, background noise. There wasn't any background noise. The acoustics were, at a guess, subterranean. The young woman pleaded and sobbed.

It was Jemma.

Belsey turned his attention to the buildings. He recognised four of them immediately: Centre Point, the modern annexe containing St. Pancras Library, the BT Tower, a black-sided office block that had to be the Archway Tower. The six others he couldn't ID. He printed them out, spread them on his desk and they formed a sea of bleak concrete.

Brutal. What was it Monroe had said? *Masterpiece of the Brutalist style*. Belsey called the journalist's mobile. He was sent to voicemail after two rings.

"Listen, Tom, stop being a cock. Get back to me."

He hung up.

"Is there a press conference on the missing girl?" Belsey asked the office. "Reporters waiting anywhere?"

"I heard they were at King's Cross," Aziz said.

"They were told something about the library," Rosen added. "Council was going to give a press conference. Then decided not to. Idea was squashed."

"Squashed?"

Rosen shrugged.

Belsey made a few calls. Eventually he pieced together what had happened. Camden Council announced there would be some kind of statement, then at quarter past two they sent a memo: it was called off. No explanation given. A lot of journalists left kicking their heels around St. Pancras. And Belsey saw what was happening. This was what Ferryman wanted—attention on the tunnels; men and women congregating on the border of secrecy, pressing at the silence and waiting for it to burst.

THE BORDER OF SECRECY RIGHT NOW WAS THE STRETCH of dirty pavement between Chop Chop Noodles and Camden Town Hall. There was a lot of confusion around the library. One satellite broadcasting van waited across the road; hacks were engaged in a casual standoff with council security and half a dozen uniformed police wearing "nothing to see" expressions. It was 3:30 p.m.

"What are they saying?" Belsey asked a news reporter sharing pizza with her cameraman.

"They're saying we should contact the Yard press office. It's a bloody shambles."

"What's the Yard saying?"

"That it's not for them to comment."

"Seen Tom Monroe?"

"Try Chop Chop."

The noodle house was a King's Cross institution, staffed by black-shirted waiters whose task was to get you out of there as quickly as possible. Monroe wasn't playing. He had the back corner, his phone and notebook out, and he was nursing prawn crackers and a bottle of Tsingtao. Belsey sat down. Monroe rifled the crackers.

"I hope you got good money for it, Nick. I'm getting fucking death threats off my editor now."

A girl slapped a laminated menu in front of Belsey. Belsey moved it to the side along with the crackers and beer. He spread Ferryman's photos across the table.

"Here's a game. What have they got in common?"

Monroe glanced at the pictures.

"You fucked me over."

"Want to go to the press conference instead?"

"Is there one?"

"No. Do you think your friends out there have any idea what's going on? No one's being told anything."

Monroe looked at the printouts more closely.

"And this is the scoop? Post-war architecture got ugly?"

"I don't know what it is. That's where you're going to help me. You said something about the style. Brutal."

"Brutalist."

"Go on."

"It's a style of architecture: concrete, modern, pure."

"Pure?"

"Pure of line."

"Centre Point is Brutalist."

"I'd say."

"The library up the road?"

"Brutal as they come."

"Are these all Brutalist?"

Monroe lifted a picture then moved it to the side.

"Yes." He shuffled the images into configurations. "These are telephone exchanges: Moorgate, Baynard House, Colombo House in Waterloo."

"Telephone exchanges."

"I think so."

Belsey looked at the cold, concrete monoliths. He understood now why they seemed so unhuman; homes for machines. "Does anything connect them all, apart from the style?"

"Well, they would have all been built within a few years of each other," Monroe conceded. "They capture an architectural moment, shall we say."

"Is Brutalism defensive?"

"What do you mean?"

"Is it used for bunkers? For protecting high-security installations?"

"It was meant to be about boldness, simplicity—a new, rational aesthetic."

"Pretty solid too."

"No doubt."

"They'd work, as bomb-proof structures."

"They certainly wouldn't fall over very easily."

"Even in a nuclear blast."

"No."

Belsey watched through the window as another broadcasting van pulled in and was immediately directed away. The journalists had begun to disperse. His waitress reappeared and he ordered a number at random.

"Douglas Argyle," Belsey said. Monroe smiled.

"Know something about the rumours?"

"Maybe. What do you know?"

"Last seen going into a posh block of flats in Westminster. Not his own home. No reason for him to be there.

According to his wife he'd left home Saturday night, anxious. Someone wanted to meet him. She's convinced he was being blackmailed by a mistress. He gets a cab straight to Horseferry Road: he's on cameras walking into this luxury block just before midnight—Westminster Green Apartments. Never seen alive again. The police were going through the whole place knocking on doors, so of course it made a lot of noise and some of us got curious. Then the gagging order came."

"You're not allowed to write about it?"

"No."

"Why do I know that block—Westminster Green?" Belsey searched his mind. He imagined his way through that odd, exclusive area between Victoria and the river.

"Used to be Westminster Hospital," Monroe said.

Belsey got his phone out. *Westminster Hospital* . . . He knew it had been mentioned. Which website had it been on? He fired off searches until he hit one of the amateur sites: *Tunnels had been extended from the Cabinet War Rooms to a new subterranean complex under Victoria, beneath three 1970s office blocks on Marsham Street, with an emergency exit in the basement of the old Westminster Hospital.*

"What was Argyle involved in exactly?" Belsey asked. "During the cold war?"

"Lots of things. He helped develop the Ballistic Missile Early Warning System; converted the RAF base at Aldermaston to the Atomic Weapons Research Establishment. At Porton Down he instigated studies into fallout and radiation. He basically re-engineered the military for nuclear war. How do you think this connects?"

"Westminster Hospital contained an emergency exit from government bunkers." He showed Monroe the web entry. Monroe studied it. "There's no record of Argyle's death," Belsey said. "I think he used some basement access that survives in the apartment block, an old route into the tunnels. Someone lured him down there. His body was dumped beneath Centre Point in the early hours of Sunday morning. It's been wiped off the police system."

Monroe maintained a poker face. A plate of gelatinous noodles was slammed down.

"Did you know a writer called Duncan Powell?" Belsey asked.

"Of course. Duncan was immense." And then Monroe frowned. "He was hit by a car, Nick."

"His prints were under the library." The frown didn't shift. Monroe was momentarily lost for words.

"Are you sure?"

"Yes."

"You printed the place?"

"Not all of it. What was he working on recently? Any idea?"

"No."

"I sent Ferryman an email. I asked why he killed Duncan Powell. He sent these."

"You think Duncan . . ."

"Yes."

Monroe turned back to the photos of the buildings. He moved the images again, studying each one in turn as if he was trying to memorise the sequence.

"They all have at least some government connection," he said, finally. "Centre Point contains government offices on the ground floor. This is a shot of the three towers on Marsham Street in Victoria, close to Westminster Green Apartments—used to be Department of the Environment. Demolished now. This was the old Home Office building on Queen Anne's Gate. Now houses Ministry of Justice."

"Archway Tower?"

"Archway Tower used to be government property. And if you're thinking tunnels, it sits right on top of the tube station."

Belsey studied the bleak structure with fresh admiration.

"But you said these were telephone exchanges." Belsey pointed to the three buildings Monroe had singled out.

"Telephone exchanges would have originally been government-controlled. They belonged to the General Post Office. The GPO was a government department, in charge of anything to do with communication: post, telephones, telegrams." Monroe pressed his finger on the picture of the BT Tower. "Until the nineties, you wouldn't find the BT Tower on any maps. Technically it was covered by the Official Secrets Act. Get an *A-Z* from the eighties and it's not there. You know why it's round? To withstand nuclear blasts."

And now Belsey saw the Central London skyline again: the BT Tower conquering the air alongside Centre Point, less than a kilometre away. Two silhouettes you couldn't escape. As a child, taken to town for the day, he could never believe there were people in the BT Tower. It looked more like technology than architecture. The Post Office Tower, as it had been known then. The Post Office . . .

And then, in the recesses of his brain, another post office-related puzzle glimmered into significance: why steal a chef's van from behind a postal depot at 10.15 in the morning? A strange MO and now getting stranger. Could they connect? It felt like a lead, but usually with a lead you had some sense where it was leading, it wasn't a path fading out into the mysteries of the nuclear age.

"I'll be in touch," Belsey said, putting a fiver by the noodles and getting up.

"I'll be here," Monroe said, unwrapping chopsticks.

Belsey phoned the station from his car and got the number for Victor Patridis, owner of the missing Vauxhall Vivaro. He dialled. A woman answered.

"Is Mr. Patridis there?"

"No," she said. "Who is this?"

"It's the police. About the stolen van."

"He's at work."

"At Mount Pleasant?"

"Yes," she said impatiently. "Where else would he be?"

ROYAL MAIL MOUNT PLEASANT SPRAWLED OVER A square kilometre between King's Cross and Farringdon, once hub of the UK's postal system and Europe's biggest sorting office. Belsey parked overlooking it. He could just see the back road where the van had been stolen. He watched the endless fleet of red Royal Mail lorries coming and going in the soft light of 5 p.m. The depot had the faceless enormity of an industrial works. He used to drink with some posties in The Apple Tree. They referred to the depot as Coldbaths, after the Victorian prison that used to occupy the site. It hadn't shaken the ambience.

25

The General Post Office, Belsey thought. And what did you do in the cold war?

He approached security on the north gate with his badge out. They suggested he make his way to the manager's office and pointed him across five hundred metres of tarmac to the one human-sized entrance beside the bays. They ran a swipe beside the gate and it opened for him.

The manager's office was on the third floor, above the chaos of trolleys and sacks. He was young, taut with responsibility, neck shaved raw. His office was bare but for a large desk, the only items on the walls a plan of the depot itself and a chart of monthly targets. He peered anxiously at Belsey's ID.

"A guy robbed?"

"Yes, a chef. Victor Patridis. Is he here?"

The manager checked a binder.

"Patridis . . . There's three thousand men and women who work here," he said, with the air of someone who's been given a big present they haven't figured out how to use yet. He gave up on the binder and looked through a spreadsheet on his PC, then went over to a map on the wall. "Three bloody canteens," he muttered. "Why do we need *three*?"

The manager flicked through a second ring binder until he had an extension. He dialled.

"Yes, can he come up now? No, the food's fine, it's about the theft of his van."

The manager didn't look optimistic when he hung up. He probed Belsey about the crime while they waited, whether it had any implications for the smooth running of his depot. Patridis appeared five minutes later: squat, unshaven, in a hairnet and disposable blue gloves. He stood with his feet apart and smelt of chip fat. Belsey showed his badge.

"You had a van stolen."

"Have you caught him?" he asked.

"Not yet. Tell me what happened."

"I stopped to get some cash out, came back to the van and he jumped me. He must have been waiting round the back."

"Did he say anything?"

"He said, 'Give me your wallet.' Which was stupid. Thing is, the cash I've got out is in my hand—250 quid. He sees it but doesn't take it, dozy twat."

Belsey considered this.

"Why do you think he wanted your wallet, then? If he left the cash?"

"I have absolutely no idea. I've cancelled all the cards. I told him the van was empty apart from some bread. It's not worth anything. You're not going to get money for it."

"What was in the wallet?"

"Debit and credit card, Tesco Clubcard, driver's licence, swipe."

"Swipe for the depot?"

"Yeah."

"Anything on the van to link it to the depot?"

"No."

"How often do you make the journey?"

"Five days a week."

"How often do you stop to get cash out?"

"Each day."

"So if he was watching he'd know you worked at the depot. He could see you go from the cashpoint into the depot itself using your swipe."

"I suppose so. Why?"

Belsey turned to the manager.

"Did you block the swipe?"

"I'm not sure I was ever aware of this. I'll speak to my head of security. It would involve resetting more than a thousand cards, you see. We can't do that—the cost alone, the time."

"Have you had any recent thefts from within the depot?"

"Nothing for weeks. I've cracked down on that."

Belsey got up and went over to the plan on the wall. The depot was a complex machine. He followed it down with his eyes, from the offices to the hangar-sized sorting rooms, to the equipment and maintenance in the basement, to a tunnel. The tunnel was shaded with red diagonal lines. *CLOSED 2003.*

"What's this?"

The manager came over.

"The old Post Office Railway."

"Go on."

"It was an underground system, connecting the post offices and railway stations. Meant they could avoid the roads. Before my time."

Belsey stepped back, stared at the depot plan. Once again, his home city revealed itself as alien.

"And it closed in 2003."

"Apparently so."

"Could a person get around the tunnels?"

"Walking? Why would they want to?"

"Let's say they did."

"Maybe."

"They're small," Patridis interrupted them. "It just carried post and parcels. The trains were driverless. Not like proper trains."

"How were they operated?"

"From control rooms at each station, I think."

"Have you had any trouble with it recently?" Belsey asked the manager. "Anyone down there, messing about?"

"Not that I've been aware of."

"Where does it go, exactly?"

The manager produced the biggest, most dog-eared binder yet; this one was apparently passed down the generations. He flicked through it for a moment then gave up and went online. He found a map on a website devoted to Post Office history: Mail Rail. 1927–2003. Belsey walked around to the screen. So did Patridis.

"From Paddington in the west to Whitechapel in the east, via Oxford Street, Liverpool Street. Nine stops in all."

"Does it connect to other underground systems?"

"Like what?"

"The tube, or any other tunnels?"

"I don't know. Why would it?"

"Let's take a look down there."

"Now?" The manager looked flummoxed. He checked the map of the depot then started searching for keys.

"What's it got to do with the van?" Patridis asked.

"It may be why he wanted your swipe."

The chef thought about this.

"Can I see it?" Patridis asked the manager.

The three of them walked down the corridor to a stone stairwell at the back of the building. The stairs were unlit. They descended several floors below ground level to a fire door. The manager spent a moment looking through his bunch of keys, forced one in, but the door was already unlocked.

It opened into a loading area littered with palettes and discarded sack ties, an old lifting truck in the corner. The space was cold and dark. Half-open steel concertina doors revealed the platform.

The manager searched for the lights and seemed surprised when the station appeared in flashes, twenty or thirty strip-lights flickering back to life. It was an underground train station, but everything was half-size. One train still waited on the narrow-gauge track, three feet high. Its main body consisted of cages for holding parcels. There was no driver's cab, just windowless engines at the front and back. It was like something from a bad funfair; a grimy, steel children's ride.

The chef chuckled to himself and took a picture on his phone. The manager looked around curiously, hands in his pockets. Belsey walked along the narrow platform. He found the Perspex front of a control office. The door was open. It contained antiquated grey equipment with red and black knobs, a swivel chair, another map of the system.

"How deep do you reckon we are?" Belsey asked.

"I don't know. Maybe seventy feet beneath street level."

"And no security issues with it recently?"

"Not that I'm aware of."

Belsey jumped down to the tracks. He stared into the tunnel. It was smaller than the ones he had walked through, but still tall enough to stand. Tall enough to move in. He walked to the entrance and stepped across the threshold. Listened for screams.

"I wouldn't go too far," the manager said.

"Why not?"

"I just mean, I'm not sure how safe it is."

QUARTER PAST SIX. HE DROPPED INTO THE STATION
and ran a search for any crime reports involving
Mount Pleasant. There were only two since the
van had been stolen—a phone gone missing from
a locker, a fight in the canteen. A similar scattering of minor offences over the preceding months.

Then one curious record from
six years ago.

26

December 2007, a man was
doing temp shifts over Christmas. This was a common enough
source of crime: turn up at the
Jobcentre mid-December and
you were sent to Mount Pleasant. In certain pubs they referred
to the place as Santa's Grotto, so
easy was it to slip cash from Christmas cards.
But this temporary employee had bigger ideas.
He went AWOL mid-shift. Four hours later he
turned up in the basement of Merrill Lynch, one
and a half miles away. According to the security
guards who discovered him, he was covered in
dirt and was carrying a digital camera and a
hand-drawn map.

The man in question was Kyle Townsend, a
repeat petty offender of mild notoriety. He'd
been twenty-three years old at the time of his

postal explorations. Belsey had briefly crossed paths with him during a Soho shakedown. He could picture Kyle spitting rocks of crack into the hands of a Drugs Squad officer. Belsey located the Merrill Lynch HQ on a map—EC4, next to Paternoster Square, St. Paul's Cathedral, heart of the Square Mile. A strange place to find yourself after a shift at Mount Pleasant.

Belsey drove over. Early evening in the City was civilised, smart congregations outside pubs, ties loosened. He passed Chancery Lane and St. Paul's. The wealth managers of Merrill Lynch occupied an appropriately grand Edwardian building, next to the ruins of Greyfriars. He showed his badge to the burly guards in black suits and hi-vis jackets and said he needed to check the basement.

They weren't having any of it, not without a warrant, not from an officer who wasn't one of their friendly local City police. Belsey walked around the building wondering about back entrances when he saw a statue. A plucky, waistcoated gentleman in brass surveying the world from the pavement in front: "Rowland Hill—Postal Reformer, Inventor of the Postage Stamp." It seemed whimsical of Merrill Lynch to celebrate Britain's postal heroes. Belsey walked the perimeter again and saw a founding stone amid the ornate flourishes:

Edward VII King of Great Britain and Ireland and the British Dominions beyond the seas, Emperor of India, laid this stone of King Edward Buildings, Headquarters of the General Post Office, on the 16th Day of October 1905.

Merrill Lynch occupied the old Post Office headquarters, then—the penultimate stop on the Mail Rail map. The stone grandeur was bizarre compared to the post offices Belsey knew: worn, beige retail operations for pushing lottery tickets and packs of stationery. He found the Mail Rail enthusiasts' website on his phone. Building purchased by Merrill Lynch in 1997, they reckoned. Occupied by finance ever since.

Belsey sat on a bench by the west wall of the cathedral. He called in and got Aziz.

"I need the record sheet for Kyle Townsend," Belsey said.

"OK. The Sarge was asking after you."

"What's she got?"

"Someone come forward about something."

"Who?"

"Flatmate of the missing girl."

Belsey felt a pang of dismay.

"Jayden Culler?"

"Exactly."

"I let him go."

"Well he's back, of his own accord this time. He wanted to talk to her. Fuck knows what his game is." Belsey digested this uncomfortably. "What was it you said you wanted?" Aziz asked.

He emailed Belsey Kyle's record sheet. Belsey took a breath then tried to focus. At the time of his Mount Pleasant escapade Kyle had already served eight months for a series of street robberies. Since 2007 he'd done time for intent to supply and, two years ago, for an attempted smash-and-grab in which he'd driven a moped at the window of a Dolce & Gabbana boutique and broken his neck.

He didn't do time for his visit to the underside of Merrill

Lynch. In fact all charges were dropped. There was no sign of his interview on file.

Belsey called Snow Hill police station, which had had the honour of dealing with Kyle on that occasion.

"Can you pull up details for the Kyle Townsend arrest, December 2007?"

They tried.

"They're not here."

"What do you mean?"

"The file's missing."

Belsey searched for Kyle's current whereabouts. According to the system, Kyle was acting shy. He'd been arrested for assault on his fiancée in May and then skipped bail, maybe knowing he was looking at a proper stretch now. Belsey made some calls. No one wanted to help. He called the chemist.

"Does the name Kyle Townsend mean anything?"

"Many things to many people, I imagine."

"Where can I find him?"

"I couldn't say."

"What could you say if I offered you half the stash on a free?"

"What do you want?"

"Kyle."

"He's at his sister's. Know Lacey Townsend?"

"Unfortunately."

"If he's not there check the loft. It's his birthday."

"Is that a family tradition?"

BELSEY ARRIVED AT LACEY Townsend's large, bare semi-detached home between Holloway Nag's Head and the

Seven Sisters Road. There was a broken tricycle parked up in the weeds of the front drive. He could hear singing inside. He rang the bell, heard the steps to the door, and then the singing stopped. He counted the thirty seconds it would take for their lodger to seek refuge, then an old man answered the door with a baseball bat over his shoulder.

"Who the fuck are you?"

"I'm looking for Kyle." Belsey walked past the batsman into the birthday party. Twenty people, four generations, all high as a kite. Party poppers had been fired and the streamers lay among empty bottles. There was no furniture. There was a cake on the floor in the shape of a Rolex. Belsey took a slice and went for the stairs.

"He's not here," someone said.

"OK."

Up the stairs to the loft. By the time Belsey made it in, Kyle's legs were dangling from the skylight. He was in shorts. Belsey cuffed his ankle to the skylight's handle. This presented Kyle with the awkward choice of remaining half on the roof or falling back with his leg dangling in the air.

Belsey looked around while Kyle pondered this crossroads. The loft was quite a priest hole, rigged for comfort. It had *Call of Duty* paused on the Xbox and a spliff burning in front of a sagging sofa. Belsey dropped onto the sofa.

"Happy birthday, Kyle. I brought you some cake."

"Get this off me." He kicked out with his free leg. There was a child's face tattooed on the calf.

"I'm not here to arrest you," Belsey said. "I'm here to absolve you of your sins, Kyle. In return for your knowledge."

"I don't know anything. Who the fuck are you?"

"I think you know about things most people don't even realise exist."

"Get this off me."

"I hear that if I lay a coin on your tongue you'll sing of sights I've never set eyes on."

"What the fuck are you on about?"

"I need you to cast your mind back. You were in Merrill Lynch. Not like that, of course. You were under Merrill Lynch. But you started at Mount Pleasant."

"They said I wouldn't get done for that."

"Who did?"

"They did."

"Why not?"

"I don't know, do I."

"What were you after?"

"I was told to take a look."

"For what?"

"That was the point. To see what was there."

"What do you mean?"

"I was casing it. Take the fucking cuff off. I don't know anything."

"You had a map."

"Yes."

"Who gave it to you?"

"Terry Condell," he snapped.

Belsey sighed.

"Terry Condell? Don't mess me around."

Kyle eased himself back to hang next to Belsey, leg in the air, grinning upside down at him with yellow teeth. It was funny—Kyle thought it was funny—because Terry Condell was untouchable; very dangerous, very criminal and generally regarded as a waste of police time.

"You're winding me up," Belsey said.

"I'm not." A look of hurt returned. "Terry gave me the map."

"And what was on this map?"

"Something three."

Kyle said it casually, but when he saw Belsey's expression he tried the words again. "That's it. Three something."

"Site 3."

"He wanted to know what it was."

"What was it?" Belsey asked, trying to sound only mildly curious.

"No idea. I never got there, did I?"

"Where was it?"

"Underground somewhere."

Belsey released the cuff. Kyle fell tumbling into the Xbox. He lay on his side, holding his head. Belsey gave him the cake and walked back out through the party.

TERRY CONDELL ORGANISED THE robbing of banks. Sometimes, for variety, he did bonded warehouses and safety deposits. He'd expanded from a base in south-east London across Europe. He was at the top, where charges didn't stick. The last job Terry Condell was associated with concerned four million pounds' worth of gold bullion stolen from an Antwerp Airport security depot in January. Associated, but nothing more. He shot a police officer in his front garden in 2001 and ended up being paid damages. Those were the lawyers Terry had.

Belsey called Rosen again.

"Send me through the file on Terry Condell."

"Kirsty wants to speak to you."

"OK. Email me the file. I'm just going to try getting killed first."

Condell's file was two hundred pages long and almost entirely speculative, from circulating fake five-pound notes as a twelve-year-old, to the ongoing investigation into the death of a former accomplice whose charred body was found in Tenerife three years ago. One of the few crimes Condell had been successfully prosecuted for involved the theft of six undelivered packages of perfume. That was December 1975. Stolen from work. Terry Condell had been a postie.

Belsey called the mobile of DI Andrew Redditch, Serious and Organised Crime.

"Terry Condell still in Hadley Wood?"

"He hasn't sent me any change of address," Redditch said.

"Do you have that address?"

"Sure." Redditch gave him the address. It involved a road called The Beeches. It seemed he didn't have to look it up. "Why?"

"I want to ask him something."

Redditch laughed. "What are you going to do? Pop round?"

HADLEY WOOD WAS SUBURBIA ON STEROIDS, DISCREET
on the outskirts of London, roads lined with co-
niferous trees between which you sometimes saw
fences but never the houses themselves. It was
popular with footballers and other people rich
enough never to meet their neighbours. The
place was clean and silent.

27

Terry Condell's home wasn't
easy to find but eventually Belsey
came across what looked like a
raised drawbridge with an ent-
ryphone beside it. He rang and a
woman answered.

"Who's that?"

"My name's Nick Belsey. I
wanted to talk to Terry about
Post Office tunnels."

"About what?"

"Tunnels. The Mail Rail."

There was a moment as this apparent nonsense was conveyed. Then the gate divided.
Belsey watched the miracle uneasily. He walked
through and let it close behind him, then continued along a curving drive past a Jeep and two
Porsches, what appeared to be a putting green
and a goddess spouting water. He wondered at
what point the last police visitor got shot. A few

seconds later he arrived at a house in the style of a package-holiday villa. A lot of dogs started barking before Belsey reached the front door.

"Stay there," someone said. The voice belonged to a young man in a white T-shirt with a Colt .45 in his hand. Belsey moved his arms away from his body. He could just make out a shorter man waiting in the doorway.

"Nick Belsey, Hampstead CID. I just had a few questions about the Mail Rail," he said. The guard fished Belsey's badge from inside his jacket.

"He's police." The guard held up the badge like a red card.

"Let me see him."

Belsey stepped forward. Terry Condell came into view wearing a grey tracksuit and slippers. Pomeranians yapped at his feet. He was fat, with little eyes that twinkled and made him look gleeful, as well he might be. His head looked like it was made of a soft material that had been repeatedly dropped. He burst out laughing.

"You fucking walk in here . . ." He coughed and spat phlegm into the grass. "Search him."

The guard patted Belsey down. He took Belsey's phone and nodded him towards the house.

"Get in here, then," Terry said.

The dogs continued to bark. The guard closed the front door behind Belsey and looked out through the window to the drive. An Asian woman in a silk dressing gown appeared at the top of wide, white stairs.

Terry turned. "Don't worry, sweetheart, it's only the police." He winked at Belsey.

They went down a lot of softly lit corridors, Belsey watching the folds at the back of the criminal's head, thinking: I am in Terry Condell's house. This is ridiculous.

Terry led the way through a bright white kitchen, down ornate spiral stairs to a games room: snooker table, signed football shirts in frames, leather sofas and a corner bar. A glass wall at the far end revealed a swimming pool lapping emptily against the smeared partition. Terry gestured to a sofa. The place felt lonely and it gave Belsey hope. First lesson of the interview room: everyone needs someone to talk to.

"Which branch of the Yard are you?" Terry asked.

"I'm not Yard. I work at Hampstead police station."

"Just Hampstead?"

"It keeps me busy enough." Belsey kicked a chewed dog toy out of the way. He could smell chlorine. There was a box of Montecristos on the coffee table.

"Just Hampstead CID," Terry mused, as if the confines of such a life were barely imaginable. Finally he said: "Drink?"

"I'll have what you're having."

"I was having tea. What do you want?"

"I'd like your finest cognac."

"That's more like it."

The bank robber set up golden tumblers and collapsed onto the sofa opposite Belsey.

"Can I have a cigar?" Belsey asked.

"Be my guest."

Belsey lit one up. Terry slid an ashtray across.

"So, Detective Constable Belsey of Hampstead CID, you're interested in the Mail Rail. Why's that then?"

"I think someone's messing around down there. Probably holding someone hostage. Call me Nick."

"Down in the tunnels?"

"That's right." Terry looked impressed. He seemed to give it some consideration. "It's a young woman," Belsey elaborated. "Twenty-two years old. She's called Jemma Stevens."

"And what do you want from me?"

"I got an idea you might know something about this system. Maybe more than most."

Terry Condell gave a curious, lopsided smile. "So who've you spoken to?"

"Kyle Townsend."

"Bloody hell." He shook his head. "How's Kyle?"

"He's doing really well."

"Never work with fucking crackheads. Life lesson for you, Nick."

Belsey shaped his cigar ash on the tray.

"Kyle had a map. He was looking for Site 3. He's erased from records. What were you up to?"

Terry leaned back, hands behind his head. His eyes went a little misty. Belsey gave him time. Professional criminals grow old; they dwell on career highlights and the jobs that got away. None were such nostalgia-bores as armed robbers. Most ended up doing long stretches or in exile and maybe this bred it. Maybe they knew their world was over generally, that some kid with an Internet connection was robbing more than they could with all the bagmen in south London. Belsey was ready to exploit this weakness.

"I just thought I'd have a sniff, you know. I'm curious. About history."

"For a job."

"Maybe." He spent a good moment running a hand over his skull, summoning up the knowledge like static electricity. He picked up his Cognac. "I joined the Post Office in 1972. The General fucking Post Office. We were responsible for more than you would believe. And there was something moody about it from the off. First thing they made you do was sign a confidentiality agreement. Before you even had the uniform. I thought: what's that about?"

"What was it about?"

Terry drank and looked almost bashful.

"I don't get you, Nick. I'm still wondering if you're mad or just stupid."

"Just stupid."

Terry smiled.

"I'd worked there a few years when I started hearing things that made me curious. There was more than just the Mail Rail. First it was rumours about blind tunnels under Trafalgar Square post office, old passages blocked off. Same at Mount Pleasant, running under Cubitt Street. I bided my time, Nick. 1981 they separated it all. You're a young man, you won't remember any of this. 1981. The Post Office became Royal Mail, Post Office Telephones became British Telecom. Government wanted rid. Anyway, the old GPO files get shoved into storage and I saw where a load of them got shoved. I thought—being a man who's interested in history—I'd take a look. In particular, at those pertaining to underground tunnels."

"Being a man interested in tunnelling under things."

"Perhaps. Either way, I made one or two discoveries."

"Like what?"

Terry watched the smoke curl. "How's the cigar?"

"Smooth."

"They were a gift from my accountant. I hardly ever smoke them myself. Makes my teeth sting."

"It's great. What did you discover?"

"A legal case that no one ever spoke about. Big one. 1952 the GPO gets sued for tunnelling under the Prudential insurance offices on High Holborn without permission. You know the big red-brick building near Chancery Lane?"

"That would have the telephone exchange beneath it."

Now Terry visibly relaxed. It was as if Belsey had said a password and they could drop pretences.

"OK. You've done your homework."

"I'm trying."

"The Chancery Lane exchange was built between 1952 and '53. A year later the government authorises an extension leading out from it."

Belsey rested the cigar in the ashtray, took out his *A-Z* and uncapped a biro.

"Where?"

"Down to Covent Garden. To another telephone exchange under the Opera House on Bow Street. But it doesn't stop there."

"Where does it stop?"

"This particular stretch of tunnel stops at Trafalgar Square. Under Trafalgar Square is a junction. It's a big space down there, but not an exchange. One of the tunnels off it they call Q-Whitehall, runs between the Treasury, the MOD building and Charing Cross station. Hang on." Terry hauled himself up and fetched a pair of reading glasses that sat incongruously on his blunt face. He stood beside Belsey, took the biro and marked the route from Chancery Lane to Trafalgar Square. He then connected Trafalgar Square to Whitehall.

"Then it goes on. Tunnels lead off from Trafalgar Square in all directions. I know there's one east into the City."

"To where?"

"Baynard House—the big telephone exchange by the river." Terry pointed it out on the map. "By Blackfriars. I had a mate who worked there, an electrician. Said it went down seven floors below the pavement. In the lift you had numbers going down—minus one, minus two. Only, on minus three and four the lift never stopped."

"Why's that?"

"He was there half a decade and never knew. Then one day it did stop. The doors open and there's just beds. Rows and rows of beds with some partitioned off. And, at the side, stacks of cardboard coffins."

Belsey nodded as if he expected nothing less. "Coffins."

"So he says."

"In part of the telephone exchange."

"In part of fuck knows what."

"So it goes east into the city. Where else?"

"At Baynard it splits; a tunnel goes south, under the river to Waterloo, and another one goes north under the City to the telephone exchange at Moorgate. Moorgate was one of the hardened war exchanges, extends under the Barbican."

"And does that connect back to Chancery Lane?"

"Yes. Here."

He marked in the tunnel routes. The map now looked like a creature with tentacles. Trafalgar Square was the body. It reached a tentacle up to Holborn, down to Whitehall, then extended another east into the City of London, an arm that coiled back round upon itself, up from the river to the Barbican.

"What about beyond the centre? There's deep-level bomb shelters connected to Northern Line stations, around Camden and then down in Clapham. Are they part of it?"

"Probably. Never saw the paperwork myself but yeah, why not?"

"How did you find all this?" Belsey asked.

"It was just a question of knowing which files to open."

"And how did you know?"

"It sounds silly. They were all marked 'Jigsaw.'"

Terry picked up his drink. The pool rippled glumly behind him. Cigar smoke knotted in the air.

"Jigsaw," Belsey said.

"J-I-G-S-A-W. Like that. An anagram."

"An acronym."

"That's the one."

Terry must have registered the effect this had on Belsey, because he frowned. "Know it?"

"London is a jigsaw puzzle."

"What do you mean?"

"I don't know. What does it stand for, the acronym?"

"No idea."

Belsey looked at the map again.

"What's it all about?" he said. "What's the idea?"

"To escape. When everything else is obliterated. A city below the city. I don't think it's about the Post Office: we were a useful cover for the government and military. The exchanges are just entrance points. And no one's going to bat an eyelid at the GPO digging cable tunnels are they?"

"And Site 3? That's what Kyle was after."

"Site 3." Terry let this linger. They had reached another precipice of knowledge. "You're the only other person I've met who knows about it."

"I don't."

"I don't either. But I've got some funny ideas."

"I could really do with a laugh."

Terry removed his glasses. Belsey was surprised by the softness of his gaze.

"Hardest files to get your hands on are the Sites. They're the big boys, the last refuges when everything else is gone. Site 1 was the Whitehall exchange, under King Charles Street. It was never referred to by name. Chancery Lane is Site 2. But Site 3 is bigger. There were specs for it in the files. More than five times the size of the other two put together. I don't know what it is or what it's under, just the specs. Anything that might suggest where it was had been removed or inked out. Big black lines."

"But you've heard other things about it. Right?"

"Just rumours."

"Tell me the rumours."

"Engineers who serviced it came in from the MOD. Someone said they had to be blindfolded in and out."

"Blindfolded."

"To and from. That's what I heard. And no one went there twice. You did the job on a small bit of the electrics or the cables and never saw the place itself. Maybe it was deeper than the others, that was the thing. I thought maybe it wasn't so much for people as for money, art, gold reserves—all that. Might be where they'd stick valuables, in case of a nuke. Maybe it related to Bank of England goodies. There's something at the core of it, I think. Especially sensitive."

"Core?"

"Gives you an idea of the scale, doesn't it? Core where they keep the real goodies."

"That's what you were after?"

"I never forgot what I read in those files. Years later I was in Cancún. Know it?"

"Not as well as I'd like to."

"Beautiful little place. I got speaking to a Merrill Lynch chap over there. Says he's shown around the week he starts at King Edward Street and told that in the basement they've still got the Mail Rail stop and trunk exchange and that no one's allowed to touch any of it. Government stipulations. No one goes down there. He thinks that's a bit strange: the rail's been out of use seven years. And all this got me thinking again. Maybe this was Site 3. Close enough to the Bank, right. And it's next to St. Paul's tube station. Those deep shelters you were on about. Don't know about Camden or Clapham, but when I was doing my nosing about there was a file: 'Deep Shelter—St. Paul's.' Top sheet said: 'St. Paul's: site abandoned, no works commenced.' The story they gave was that they were concerned about damaging the cathedral's foundations. Nonsense. So when I heard about that space under King Edward Street, I thought maybe they hadn't abandoned it at all. That it was the big one."

"But it's not."

"Not from what Kyle saw before he had his collar felt. But there must be something serious near there, because they never chased up his misadventures. I remember, a couple of days after it happened, someone spoke to me for about three hours: what did I know? What had I seen? He had the map I'd drawn Kyle. He wasn't CID, I could tell that much. Never known the filth wear Savile Row. Never known any serving coppers who walk with a stick. Then that was it. Never heard about it again. Strange, isn't it. You've got to hand it to this kidnapper of yours, though. If you're going to take a girl, the system's a good fucking place to hide her."

"How would I get down there?"

"You might try some regular post offices. Russell Square, I think. Aldwych, Trafalgar Square. Those are the Royal Mail buildings I know with ladders down. There's something under the old Post Office Research Station at Dollis Hill. But I imagine it's all bricked up now."

"When did everything start getting bricked up?"

"Mid-eighties. 1984, 1985."

"Why?"

"No idea. I think there was some pretty odd stuff going on in the name of JIGSAW. I really don't know what."

Terry got to his feet. Visiting time was over. Belsey sensed something like morning-after regret. He took a last puff on the Montecristo before being led back upstairs. His phone was waiting by the door. No sign of the guard. Terry picked up the mobile and held it.

"Three hours I was in that interview room after they nabbed dear old Kyle, being asked what I knew. No lawyer, no cup of tea, no pack of fags on the table. It wasn't police talking to me in that room. I've been interviewed twenty-six times. That was the only one where I thought, this guy could do what the fuck he wants with me." He handed the phone back. "I'm just saying, you're not on an official investigation. I can tell that much. Might be saving you more than trouble if you find a new hobby."

BELSEY SAT IN HIS CAR BESIDE TERRY CONDELL'S drawbridge. A new hobby sounded a fine idea. It had gone 8:30 p.m. and Hadley Wood was easing itself into a night as quiet and empty as any other time of day. Kirsty Craik would be processing his arrest warrant: either Jayden Culler had made a tasty accusation, or she'd chased up the CCTV from Costa and seen what it had to show, or both. He had nothing but a puzzle.

J.I.G.S.A.W.

He called Jemma's phone. It went to voicemail. He looked at Terry's markings on the *A-Z*, then drove back south, into the city. One last look, he thought. The next time he passed through London it could be in the back of a Serco van.

It felt too bright for the hour. Light was thickening rather than dispersing. After-work drinks were over and those remaining seemed to have run aground. It was Wednesday. Belsey kept his *A-Z* on the dashboard and followed the tunnels. Drove the X-Ray. Chancery Lane, past the Prudential Building. *1952 the GPO gets sued for tunnelling under the Prudential Insurance of-*

fices on High Holborn without permission. The offices were still there, silent in their Victorian pomp. A few metres further east he saw the winch on Furnival Street, like a giant gallows folded away. On, through the Square Mile to the river. The sun was dipping behind Baynard House, the telephone exchange's long layers of concrete stacked in silhouette. A plaque told Belsey he was on the site of a Norman castle. He tried to remember what Terry had said about the building. Three floors down, the lift opens, cardboard coffins . . .

Belsey walked around the windowless concrete of Baynard to the Thames and looked across the grey ripples to the southern embankment. He imagined the tunnel as it passed beneath, to the exchange under Waterloo. He had a sense that if he could just find the right way in, the front entrance, he would have access to it all. That you could break through, as Ferryman had done, and the kingdom was yours to wander.

He got back in his car. His phone buzzed: a message sent from Jemma, supposedly.

Find me.

Attached was a blurred photograph of tall, narrow silhouettes against a low sun. Tower blocks? But they were too rough and misshapen. And there were no buildings either side. Belsey adjusted his sense of perspective. He thought they looked like standing stones. That book, he thought: *Guide to the Standing Stones of Wiltshire . . .* What was Ferryman saying?

Then the message was replaced by an incoming call. Kirsty Craik.

He let it ring. He followed the tunnel along the river to Westminster. The Houses of Parliament looked soft as cake. He imagined London crumbling until only the tunnels remained, like the veins of an anatomical model. A minute later he arrived at Westminster Green, the old hospital. You wouldn't have guessed its previous existence from the neat red bricks of the apartment block. A guard sat in the lobby. But it wasn't a lobby made for a guard. He was at a table squeezed in by the door. He'd been recently installed: army haircut, radio handset, vigilant. He noticed Belsey loitering within a second.

Belsey drove on, up through Whitehall. Over Q-Whitehall. He wondered how you lured a former Chief of the Defence staff down into tunnels alone. What you'd have to say to him. What secrets he might be protecting. He slowed past Trafalgar Square—imagined the confluence of the tunnels beneath the splashing fountains, the tourists posing for photographs—reached the Opera House, turned, headed east again, back into the City.

The Moorgate telephone exchange had vanished, its form preserved in scaffolding and flailing, translucent sheets of plastic. Decrepitude spread from the demolished exchange. The raised walkway into the Barbican had been closed. Belsey climbed over a plastic barrier, up the steps. The whole walkway with its offices and shops was dead.

He went down to street level again, to a very new bar by Moorgate station that offered to serve you two hundred different types of vodka. The bar was all glass, as were the office blocks around it. He saw the glass now as a very slow tide, eroding the concrete. The bar was dark with occasional spotlights, filled with people for whom the past was not a profitable concern. Belsey got a taster menu of three infused vodkas and drank off his anxiety. He listened to healthy men talking about their children's schools and up-coming holidays. Sky News reflected in the floor-length windows: Jemma, then Jemma on London Underground CCTV, walking through Belsize Park tube station on her way to meet him.

His phone rang again. Kirsty Craik. Belsey finished his vodkas and drove to Hampstead.

CRAIK WAS IN HER office. Belsey went in and closed the door. A statement by Jayden Culler lay in the centre of her desk.

He sat down. She stared at him. Of course it would be conceivable to her that he might kill a young woman. What had he shown her to make it unlikely?

"Do you know where Jemma Stevens is?" Craik asked.

"No."

"Do you know Jemma Stevens?"

"Yes. I took her down there, into the tunnels."

Craik's expression was cold, holding off dismay.

"And killed her?"

"No."

"You let Jayden Culler go. Rob had him in for question-ing."

"Whatever's happened has nothing to do with Jayden Culler."

She moved Culler's statement to the side. There were more papers underneath.

"You arrested Jemma Stevens on the afternoon of the first of May, while she was attending a protest against the police."

"That's when I met her. Over the following weeks we saw each other a few times. I visited the bar where she works."

Craik checked her notes: "That was Saturday the eleventh of May. Then you visited again on the Friday of the following week, Friday the seventeenth."

"Sounds right."

"And she was your date that night, Monday, when I saw you."

"Exactly."

"Why have you been giving me nothing but bullshit?"

"Because you're a good enough detective to see that everything points to me being guilty."

"And I shouldn't believe that?"

"You can believe what you want. I'm not the one who abducted her."

Craik turned through the paperwork again as if trying to find something that wasn't damning.

"Did you request the CCTV from Costa?" she asked.

"No."

"Maybe I should."

"Of course you should. It will show me with Jemma Stevens about fifteen minutes before she goes missing. This is what I'm saying. I'm not stupid, Kirsty. I know how it looks."

"All the stuff about Soviet spies, government secrets . . ."

"That's true. Why do you think this investigation is being blocked? There's something seriously odd going on with these tunnels. I just spoke to someone about a General Post Office scheme . . ."

"Nick." Craik winced. "Stop. Please. I think this is about secrets, not governmental ones." Her eyes aimed angry points of light. The tide of credibility had turned. "Did you attack me down there?"

He saw how far she'd speculated the case against him.

"No. And I didn't send the hair in."

"It would be a pretty good ploy."

"It would be amazing. Do you think I did?"

"I don't know. But, as you point out, it doesn't make a difference what I think. I could have a guy walk in covered in blood making a confession, but it's still you taking her down into tunnels then removing all evidence of it. I've had three journalists calling in the last half-hour. We put a picture of her out there. This is going front page and I can't see what you expect me to do, Nick."

"Arrest me."

"Is that meant to be a challenge?"

"No. What else are you going to do? Place me under arrest. I'll be off your hands soon enough. Or get Derek Rosen to do it. I'd do it myself but I can't be arsed with the paperwork."

"It's not funny, Nick."

"No."

He picked up Jayden Culler's statement. Then he saw, beneath it, a file with the name: Duncan Powell.

"You got the file on Duncan Powell's killing."

"I got it. I spent an hour chasing a crappy attempt at a hit-and-run investigation. Now I'm wondering why you were so keen on having me do that."

Belsey opened the file. It was the full investigation, seven sheets. The unenthusiastic attempt by Barnet CID. But not entirely feeble.

"It won't be much use to you, Nick. Not unless your suspect is in Wiltshire."

Belsey stopped, his hand above the file.

"Why Wiltshire?"

"Take a look."

Belsey read. Craik watched him, perturbed by this sudden intensity. Barnet had accessed records of all calls Powell made in the days and hours preceding his death. One area code was conspicuous—01373.

"Whereabouts in Wiltshire?"

"A village called Piltbury."

"We've got him," Belsey said quietly. Craik didn't look impressed by this breakthrough. "We need to dial it."

"You can dial it all you want. It's a phone box."

"In Piltbury?"

"Yes. You're saying the answer lies in a village in the West Country? That's nice. I thought we were looking for someone who was in Belsize Park on Monday."

"The suspect has come into London," Belsey said. "He's not a Londoner. He doesn't sound like a Londoner." He examined the phone info again: three calls, one a day in the three days leading up to Powell's death. Long calls. The first lasted twenty-one minutes, then a forty-five minute call on Sunday the ninth, then a nine-minute call at 10 a.m. on the Monday. They must have been arranging to meet. It was seven hours before Powell was killed. Enough time for someone to travel from Piltbury to London.

Belsey put the number into his phone and went to his PC. He found a map of Piltbury. The village was twenty miles west of Swindon, ten miles east of Bath. It was tiny, population of less than a couple of hundred, he guessed. The screen was mostly white. The towns a few miles either side seemed to crumble into scattered fragments surrounded by nothing, a void.

He took out his phone and found the most recent communication from Ferryman: a photograph of standing stones. How low was the sun, he wondered? How recently was it taken? He's there. He's telling me he's there.

Think outside the box.

Belsey imagined someone amid all that white, filling it with thoughts of London: London tunnels, London police, its government and its secret service. He imagined the sense of invulnerability, diving in and out of the capital. Commuting. Best of both worlds: the civilised peace of the countryside, the hardened nuclear war defences of London. He imagined being in Piltbury, thinking of all the Met detectives searching the big bad city, running around your maze, tying themselves into knots. And you've got your captive amid all that space.

He walked over to Craik's office. She looked at him. She didn't say anything. He went down to his car.

ALMOST HALF TEN. QUIET ON THE RADIOS. NO HOMICIDE news in London. Belsey hit the M4 in minutes.

Nearest police station to Piltbury was in Chippenham, five miles away. He called Wiltshire Police and got put through. They didn't know of anyone suspicious in Piltbury. No click on the vague suspect description Belsey gave. No incidents in the area recently, of any kind.

29

He refilled the Skoda at Reading services and wondered what he was doing. The fields beyond the service station were very empty. The night air smelt sweet and utterly foreign. He was being steered onto someone else's territory, alone.

Belsey checked his cuffs and spray and began to drive again. Half an hour later Swindon appeared, a brief, orange smudge on the horizon. He passed signs for deer, theme parks and stone circles. Then he reached the turn-off for Piltbury.

The village was visible in the distance as you left the motorway, a thin stretch of grey houses backed up against a steep hill. A square church tower broke the line of roofs. Then as you got closer the road sunk between hedgerows and the view was lost. The next time you saw the village you were in it.

Belsey passed through a scatter of newer homes on the outskirts, obediently conforming to the slate-grey of the older cottages. They led to a main street with a convenience store and a tea-shop. *Recommended by the Wiltshire Tourist Board*. The place wasn't Cotswold classic though, no village of the year awards going to Piltbury. Station Approach led to a small building with empty hanging baskets and a low platform. The main road ended at a roundabout with bare hillside and flowers blown flat in each direction.

Belsey returned to the high street and parked. There were no people, it seemed. No streetlights. Once the door of the Skoda closed behind him all artificial light was gone. Thousands of stars appeared as piercings in the sky. The hill rising above the houses thickened the darkness. He listened to the sound of a world without humans: branches and water. He considered knocking on doors then took his mobile out and dialled the Piltbury number. Somewhere in the distance a phone rang.

Belsey followed the sound. He cut down a path between houses to the church with the square tower that he'd noticed. He dialled again and the phone was a lot closer. A minute past the church towards the village's northern edge and there it was, a red telephone box, its concrete platform subsided into the earth so that it stood unevenly in front of a steep wood.

Belsey opened the box and stood in it. He wasn't sure what he expected. It didn't have the urinary smack of London boxes. He lifted the receiver. It was still working. Not too many vandals in Piltbury he guessed. He stepped out. There was more water flowing somewhere in the wood. He listened, wondering what he was going to do now, then heard a more familiar sound. A bell rang. Belsey checked his watch. Last orders.

He walked faster now, chasing this new sound back to the roundabout. After another moment he saw a low, thatched pub. The Quarry House. He walked in. Five locals huddled at the bar, four large men with pints, one woman on a stool with a brandy. A younger couple were playing dominoes at a back table. It was warm, with rusted implements of industry and agriculture decorating the wooden beams. The bar was a small shrine of beer mats and postcards of other places. Belsey studied the crowd but didn't see a man young enough to be his suspect. All were either too tall or too broad and most had facial hair. He showed his police badge to a teenage barmaid.

"I'm looking for a man about my height, usually clean shaven, might wear a hoodie. He's been in London a lot recently. Anyone in the village fit that description?"

She shook her head, eyes wide. Her customers had started gathering around. Belsey repeated the question, got nothing but frowns and more shakes of the head.

"Seen a van about? A white Vauxhall Vivaro?"

"What did you say he's done?" a man asked. He had a local accent, tanned forearms, a shirt open halfway down his chest.

"He's wanted in connection with two murders in London," Belsey said. "Right now it's possible he's abducted a young woman and is holding her hostage."

There was a gasp, some urgent muttering.

"And he's from Piltbury?" the woman on the stool asked, slurring slightly. She was wearing a lot of make-up.

"I don't know. It's one possibility. He's been using the phone box over by the church."

The pub was quiet. He had their attention now. Two of the men began to confer, the one in the open shirt and a taller man whose bald head almost brushed the low ceiling. They turned and spoke to the others.

"That fellow. Walks around sometimes."

"It could be."

"Tell me about this fellow," Belsey said.

"Seen him about at night."

"Not a local?"

"Told me he was," the woman on the stool said. "Think he had family around here."

"What else does he say?"

"Nothing."

"Know where he's staying?"

"Hill View," one of the men said. There was some more consultation. "Yes, Hill View."

"What's Hill View?"

"It's an old farmhouse," the tall man said. "You can rent it. Over the other side and past the phone box."

It was him then, Belsey thought. He was in the right place.

"You've seen him about?"

"At night."

"I saw him buying food once," the woman said. "In the store."

"Who's he killed?" the barmaid asked, slow with disbelief. The couple had abandoned their dominoes and were on the phone: "Darling, make sure all the windows are closed."

"Where is the farmhouse in relation to the road?" Belsey asked.

"A little way on from the phone box you'll see a track," the bald man said. "Cuts through the trees. That will lead you to the gate. You'll see the house from there."

"OK."

"Are you going on your own?" the barmaid asked.

"Anyone want to come with?"

There were no offers. Belsey left his name and number to call in case they needed him. He didn't add: and so you know who the corpse belongs to. He told them all to keep an eye out, not to approach anyone, to contact local police if they couldn't get through to him. He checked the clock.

"Am I in time to get a large Jameson's?"

The barmaid put the whisky on the counter. He offered a fiver and she just stared at him. Belsey downed it and left. He heard the door being bolted.

He walked back to the phone box. The track began a couple of metres beyond it, a narrow dirt path leading into the trees. Belsey followed it through the rustling darkness of the small wood and out again to fields. It continued along the side of the hill to a gate, and beyond the gate to the farmhouse.

The house stood alone, facing away from the village, with its lights on. Fields continued rising behind it, becoming rocky and treeless. The gate was fastened with a loop of string. Belsey closed it quietly behind him and approached.

The curtains were drawn. It was an old slate farmhouse. He watched for movement behind the curtains, then circled the house to a garden portioned off from the surrounding hillside by a low fence.

The French windows at the back of the house were open an inch. The curtains were drawn here too. He could see movement through the crack between them. Belsey took a step nearer and heard music playing. He touched the back of the curtains, then swept them to the side and walked in.

A woman screamed. A florid man in a shirt and a cardigan spun from shopping bags. The woman wore a dressing gown.

Belsey produced his badge.

"Jesus Christ!" the man said. Belsey appraised the scene: a bottle of Shiraz on the go, suitcase open, everything cosy.

"Is this your home?"

"No."

"What are you doing here?"

"We're on holiday."

"How long have you been here?"

"About three hours," the woman said, indignantly.

"Do you know who was here before?"

"I've no idea. What's happened?"

Everyone took a breath. A holiday cottage. He'd been lured to a holiday cottage. Why?

The house was snug: kitchen at the back, living room with a basket of logs and a working fireplace. But a sense of wooded isolation seeped in. Three hours, he thought. The place had been cleaned before that: J-cloths over the taps, drying rack empty, floor swept. In the centre of the kitchen table was a guestbook. Belsey flicked through. The last entry had been signed 24 May: Mr. and Mrs. Wilton found the cottage delightful if a bit cold at night. That left a gap of almost three weeks.

"Who runs the place?"

"The owner, Caroline."

By the guestbook was a note from her: *I hope you enjoy*

your stay at Hill View House. In case of emergency, call me.
Caroline Mitchell. Belsey took his phone out. No signal.

"Does she live nearby?"

"In the next village along. Tilherst. Signal's awful here
and there's no landline."

They all checked their phones.

"Here," the woman said, hovering close to the French
windows. "I've got a bit of signal." She dialled, and by the
time she passed the phone the owner had already answered.

"Hello?"

"This is Detective Constable Nick Belsey. I'm at Hill
View House. Was there a man staying here recently?"

"Yes. Why?"

"On his own?"

"Yes."

"What was his name?"

"Mr. Ferryman. I never knew a first name."

Belsey sighed.

"When did he leave?"

"Last week. Friday morning. Almost a week ago."

"How long was he here?"

"Two weeks exactly."

"Could you describe him?"

"Not well, I only saw him twice. Reasonably tall, lightish
hair. Very pale. I'd say he was in his late thirties."

"You didn't see him when he left?" ·

"No. They just pop the key back through the letter box."

"Could you come to the cottage? I'd like to ask you a few
more questions about this man."

"Why?"

"I'll explain."

"Now?"

"Immediately."

Belsey explored the house. Narrow stairs twisted up to a single bedroom with a quilted bedspread beneath sloping beams. Everything was spotless. Beside it was a bathroom. The paint was new, everything new, but the taps were rusted. So was the metal trim on the cupboard and mirror. He ran his finger over the rust then went back to the garden.

The only problem with the location of Hill View House was that you were on a near-vertical incline. But you had a view over the village and could see moonlight on the thin river at the bottom. Belsey imagined his suspect enjoying this, lording it over the little houses. Plotting and planning. He climbed over the fence and walked to the crest of the hill. It was windy. You could see what might have been Tilherst to the west. You could just make out the lights of the M4. The hill continued in a long ridge to the east, a plateau of rocky ground with heather and gorse clinging on. Hard digging. No obvious burial plots.

Belsey felt very distinctly that he was a long way from where he should be.

He walked back to the cottage. A place to retreat as you start your campaign. To keep police at bay as you prepare the game for them. He watched car headlights turn onto the track, moving through the pines to the gate. By the time he was back at the house the owner was climbing out of a mud-spattered Volvo. Caroline Mitchell wore green corduroy trousers, and a waxed jacket; she had blonde-grey hair, glasses on a chain. She looked aghast already.

"What's he done?" she said.

"He's in some trouble. What do you remember about him?"

"Nothing. I thought it was slightly strange, a man here on his own. That's all."

Belsey ushered her inside. Everything was a little tense with the guests there; drama wasn't part of the holiday they'd been sold.

"How did he contact you?" Belsey asked.

"He called one day, said he was in the area and he'd seen one of my adverts in the village. He enquired about renting the cottage. It was just what he needed."

"For what?"

"To get some peace and quiet. Seclusion."

"Why did he want seclusion?"

"To work, he said."

"What did his work involve?"

"I don't know. Research, he said. He told me he'd be popping to London regularly, not to worry if he was away for a few days. I said I wouldn't be interfering. Better things to do than nose."

"But you took a look. A man here on his own, you'd swing by, check the place was OK."

"Yes," she conceded. "I had a look in, once. The place was full of papers."

"What sort of papers?"

"Work papers. Photocopies."

"Of what?"

"I don't know. Of whatever he was researching, I suppose. The papers were everywhere. Photocopies, letters, maps. You couldn't see the carpet. It was a bloody mess."

"Do you have any address for him? Contact details?"

She fished a piece of paper from her jacket pocket. She needn't have bothered: "Mr. Ferryman, 12 Jigsaw Lane. London."

"I don't suppose he used a cheque or bank card?"

"No. He paid up front. In cash."

"What a surprise."

Belsey sat down on a low sofa by the cold fireplace. The other three remained standing as if they were visiting him and he was unwell.

"The metal in the bathroom is rusted," Belsey said.

"I saw. Never used to be like that."

"Not before Mr. Ferryman's stay."

"No. What's it from?"

"Did he leave any rubbish? Empties? Packets or bottles?"

"A few bits and pieces."

"Was there icing sugar?"

"Yes!" Now the owner of the cottage looked impressed.

"Vaseline? Bleach bottles? Vinegar?"

"Bleach, yes. Maybe vinegar. I didn't itemise it all. How do you know?"

"Do you still have that rubbish?"

"It was collected this morning."

Belsey pulled himself awkwardly to his feet and returned to the bathroom. He ran a finger along the shower head and down the pipes, then sat on the edge of the bath. So Ferryman wanted to show Belsey his lab. The rust was from exposure to chemical reactions, fast oxidisation he'd only ever seen in less cosy places stocking more martyr videos. Experiments in bomb making. Maybe there was one going off in London now. Maybe that was the punchline. When he looked up there were three faces at the doorway, peering in.

"Are we safe?" the male guest asked.

"I have no idea. Where can I get signal?"

"Up the hill," the landlady said. She pointed him back to the garden. Belsey went downstairs, through the garden and over the fence, wondering whether to give a heads-up to the local police first or call Counter Terrorism and introduce them to Ferryman. Or perhaps just disappear, dive into the inviting and infrequently lit night of Wiltshire. He got two bars on his phone. He'd got twelve missed calls.

Seven from Kirsty Craik, five from Hampstead CID. Craik hadn't left a message. The station had: "Call now."

He tried Craik's phone and it went to voicemail. He was about to dial the station when his phone rang. Trapping.

"Nick, where are you?"

"Why?"

"Are you with Sergeant Craik?"

"No. Why?"

"She's gone missing."

"What do you mean?"

"You're cutting out."

"I can hear you."

"No one . . . where she is."

"When did anyone last hear from her?"

"Nick? . . . phone . . ."

BELSEY TOLD CAROLINE MITCHELL AND HER GUESTS
he'd be in touch. He cut back across dark fields,
stuck his sirens on as soon as he hit the motorway. He got a signal the moment Piltbury's rocky
hillside left his rear-view mirror. Trapping answered in the CID office.

"Nick, where are you?"

"Coming back to London
from Wiltshire. When was Sergeant Craik last seen?"

"We're not sure. She was in
the office briefly. We're getting
all the information we can."

"Has anyone checked her
home? The suspect knows where
she lives. He broke into her car
and saw post addressed to her."

"There's no one there. No indication she went
home."

Belsey was out of Wiltshire in half an hour.
He coaxed the Skoda to one hundred and twenty
on the M4, mind already searching London. Last
missed call from Craik was 11:42 p.m. He tried
to imagine Ferryman plucking her off the street.
Not a woman who'd go without a fight. Could he
have lured her somewhere? Would she have gone
back down into the tunnels? She'd have told
someone she was going. The west of the city

closed around him. He was in the centre at 2:15 a.m., Hampstead five minutes later.

The CID office was on edge but they hadn't called in other units yet. Reports were coming in from patrol cars: "No sign of her . . ."

Rosen said: "Northwood's upstairs. He's worried."

"About time."

"Wants to know what you know—about these tunnels, this suspect you were chasing."

"Where was Sergeant Craik last seen?"

"She was here, Nick. She got some kind of tip-off about Jemma Stevens."

"Saying what?"

"Someone knew where she was."

"Who?"

"I don't know. Kirsty legged it. No sign of her Mondeo."

"The Mondeo was broken into. It had a smashed window. She wouldn't have been using it."

No one had checked what vehicle she was actually driving. Craik hadn't signed anything out. Belsey called the duty Sergeant downstairs and told him to see if any CID pool cars were missing. He called back a moment later and said the Mazda estate was gone. Belsey checked traffic reports. Then he called the control room at the borough headquarters in Holborn. The Mazda would have Automatic Vehicle Location installed. Holborn said they'd establish its whereabouts and get back to him asap.

He called the storeroom. Craik had taken a new battery pack for a Taser at 10:15 p.m., not long after he'd left her.

Trapping entered the office holding a coffee, looking at Belsey with uncharacteristic alarm.

"Nick, you know Northwood's upstairs . . ."

"The man we're looking for was in Piltbury, Wiltshire, between the twenty-fourth of May and the seventh of June." Belsey gave the cottage address. "He was making bombs. I still don't have a name for him. Calls himself Ferryman. He's the one who dropped off the package of hair on Tuesday night. He hasn't come out of nowhere. Who the fuck is he?"

Belsey looked on his desk for a message from Craik. He couldn't see one. He checked emails. Nothing. He went into Craik's office and searched the place. On top of a messy pile of papers was an unopened envelope from Costa Coffee, labelled: *CCTV footage from 210 Haverstock Hill Store*. It had a disk inside. He pocketed it fast. There was nothing else connected to the investigation. So she'd got a tip-off and not written it down? Told no one?

Holborn control room called back.

"The Mazda you were asking about is on Amhurst Terrace, by Hackney Downs. It was involved in an accident."

"What kind of accident?"

"I don't know."

"Is the driver OK?"

"I couldn't tell you. All I know is the car's there now."

Rosen interrupted. "Nick, Northwood."

Belsey ran up to the meeting room. Northwood was sitting at a large, bare conference table, looking hot and uncomfortable. A thinner man in a grey suit sat beside him. Belsey didn't recognise the thin man. He looked like Homicide Unit. He had greasy lead-coloured hair swept over his scalp. The room was stuffy.

"We've been trying to get in contact with you," Northwood said.

"I was out of signal."

"Do you have any idea where Sergeant Craik might be?"

"The car she was driving is in Hackney. There was an accident of some kind."

"What was she doing there?"

"She was responding to a call, a tip-off. I don't know any more than that."

"How do you know it's there?" Northwood asked.

"A bit of detective work." Belsey felt his teeth grit. Time was being wasted.

"When were you last with her?" Northwood persisted.

"Last night, in the office."

"How long have you known Sergeant Craik?" the thin man asked. He spoke languidly. There was something malnourished about him; chinless and disinfected.

"I mentored her a few years ago. I think we should check the Hackney location."

"What have your movements been over the last two hours?" he asked. Belsey gathered himself. He'd spent three days braced for accusations and now he'd been caught off guard.

"I've been to Piltbury," he said. "In Wiltshire."

They looked at him more intently now. No one moved, yet the physical relationship between the three men shifted. Belsey checked the pair for kit: no cuffs, no radios. He doubted either of them had made a physical arrest in the last twenty years.

"Why were you in Wiltshire?" the man continued.

"The suspect was renting a cottage in Piltbury." The man's nostrils flared as he breathed in this information.

"What suspect?"

"I don't have a name yet."

"But you know where he takes his holidays."

"We haven't been introduced," Belsey said.

"This is Detective Inspector Gary Finch," Northwood said. "Answer his questions."

Finch's eyes were flat. He stared at Belsey and didn't blink. Well I never, Belsey thought. DI Gary Finch—the investigating officer on the Powell hit-and-run. The man who had swept Powell's death under the carpet. He wasn't Collision Investigation, that much was clear.

"What have you done with her?" Belsey said. He felt the muscles in his hands tense. Finch looked curious and amused. Belsey stopped himself walking over to the man and grabbing him.

"What have *I* done with her?"

"Yes."

Finch stonewalled: "Can you explain what this was doing in your hotel room?" He loitered on the word "hotel." Then he reached beneath the table and produced a plastic evidence bag containing Craik's bloodstained blouse. It had been stained in the course of her Tuesday-night foray underground, but that wasn't what the blood seemed to say right now. Belsey felt something heavy heading towards him fast. It involved two tight, elegantly interlinked homicide cases with himself at the centre. "Her clothes were in your hotel room."

"Yes."

"Could you explain how that came to be?"

"She took them off there. Did you have a warrant to go into my room?"

"Yes," Finch said.

Belsey knew what was coming. He saw himself sat in custody, staring at the cell graffiti and translating each minute into Ferryman's escape.

"You were seen with her last night, involved in some kind of disagreement."

"Were we?"

"In her office. Was it about Jemma Stevens?"

"What makes you say that?"

For his final trick the man produced Jemma Stevens' purse. What a hand, Belsey thought. What a flush. He wanted to clap.

"OK. You win. There's some documents I think you're going to want. Maybe that will help." Finch gave a slight nod. Northwood turned between them, confused.

"If her life is in danger," Finch said, "I think that's the best thing you could do. To step away from anything inappropriate."

"I need to cooperate to ensure her safety, you're saying."

"I'm saying it would be wise if everyone did what they could to resolve this situation as quickly as possible."

Belsey nodded.

"I'm going to be deeply appropriate," he said. "All the way. I'll get those papers. Then I want legal representation. One moment, gentlemen."

He went down to the main office before they could protest, scooped up his bag and stepped onto the fire escape. The sky was edging indigo. He paused for a fraction of a second and felt himself signing a confession. Then he felt the clock ticking and went down to his car.

THREE A.M. MISSION INTO HACKNEY. IT HAD BEEN A while. Through Canonbury, descending east, gentility loosening into the low-rise clutter of Kingsland Road. Hackney was oblivious to the night, grocers and kebab shops sailing neon-bright through the small hours. Insomniac as ever.

Finch, he thought. What grim crevice had he flown from? A well-connected one, it seemed. Belsey heard his own name on the police-band radio. "Arrest on sight."

31

He sped deeper into Shack-lewell. Past the Nando's, onto Shacklewell Lane; past the mosque. Amhurst Terrace was dark and narrow, lights flashing at the far end: yellow recovery vehicle lights, blue police lights, no ambulance. The road was residential until the houses ran out; then you were heading for locked gates, an industrial estate, Hackney Downs. Black tarmac shimmered with petrol.

Belsey parked on the forecourt of a disused laundrette and walked towards the wreckage. He found the point of collision, identifiable from the glass diamonds in the road. You'd expect a

T-junction. It wasn't a junction at all. Belsey crouched to see the tyre tracks. Two sets, parallel. Craik had been side-slammed.

He approached the damaged Mazda. The two police officers beside it nodded at his badge indifferently. They appeared to be out of the loop as far as Belsey's new renegade status was concerned.

"Know what happened?" Belsey asked.

"Just got here."

Belsey borrowed a torch and circled the damaged car. He could see the scrape lines on the bodywork. They were relatively high. So she'd been hit side-on by something large, like a Land Rover or SUV. There were traces of black paint in the dents. The wall on the far side of the Mazda was also scraped. She'd been trapped against it. No evidence of a front collision; no impact with the windscreen. No blood on the glass.

He gave the torch back.

Belsey looked for potential witnesses and saw a man wearing a bulging polo shirt and smoking in a bright doorway. As he got closer he saw it was an old schoolhouse, two entrances, one carved with the word "Girls" the other "Boys." Girls was bricked up. Through the boys' entrance, behind the smoker, was a reception painted acid yellow. Above the front desk he could make out the words *St. Matthew's Hostel*, with its motto: *No Drugs or Alcohol on the Premises*.

"No one in after midnight," the man said.

Belsey produced his badge. It occurred to him that he hadn't shaved for a while. The man apologised.

"Did you see the accident?" Belsey asked.

"Heard it. I came out."

"What did you see?"

"A woman. Looked like someone piled into her."

"Was she injured?"

"Shaken."

"But she could walk."

"She was walking. They were helping her walk."

"Who were they?"

"No idea, mate."

"They were from the other vehicle?"

"I guess so."

"See it?"

"No."

Belsey turned back to the road as if to catch some ghostly impression of the incident.

"Were they men? Women?"

"Looked like two men."

What was she doing here? Where could she have been going? He looked around as if the weak neon from the hostel might illuminate a destination. Then he turned to the hostel itself. The light flickered. The hostel manager tossed his cigarette into the night and retreated to his surreal chamber— the yellow walls, chessboard floor. The chessboard was spoiled only by semi-circular prints from the heel of someone's shoe. They led across the reception, heading out of the hostel from a door marked *Residents Only*.

Belsey stared at them. Not mud, the print was too clear. A dark, viscous fluid. There were only so many of them in the world.

"Any trouble tonight?" Belsey called after him. The manager turned.

"Here? No."

Belsey pointed to the prints.

"What are those?"

"I don't know." The manager poked the toe of his shoe at a print and smeared it sideways.

"Mind if I take a look?" Belsey asked.

"At what?"

Belsey followed the shoe prints through the door to wide stone stairs.

"When did you last go up here?" he asked.

"About an hour ago."

Belsey climbed the stairs, past an empty TV lounge, a large kitchen, closed dorms and more notices about health checks and drugs. He got to the second floor. Someone had walked blood down the corridor. The shoe prints began at the door for Room 23. Belsey opened the door.

A man sat on the floor in the corner. Brain tissue dripped down the wall beside his head. He was old, gaunt, his grey hair streaked with scarlet, mouth gagged with duct tape. His shirt had been unbuttoned, exposing ribs and white skin. Blood pooled beneath him, spreading in neat lines along the grain of the floorboards.

The manager retched. Belsey stepped inside. The room had three camp beds set up, an old fireplace, a sink. Belsey moved around the body and saw slick shards of skull where the head had been caved in. The hands were also mutilated: fingers cut with a blade of some kind, pierced and pricked. Belsey caught something out of the corner of his eye and turned. The wall beside him was smeared, floor to ceiling, with blood: daubs, smudges, finger lines. As if the victim had tried to claw his way out. Or to draw something.

Belsey stepped back into the corridor. The manager was on his knees, bending over a pool of pink vomit. Belsey squatted beside him.

"Any idea who did this?"

The manager shook his head. He fumbled for an inhaler, wiped his mouth and took a suck.

"Who's the victim?"

"Bill."

"Who was Bill?"

"Just one of the regulars."

"Know why this might have happened to him?"

"He was talking earlier about having to make a call. To the police. But they're all saying stuff like that, half the time."

"What did he want to say to the police?"

"I don't know. Bill . . . He was an odd one. I don't know who'd do this."

Another regular, swaddled in a padded coat three sizes too big for him, had come to see what the fuss was about. He was barefoot, his mouth open and toothless, a Rizla twitching in his hand.

"Holy fucking God, man, Bill. Fucking Bill!" His voice rose. "Boys, it's Bill!" He flapped his way downstairs. Belsey lifted the manager to his feet.

"You've got to keep everyone in their dorms. Someone might know something. No one moves, no one comes up here. OK? This is sealed now."

The manager headed down the stairs to enforce some kind of order. It was too late. Residents pushed past him; doors were flung open. There was shouting. Someone ran into the street.

Belsey could see the lights of the crash scene through the hostel windows. More police would be here soon enough. He couldn't afford to be spotted. Time to disappear into the night. To find out where those helpful men had led Kirsty Craik. He ordered the curious back downstairs then took a final look at the scene: the body, the blood scrawls resolving themselves into a diagram of some kind. He felt sure now. A floor plan. There were squares, doors, arrows. A route. Belsey took his phone out. He was about to take a picture when he heard someone else's phone click behind him.

Belsey turned. A man stood in the doorway, holding a Nokia, angled to see the scrawls.

"This is a crime scene. Get downstairs," Belsey said.

The man lowered his phone. He looked at Belsey. He was pale, his short hair light brown. His skin had an almost translucent quality, the pinks and blues rising up from somewhere beneath the surface. His face was all bone: high cheekbones, deep-set eyes. He wore a white T-shirt, a small black rucksack over one shoulder, grey hoodie tied around his waist. A smudge of dried blood remained in front of his left ear.

He watched Belsey steadily.

"Ferryman," Belsey said. Still the man didn't move. Belsey took a step towards him. "Let's talk."

The man nodded. Then there was a noise from the stairs and he turned. Two uniformed officers appeared, red-faced, breathless, one young, one old. They looked straight at Belsey.

"It's him," the younger one said. "Belsey." The man with the rucksack stepped backwards, past them.

"Stop him," Belsey shouted, lurching forward. Fat hands grabbed him. He shrugged the first constable off, smashed his elbow hard into the next one's mouth, then sprinted downstairs in time to see Ferryman jumping into a squad car. An officer lay on the ground beside it clutching her face. The taste of CS spray hung in the air. The squad car reversed fast in Belsey's direction, then it swung around and veered towards Kingsland Road.

HERE WE GO AGAIN, BELSEY THOUGHT. HE JUMPED BACK into his Skoda and tore past the crash scene, onto the high street. No losing him this time.

4:07 a.m. Night still and silent. And they were churning it up. Belsey caught up with the squad car at Dalston Junction. He rammed into the back of it but failed to cause a tailspin. His competitor had a more powerful vehicle and used it to accelerate away. Kingsland Road was straight and empty. Belsey matched him over the hundred mark, close enough to see the man's eyes in the rear-view mirror. A couple of drunks dived from the road. Nocturnal seagulls flapped, startled, out of mountains of rubbish. The Skoda did its best, but Belsey couldn't close the gap again. A night bus screamed in sideways. Ferryman went straight over a traffic island, sending a plastic bollard flying. Belsey followed. Then Liverpool Street arrived. They swung a hard right around the station, through Moorgate onto High Holborn, forcing a lorry into a news kiosk.

Belsey swerved around the lorry. This was tunnel territory now, heading into town. They had terrified company on the roads. Past Chancery Lane, into the back streets of Holborn, sharp left again around the British Museum. He's trying to kill us both, Belsey thought. Then his target hit the brakes. Middle of a junction, top of Shaftesbury Avenue. Traffic skidded and blared. Ferryman was already out and running.

Belsey sprinted after him. He saw him turn off the main road, rounded the corner a few seconds later and the man had gone.

He swore. Then he saw it. On the corner of Museum Street and New Oxford Street: not a building so much as an entire block obscuring the sky, grey and disused. Brutal. The glass of the upper floors was dirty. The ground floor had been sealed with black-painted panels. There was a small door open in the closest panel. *Hard Hats Must Be Worn at All Times.*

Belsey stepped into semi-darkness. He had been in cathedrals smaller, mortuaries less gloomy. Square, grey pillars divided the space. Cans and bottles littered the floor.

He picked up a bottle and held it by the neck. Every pillar cast a shadow thick enough to hide in. He stepped between them, turning as he walked.

"Just us now," he said. His voice echoed. "Not sure how long I'm in the game for. Kirsty Craik's gone. Did you know that? They got her. You've put me in a tricky situation. Does that mean you've won?" No answer. "Can I speak to her? There's an arrest warrant out for me. You're going to be on your own now. I'd like to speak to Jemma before I get arrested. Then you're on your own."

Belsey stumbled into metal. A row of trolley cages clattered angrily into a wall. He read a torn notice pasted to the wall: *Royal Mail: Ten Steps to Gold Standard Service.*

The New Oxford Street postal depot, then.

Glass smashed. Belsey chased the sound to broad stone stairs at the back. Footsteps hurried down. Belsey followed. After six turns of the stairwell he couldn't see a thing. He lit his phone screen, then decided on discretion and continued blindly. It must have been twelve floors before the steps ran out. He was in a large space, he could tell that much. There was the faintest of draughts. He wondered if his eyes would adjust. He smelt propane gas.

A lighter scratched and then there was a roar. The hard blue flame of a blowtorch appeared, ten metres away and getting closer. Belsey moved sideways and hit another trolley cage. He got behind the cage and pushed.

He kept pushing. His target must have moved. Belsey felt as if he passed through him, and then he was falling. The cage fell first; he landed on top, then it was on top of him and his ribs slammed into cold tracks. The propane hiss got louder. He was winded. He couldn't tell which way was up or how to go about getting there. So, Belsey thought, that was life. The pain would render him unconscious quickly enough. He considered praying. Then the hiss was extinguished. There was no light. Footsteps faded into the tunnels.

It took Belsey a minute to shift the cage and pull himself back up to the platform. He got his phone out again and saw, in its weak light, that he was in a disused loading area almost identical to the one at Mount Pleasant. Eventually he found the stairs again. By the time Belsey got out of the depot it was dawn and there were six police officers circling the abandoned squad car. Senior command were pulling up.

Belsey didn't wait to gauge their reaction. He legged it to the Skoda and set off towards Oxford Street lifting his radio.

"I need Gold level control, Central London, all units. Put me through to Major Incident Coordination."

"Who is this?"

"Chief Superintendent Northwood. I've got a triple-homicide suspect just entered the Mail Rail tunnels at the disused New Oxford Street depot. We're going to block his exits."

He was put through to MIC.

"Sir?"

"Get a map of the Mail Rail up," Belsey said. "It's a disused Post Office railway. It runs from Whitechapel to Paddington through central London. Get officers to each old postal depot with a station beneath it, functioning or not: Paddington, Wimpole Street, Rathbone Place, Mount Pleasant, King Edward Street, Liverpool Street, Whitechapel. They won't all look like Royal Mail property—some are disused, some have been sold off. Have you got that? Get the dog unit to the New Oxford Street depot and Mount Pleasant. Suspect is six foot, white with light-brown hair, white T-shirt or dark grey hoodie. He'll probably have a black rucksack with him."

He heard them radio this instruction through.

"Put an alert out to patrol officers, Code Seven, all Met units: stop him if seen, approach with caution. He may have a hostage with him. If he's heading north he'll hit Mount Pleasant. He's used that depot before to enter and exit the system. And the Chancery Lane area: he may be able to surface from an underground exchange there. And Centre Point."

"Centre Point?"

"And I want Transport Police at all Northern Line stations, in particular those close to deep-level World War Two bomb shelters: Belsize Park, Camden, Goodge Street."

An older man cut in: "Who exactly are we looking for?" Belsey recognised the bark of the Assistant Commissioner.

"Sir, the suspect's connected to at least three murders and an abduction. He may be armed. If he's alone when apprehended, we need him alive. We need to know where the hostage is."

Belsey checked his *A-Z*. The nearest Mail Rail stop from New Oxford Street was Rathbone Place. He doubled back and drove past two patrol cars parked beside the Rathbone Place depot. That was good.

He continued east, past Centre Point. No armed support there yet, just a confused-looking constable. Then down Chancery Lane to Merrill Lynch: two City police drove up as he watched. It wasn't clear to what extent they understood the operation. But they were present. No one was getting out easily. This was chaotic but it might actually work, Belsey thought. He allowed himself that brief hope. Trap him. Smoke him out. Belsey turned and headed back along the Strand to Trafalgar Square. That was when he clocked a black Land Rover in his rearview.

IT WAS A BOXY DISCOVERY 4, CUSTOMISED WITH A BULL bar. Heavy tint on the sides. Driving too close. The Land Rover circled the square behind him. Then a debate started on the police band-radio.

"It's Nick Belsey's I reckon, sir."

"Nick Belsey's voice."

"His call sign . . ."

". . . wanted for questioning."

"Call it off," the Assistant Commissioner instructed. "It's a hoax."

Belsey punched the steering wheel. His pursuers weren't letting him out of their sight. He cut sharp right, then left. The accumulated mess of his car went flying. Something jammed beneath the pedals. He reached down and pulled out the spray can he'd retrieved from Centre Point. The Land Rover caught up again. Belsey swerved the wrong way onto St. Martins Place then hit the brakes. The Land Rover slammed into his back. Belsey jumped out with the spray can. He walked around to the Land Rover, tore the windscreen wipers off and sprayed the windscreen red. Two men inside stared at him. They both wore suit jackets over T-shirts. They disappeared behind the paint. Belsey got back in his car and slipped west into Chinatown.

They had Belsey's name and a full description out on the Met-wide police band. "Detain if seen . . ." He imagined various friends and former lovers tuning into that with a roll of the eyes. He stopped behind the Trocadero and caught his breath. Half six in the West End, surreal at the best of times. The confused and desperate and drugged. Find yourself by Leicester Square at six thirty in the morning and you knew something was going wrong with your life.

So, Belsey thought: Kirsty's crash—that looked like it might have been caused by a black Land Rover. Only witness to Powell's death was a man in a Land Rover who wasn't answering Belsey's calls. What if we flip the incident on its head, he thought. You've still got Powell and another man running, only both are being chased. Powell gets struck by the Land Rover. The other man, understandably, gets back in his stolen BMW and bombs it. Down North End Road, down Heath Street. Past a detective trying to get some peace.

It was time to go under the radar. Belsey scribbled down the numbers he needed, then took the battery and sim card out of his mobile. He tore the rear facing police lights from his back windscreen. He went to a cash machine in a twenty-four hour Costcutter and withdrew the maximum daily amount of three hundred pounds. He bought new batteries for his torch. He asked the kid behind the till if they sold screwdrivers and, after a moment's searching, he found an all-in-one pack beneath the counter with three screwdrivers and a pair of pliers.

Belsey drove around the back of an Angus Steakhouse.

Rats scattered. There were three cars parked. He unscrewed the number plates on a VW Golf and switched them for his own. It meant he could keep access to police-band radio while deflecting attention from any Automatic Number Plate Recognition technology.

It was time to sample the delights of the Golden Pavilion.

He left the car behind the Steakhouse and walked down Gerrard Street to the Golden Pavilion, a good restaurant on the corner of a piss-stained alleyway. Its lights were out, but a slice of neon cut into the side street from its kitchen door. Belsey knocked and pushed the door. A waistcoated man sat at a table just inside. He had a bow tie hanging loose around his neck, a sheen of sweat over his pockmarked cheeks.

"Play?" he said.

"Mr. Andrew here?"

"Not tonight."

"I wanted to buy some things. I need a phone," Belsey said, "Pay as you go, but web-enabled. And something I can use for self-defence: small, but effective." He showed money.

"Weapon?"

"Weapon and a phone, for under a hundred quid. If you can do some kind of early-morning deal."

The doorman led Belsey to the back of the kitchen and opened a second door into a brightly lit room with fifteen men playing Mahjong and Pai Gow poker, a lot of smoke and paper money around. The walls were peach-coloured. The men were all either very fat or very thin. A young waiter with an empty tray appeared and the first man said something in Cantonese. The waiter looked at Belsey, then disappeared. He came back a few moments later with a fake

Samsung Galaxy and a leather-wrapped cosh. The cosh felt good to hold, with a wrist-strap and spring handle. Belsey checked that the phone got him online and haggled the whole thing down to ninety.

When he was back in his car, he tried calling Jemma's number from the new mobile. No answer. He left a message explaining that he'd changed phones. Tried Kirsty. The same. He dug through the Umbro bag for the phone number he'd obtained for Gary Finch. It was a landline. It wasn't local to the hit-and-run and it wasn't New Scotland Yard. He dialled. No one answered. Belsey tried again. This time, after 0207 for central London, Belsey dialled the first three numbers of Finch's phone followed by four zeros. Someone did answer.

"Yes?"

"Is this the right number for Inspector Finch?" Belsey asked.

"This is the reception of Tintagel House."

Belsey hung up. Tintagel was home to the Confidential Intelligence Unit. So now he knew who'd been looking into Powell's accident. The exact details of CIU's remit were opaque for obvious reasons. They had inherited a lot of Special Branch files. They also inherited Tintagel on the Albert Embankment, the ugliest office block in police hands. The place was known jovially among officers as Tinkerbell. It was a hop across the river from MI5, ten discreet steps to MI6, and it accommodated men and women from both. From a police point of view the unit drew in members of Covert and Firearms and Counter Terrorism who disappeared off police books and changed their phone numbers.

They gathered intel on what had been called subversion when Belsey joined the force and was now referred to as extremism. He guessed he was being extreme.

One thing was certain, however. Finch was a dogsbody. Someone on the other side of secrecy was running the show.

He watched Sky news through the window of a cafe as it prepared to open up. No news on Craik. No news on St. Matthew's. Full-blown Jemma appeal, parents crying and holding on to one another. Jemma took after her mother. Belsey remembered her saying she hadn't spoken to her parents for two years, that they were born-again Christians who'd found sex toys in her bedroom; they lived in Peterborough. They'd been reconciled with their daughter in her absence, it seemed. The parents' appeal was followed by shots of Euphoria with the house lights up, which didn't flatter it.

Missing since Monday night.

No point holding on to incriminating evidence. He found the envelope containing the CCTV footage from Costa and wondered how best to dispose of it. Burn the envelope, break the disc. He shook out the disc and a note came with it. He walked outside, put his lighter to the note then saw what it said.

Customer account: Ms. J. Stevens.
Last use: Tuesday, 11 June, 18.10

That was almost twenty-four hours after he lost her.

Card no. 94406. Customer account: Ms. J.
Stevens.
Last use: Tuesday, 11/06/2013, 18.10. Store:
210 Haverstock Hill, Belsize Park.
Transaction: £6.30.

So, according to Costa, she
was buying coffees thirty-six
hours ago. This was the transaction on the footage they'd sent,
not her with Belsey. He wondered if they'd made a mistake.

He put the disc back in the
envelope and looked around.
Where to play a DVD in Soho at seven in the
morning? Plenty of *24-hour* signs flashed untemptingly. Only the Flamingo advertised XXX
Film Shows. It was worth a shot. Belsey found its
doorway, between Genuine Models and We Sell
the Blue Pill. Narrow red stairs led down to a
UV-lit bar with elaborate group sex up on a projector screen. It was empty. The UV picked out
dust. He could see stains on the red-cushioned
seating. Then the staff woke up. The scene assembled itself for his benefit. A woman in a short

dress got onto a low stage and started to gyrate. After a few seconds she was joined by a friend who wanted to rub their bodies together: one blonde and one brunette, equally toned and glazed. Shadows crossed on the projector screen.

Belsey took a stool at the bar. Eventually the dancers stepped down and sat either side of him. It was a buyer's market. 7 a.m. in a Soho clip joint, and he felt safer than he had for a while. They fussed with the lint on his jacket. A barman appeared, looking more like security with a bow tie. He wiped a dirty rag down the bar, as if the whole place was a museum of insincere gestures.

"Drinks?" the barman prompted.

"I'll have a coffee," Belsey said.

"Minimum spend is fifty pounds."

"Then make it a large one. I need to play this." Belsey put the disc down. The barman considered the request.

"Do you like champagne?" one of the women asked.

"I love champagne. I love watching other people drink champagne." Belsey laid one hundred pounds by the disc. That was two thirds of his crash money gone and he was still on Berwick Street. "We can get whatever we want if this gets played."

The barman took the disc to a laptop at the side. The orgy disappeared, replaced by the Belsize Park Costa, ten feet by ten. The women exchanged looks.

The CCTV footage came from a ceiling camera above the service counter. It covered the entrance and the tills and a fair slice of store. A good shot of customers ordering, also the front tables and window seats. Date stamp: 11 June.

Ferryman walked in at 17.58. He was in a suit, no hood,

but it was him. The best shot of him so far. Short, neat hair, eyes deep-set and a little far apart. He walked in and looked around, checking people. He was searching for someone. They weren't there. He chose a table close to the front window. It was to the right of the shot but comfortably within range. He borrowed a third chair from an adjacent table.

Belsey's fifty-pound coffee arrived. The barman placed flutes of champagne in front of the women and set up an ice bucket. They were all watching the footage.

Ferryman didn't buy anything. He sat stiffly and tried to figure out what to do with his hands. He straightened the other seats. He glanced at the door as Joseph and Rebecca Green walked in.

Belsey stared. Dr. Joseph Green, proud owner of the BMW that had broken his peace three days ago. Green headed straight over to the man who had stolen it and placed a hand on his shoulder. His wife followed and hugged him.

Belsey walked up to the projection. Rebecca wore a white sundress. She held a straw hat. Joseph wore a creased white shirt and linen trousers. Rebecca sat down and put a hand on Ferryman's arm. Green took a seat too. The three of them had a chat.

After two minutes Ferryman stood up and got three coffees. He took a wallet from his back pocket and slid out Jemma Stevens's reward card. You could see the card in his hand as he waited to pay. He tapped its edge against the counter. Belsey stared at the card, at what felt like a display for his eyes now, here, two days later. The rectangle of plastic was a link to a different world, one they shared. Ferryman paid and checked as the card was swiped. He returned it carefully to his wallet. He took a tray with three lattes in tall glasses to the table and sat back down with the doctor and his wife.

The three of them spent another fifteen minutes in the cafe. At one point the doctor appeared to cover his face with his hands in exasperation. He left with his wife at 18.27. You could see their legs outside the window, upper halves blocked by a sign. They went north up the hill. Ferryman sat for forty seconds at the table then left and went south. The three coffees remained on the tray, untouched.

Belsey went around the bar to the laptop. His companions had lost interest. The barman was refilling the ladies' glasses with the businesslike expression of someone pouring alcohol down the sink. Belsey ran the footage back to the start—to Ferryman walking through the door, suited, hot, anxious. He watched the screen, beyond the stage and its pole and its drifting coloured lights. Then Belsey knew where he'd seen him. Emerging, awkward, from the consultation room on Windmill Drive. He was Joseph Green's patient.

THE FRONT DOOR WAS ON THE LATCH AT WINDMILL
Drive. Belsey stepped inside. He could hear two
voices, Joseph Green with another man. They
were in some kind of argument. Belsey felt for
his cuffs. Then he recognised the second voice; it
was the disciple. The argument was an intellec-
tual one.

35

"How is this relevant?"
Green asked gently, wearily.
"I've told you I attended his lec-
tures in Paris. But I hadn't encountered Brodsky's theory of
the ego when I wrote *Unnatural
Man*."

Belsey walked to the waiting
area and watched through the
study doorway. Green stood, staring out of the
window like someone at the bars of their cell.
The disciple was sitting in front of notes, glowing with combative delight. Coffee and crois-
sants waited on a tray at the side.

"It is entirely relevant. You see, this is crucial
to the development of your theories. This is your
major influence, and if you don't mind me saying, its omission in your account is striking."

"I've never denied my debt to Otto Brodsky.
But if you think his theory of the ego underlies

my work then you've either misunderstood his writing or mine."

Belsey walked in.

"Doctor Green, I need to speak to you." Green spun towards him, trailing irritation. The disciple watched with proprietorial eyes as if Belsey might have a few theories about Brodsky's ego up his sleeve.

"We were just going to give it five more," the younger man said.

"Didn't sound that way."

"Is this about the car?" Green asked.

"It's about a patient of yours who may be in trouble."

A second's silence. Belsey felt the disciple's ears pricked for more.

"Hugh, would you mind leaving?" Green asked, not gently. Hugh looked indignant.

"I'll wait in the kitchen," he said.

"You'll go, Hugh. Please. I'll call you if I wish to cooperate any further."

The disciple's eyes widened as he analysed this choice of words; he flushed, then shook his head and began gathering up notes.

"Well," he muttered, "now I can't find half the . . ."

Eventually he left. The front door slammed.

"There was a patient in session when I came here on Tuesday. Who was he?"

Green looked taken aback.

"Why?"

"He's a suspect in a major investigation."

"Who?"

"I don't know his name."

The doctor adjusted himself to this fact. He regained some balance.

"What makes you think he's done anything wrong?" Green asked.

"I don't have any doubt that this is the individual I'm looking for. He's holding a woman hostage somewhere. He just attacked me with a blowtorch in a disused postal depot. Prior to that he killed a resident in a homeless hostel. There are at least two other deaths he's involved in."

It was overkill, Belsey realised. He sounded desperate. Green blinked and looked almost embarrassed.

"Do you have a warrant?"

"I need his name. The man who was seeing you when I arrived the other day. Who was he?"

The doctor studied Belsey's eyes. Belsey's skirting the warrant issue hadn't gone unnoticed. And Belsey sensed that most stubborn thing: an instinct turning into a principle.

"Have you heard of patient confidentiality?"

"This is more important than patient confidentiality."

The doctor nodded slowly, but not as if he agreed. He picked up a sheet his disciple had left behind and glanced across it.

"I have people devoting their working lives to my ideas: where they came from, what they mean." He put the sheet carefully to the side. Then he transferred his gaze to Belsey. "In truth I have only one idea. Trust. I create a space of privacy in which people can speak of things they would not say anywhere else. That is the whole of it."

"Trust me."

"I can't turn over what is most personal to someone, hand it to the police, without being legally compelled."

"Their name and address isn't personal."

"Their address is their home."

Belsey felt a wave of fury. This was all the doctor had, he thought: this bastard wisdom. This act. The faded blue eyes. It was what he charged for. Nothing was as immovable as a meal ticket. The anger steered him into a bad move.

"I have CCTV of you meeting him at Costa Coffee in Belsize Park yesterday. What was that about? Did you know it was a patient who took your car?"

The doctor continued to stare, but building from compassion to quiet outrage, the moral victory of outrage. He narrowed his eyes.

"You never did say why CID were going to so much trouble over a stolen car. When you came here with the magazine. That is a lot of police effort for a vehicle theft. Now I ask myself: why would you be coy? Detective Constable Belsey, my patient believed he was being harassed by the authorities."

"I think he's right."

"He believed he was being monitored. I hadn't taken him seriously until now."

"I think he's being monitored by people a lot less friendly than I am. I highly recommend you let me get to him first. I think he may have stumbled upon something that's dangerous for him to know."

Green took a pencil from his jacket as if he might write some kind of cheque and sort this out. But he was looking for a prop. He balanced it between his fingers in a practised pose.

"But that's not what you were saying. You were telling me he is some kind of psychopath. Who is he at risk from, do you think?"

"The state."

"And what, exactly, are you?"

"Not very much to do with it."

Green twirled the pencil. It was missing its eraser. All his pencils were like this, Belsey saw, looking across the desk. Either Joseph Green didn't make mistakes or he didn't believe in revising them. That sounded right. The doctor caught him staring and put the pencil away with the first touch of self-consciousness he'd displayed. But it only sealed the defences. Belsey had never got what he wanted from an analyst. His luck wasn't going to start now.

"Why *don't* you have a warrant?" Green asked.

"Forget it." Belsey stood up.

"Should I?"

Belsey went over to the window, opened it and took a breath. The garden was big enough to neglect and still look splendid, teetering snapdragons, a gnarled apple tree. He breathed again, then turned and admired the organised chaos of the study itself. The files, the paperwork, notebooks on the desk, an old PC. On the floor by the desk was a box of Dr. Green's own *Living with Others, Living with Ourselves*. Green's face smiled up from the dust jackets, looking a lot more amenable. *When you're ready to begin the journey of recovery* . . .

"What?" the doctor asked, watching Belsey carefully.

"It's a nice study, that's all. When I was sent to counselling it was all white walls and IKEA furniture. It was like an interview room. I used to think it must be strange hearing so many confessions and not prosecuting anyone."

Green allowed himself a cold smile. He was waiting for Belsey to leave. Belsey reached over the photo frames and placed his card on the desk.

"If you feel there's anything you want to share."

He walked out of the house, gave it a minute then threw a stone Buddha at the front window. Glass smashed. He cut to the side, climbed over a gate into the back garden. The study window was still open. Green had abandoned his post. The old tricks were best. Belsey climbed through the window, stepping down via the couch. He closed the study door and rammed a chair underneath the handle. Then he took his card from the desk and began to search. He started with the desktop, progressed down the drawers. He found an appointments book in the middle desk drawer and tried to remember exactly when he'd first visited Windmill Drive. Tuesday, around 3 p.m.

Tuesday 2–3 p.m.—Michael.

He flicked back through the preceding pages. "Michael" three times a week, 2–3 p.m. Going back six weeks to 22 April.

There would be an address somewhere. Belsey pulled the files down from the shelves, rifled through, tossed them to the floor. He opened a cupboard beneath the shelves and found a stack of ledgers, black hardbound books each labelled with a name on a white sticker. Inside were notes on treatment. Case histories. Only one initialled M.

M. Easton.

The door handle rattled. Belsey opened M. Easton's case notes.

Session 1

Patient 37 yrs old. Reports increasing levels of anxiety over past year. Fears for own mental health.

Describes himself as possible object of surveillance by unknown individuals. Asks whether this sounds irrational. Alludes to something confidential he may have uncovered—something that places his life in danger.

High intelligence. Left job last year. Not in a relationship. No previous history of mental illness.

Michael Easton. So much less mysterious than Ferryman. So much more vulnerable.

No address, though. Green was banging outside. The barricade flexed. It wasn't going to last long. Belsey looked around for the place he'd keep patient addresses. Then something hard slammed against the door. Wood began to splinter.

He took the case notes and went back out of the window, through the garden, over the gate.

HE DROVE FOR A minute, down the hill, into the grey bustle of Archway. Past the hostile stare of the Archway Tower itself, a little more unnerving now he knew it played a role in the underground scheme.

Alludes to something confidential—something that places his life in danger . . .

Belsey continued along Junction Road, through the everyday hubbub of greasy spoons and Irish pubs. He parked behind a Cash Converters and sat in the driver's seat, skimming the case notes. He searched for any suggestion as to who Easton was, for clues to tunnels, Site 3, JIGSAW. Green's summaries were terse, sometimes telegraphic, evidently written during sessions or immediately afterwards. The writing was cramped but legible enough.

Session 3

M talks at length about nuclear war. Acknowledges something bordering on obsession. He traces interest back to childhood. Age ten he saw a documentary about the atomic bomb and it produced feelings which he struggles to describe—familiarity, comfort, recognition. He has researched the topic and is adamant that there is a great deal we have not been told—about tests carried out, knowledge acquired. Recently this theme has gained fresh importance for him, providing a possible explanation for his trouble. His lifelong interest in the Bomb has made someone uneasy.

Another week in and the doctor was more cautious.

Session 5

Further attempt to articulate his relationship to what he has begun to refer to as the "central secret." M claims the confidential information is within him. Either he was born with it or someone implanted it, somehow. Asks whether, through analysis, we might gain a sense of what it is and how it might be removed so he can live normally.

This is the first step to alleviating his suffering. He has read my work on trauma and believes that a similar course of treatment might rid him of this traumatic and confidential knowledge.

Wants me to extract it from his unconscious like it is a tumour.

A sheet of yes/no tick boxes had been folded in: the Borsch-Chapple Early Psychosis Indicator Test. *I have trouble speaking the words I want to say, or I am able to speak but other people have told me that what I say is incoherent . . . I see or hear things that other people cannot see or hear . . .* It went on for fifteen questions. From what Belsey could tell, Easton wasn't psychotic. Not according to Borsch-Chapple.

Belsey tried to match what he could glean of Michael Easton the patient to Ferryman the killer. Was there genuine desperation? It was hard to tell through the cool filter of the doctor's notes. But all the talk of secrets within him—it didn't chime convincingly. It sounded like another game.

Session 6
M keen to elaborate his theory. Provides new "evidence." Claims he dreams of places before he's seen them. So convincing are these dreams that he attempts to draw maps when he wakes, mapping the journeys he has dreamed. Sometimes he can wander London and find the buildings he's dreamed of. But in the dreams London is always empty. Swears me to secrecy with regards to this. In his dreams he sees London, empty and abandoned.

Belsey's radio crackled:

"Break in—Windmill Drive."

Green had reported him, then. Belsey listened, to see exactly where police were searching. Then he turned it up and listened more closely.

"Break in—Windmill Drive—individual detained."

HE DROVE IN THE DIRECTION OF GREEN'S HOUSE, parked around the corner and walked. There was a squad car outside. Belsey could hear someone remonstrating in the back seat. One restless-looking special constable, no older than twenty-two, hovered nearby. Not someone Belsey knew.

He risked showing his badge.

"I got the call late. Is it under control?"

"I think so."

"Who've you got in the car?"

"A nuisance."

"Suspect?"

The man laughed.

"No. A guy, knows the victim, got in the house while we were here. Says he was trying to help."

Then Belsey heard the nasal voice of the disciple: "I'm telling you, I think I know what's going on . . ."

"There's some kind of grief between him and the householder. Things got a bit antsy so we're letting him calm down before taking him home."

"What was it about?"

"Some kind of tiff between them. Not what we need."

"What's he saying?"

"Haven't the foggiest. Reckon he's just a bit of a character. Wouldn't read too much into it."

And Belsey remembered that first visit to Windmill Drive
once again—he had stood beside the disciple while they
waited for Green. And then the patient—Ferryman, Easton—
had emerged from the office. And the two had exchanged a
glance. Belsey heard the joking, the disciple asking Easton:
"What would you say? Is Joseph any good?" They knew
each other.

Belsey looked towards the squad car. He wondered if he
should ask to speak to the disciple. Then he saw two DCs
from Highgate station coming out of the house. They knew
Belsey. They'd know the score. Belsey turned his face away
from them.

"You say you're taking him home?" Belsey asked the Special Constable.

"In a minute."

"Did you get his full name?"

The Special checked his pocket book.

"Hugh Hamilton. *Doctor* Hugh Hamilton."

BELSEY RAN A SEARCH on his pay-as-you-go when he was back
in the Skoda. According to Dr. Hugh Hamilton's website he
was a member of the British Association of Psychoanalysts,
Kleinian in orientation, "a solution-focused practitioner in
integrative therapy." It listed his publications: "Joseph Green
and Regression," "Green and Klein: the Missed Encounter,"
"Joseph Green: Unspoken Debts."

There was an address advertised as a clinic on Langford

Place in St. John's Wood. Belsey drove over, careful as he crested Hampstead, down through the heartlands of psychoanalysis, along a tightrope of north-London wealth. Deep among the townhouses of St. John's Wood he found a ground floor flat. It seemed Dr. Hamilton worked from home. A woman answered, blonde and anxious. She stared at the Skoda then at Belsey.

"I'd like to speak to Hugh Hamilton," Belsey said, badge out.

"He's not in."

"It's OK. He's on his way back."

Belsey moved past her into the flat, taking the case notes with him. The flat had the same studious clutter as the Greens', but glossier and more considered. A large dining-room table at the back supported piles of books and papers.

"Does Hugh know someone called Michael Easton?" he asked.

"Michael? He was a patient. Hugh saw him once before he began treatment with Joseph Green."

"Where does he keep patients' details?"

"I don't know."

A phone rang and the woman answered.

"Hugh? OK . . . Well there's another one here. Yes, a police officer . . . I don't know. Just come home. Please."

Belsey found himself a seat at the table and began sifting through the papers, a landscape of research on Green's theories. The first book he picked up was Green's own *Living with Others, Living with Ourselves*. Chapters ranged from "The Shattered Narrative" and "Fortress Personalities" to "Faith in a Future" and finally "Beyond Trauma." Belsey

turned the pages, wondering what convinced Easton that
Joseph Green was the man to treat him.

> We all carry trauma. Trauma is the failure of memory;
> it is the undigested fragments of experience where nei-
> ther our waking mind nor our dreams have completed
> their task of processing . . .

He was still on the introduction when Hugh Hamilton
walked in. Green's disciple held a briefcase and looked fever-
ish. A squad car pulled away, past the front window. Hamilton glared.

"You."

"Me."

"What's going on?"

"Who's Michael Easton?"

"I don't need to talk to you."

"Sit down," Belsey said. Hamilton sat down across the
table from Belsey. "I need to know about Michael Easton, an
address to start with. Or you're back in a police car for obstructing inquiries into a multiple-homicide investigation."

Hamilton's eyes widened. He pressed against his goatee
as if it might fall apart and everything else would follow.

"I never had his address."

"For Christ's sake. You saw him, before he started with
Joseph."

"Yes. He had a consultation session with me. What's he
done?"

"Abducted someone, killed others, possibly upset the security services. I think he's making bombs now." Hamilton

absorbed this. He looked dismayed, but not quite incredulous. "You were telling the police you had an idea what was going on."

"I knew it would be something about Michael. I heard you say that a patient was in trouble. It could only have been Michael Easton. Joseph has had concerns for a while. I think he feels very exposed."

"What kind of concerns?"

"That he had got it terribly wrong. That Michael was far more dangerous than he had initially realised. Michael had one session with me, but it was Joseph he wanted. Michael had read all of his work. He quoted from it. I'm sure Joseph loved that. Michael came to London for him. Because he thought Joseph would help, you see. That's what he said. He begged me to refer him to Joseph. Joseph doesn't usually take on new clients without a referral."

"He thought Joseph would help with what?"

"He thought he was dreaming state secrets," Hamilton deadpanned. "And they were placing him in danger."

"Did he say what these secrets were?"

Now Hamilton hesitated. "Something about a forbidden place, underground."

"Did he say where he thought it was?"

"No."

"When did you see him?"

Hamilton checked his diary.

"April 17. I spoke to Joseph that evening and he agreed to see Michael the following week."

"Why did he agree?"

"Michael offered to pay three times the usual fee. He was

desperate. I think Joseph was . . . Let's be generous and say he was intrigued. Concerned. But it was bound for failure—a situation like that. I know that recently there had been a deterioration. Michael wanted to terminate analysis. Joseph was concerned about this. Michael was becoming increasingly paranoid."

"Joseph and Rebecca Green met him in a cafe on Tuesday."

"He'd said he was done with it all. I think they were trying to persuade him to return. Not to do anything rash."

"Like what?"

"I don't know. Michael had some violent fantasies."

"No kidding."

Belsey placed the case notes on the table between them. Hamilton stared.

"Take a look," Belsey said. Hamilton plucked a tissue from an ornamental Kleenex holder and used it to open the notes. He read a few pages, nodded, pressed his goatee again.

"What do you make of them?" Belsey said.

"They're what I'd expect. When he saw me he asked a lot of questions about the practicalities of psychoanalysis. How do you learn about the unconscious? How do you explore it? Is it like a place?"

"What did you tell him?"

"I said you cannot explore the unconscious itself, by definition, but you can follow its edges: the moments when memory falters, or narratives unravel. He seemed to understand. He seemed fascinated. Do you know what I think he wanted?"

"What did he want?"

Hamilton closed the notes.

"He wanted to know how to manipulate us. He wanted to be famous and thought Joseph would write him up. Joseph wrote up every other oddity that came to him. Michael wanted Joseph to disseminate his message to the world."

Belsey considered this. The sources of crime and fame weren't so far apart. Still, he found himself having too much respect for Easton to write him off as a wannabe. As if anticipating his objections, Hamilton continued:

"Michael is clever. He was communicating *something*. He was giving Joseph something to interpret. Because he knew how Joseph worked, you see. That's always dangerous."

"What was the message he wanted disseminated?"

"I don't know. It wasn't a game I was prepared to play. Joseph . . ." Hamilton sighed. "Joseph, perhaps, is too seduced by his own powers. This is what I have always said. There is a lack of theoretical rigour to his work."

"What were you arguing about when I arrived today?"

"Just that."

"Brodsky."

"Otto Brodsky. Joseph's whole training, or lack of it; his plagiarism, his buried influences." Hamilton seemed almost weary with his duties as iconoclast. "Joseph Green is not the infallible figure he likes to present to the world. When a reputation unravels it begins with one thread. Now Michael will do more damage than Joseph has ever had to fear from my work."

Belsey thought of those pencils again, their torn-off erasers, and supplied his own analysis: anger. Joseph Green knew he had made a mistake and couldn't correct it. It was a stress tell, erupting from beneath that sage exterior. Belsey imagined trying to heal someone and realising you'd been played, that your hard-won reputation was out there, murderous, running underground.

Then he thought of Centre Point. Site 3. State secrets.

"What if there *was* something to Michael's theories?" Belsey said. "And maybe he felt this was the only way he could communicate them?"

Hamilton arched an eyebrow. He flicked through the case notes once more as if he might have missed the convincing bit.

"So you've been seduced too," the disciple said.

"Maybe."

"Michael Easton plays figures of authority: psychoanalysts, now police. It is a way of allowing small men to feel powerful. He's sucked you in as well. Do you see?"

Belsey sat back and wondered. Then the blonde woman appeared and looked at him.

"I think somebody's trying to steal your car," she said.

BELSEY STEPPED OUTSIDE. HE NEEDED A LOT OF things right now, a car thief wasn't one of them. The man was getting busy with his passenger door.

"How's it going?" Belsey asked. The man looked up. He was white, with short, dark hair and gym muscle under a black fleece jacket. He saw the case notes in Belsey's hand.

"Give me the notes," he said, calmly. Then he pulled a gun.

37

Belsey took a second to process this. He walked up to the man, holding the notes out. Then he tossed them onto the roof of the Skoda. Not a killer move, but confusing enough. The man glanced. Belsey punched him in the face. Men with guns don't expect to be punched. Belsey grabbed the gun wrist and slammed his forehead into the bridge of the attacker's nose. He steered him to the ground in standard arrest procedure, then kicked his head against the railings in a less orthodox move. The gun fell. It had a silencer. Belsey saw Hamilton watching from his window, then a reflection in the window. Belsey took the gun and turned. The second man looked Mediterranean, with a shaved head, wearing a grey Adidas sweater. He saw the gun, hesitated, then turned, walked back to the corner of the road and disappeared. There was the sound of a car screeching to a halt. A second later Belsey heard it start up again, tearing east towards the Finchley Road.

The first man was on his side trying to gather in the blood streaming from his face. Belsey sat him up, pulled his arms back and cuffed them to the railings. Blood ran from the man's hairline into his eyes and from his nose down into his mouth. He was wearing a concealed holster, with a neat pocket for the silencer. The gun was a Sig-Sauer P226; pristine, not a convert, not second-hand. Belsey removed the clip and saw live rounds. He slipped the clip back in and stuck the barrel in the man's eye.

"What's going on?" he asked. The man shook his head. "Where's Kirsty Craik?" The man licked blood from his lips. He breathed in shallow gasps.

Belsey searched him: no ID, no wallet, not even house keys. He took the clip back out of the Sig, placed the gun at his attacker's feet, went to the Skoda and saw he'd succeeded in getting the door open. Belsey took the notes from the roof and chucked them in, then checked for brake fluid on the road, tools left lying about, any signs of tampering. He crawled underneath the chassis. There was a tracker on the driveshaft, size of a cigarette packet, magnetic. Belsey tore it off. He walked back to the injured man, forced the tracker into his mouth. Then he climbed into the Skoda and drove fast.

THROUGH MAIDA VALE TO the Harrow Road. He parked at the back of a derelict MOT garage now being used as a Pentecostal church. The sign was up: *New Hope Ministries.* Hymns escaped among stacks of tyres and a burnt-out Ford Focus.

Give me the notes. That was clear enough. Well spoken even. Belsey took them out and searched for whatever it was they wanted so badly.

Session 7
Dreams. London is often empty and he must walk for miles before finding someone to ask about this. The person he finds is a young girl. M describes her as like a sister. She tells him: they are not missing, you are missing. She points up and M sees that there is no sky. He continues to walk, trying to understand where he is. He is underground. But there are streets, streets and houses. Then there is nothing any more.

Between 6 May and 13 May Easton started having nightmares that involved loved ones trapped and dying. Their cries came from cells and holes in the ground. When Easton heard them he realised, to his horror, that he had thought they were already dead. In fact, this was the problem: he had locked them up and then forgotten to release them. His premature grief was forgetfulness of the worst sort. So he would race to let them out before it was too late. He would be trying to get back to them when he woke. These dreams troubled him to the extent that he stopped going to bed. He spent the night walking the city.

On 15 May, Session 12, the guilt-dreams ceased. His own visions went underground again. He walked past subterranean shops and schools and gardens, into a home, the occupants decomposing in front of a television. Up, past the corpses, to a bathroom where he stood before a mirror and saw that he was in uniform. This was a shock.

And then, as soon as he had woken, it felt to M like a revelation. A past life in the military would explain everything. And now he claims he can recall details of this life. He can smell the wet canvas in the bases and taste the army food. M's theory now—he was involved in a secret mission. He was involved in army communications. What if, as a signals engineer, he devised a way of communicating that could project classified information into the future, to be picked up at a later date? These messages are the dreams. The dreams are military signals he has sent to himself. Asks whether I think this is possible.

Signals engineer. Why did that ring a bell? Belsey found the copy of *Military Heritage*. He turned through the pages until he saw the one it had been opened to: the adverts, the black and white photograph that took up half the page. It showed around thirty uniformed men and women, but mostly men, standing in front of a bar.

Were you here? Did you or any family members serve

in the 2nd Signal Brigade, 81 Signal Squadron between 1979–1983? Please get in touch. Reunion planned South-East, weekend of 8–9 November.

If it weren't for the uniforms they could have been any gathered pub crowd, one of the women acting as barmaid, laughing. The pub was ornate, its Victorian bar partitioned with screens of etched glass. They were gathered for the start of something: uniforms crisp, smiles fresh. It clearly belonged to the era in question: 1979–83. There was a large radio cassette player on the bar. The hairstyles were short but not shaven on the men, a little long at the back. Moustaches were popular. The women wore their hair scraped back under berets.

He looked across the faces in the advert. Then one face made him feel very cold. The man stood just to the right of centre. He had his shoulders back, a tankard held at waist height. The posture suggested he was about to laugh or say something, but that wasn't what the face said. His expression was wary. Belsey stared at the face and tried to remember Easton in the unforgiving light of St. Matthew's Hostel, on the Costa CCTV: the cheekbones, the half-smile.

It was him in the photograph.

Which was impossible. Belsey got out of the car. The congregation in the garage was speaking in tongues. He took a deep lungful of air and tried to remember when he last ate or slept. He retrieved a warm bottle of mineral water from the back seat and poured it over his head. He's infected me with his madness, Belsey thought, dripping into the faded oil

stains. He wondered about the Site 3 pill bottles and exactly
what he'd taken.

Then he looked at the picture again. It was still Michael
Easton. With a group of army personnel sometime between
1979 and 1983.

Belsey took his new mobile out. The military liked to keep
watch over their own. Online, he found a number for the
Royal Military Police. He had a contact at the RMP—Steve
Hillier. Their last meeting had involved a squaddie gone
AWOL, found conversing with angels on the roof of a Vauxhall nightclub. Belsey helped talk him down and had never
quite forgiven himself for it. He dialled the RMP headquarters at Southwick Park and got put through.

"Steve, can I call in that favour?"

"Of course."

"2nd Signal Brigade, 81 Signal Squadron. Mean anything to you?"

"Not off the top of my head, Nick. Where are they based?"

"I don't know. I've got an advert about a reunion in November. Class of 1983."

"Right. Planning to go?"

"I need to know who these people are, if there's any way
of contacting them. I need to find out what they were doing
at that time. 2nd Signal Brigade, 81 Signal Squadron, 1979
to 1983. I'll send you a picture of the advert."

"OK. I can get you a number for their base at least."

Belsey wrote down Hillier's mobile number and sent
through a rough shot of the advert taken on the new phone.
He flicked through the case notes again with the radio on;
no news on Jemma. No mention of Kirsty.

Hillier called back ten minutes later on a different line.

"What is this?" he asked, quietly. Belsey could tell from his voice that something was wrong.

"You tell me."

"Well, it's going to be a strange kind of reunion."

"Why's that?"

"They're all dead."

Belsey took the magazine from the passenger seat.

"What do you mean?"

"I mean they're no longer on this earth with us. Who placed the advert?"

"I don't know."

"Someone with a dark sense of humour," Hillier said. "There are copies of thirty-seven death certificates here. They all died on the same day, ninth of November 1983."

Belsey looked at the pub scene again. Then at the face that troubled him more than any other.

"What did they die of?"

"It was an air accident."

"A crash?"

"A mid-air explosion."

Easton stared out. Cautious. Quizzical. 9 November 1983. Belsey saw the calendar in the Control Bunker, crossed out to 11 November. Remembered Riggs observing the two-minute silence deep underground. *It just ended. Suddenly. No reasons given.* Exercise Able Archer.

"Nick," Hillier said. "I don't know what this is, but you haven't spoken to me, OK?"

"OK."

"The brigade is disbanded. There's nothing else I'm going to be able to get." He hung up.

Were you here? . . . Reunion planned.

Belsey dialled the number at the bottom of the advert. His heart was beating fast. A machine clicked in. Someone awkward with technology cleared their throat.

"Hello," the voice said, "you're through to Duncan Powell. Leave a message and I'll get back to you as soon as I can."

BELSEY FELT HIMSELF ON THE VERGE OF SPEAKING. HE had an overwhelming urge to try, to test the possibility that Powell might hear him, the call reaching whichever subterranean exchange could make the connection. Finally he said: "Andrea, if you're there, please pick up."

38

She didn't. It recorded his waiting. A squad car passed and slowed. He heard it stop at the end of the street.

Time to move on. He cut through to the other side of the estate, under the Westway into Paddington, fast past Paddington Green police station, along the Harrow Road. After five minutes' twisting through the back streets of Bayswater he felt safe enough to stop again. He walked into a newsagent's, searched for *Military Heritage* among the magazines. It had *Collectors' Monthly, History Now.* No *Military Heritage.* The woman behind the counter said she'd never stocked it, didn't think many places would. She recommended contacting the magazine directly and requesting a subscription.

Belsey called the number listed in the magazine. A man answered.

"I'd like to speak to the subscriptions department," Belsey said.

The man laughed.

"There's only one department here. How may I help?"

"This is Detective Constable Nick Belsey. I'm trying to track down someone who may subscribe. His name's Michael Easton."

Belsey waited while he checked.

"Easton. Mr. M. Easton, yes. He ordered a back issue."

"Just the one?"

"Yes. The February issue this year."

"What's the address you've got?"

"103a, The Beaux Arts Building, Holloway."

Belsey scribbled it down.

"One more question," he said. "There was an advert in that February issue—a reunion for a Signals regiment. Do you remember anything about it being placed?"

"I remember the guy."

"Did he say why he wanted it in?"

"For a reunion. Why else would it be?"

BELSEY GOT TO THE Beaux Arts Building in fifteen minutes. It was off Holloway Road, a grand Edwardian pile that had clearly served some municipal purpose before being converted into flats that sold for half a million. It was the size of a castle, with a gym lit behind basement windows and a concierge visible through the glass doors of the entrance hall.

Belsey waited for a man struggling with Waitrose bags to punch the entry code, followed him in, nodded to the concierge and found a lift. Empty off-white corridors circled the first floor. It struck him as a good place for someone returned from the dead.

Doors looked solid. 103a was identical to every other one. He stood before it wondering whether to ring. Then he saw it was open a crack. Belsey listened. He pushed the door open another inch and got a whiff of stale air. He walked inside.

Bare hallway, no bulb in the socket, no coats on the hook. He opened the door into a small living room. Thirty-two faces stared back at him. The open door made them flutter. Each occupied an A4 sheet attached to the wall by an inch of tape, floor to ceiling in six rows of five. Most belonged to men in military uniform. It was Easton's old regiment, taken from the reunion advert itself; a gallery of the dead. There was Easton himself, close to the top. This had been his sole attempt at decoration. A mattress lay on the floor draped with a sleeping bag, books piled against the wall beside it: *On Thermonuclear War, Voices from Hiroshima and Nagasaki, Strategy in the Missile Age.* There were dictionaries of Russian, German, Czech and Hungarian. The carpet was cigarette-burnt. The small kitchen hadn't been cleaned for several months. Belsey opened the fridge. It contained milk halfway to solid and a green loaf of bread.

He opened the door to the bathroom. The bath was filled with ash. Ash and scraps of paper, with burn marks up the side.

Tools filled the rest of the space: seven different screwdrivers in the sink, a length of rope and a grubby head torch on the floor. Propped against the bath was a yellow contraption that looked like a heavy-duty litter picker. It was labelled *BT Handylift*. Belsey experimented with it until the metal ends opened and he could see how the device might be used for lifting manhole covers.

He returned to the main room and looked at the faces. Blown up to A4 you saw the variety of expressions across the group—wry, amused, uncertain. Each hung alone. There was no letter box in the door to the flat itself. Belsey went downstairs. Beside the front entrance was a room of post boxes with some broken furniture stacked in one corner and a residents' noticeboard beside electricity meters. It wasn't hard to spot Easton's post box; only one of them was overflowing. There were envelopes sticking out of the flap, several fallen to the floor beneath it. Belsey pulled one free and tore it open. The letter was on headed Ministry of Defence paper.

Dear Mr. Easton,
I am writing with regard to your recent enquiry for the following information under the provisions of the Freedom of Information Act 2000.

You requested information about any experimental research connected to MOD property Site 3.

Unfortunately the relevant material is covered by Section 24 of the Freedom of Information Act and remains unavailable for public consultation.

Belsey opened another. Royal Mail Head Office this time:

Dear Michael Easton,
You requested material from the General Post Office Archive concerning Site 3 . . .

Again, it provoked a polite refusal citing the same Section 24. Westminster Council had written to him too: *The subject of this request was primarily the involvement of the council in preparations for nuclear war and any files concerning Site 3. Unfortunately, due to Section 24 . . .*

Section 24, whatever it may be, seemed a pain in the arse and an abrupt end to a lot of otherwise courteous letters.

Belsey made a sweep of all the spilled envelopes, collected up everything he could find. He took a chair leg from the pile of broken furniture in the corner, wedged it into the slot of Easton's post box and leaned all his weight on it. After a moment he could get a hand in.

He removed twenty-three envelopes. Six were final demands addressed to an elusive Mr. Bhatnagar. One was Easton's bank statement from HSBC. Belsey tore it open. Current account, 1 May to 1 June. There were purchases at cafes, supermarkets, rent to a lettings agent. It all seemed corporeal enough. There was travel to Piltbury. This was good, he thought; this was a life coming into focus. There was a payment of £176 to a company called Ammo Direct. Less good. Belsey stuffed the statement into his pocket and checked the remaining envelopes. They were stamped with the crests of government departments and public bodies. Half of officialdom seemed to be in reluctant correspondence with Michael Easton: *Dear Mr. Easton, I am writing in respect of your recent enquiry . . . Dear Mr. Easton, Thank you for your request . . . Dear Michael Easton, Unfortunately the department was unable to release the relevant information . . .*

BELSEY WALKED OUT OF THE APARTMENT BLOCK, cramming envelopes into his pockets. He checked underneath the car again. He used the Samsung and called Rapid Solicitors on West End Lane. Rapid specialised in custody calls, prisoners' rights, police misconduct. They'd twice represented individuals making claims against Belsey, but there were no hard feelings.

"It's Nick, from Hampstead CID. Is Vikram there?"

39

"Speaking. How's it going, Nick? You sound a little breathless."

"I'm fine. Do you know about Freedom of Information requests?"

"Of course."

"What's Section 24?"

"How fine are you exactly?"

"Not at all."

"Section 24 is the national security exemption."

"Covering what?"

"Pretty much anything the government doesn't want you to know."

"There's a list?"

Vikram laughed. "Maybe somewhere, sure. But the government has discretion. The way they see it, if they don't want to let something out, then it's a threat to national security."

"If someone's a time waster, a crank, sends FOI requests all over the place just for a laugh, would anyone pool that information?"

"I don't reckon. No."

"Who oversees them?"

"The FOIs? There's an Information Commissioner's Office, but it doesn't exactly oversee anything. They go to whichever public body has the relevant files."

"OK. Thanks."

"Remember, Nick, don't say anything and don't sign anything."

"Understood."

He moved on and stopped the car behind an Argos, got out with the Umbro bag over his shoulder. He wanted it with him now. He'd turned into one of those people with nothing except the truth amassed in an old bag, clutched tight. Darkest pub on the street was the Coronet. It occupied an old cinema and they'd preserved the gloom. You almost expected ushers with torches. He walked through to the back and sat down.

Belsey turned to the bank statement first. It gave him a pattern of activity up until a fortnight ago. Only one payment in—from a company called Connoisseur Catering: £1384. Catering was a good line of work for staying under the radar. For keeping strange hours. It would have given Easton a cover that he could walk away from at a moment's notice. Belsey looked the company up. Connoisseur ran a chain of fifteen restaurants across central London, and also provided corporate and conference catering. Easton received £1384 from them on 1 May. Belsey found a number for the caterer and called. A message told him all the operators were busy.

He tried to piece together the geography of the life from its transactions. Mostly Easton withdrew big sums and presumably paid in cash, leaving little in the way of paper trails. But his two weeks in Piltbury and its surrounding localities were easily visible: Bath and Swindon—for the nearest big shops—and train fares, Piltbury to London several times a week. In London itself, Holloway and Highgate made sense. There was one pattern that Belsey couldn't understand, however. At least once a week, since mid-February, there were cash machine withdrawals in Kew, near the Botanic Gardens. Maybe Easton knew someone there, maybe family, maybe he had a thing for horticulture.

Belsey circled it.

Either way, Easton's money was almost gone by June: £215 remaining in the account when the statement ended. That could explain why it seemed a good moment to conclude his analysis. Especially if he was paying triple-rates. Maybe why it seemed a good moment to throw caution to the wind. A plan was being put into place. There were a few final purchases: the £176 to Ammo Direct two weeks ago. The same day, £200 to a company called Combat Effects pushed Easton into his overdraft. Belsey searched for a website. It advertised smoke flares for the paintball and military recreation community. Sounded fun. Why was Easton stockpiling smoke flares?

He had a lot on Easton now, but what he wanted more than anything was a location for the last twenty-four hours. Belsey called the bank, gave the requisite authorisation code and got put through to the police liaison department.

"How can we help?" a woman asked.

"Hampstead CID here. We've got a possible case of ID theft and I wanted to know the most recent transactions on this account." Belsey read out the account number.

"Well, the last transaction was certainly big."

"What was the last transaction?"

"Payment to a company called Falcrow. They received a card payment for £1886. That exceeds the overdraft limit on this account."

"Any suggestion of what kind of company that is?"

"No. They're based in London. That's all I can see."

"Any addresses for this customer on the system, other than the Beaux Arts Building?"

"No. The account was only set up a year ago."

"Can I get a date of birth?"

"Sixth of July, 1975."

"That's Michael Easton."

"Yes."

Belsey wrote down the date.

"Did Mr. Easton make any trips abroad in March?" the woman asked.

"I don't know. Are there foreign transactions?"

"Yes. Russia, Germany, Czech Republic and Hungary."

"When?"

"Between the fourth of March and the twelfth of April."

"Could you email that through?"

"Of course."

Belsey gave his personal email address. He headed out of the pub, towards the Seven Sisters Road, looking for somewhere with a printer he could use. Next to the Agora Amusement arcade was a convenience store with what it described as an e-cafe at the back. The place was fluorescent and bare, two men sitting on the floor chewing khat, nothing on the shelves apart from packet noodles. The e-cafe was three monitors, a young boy playing online poker and a woman crying into Skype. Belsey paid for half an hour and sat between them.

The bank had been prompt—there were Easton's statements, March to May 2013. Belsey opened them up and looked through. A few days into March, Ryman, NatWest and London Underground became Promsvyazbank, Směnárna Praha and Hotel Mokhovaya.

£792 to Hotel Mokhovaya in Moscow on 25 March. It looked like he was there for five days. There were also stays in the two weeks before his Moscow jaunt at Danubius Hotel Budapest, and Eurostars Hotel, Berlin. Quite a traveller. Quite a spring tour.

But the longest sojourn was Penzion Speller in Prague: £1125.68 paid on April 12. Belsey searched Penzion Speller. From its website it looked small, family run. They'd remember a man travelling on his own.

Belsey slid his chair away from his fellow customers and called. The hotel answered quickly.

"Dobrý den."

"Do you speak English?"

"Of course," a man said. He sounded good humoured.

"I need to know about Michael Easton. An English man. He stayed with you in March."

"Who is this?"

"Police," Belsey said. "London police. Do you remember that guest?"

"Michael? Yes. The student."

"What was he studying?"

"I don't know. He was studying. Researching."

"The cold war?"

"I don't know. You are police? What has happened?"

"Quite a lot. What was he researching?"

"Archives," the man said. "Libraries. That is all I know."

"Which archives?"

Either the line cut or the man rung off. Belsey looked at the statement again. He wondered if Easton was in Moscow, Budapest and Berlin for the same reason. Researching. He pictured Easton sifting through the scraps of Soviet intelligence that were making their way into the public domain. Trying to find out why he died in November 1983.

Belsey looked through the rest of the email. They'd helpfully sent the last twenty-four hours' transactions. Last payment was Falcrow, as they'd said. Belsey searched the company online. It was a building supplies depot in South London. Belsey's first thought was: cement, bricks, digging tools; the disposal of bodies. Then he checked when Easton had been there. It was forty-five minutes ago.

HE DROVE OVER FAST. Falcrow Building Supplies was based in a long warehouse that backed onto the railway line south of

London Bridge. It also had a yard with towering stacks of bricks and timber. Cigarette smoke hung in the air between them.

"Hello," Belsey called. A grey-haired man appeared from among the stacks, carrying his cigarette and a polystyrene cup. "Are you the manager?"

"Who wants to know?"

His face was lined, jaw dusted with white stubble. Belsey showed his badge. He told him about the £1886 transaction.

"Yes, he was just in. Hour ago. Been a few times."

"Was he on his own?"

"Always."

"What did he buy?"

"It was a plasma cutter today."

"What about other times?"

"A propane torch, goggles, gloves, angle grinder. Drill, too, I think. Top of the range stuff. Big spender."

"Did he say why he wanted them?"

"Converting an old building. Is he dodgy?"

"Did he seem dodgy?"

"No."

"How did he seem?"

"Fine." The man flicked his cigarette away and took the lid off his cup.

"Did he say where he was going?"

"No."

"Was he anxious? In a hurry?"

"No."

The man sipped and grimaced.

"How did he transport the equipment?"

"He had a van."

"A Vauxhall."

"That's right. What's he done?"

"See inside the van?"

"Briefly. Helped him load up."

"No one in the back of the van?"

"No. No one with him at all."

A lorry honked its horn. Belsey followed the manager as he unbolted the other half of the gates to let it in.

"Besides the orders, did he say anything else?"

"He asked about getting spare blasting caps. For PE4. You know what that is?"

"Plastic Explosives."

"Well done."

Belsey felt the edges sharpen once again. He knew PE4 from the jihad-infused days of late 2005, when he found his skills briefly employed in the service of Counter Terrorism. Composition 4–style explosive, cyclonite and plastic binding.

"How many caps?" Belsey asked.

"Seven, with electric detonators. Short delay."

"Do you sell them?"

"No." The lorry passed. The man straightened and faced Belsey again. "So he said he'd have to get some ammonium nitrate." He grinned.

"Fertiliser."

"It was a joke. I told him we'd need to inform the authorities. And he had det cord in the van."

"You saw detonating cord in the van?"

"Yeah."

"How much?"

"Two reels."

Belsey thanked him and returned to the Skoda. He sensed a cold, methodical kind of preparation. And a clock ticking. Tooled up like that you're not going to sit on it. The statements with their diminishing balance and swelling armoury said endgame loud and clear.

He called Hotel President. Martyna answered and her voice sounded sweet as any voice from a home you weren't going to get back to.

"Martyna, it's Nick"

"Nick? There are police here. They want you."

"I know. Make sure they don't give you any trouble. Can they hear you now?"

"No. Have you done something bad?"

"Not as bad as they think. Do you know if anyone's tried to contact me at the hotel?"

"Yes."

"What did he say?"

"She. It was a woman."

"Who?"

"I don't know."

"When was this?"

"An hour ago. She was a colleague, I think. Asking if you were here. She sounded . . . I don't know. It was quick."

"What else did she say?"

"Nothing."

"She sounded scared?"

"I'm not sure. She was speaking quickly, quietly."

Of the two women currently on his mind, that sounded distinctly like Kirsty Craik.

"Did she leave details?"

"No."

"But you can see the number calling you. On your phone."

"Yes, I have it here. A mobile number."

She read it out. He wrote it down.

"What should I tell the police, Nick?"

"Tell them I'll be back in five."

He tried calling the number. A woman answered abruptly.

"Yes?"

"Who is this?" he said.

"Who is *this*? Why are you calling this number?" She sounded Filipino and up for a fight.

"I received a call from this phone. Is a Kirsty Craik there?"

"No."

Belsey was wondering if he or Martyna had got it wrong. He heard a trolley rattle in the background. Linoleum squeak. Doors swinging.

"Where are you? Is that a hospital?" he said.

"What do you want?"

"Is there a police officer at the hospital? She was in a road accident. I think she may have used your phone, maybe without you being aware."

"This is a joke? Waste my time?"

"Which hospital do you work at? Please tell me."

"Cromwell."

"The Cromwell Hospital in west London?"

"I did not call you. Please do not call this phone."

She cut the line.

THE CROMWELL WAS A private hospital in one of the more dishevelled enclaves of west London—which didn't make it any cheaper and wasn't going to make it any easier to get into. Belsey drove past peeling hotels and bureaux de change, souvenir shops, discreet brothels, squatted townhouses. He parked on Cromwell Road, bought overpriced flowers from a store specialising in Iranian food and approached the hospital as casually as he could manage. They had security right at the front: a roulette wheel of revolving doors with visible guards.

Belsey cut to the side of the building and watched an ambulance slow for a barrier. He stepped up onto the running board. It took him down a ramp. They stopped by doors into a basement level. He jumped down while they unloaded a wheelchair, moving fast through automatic doors into the light of the hospital. It was much like any other, but your money got you a smile from nurses and a pleasing combination of white paint and pale wood. Belsey moved past Radiography to back stairs.

Where to start? He went up a floor, out into what he soon realised was Maternity. The ward matron saw him, saw the flowers.

"Can I help?"

"I'm looking for Kirsty Craik."

"No one on this ward by that name."

"Can you check if she's on any other wards?"

The matron paused to study him more closely.

"What was she admitted for?"

"She was in a car crash. I'm not one hundred percent sure."

"How did you get in?"

"I think I've got the wrong hospital. Sorry."

Belsey left the ward fast, returned to the stairs. He ran up them, staring through the glass strips in the doors to each floor until he saw one with conspicuous security: suits with earpieces crowding the corridor. He was wondering what to do when Gary Finch emerged from a room on the corridor. He had a younger, more elegant companion with him. Belsey ran back down a flight. He heard the door above him open and the two men join him on the emergency stairs.

"Those aren't my instructions," Finch said. "They're Lord Strathmore's."

"My concern is that those who will ultimately be held accountable remain informed of developments." The younger man was a lot smoother of voice. They were coming down the stairs towards Belsey. Belsey kept a flight ahead.

"They don't want to remain informed."

"My fear is that his Lordship is overestimating the influence he still wields."

"A DA Notice will solve nothing and involves notifying the Permanent Secretary."

"But there is a standing notice. We could alert the press to their responsibilities."

"Alert them is precisely what we are *not* trying to do."

The stairs ran out. They were at the car park. Belsey dropped to the stained concrete and slid under a stationary minibus. He watched Finch's shadow.

"No one's pretending this is ideal. We will find him, and the situation will be a lot more stable. I'll speak to Lord Strathmore now."

Then the shadow receded, followed by a car, and he was left with neon-lit silence. Belsey slid himself out. He walked up the ramp and ducked under a barrier to Cromwell Road. He thought about how Finch's voice had sounded: anxious, obnoxious; the voice of someone trying to borrow authority from a figure who made them nervous. Strathmore. Whoever that was.

Belsey got back into the Skoda and checked through the printouts. No Strathmore. All that was left in his bag were the med bottles, Easton's case notes and Monroe's book. He flicked through the book's index to S: Secret Operations, Sleeper Agents, Stasi, Strathmore.

"Strathmore, Edward" with a subentry: "J.I.G.S.A.W., 125."

Belsey turned to page 125 very fast. JIGSAW. The pieces were coming together. And then they didn't.

The index had directed him to a page on Able Archer. Belsey read it three times. There was no mention of Strathmore or JIGSAW on the page. No suggestion even as to what JIGSAW might be. Belsey checked adjacent pages. It was hard to focus. He assumed it was adrenalin blinding him to the reference. But after two more attempts it was clear: there had been an infuriating and intensely curious mistake.

Belsey called Monroe. The journalist answered on the second ring.

"Nick."

"No names or places. Your phone probably isn't secure."

"I've been trying to get hold of you."

They needed to meet. Belsey wondered how they were going to arrange this without acquiring unwanted company.

They needed refuge. There was one place, of course, that had always given them refuge. It wasn't going to be pretty.

"I think we should get a drink," Belsey said. "For old time's sake."

"Nick?"

"Only it's past closing time."

"It's quarter to four in the afternoon."

"I feel like it's gone four in the morning," Belsey said. "Soon it's going to be getting light." Monroe groaned. "We need somewhere that's going to serve us at this kind of hour."

"This better be good."

"Don't get followed."

EAST, INTO THE CROOK OF THE RIVER, THE TANGLE OF
sullen development that ran between Docklands
and the Isle of Dogs. Belsey parked on East India
Dock Road, stole some tarpaulin off a skip and
covered the car. He weaved a labyrinthine route
down soulless streets, past the DLR and the new
plastic apartments that crowded
the place before you turned a
corner and looked up and realised you were in the foothills
of Canary Wharf.

40

Through to the fish market.
No one was following.

He hadn't been under the
market for a while, past the
heady tang of marine life, down
the crooked stone stairs, rapping on the door
that gave you access to the Ship. Mrs. Kavanagh
opened up. She was still alive, painted to resem-
ble an eighty-year-old drag queen. Belsey checked
she put the bolts back on.

"Nicholas, well I never."

Déjà vu.

The tribes were as he'd left them: off-duty
ambulance drivers, raucous cabbies, some dying
stars of musical theatre. He glimpsed the men in
dark corners, gold teeth flashing. The corners of

the Ship were still truly unlit. It was mid-afternoon outside, but in the pub's time zone it was a few minutes to midnight. People were lively. Motown played and someone had plugged in the fairy lights. Two women in transparent platform heels danced with men in bloodstained white coats.

Monroe stood stiffly at the bar. He glowed with greasy light from the heat lamps of the all-day carvery. He was watching the dance.

"I could have managed without this flashback."

"It worked."

A security screen beside the pork scratchings broadcast grainy images of the outside world. Next to it was Dennis Kavanagh himself, who looked increasingly like the greyhounds he used to train.

"I've got a bit of a child support issue," Belsey explained, slipping him a tenner. "Few people I don't want finding me here."

"They're fucking vultures, Nick."

"Back door still good?"

"It's open."

"Maybe only regulars in tonight. Let me know if anything else turns up."

"Right you are."

They got bottles of Nigerian stout, which were a safer bet than the taps. Belsey had used the emergency escape route twice, when the Ship had been raided. It brought you up behind the market. They took a table close to the back door, among decorative netting and lobster pots, but still with an angle on the security screen. Belsey lifted his bag to the table. He found his copy of *Britain's Most Notorious Spies*.

"I didn't know you were a fan," Monroe said.

"Edward Strathmore. He's in the index, along with JIG-SAW." Belsey passed the book over. "They're not in the text."

Monroe checked both these facts.

"It shouldn't be in the index. I was asked to take it out."

"Why?"

"No reason given. Week before it was due to be printed the Attorney General's office requested a preview. They demanded that everything about Strathmore had to go. That was a lot of interesting research spiked."

"JIGSAW?"

"The Joint Inter-Services Group for the Study of All-Out Warfare."

Belsey repeated this to himself.

"What was it?"

"The Doomsday Department. Strathmore's baby." Monroe took a pull on his bottle. "Strathmore was an air marshal in Bomber Command during the Second World War. He was one of the first to visit Nagasaki after it was destroyed, with the Atomic Bomb Casualty Commission, and he returned two years later with the After-Effects Research Council. Early 1947 he tries to convince the British government that they need to start preparing for the worst. He's a civil servant now. His message falls on deaf ears. In 1950 he commissions a report into the likely consequences of a nuclear attack on Britain: fifteen 10-megaton bombs, 12 million dead, half of industrial capacity destroyed. It leaves 40 million survivors living in siege conditions and a blanket of fallout over the country making movement impossible. The report's presented to government. Within six weeks Strathmore was made permanent secretary and given a blank cheque. The Prime Minister, Attlee, tells him to start writing the War Book, the national plan for the event of nuclear attack."

A singalong started. A prostitute said they looked too serious and offered them a line. They declined. She went to dance.

"Over the next decade there are millions of pounds unaccounted for in civil defence spending," Monroe said. "Duncan Powell was one of the first to look into this. It seems likely that it was heading to JIGSAW projects. Everything was kept off the books. Strathmore recruited army men, war gamers from the Admiralty, but also thinkers: sociologists, anthropologists—the best and brightest, and then some less straightforward souls. Edward Strathmore wanted people willing to stare into the abyss with him. Men for whom the Second World War never ended. I spoke to retired civil servants who remember JIGSAW being whispered about like a clique, a private club."

"And Douglas Argyle was part of that?"

"Argyle was their man in the MOD. He first proposed the concept of Breakdown, the level of destruction at which a country would no longer be able to function as a coordinated whole. Argyle estimated that about thirty percent destruction of a city renders the whole city population 'ineffective.' Meanwhile, the latest research from his teams at Porton were suggesting that fallout and biochemical contamination could make it necessary for people to stay underground for a year or more if they hoped to survive. A year, and then they could emerge to divide the wasteland between them."

Monroe sipped the stout again. He looked around. People were smoking. He lit a cigarette.

"Individuals central to the work of JIGSAW were given cover positions within governmental departments. That was how they drew their salaries. No reference was made to the committee in government correspondence. The armed forces denied it existed and military intelligence assigned the organisation a new level of confidentiality: Top Secret—ACID. The War Book wasn't even seen by cabinet members. It was kept to about twelve people who were fully initiated into what they called the central secret, code-named Operation Black Wing. That was the last resort, the wholesale transfer of government and the civil service. No one knew who was in, who'd be selected, where they'd be going. An angel would come down and touch you on the shoulder, lead you through the next steps. Get you where you needed to be."

"To Site 3. London is a JIGSAW puzzle."

"What's that meant to mean?"

Belsey enlightened him.

"In the 1950s and '60s the government was tunnelling under London using the cover of the General Post Office. This was when the Brutalist buildings were commissioned. I had a word with a bank robber. He'd found files in the GPO archives. I think there are three ultra-top-secret sites relating to nuclear war—Whitehall, Chancery Lane and a third one—Site 3. Mean anything to you?"

"No."

"It must be where the High Command would go. What we're seeing are the ways down. They must have wanted all officials within reach of the tunnels—via postal depots, council buildings, hospitals; anywhere in government control with subsurface access."

Monroe was feeling this. He smoked while he thought.

"It makes sense," he said. "There may have been less than an hour or so's warning. And of course it makes the whole operation invisible. They're immediately protected from fallout and from surveillance. Damage to roads or rail is no longer an issue." He nodded. He drank. There were voices raised on the dance floor, the prostitute and one of the women in platform heels having a misunderstanding.

"Why are you talking to me?" Belsey said.

"What do you mean?"

"You know what I mean. Why's all forgiven?"

Monroe downed his drink and ashed in the bottle.

"You were right. I asked around about Duncan Powell. He'd told his publisher to expect a manuscript in August— that it was going to be big news and they'd need lawyers with experience in fighting injunctions. It had something to do with a new theory: Line X was dedicated to sabotage. You know Line X?"

"I read your book. Line X is what Ferryman was working for—the network of Soviet spies. So Ferryman sabotaged something."

"It would make sense. Maybe something to do with these sites of yours, trying to put the kybosh on all this planning. By the late seventies Moscow could see they'd lost the arms race. Sabotage was a way of striking at the centre. But it depended on insiders."

Belsey slid the copy of *Military Heritage* over.

"Duncan Powell placed this advert in February."

It was strange seeing Easton's face in the pub darkness. Every time he took the magazine out he expected it to have disappeared. Belsey didn't mention this aspect of it all, the resurrection. It was possible that a lot of people were about to paint him as mad and bad. They didn't need more help.

"Why?"

"I don't know. The individuals in the photo are all dead. They died in an air accident on November 9th, 1983. This is what Powell was working on. So my guess is that this somehow connects to Line X, to his research there, right? To Ferryman, to sabotage." Belsey let Monroe digest this. "Date ring a bell? November, 1983?"

"Able Archer." Monroe looked across the faces. "Duncan Powell, you poor fucking genius," he said.

"What are you thinking?"

"It would make perfect sense. A sabotage of the exercise somehow. Able Archer sent the Soviets crazy. They believed the simulation was cover for an actual nuclear strike. That's how full scale it was. NATO forces went through all alert phases, DEFCON 5 to DEFCON 1. There were procedures the Russians had never seen before. And you think Duncan connected this to Ferryman?"

"That's what I'd imagine." Belsey tapped the advert. "Could one of these people be him? The mole?"

"Ferryman? No, they're too young. Ferryman was recruited in the sixties. Early sixties. No one here is older than mid-thirties. And you say it's 1983."

Belsey took a cigarette out of Monroe's pack. The dance floor was friendly again. There had been a reconciliation.

People swept ice cubes and broken glass to the side with their feet.

"How would the Soviets have recruited him?" he asked, after a moment. "Someone who ends up right at the centre of secrecy: what's the process?"

Monroe shrugged and offered a light.

"It depends if he was blackmailed or idealistic. Often the spymasters will have uncovered a personal misdemeanour and used that as leverage. Alternatively they'll have picked up a sense that he's sympathetic to the cause, some bright Cambridge undergraduate uncomfortable about the suffering of the world's poor. One day he'll get a tap on the shoulder, maybe abroad, maybe in a communist country. A man takes him aside and makes him a proposition: cash under the table and his name engraved in history when it's over. In return for doing what he was going to do anyway: go home, work his way into the establishment."

"You must have some theories about who he was."

"I don't care who he was. If I knew, I'd leave him well alone. I'm sure the current intelligence services feel the same. Whatever he did was a deep embarrassment for them. What are they going to do now? Trade him? Sweat him for thirty-year-old information? It's not like he's the only retired spy out there. The music stopped, people froze, dust fell. The world moves on and it turns out everyone dies anyway."

"Maybe our suspect knows who he was."

"I very much doubt that."

One of the dancers was on the bar, one of the men with gold teeth trying to get her down. Belsey checked the security screen; no one appeared to be waiting for him outside.

He finished his cigarette, dropped it into the stout and watched the smoke coil.

"I'm going to need your help on this, Tom. You can take your pick of exclusives. My colleague, Kirsty Craik, was in a crash last night. I think she was side-slammed on her way to a man who claimed to have information for her. She's now being kept under guard in Cromwell Hospital. Only nobody told the police—as far as we're concerned she's a missing person." Monroe wrote this down. "The man she was trying to get to was killed. He was a resident of St. Matthew's Hostel in Shacklewell, and is yet to turn up on any news. The crash was caused by people trying to stop Kirsty investigating this. One man responsible is Detective Inspector Gary Finch, from the Confidential Intelligence Unit. Finch was at the hospital earlier. I'm pretty sure Finch and his team killed Duncan Powell. Finch is taking instructions from Lord Strathmore."

Monroe stopped writing.

"Strathmore?"

"Know where I'd find him?"

"No."

"The man currently calling himself Ferryman is an individual named Michael Easton. I'm trying to find out what I can about him. I want attention on Kirsty. I want her crash to be reported, and I want Gary Finch and Lord Strathmore and whoever else to know that they're out in the open; we can see them. I don't want them being able to act in secrecy." Belsey gave Monroe his pay-as-you-go number. "They'll try two things: they'll throw a gagging order at you and then they'll say I'm responsible."

"You're responsible?"

"You're going to hear things about me. Don't believe them."

"Like what?"

"About a girl. It could turn nasty."

"What is it now, exactly?"

"Not as nasty as it's going to be."

IT WAS 5:35. BELSEY EMERGED FROM THE SHIP, got the old daylight whiplash and caught his breath. Blank cloud reflected in windows. The ice mountains of Canary Wharf provided an ominous kind of cover.

He walked into Limehouse, tore the tarpaulin off his car and climbed inside. *Joint Inter-Services Group for the Study of All-Out Warfare.* He scanned the notes.

41

Session 14
Deterioration in past few days. M still "receiving signals" from a past war. Requests increase to five sessions a week. Complains I am not trying hard enough.

Session 20
Anger. He has been turning up for sessions either early or late. Today I arrive and he is sitting behind my desk. Begins asking questions about my family, my relationship with my wife, how we met; purposefully intrusive.

I realise I don't trust him any more.

Then suddenly "M" was a different person altogether. Pious and chilling.

Session 21
M speaks at length on a topic he has not shown any interest in previously: guilt and the possibility of redemption. He asks whether I believe in hell, whether killing can ever be justified, whether there is a limit to forgiveness.

Asks if I'd forgive my own killer if I met them, before or after death.

He still claims to be sleeping only 2–3 hours a night. London is at the centre of his anxiety. I suggest a break from London.

Session 22
M does not arrive. I receive a call at 2.30—he is in the West Country. He has taken my advice. He reports first feelings of tranquillity in a long time.

This was followed by a fortnight's gap in the notes. As Easton, offstage, presumably strolled Piltbury Down, checked its standing stones and experimented with bomb-making while he got his head together. There were only two further sessions. Apparently Michael returned calmer. He had what Green described as "the unnerving tranquillity of a suicide risk."

Belsey turned to the final entry.

Session 23

M tells me he is leaving treatment. Apologetic. This is the wrong place for him. Suggests he has found answers elsewhere. Misses the countryside since returning to London. Reports a new interest in nature. He speaks like someone who has never noticed it before. Has been spending time at the Botanic Gardens in Kew. Says they are teaching him patience. Plants emerge without trying. Everything breaks through eventually. Even government secrets have their own seasons—they will surface when it is time. In his dreams or someone else's. In slips of the tongue.

Kew. So was this what he was doing there? Finding a new metaphor? There were no more notes—apart from an illegible scribble at the bottom of the page, a word that began with what looked like "Defe." Deferral, perhaps. Or Defeat.

Belsey closed the notes. He wasn't playing to his strengths. He was a detective; he needed something concrete.

Easton had been involved in at least one form of official employment. Connoisseur Catering. Belsey had seen the payments; Easton was caught in that web of the mundane that divides the living from the dead.

Belsey called the tax office. After ten minutes on hold he identified himself as a police officer and things went a little more briskly.

"I need some details in relation to a homicide investigation. Michael Easton, 6 July 1975. Has he got a National Insurance number?"

"Yes."

Belsey took down the number. "What other details do you have?"

"Just one address. Been in the system since he turned sixteen."

"Can I have it?"

The address was in Cumbria, in a town called Maryport on the Solway estuary, the very north-west coast of England: 27 Kirkby Terrace, Maryport. HMRC had the address registered in 1991 when Easton turned sixteen and they sent him his first National Insurance card.

That was the accent Belsey had picked up on the phone: not quite the twang of the north-east, a softer lilt. They still had a landline for the address. Belsey dialled and got through to a creaky-sounding woman who said the Eastons were the previous owners, a couple and their son. The parents died several years ago. The son sold her the house in February. That placed it around the time of Powell's advert—a few weeks before Michael Easton's foreign travels.

"Did you meet him?"

"Yes."

"What was he like?"

"Nice. Polite."

"Anything strange or suspicious?"

"No."

"How did the parents die?" Belsey asked.

"I don't know."

"Did he say why he was selling the house?"

"He didn't need all that space for himself."

"He was single?"

"I think so."

Maryport had its own police station. The Sergeant was helpful; he'd known the Eastons.

"Ian was the grocer here. Had been for thirty years. Died three, four years ago."

"How did he die?"

"Heart attack. He was on a walking holiday in Spain."

"And his wife?"

"Cancer, I believe. A year earlier. Hit him hard."

"Did you know the boy? Michael."

"Not well. Only to see. Worked in the Waverley Hotel for a few years, I believe."

"Was he ever in trouble with the law?"

"No, he was a quiet kid."

He had left quietly too. The Sergeant had no idea where Easton had gone. He didn't know anyone who would have kept in contact.

Belsey thanked him and said he might be in touch again. He studied the reunion advert, its dates, then the face to the right of centre. The dates would fit a father, but Ian Easton had been supplying Maryport with its fruit and veg until a few years ago. Everybody in the photo had died on the same day in November 1983. Belsey felt another potential solution slip beyond his grasp.

He called the General Register Office, got put through to Birth Records and asked what they had for Michael Easton, born 6 July 1975.

It took them five minutes to check their files and plunge him deeper into confusion.

"We don't have a Michael Easton born that day."

"Are you sure?"

"Yes, sir."

He had them search adjacent days in case there was some discrepancy logging it. But there was no Michael Easton. Undead. Unborn. Belsey thanked them for trying. When they had hung up he shut his eyes. He watched the patterns formed by his eyelids and thought of the deep shelter darkness and after a moment realised he was still holding the phone to his ear.

He put it down. Michael Easton didn't enter this world. Not as Michael Easton, anyway. Maybe he arose from the tunnels, the soul of a dead soldier reborn, sending victims back like some kind of payment plan. There was another explanation, however, slowly emerging from between the clouds. Belsey looked at the magazine again. The man in the photograph was his biological father. Easton had been adopted.

He opened the phone's browser, typed in *2nd Signal Brigade* then the date Hillier had given him for their deaths: *9 November 1983*.

Two hits.

The first was Powell's advert preserved on the *Military Heritage* website. The issue had been digitised, an appeal suspended in cyberspace with its message pitched to the hearing of those who would understand. Only when Belsey clicked on it, the page was unavailable.

The second result came courtesy of the *Bedfordshire and Hertfordshire Advertiser*: *Victory in Campaign for Memorial. Relatives Granted Ebsey Cemetery Site.* This web page was also currently unavailable. Belsey tried other pages from the newspaper and they worked fine.

He read the headline again then looked up Ebsey Cemetery. It was located outside a town called Shefford, an hour's drive north of London. He retrieved a torn road atlas from beneath the passenger seat and tried to think of anywhere better to go.

BELSEY WONDERED WHAT HE WAS GOING TO DO IN A cemetery. Interrogate the gravestones. While someone with an ambiguous relationship to existence fed him to the secret services. While they took his life apart, sitting on enough ammo and explosives to undo a few more while they were at it. Head to the graveyard, beat the rush. It was 7:05 p.m. Belsey kept the radio tuned to the news. No reporting about Kirsty Craik yet. Plenty on Jemma. "Police insist that, as things stand, this is a kidnap investigation and they have every reason to believe the victim is alive. They have what they describe as a 'significant lead' and expect to be able to give more information later this evening." No suspect name released. Was that meant to be some kind of message directed at him? That there was still time to turn himself over to the forces of silence?

No mention of tunnels.

Belsey followed the cars driving away from the city, gliding through a sudden shower back to commuter-belt homes. He was the only one who turned off at the cemetery. The graves arrived before Shefford itself. They sat amid flat fields, beside an industrial works. He parked at the front gates. The rain stopped and the sun appeared, low in the sky. He climbed out.

The gates were open, the cemetery empty and disarmingly lush in the wet light. Rainwater dripped from branches, splashing in sawn-off bottles filled with dead stems. Headstones spread out from a new-looking crematorium in the centre. An older section of cemetery lay to its right, with softened crosses and stone seraphim. To the left were neater rows.

Belsey walked along the sleek modern avenues. Where would you place a memorial? He found an ivory-white Commonwealth War Graves Cross of Sacrifice in the far corner. Beyond it was a newer monument formed of two blocks of black granite. Each had rows of names leafed in gold. At the base was a plaque.

In Memory of the Thirty-Seven Individuals who Lost
Their Lives in the Air Accident of
9 November 1983.
They Gave Their Lives in the Service of Their Nation

Belsey looked down the engraved columns of surnames. Eady and Ellison, no Easton. He read the dedication again. It struck him as oblique, even by the standards of memorial plaques. Which of their nation's many needs demanded their lives? Two steps led up to the memorial. A bouquet of white tulips lay on gravel at the top, petals starting to curl.

Belsey studied the flowers. They had been there more than forty-eight hours, less than five days. He turned the bouquet over and found a handwritten note in a plastic pocket. *Would whoever is leaving these flowers please contact me?* It gave a mobile number. It didn't give a name. Belsey put the number into his new phone.

He dialled it halfway back to the gate.

"Hello?" a man answered.

"Hi," Belsey said. His voice seemed loud. For some reason he wished he hadn't called from inside the graveyard. "This is Detective Constable Nick Belsey. Who's this?"

"Malcolm—Malcolm Walsh."

"I'm at the memorial in Ebsey Cemetery. I saw this number with the flowers. I wanted to speak to someone about the accident."

"Why? Do you know something?"

"Maybe."

"Come to my place," Malcolm said, quickly. He gave an address.

"I can be there in five. It's not far from the cemetery."

BELSEY FOLLOWED THE NAVIGATION program on his new phone, past a cinema and bowling complex preparing to offer Shefford its entertainment for the night. The address he'd been given was part of a 1930s housing development, identical semi-detached homes arranged around a recreational ground. The houses gathered beside the thin grass, backs to the world. A few tried to fly a Union Jack in the breeze. He counted three cars with a *Support our Troops* sticker in the window.

A black van in Malcolm's driveway advertised MW Roofing and Loft Conversion. A man in his fifties answered the door wearing a polo shirt displaying the same roofing company logo as the van. He was someone who had been well built and was now just large, with plaster in his hair and up his arms. He shook Belsey's hand and pulled him into the house.

"Come in. I'm Malcolm Walsh. I just got back."

Malcolm shut the door. Belsey wiped his feet. The inside of the house was catalogue clean. It smelt of oven chips. A strip of clear plastic led along the corridor to the front room.

"Take a seat in there. I'll be with you in a minute," Malcolm said.

Belsey sat on a pink sofa. Family photographs seemed to have reproduced themselves in the warm atmosphere, many in heart-shaped frames. He thought of Easton's flat and its naive attempt at decoration. An attractive, thin-faced woman in her forties glanced in at him then disappeared. Belsey heard children's voices, then an instruction to stay in their rooms.

Malcolm returned and drew the curtains. Belsey felt unprepared for whatever ritual was about to unfold.

"You said you knew something," Malcolm said, taking an armchair, leaning forward.

"I said I wanted to talk to you."

"What is this about?"

"There's a possibility someone I'm investigating has connections with the brigade."

"What kind of connections?"

"I don't know. I need you to tell me what you know about the accident."

"John's on his way. He helps run the campaign. He lost his brother."

"You lost your—?"

"Sister."

"What exactly happened?"

"It was a Hercules plane, a C-130. It exploded over Montenegro."

"Ninth of November 1983."

"Yes."

"What caused the explosion?"

"That's what we've been trying to find out for thirty years."

He kneaded his hands. There was a lot of nervous energy underneath the stocky exterior.

"Why did you want the person leaving flowers to call you?" Belsey asked.

"To see who they were. We spoke to everyone, all the relatives, and no one knew who was leaving those flowers. So obviously I wondered who they were and if they knew something."

"Where were they going?" Belsey asked. "What were they doing on that flight?"

"It's not clear. Officially it was for training. But training for what, we don't know. They were being flown to Cyprus. First story we were given was that it was an R&R break."

"Where in Cyprus?"

"Akrotiri. There's a British army base there."

"So why's there been so much secrecy surrounding it?"

"I don't know."

"Have you come across this?" Belsey took the copy of

Military Heritage from his jacket and passed it over. Malcolm's eyes moved slowly between picture and text then back again. His mouth opened.

"That's the photograph my sister sent. What kind of . . ."

"The number connects to a writer named Duncan Powell. Did you know him?"

"I'm the reason he has the photograph. I gave it to him to copy. He was here, writing about the crash for a book. What's he done this for?"

It seemed Malcolm was unaware of Powell's recent road accident. Belsey decided to keep the news to himself. The house had enough unexplained death in it for the moment.

"Maybe he wanted people who knew about it to get in touch," Belsey said. "But he felt he had to be subtle. Maybe it was an advert intended for those who saw what was wrong with it. The date of the reunion is the anniversary of the accident."

"Maybe." Malcolm sounded unconvinced.

"When did Duncan Powell visit?"

Malcolm checked the date on the magazine. "Just before this. About a month before this. January."

"What exactly did he say he was writing about?"

"The unanswered questions: the flight, the explosion."

"Did he say anything else? About why he wanted to write about it now?"

"No. We told him he was wasting his time if he thought he could publish anything. It's all covered by military confidentiality. The incident's got a Defence Advisory Notice on it. It can't be written about."

"Why?"

Malcolm raised his hands in something more exasperated than a shrug. Belsey pressed on.

"This picture in the magazine—you say your sister sent it."

"Yes, my sister sent it just a few days before she died. She's the one behind the bar."

"Know any of the men?"

"We've identified most. I couldn't give you the names off the top of my head."

"Know this one?" Belsey leaned across and pointed to Easton's doppelganger.

"No. Why?"

"I'm interested in him."

"Who is he?"

"I'm not sure. I need to find out. Does the name Michael Easton mean anything?"

"No."

"Where are they in this photo?" Belsey asked.

"A pub somewhere, just before the accident. I don't know where."

"There was an exercise in 1983: Able Archer, a cold-war simulation of nuclear attack," Belsey said.

"It coincided, yes." Malcolm nodded. "There's no evidence of any connection. We've certainly speculated that they may have been involved in it. I'm not sure it has any bearing on the accident. The exercise wasn't mentioned in the inquiry."

"What did the inquiry say?"

"Nothing. For five hundred pages. Want to see?"

Malcolm left the room. He fetched a ring binder from the bright, white kitchen next door and for a surreal moment

Belsey felt this was part of the sterile conformity; that every respectable family should have one. "This is the lot," he said. The doorbell rang and Malcolm went to answer it. Belsey opened the binder.

It contained a copy of the inquiry and a lot more. The collection began with copies of each MOD condolence letter, identically worded, only the name changing. Then the official report, starting with the facts: the flight took off from RAF Lyneham at 07:15, 9 November 1983. At approximately 09:05 it exploded close to the coast of Montenegro. Belsey leafed through the main body of the report: "inconclusive," "technical malfunction," "recommendations to be made." They'd got a very senior military official to lead the inquiry. He was called Sir Douglas Argyle. That was convenient, Belsey thought. He had a feeling Argyle might have known exactly how to steer it.

He heard the conversation at the front door.

"He's a police officer."

"What does he want?"

"Give him a chance."

"Has he said what he wants?"

The new arrival had a gruff voice, with traces of a Yorkshire accent that enhanced his disdain. When he came into the living room Belsey saw he was at least ten years older than Malcolm. He wore a jumper over what looked like a pyjama top. He scrutinised Belsey, didn't offer his hand, lowered himself onto the edge of the other sofa.

"This is John," Malcolm said. He showed John the advert in *Military Heritage*.

"Who did this?" John demanded.

"That writer."

He scoured the page. "Look at the date of the reunion."

"We were just saying."

"Is it meant to be bloody funny?"

"Who were they, on the flight?" Belsey asked.

"Mostly men from 81 Signal Squadron," Malcolm answered. "2nd Signal Brigade. All ranks." He showed him in the binder. "Private, signaller, lance corporal, warrant officer class 2. All kinds of communications officers, radio operators, logistics; there was also a medic, a cook, a chaplain. Not from the same brigade."

"And the women?"

"Three from the Women's Royal Army Corps. One female medic."

"I don't know much about the military," Belsey said. "But that's a strange assortment."

"Yes." Belsey waited but the two men didn't seem to have anything to add to this. Belsey pointed to the job titles within the brigade.

"What do these mean?" Malcolm took the file and glanced over them.

"Systems operator—that's radio and trunk communications. Systems engineer deals with computer networks, an installation technician will look after the fibre optics and telephone systems."

"Did they ever do any work in telephone exchanges?"

"Telephone exchanges? What do you mean? They were military. This is military communications."

The binder contained a photograph of the memorial being unveiled, then another list of the thirty-seven names.

DEEP SHELTER   337

"Can I take a picture of this?"

"Be my guest."

Belsey took a photograph of the names using his Samsung. He turned back to the page of *Military Heritage* and counted the faces in the pub. Thirty-two men and women. Allowing for someone taking the picture, still four short.

"This isn't everyone who died."

"No. The children aren't in the picture."

Belsey took a second to process this. The other men noticed, their anger finally vindicated.

"You didn't know?"

"No. Go on, tell me about the children."

"There were two military families on the flight. The woman medic, Helen Kendall, was married to one of the systems engineers. Eleanor Forrester from the Women's Corps was married to a corporal in the brigade. They had four children between them, six years up to thirteen."

Belsey felt himself inching towards some theory that might almost obey the laws of time and space.

"Could one of them have survived? One of the children?"

"Survived?" Malcolm picked up the binder and flicked through to the colour shots. Deep blue sea. It took Belsey a moment to realise it was sprinkled with debris. There were twenty-five of these photographs, almost identical: vividly blue stretches of the Adriatic strewn with fragments of dull grey metal. In most of them a rocky coastline could be seen on the horizon. A few shards of aluminium glinted in the sun. The wreckage was augmented by hundreds of birds, white and grey, resting on floating fuselage and wing panels.

"That's all we were given. Hard enough just getting those pictures out of them."

Belsey took another photo.

"Where exactly is it?"

"The explosion was roughly twenty miles from the Balkan shore. Think anyone survived?"

"What were the children doing there?"

"That's what we'd like to know: what was the nature of the exercise? No doubt the involvement of children is one reason it's all been hushed up. Heaven forbid that should get out."

"And why wasn't the plane checked?" John said. "Problems had been reported with other C-130s."

"Why did it take five days to inform us?" Malcolm said. This returned them all to silence. Belsey understood. It was what you looked for as a detective, unexplained gaps. John leaned forward.

"The plane sent out twenty-four automatic messages signalling system failures in the moments before the crash. That doesn't rule out pilot error or weather conditions."

"But the weather was fine," Malcolm said.

"First we thought it was a technical malfunction," John said. "It remains an outside possibility. These planes are still being used, you see. It would cause a stink if it turned out the government had been hiding evidence of faults."

"But we think there's more they're not telling us."

"Like?"

"The nature of the posting, the role of the children. In Amy's letter, sent a few days beforehand, it seems she hadn't been fully briefed."

"What did she say?"

"Just that she might be out of contact for a couple of weeks but hadn't been told why."

Again, there was hurt mixed in with the grief, hurt at the infidelity of the dead, in their secret place, whispering among themselves.

"Any suggestions that she would be doing something dangerous?"

"No."

John said: "My brother told me he was involved in something highly important. He said he shouldn't have even told me that much. We believe they had all received extra security vetting. We know this because for at least ten months prior to deployment their letters arrived late. They'd been opened. Someone was checking them."

"Did either of them ever talk about any military or government facilities underground?"

"No."

"Anything secret?"

"We think possibly their training meant they knew *something*. We have no idea what." Belsey waited. He was learning the rhythm. He went for it.

"What if they were killed because of what they knew?" He braced himself for outrage but they didn't flinch.

"It's possible. We don't know."

Belsey looked at the photographs of the wreckage again. He imagined the plane breaking some barrier of possibility, vaporising, leaving faint traces on the waves. When he looked up the two men were staring at him.

"But what is it *you* know?" John said. "Why are you here?"

For a second, Belsey struggled to think. He was sleep-deprived. He felt himself stepping through puzzled grief again, incompetently, so that he wasn't building an answer, just trailing around other people's questions. He got to his feet. The men looked defensive now, as if Belsey had taken their money in a game of cards. He wondered if they'd let him out of the house.

"Come on then," John said. "Who was leaving the flowers?"

"I'm going to find out for you. Now. Tonight."

BELSEY SAT IN HIS SKODA WATCHING THE END OF
a sunset whose drama was disproportionate to
the town beneath it: a sky of ash on embers,
black scraps of cloud across what looked like
lava dripping over the entertainment complex.

Children.

He brought up the names of
the dead on his phone, looked
for the children: James and Ra-
chel Kendall; Susan and Michael
Forrester. Michael Forrester had
been eight years old when he
died. Son of Corporal Terence
Forrester, 2nd Signals Brigade,
and Eleanor Forrester, staff sergeant in the Women's Corps.

43

Only somehow Michael Forrester didn't die.

Was that his message? What answer could
Belsey provide that would restore Jemma to the
living? He couldn't see how the flight connected
to the tunnels. But they had all been engaged in
something sensitive before it took place.

Belsey turned to the reunion advert. There
were the adults in the pub. Thrown together. Not
much physical contact between them. Maybe
they hadn't known each other long. Where were
they? He couldn't see any military memorabilia.

There was one clock, which said *Guinness Time*, a shelf above the bar with a hunting horn, an old drum, Toby jugs. The bar was distinctive: elegantly curved and divided into three by wooden buttresses that broke against the ceiling like wooden waves. And the ceiling itself was ornate, with bowls of light set among the moulding. Not a country pub: it had an air of buttoned-up city heritage; a London pub, brass and polish. Not rough around the edges, not cosy with darts-tournament clutter either.

He took a photo on the Samsung and zoomed in. Where would you get identifying marks? He checked the mirror behind the bar. There was a heraldic lion engraved. A lion with its claws out. Belsey thought of the undelivered crates in the Belsize Park shelter, the bottles of champagne. *For Dispatch: Red Lion.*

And then he knew he'd been there. Something clicked as the name and image merged. The hunting horn, the Guinness clock . . . Belsey rifled his mind's sodden archive of pubs, working through the Red Lions of his life. The slight stiffness of the place suggested a business district, somewhere central, preserved by well heeled footfall. Now he looked again at an object on the end of the bar. It was a bell. A fine bell, wooden handled. A division bell. Belsey's memory was waking up and stretching. A bell for calling MPs and their aides back to parliament when a vote was on. It was the Red Lion on Parliament Street.

Now he saw it: the ornamental jugs had the faces of politicians. Churchill, Thatcher, Harold Wilson. He had been there several times. It was always filled with exiles from the Commons' own bars, getting drunk on expenses before smuggling their interns back to Portcullis House. A few years ago he'd stopped the daughter of a Tory whip driving her father's Audi loaded with five boxed stereos and three members of the Peckham Ghetto Boys. He'd been treated to a lot of Beaujolais in the Red Lion while her father convinced him that neither he nor his daughter were Ghetto Boys. It was a good pub in which to take a break from kettling protests. Hard to get a seat, though.

AN HOUR'S DRIVE INTO London, back from the sleepy suburbs into the airless unsleeping city. Then through, into the business heart of it, where things almost got quiet again. Westminster, Whitehall, past the taciturn monuments and ministries resting on their tunnels. Maybe that's where all the civil servants were; you never saw them out and about. He cruised past the Red Lion. Its windows glowed. Belsey parked on the first road he found that wasn't drowning in cameras and stepped into a photograph.

It was 9:30 p.m., and a greyer uniform was in attendance. Women in blouses tilted glasses of white wine at one another while a scrum of suited men occupied the centre ground. But the pub was unmistakable. Belsey squeezed himself in, knocked by the throng as he unfolded *Military Heritage*. They were here, he thought. Why? It was a long way from RAF Lyneham. He felt the ghosts mingling. The Toby jugs remained above the bar, an enhanced collection now, and there were a few other additions to the clutter: a flatscreen in the corner, a fruit machine. But he was in the right place. He pushed his way to the bar.

"Is the manager about?"

The landlord came over. He had bushy white sideburns and a moustache. He was a little flushed, a little yellow of eye, whisky of breath. Belsey laid the picture on the bar.

"I'm interested in this—whether you remember or have heard anything about this photo being taken."

The man lowered a pair of glasses from his brow and peered through them. He tilted the advert until the light was on it.

"I've never seen this picture before."

"How long have you run the place?"

"Twenty-five years. What year was this?"

"1983."

"That would have been my father's time." He turned to the front cover of the magazine then back to the advert. He stroked a sideburn.

"It's my pub, but that's not my pub."

"What do you mean?"

The landlord took his glasses off. He looked around the pub itself, came out from behind the bar and stood next to Belsey. He used the arm of his glasses to point at the photograph.

"There are no windows."

They both turned to the pub's windows, then back to the magazine. The windows would have shown in the mirror behind the bar. The clock in the picture said 3.30. Eternal Guinness Time. But there was no daylight, no windows, no outside.

"And where's the photographer standing?" the landlord added. He grabbed the magazine, marched through the crowd to the furthest corner, by the door. He climbed up onto a bench, still holding the magazine. Customers were looking now. "It's impossible."

"Yes," Belsey said.

"So what is this?" the landlord asked from his perch. "Has someone copied my pub?"

HE MADE WHITEHALL TO WILLESDEN JUNCTION in forty minutes, heading for the home Duncan Powell had left half-empty. Belsey tried to establish the chain of events as he drove. Five months ago Duncan Powell visits Malcolm Walsh. He has a theory the accident might connect to Line X sabotage, to Ferryman. He gets the sister's photo of the regiment and, one week later, he places the advert for a reunion in *Military Heritage*.

44

Meanwhile someone, somewhere, is trying to break the code of their own name. Easton types in searches, trying out combinations of words; a safecracker coaxing the mechanism. What would he have to go on? The year his old life ended. He starts with that: *1983*. And then he adds *military accident*. Nothing useful. Maybe he knows a little about his real parents: he types in *81 Signal Squadron*. And his father's face appears.

So Michael Easton calls the number. I'd like to come to the reunion. I'd like to reunite with myself, if that is possible. Duncan Powell invited thirty-seven dead people to a reunion and one got in touch.

Belsey parked at the far end of Viners Road. He rested his arms on the steering wheel and watched the orange silence of the street. And he tried to remember what it was like being eight. The memories were there, over-handled fragments worn to dullness. He imagined being a young Michael Easton—adopted, transplanted to Cumbria. How much would you remember if your past was amputated from the present? *M claims the confidential information is within him.* Your new parents give you an approximation of the truth: your birth parents were in the military. They died in an accident. And maybe for a while it suffices but it does not stop you wondering. And then, when your adopted parents are no longer around to hold the story together, deep memories grow. They are like the bacteria inside us, peaceful until we die, when they begin to consume us from within.

Cut to five months ago. Powell is stopped for speeding on 23 January—that was how Belsey got the fingerprint match. It would have been a few days after Powell's visit to Malcolm Walsh. Stopped by police, only he's not charged, just printed and filed away. So that must have been the security services already on to him. They were tracking Powell as soon as he got involved with the campaign for truth.

Meanwhile Easton sells his home. Powell has given him a lead. He's suggested that the tragic accident that stands as a gateway between Easton's identities was in fact a crime, with a name attached: Ferryman. Easton goes researching across Eastern Europe, hunting for Ferryman's identity. For any other clues as to what happened in November 1983.

He tries to find an answer under London. Tries to find one in the depths of his own mind. One night he shows Powell the

St. Pancras Library bunker and they run into trouble. The two of them surface. The two of them are chased. Powell is knocked down by a black Land Rover. Easton flees for his life, straight into Belsey's. And then, just when Easton was backed into a corner, when he had no cards left to play, Belsey hands him one more—a hostage. Now Easton can get the world to pay attention to whatever it is he and Duncan Powell are not allowed to say. All it costs is an art student and a crooked detective.

ANDREA'S FACE APPEARED IN the window beside the front door when he knocked. She opened the door but kept it on the chain.

"I need to talk to you," Belsey said.

"Why?"

"I may have discovered why Duncan died."

She let him in. She was alone; no friend around, thank God. The front room was lit by the dull glow of an American sitcom. The sofa was still being used as a bed. Belsey took a seat in the armchair. Exhaustion hit him. He felt gnawed away inside. No sleep for forty-two hours. He was on the edge of delirium. Not where he wanted to be. The power to discern reality was one of his most valued traits right now. Had it already gone? He tried to focus on Andrea.

"Did Duncan ever mention a man called Michael Easton or Michael Forrester?" he asked. She shook her head. "I think they met. I think Duncan was killed deliberately, to stop him writing about something."

Andrea sat down and seemed to grow paler still. Turning

a death into a murder is an announcement of its own, Belsey reminded himself. Into an assassination. That was moving things into a different world.

"Who are these Michaels?" she asked.

"It's a good question. That's what I'm trying to find out. I think Michael Easton was another name for Michael Forrester. I think he shared an interest with your husband. The place where Duncan was knocked down is near an entrance to underground tunnels. My theory is he'd been down there and seen something—maybe shown by Easton, who contacted him as a result of this advert."

He passed the magazine over, studying her face for any stray flickers of knowledge.

"This is Duncan's work number," she said.

"Yes. The magazine's from February. Do you remember anything Duncan might have said about work, research, around that time?"

And then the flicker came.

"Someone had contacted him. He was excited. Why didn't he tell me what he was doing?"

"I think Duncan didn't tell you because he knew it was dangerous. I need to see any notes he might have left behind."

"You already have them."

"You mean the police?"

"The Inspector already has everything."

"Inspector Gary Finch."

"Yes."

"Andrea, what did Inspector Finch say exactly?"

"He said he was investigating Duncan's death."

"What else did he take?"

"Notes, computers, books."

Belsey got to his feet. Of course. Road accident, take the fucking hard drive.

"And he asked about his work?"

"His work, his friends, where he'd been, where he'd been that afternoon, the day before."

"And where *had* he been?"

"Nowhere. The library." Belsey found the same library books, still on the floor, still waiting to be returned. Sailing, bird watching. *Birds of the Mediterranean, Bird Migration in the Adriatic.* He picked up the book on the Adriatic. There was that blue again, the dazzle of light on waves, only without the floating debris. He thought of the white birds on the remains of the Hercules.

"Planning a holiday, you said."

"Yes."

"Was Duncan always interested in bird watching?"

"What's that got to do with anything?"

"I don't know. Was he?"

"No."

Birds of the Adriatic. Belsey flicked through. *The wetlands along the Eastern Adriatic coast provide internationally important resting areas for more than twenty waterbird species.* What were they in the debris photo? He looked at the picture on his phone. He searched the book again until he had a match. Spoonbills. And his heart kicked. *One of nature's great wonders, the spoonbills undertake a flight of thousands of miles, year after year, each spring and each autumn.* But never the middle of November. Not for the spoonbills. Whatever the accident photographs showed it wasn't what happened in November 1983. Any more than the squadron in the Red Lion was drinking on the corner of Whitehall.

He had moved beyond the relatives of the dead. In a matter of hours he had moved beyond the mystery they had lived with for three decades, past the company of their anger onto new ground. They thought they had a mystery but they had just the beginning of it. And now he missed the companionship.

Only one companion left.

Belsey tried Jemma's mobile. Maybe Easton would pick up. But there was no answer. He sent an email to the Ferryman account: *What happened on 9 November 1983?*

Andrea was at the window, peering around the curtains. He felt her rising panic. A lot of half-pieces of information were stirring unfocused anxiety. He'd subjected her to the same fate as Malcolm Walsh. People die, their secrets turn up like lovers at the funeral. Memories, which you thought you got to keep, start to change.

"Should I tell someone?" she said. "Other police? The ones who spoke to me? Who can I trust?"

"I wouldn't call any other police right now. Let me see what I can find out. Try to be calm."

"Am I even safe?" She was about to cry.

"You're safe. You're here. They're not interested in you."

"Where are you going to go?"

"I don't know." He saw her expression and realised what she was asking. "Andrea, I don't think my presence is going to keep this place secure. Is there somewhere else you can go for tonight? That friend of yours?"

"She's not in London."

"I can stay for a bit if you want. You should get some sleep. I can't promise I'll be here when you wake up."

He sat down. She propped on the edge of the sofa. The sitcom ended with someone proposing and laughs all round.

Then came the news.

A man in a shirt and sports jacket stood outside Cromwell Hospital, microphone up, excited by possibilities.

"Detective Sergeant Kirsty Craik was the officer originally assigned to the investigation of missing student Jemma Stevens. Craik was involved in a car accident last night. There were rumours that she was being treated behind me at the private Cromwell Hospital in west London. No word from the Metropolitan Police yet as speculation mounts regarding possible connections between last night's events and the Jemma Stevens investigation."

Monroe had got to work, then. It was better than nothing. Unless the move was going to force Finch into something drastic, like slitting Kirsty's throat. Andrea saw how intently he was watching the report.

"Do you know about this?" she asked. "Is it to do with Duncan?"

"Maybe."

No report on the St. Matthew's doss-house murder, though. Obviously the homeless don't always make the bulletins. Still, it should have done.

Belsey called Cromwell Hospital. He introduced himself as Finch and asked to be put through to Kirsty Craik. He got a flat denial that she'd ever been in.

"And if anyone ever was here, they're not here now," a woman said, pointedly.

Belsey went outside, studied the vehicles parked on the road, took the Umbro bag from his own car, along with the cosh and his CS spray. He deadlocked Andrea's door when he came back in and told her to set the burglar alarm. He checked the glaziers had done a decent job on the side. Andrea took a blanket upstairs. Belsey spread the papers from the Umbro bag on the coffee table.

First he read through the FOI responses. Eastman had two techniques: he homed in on details until he was blocked, finding the edge of whatever remained secret; then he became more subtle. He was told information about MOD purchasing of furniture couldn't be disclosed so he asked for general budgets: MOD budgets for 1970–1980 then the spending of individual departments. Eventually he must have been left with an excess, an amount of budget unaccounted for. He'd made FOI requests on steel, stationery, labour: employment of electricians and engineers, trying to find the space representing JIGSAW and its projects.

Belsey sorted the requests into piles.

The biggest related to Site 3: twelve requests, four to local authorities, eight split equally between the Home Office and the MOD. Easton asked about equipment kept at Site 3, research carried out at Site 3, experiments concerning Site 3. None received more than a polite refusal.

Easton had more luck with a curious selection of FOIs about trains: government purchasing of railway tracks and associated employment of trackmen and track gangs. These did get a response. An information officer for MOD Procurement opened a chink. Yes, the Ministry Of Defence purchased ninety-two miles of disused railway track in 1957. Purposes undisclosed.

To run beneath the city? A city beneath the city, like Terry Condell said? With some kind of private transport system connecting the exchanges? The Sites?

Finally Easton hunted those responsible for the underground project. The clique. The Doomsday men. Obviously no one would release names, so he sent his own. Where was Douglas Argyle 1970–80? Where was Edward Strathmore 1970–80? Where was a man called William Lanzer?

More requests than any related to this William Lanzer. The name kept coming up. No title given. Lanzer didn't seem to be a lord or a sir or a corporal. Plain old William Lanzer. Easton asked: Where was Lanzer employed? How much was he paid? Do you hold any files relating to his work?

Belsey searched the name on his phone and saw why.

William Lanzer, architectural engineer, born 23 August 1919. First Supervising Engineer of the General Post Office and subsequently Chief Technical Officer at the Ministry of Public Building and Works.

Lanzer was a pioneer and uncompromising visionary who worked his way to the heart of post-war planning. He helped introduce a new, Brutalist aesthetic to British architecture, a style that was to prove as inspirational as it was controversial.

The entry was in an online encyclopaedia of twentieth-century architecture. It gave a list of buildings William Lanzer had either worked on or commissioned: Centre Point, Barbican, Archway Tower, BT Tower, Baynard House.

So he'd found the Doomsday Department's chief architect. Belsey read Lanzer's entry in full. Lanzer started his career in the research section of the Ministry of Home Security, investigating the effects of bomb blast on reinforced concrete. After the liberation of Calais he went to northern France to examine the effects of the Allied bombardment on the heavily defended V-1 and V-2 sites. In 1953 he attended the atomic weapons trials in Australia.

It was, then, a curious sideways move that found him in charge of the Post Office estate, before running things at the Ministry of Public Building and Works, where business really picked up:

> Lanzer was the central figure behind the post-war London Plan, sometimes referred to as the Lanzer Plan, involving widespread construction across the capital. Much of this work was criticised at the time, but under Lanzer the Ministry of Public Building and Works developed exceptional technical expertise. His engineering achievements included pioneering developments in air filtration, prestressed concrete and underground construction.

There were no pictures of Lanzer online. No obituary either. He'd got a CB upon leaving government service in 1985. Belsey tried to imagine the man retired somewhere, rich on twentieth-century fear. He would have his designs framed on the walls; his Brutalist vision.

Belsey turned the FOI rejections over and wrote the names of Lanzer's buildings on the back, one per sheet. Then he moved the coffee table to the side and arranged the sheets across the floor until he had central London. He tried to see the route—the logic of Site 3. Easton's taunting voice re-

peated in his head: *Jemma says she wants to visit Site 3.*
While Croydon is all cinders, and Lewisham empties of life,
London is defended from below. The machinery of government sinks down. Civilians climb under their tables and the
government climbs under the streets.

Where was the final site? The last stronghold? He tried to
remember every detail Terry Condell had given him. The
specs were more than five times bigger than the Chancery
Lane and Whitehall exchanges put together. How would
that be possible? He pictured Site 3 as monstrous, the surface of London as a placenta feeding what lay below. *There's
something at the core of it,* Terry Condell had suggested.
Belsey imagined the place centred on extraordinary tech-
nologies, mechanisms of life and death. What was Michael
Easton trying to reveal?

It was late. His mind had stopped moving to any great
effect. Belsey wandered the house, opening drawers, sifting
whatever debris from Duncan Powell's life had escaped
Finch's attention. He returned to the sofa, lay down, then sat
up and turned back to the case notes. He tried arranging
these in piles too, tearing them out. Dreams of forgetting
something crucial, of having to return, of London and
breakdown. He is breaking down. His attendance is erratic.
Session 18, in the depths of his turmoil:

I ask why he arrived late. M says he was walking and
got lost. I suggest that getting lost is a way of escaping
and he agrees. M says that when he was young he was
always trying to escape. Wherever you put him he
would leave.

Belsey ate Andrea's leftover toast, pondering these words. *They are not missing, you are missing.* He found whiskey in a cupboard under the TV and drank, then lay on the floor, hoping for sleep. He thought perhaps his dreams could pursue Easton's own.

HE SLEPT TOO DEEP and far too long. He didn't dream of anything. When he woke Andrea Powell was standing over him pointing a kitchen knife at his throat. It had gone 9:30 a.m. The TV was on, a tanned woman above a news ticker.

POLICE HUNT MET DETECTIVE

The presenter read her autocue excitedly.

"The investigation into missing art student Jemma Stevens took yet another dramatic turn this morning as the Metropolitan Police announced that one of its own officers, Detective Constable Nick Belsey, is wanted for questioning regarding both this incident and the whereabouts of his colleague Detective Sergeant Kirsty Craik.

"Belsey has been described as a maverick figure in the force, whose career has already been dogged by controversy. Attempts to locate him have, so far, been unsuccessful and the search continues. Members of the public have been warned not to approach him."

Belsey got to his feet. The knife brushed his chest. Andrea stepped back.

"Get out," she said. She'd responded quite robustly to this, he thought, all things considered. On the news they had a picture of him from God knows whose social-networking page, with a bare-shouldered woman in what must have been the Rocket or maybe even Majingo's. From the 1990s, so at least he was barely recognisable. Sadie, that had been her name. A veterinary nurse. She'd also tried to stab him, eventually.

"I'm being framed," he said. The line didn't sound as fresh as he'd hoped. He gathered up his papers and sighed. "What the fuck's 'maverick' meant to mean?"

He opened the front door and the burglar alarm went off.

ANOTHER GLORIOUS MORNING, SUN A HAZY
slick in the sky, everyone out and about, whis-
tling and thanking God it was Friday. Those
who weren't already at work were catching up
with the news, reading about killer cops.

Belsey drove into the centre of town. He
parked close to Warren Street.
There was a new attraction to an
area with three mainline train
stations out of London and a Eu-
rostar terminal. Colours seemed
very bright and he could smell
chemicals coming through his
skin. He walked into a newsagent's at the top of Tottenham
Court Road. Someone had re-
leased the story in time to make the day's front
pages. *Met Police Detective On the Run.* He
bought a selection of papers. The shop owner
didn't connect him to the headlines.

The tabloids had been on the scent long enough
to produce pictures of Kirsty off duty, looking
gorgeous and distinctly killable. These were run
alongside Jemma in her tequila girl outfit, with
the implication of some kind of threesome.

He was suddenly hungry. He looked into a
cafe, saw a lot of people with newspapers and

walked on. The next cafe was empty. It had a dirty glass roof and a lot of dead pot plants. Belsey went in and ordered poached eggs, then changed his mind and went for a full English. He continued with the papers. He felt a perverse curiosity, picking at the scab of his life. He risked putting the battery back in his old phone. Everyone he had ever known had tried to get in touch. And Jemma had apparently sent him another text: *Welcome to Doomsday—I will die at 6 pm. Site 3.* It had been sent half an hour ago.

It was already ten-forty and he had no ideas.

His food arrived. He ate what he could, looked up and there was Centre Point, beyond the roofline opposite, mocking him. Indestructible. Clever old William Lanzer.

Belsey checked William Lanzer again online. Eulogies, aesthetic condemnation, encyclopaedia entries. No death announcement. But no postal address either. He didn't come up on any online directory. The most useful lead was in an article from nine years ago on the Academy of Engineering Innovation website: *Lanzer still lives with his sister, Miriam, whose interest in marine life he credited with inspiring his research into chemoautotrophy.*

Belsey typed in *chemoautotrophy*. It was the biological production of energy by means other than photosynthesis. Energy without sunlight.

A Miriam Lanzer *did* come up on a search of the BT directory. Belsey almost choked on his egg. There was a landline and home address. The address was on Wandsworth Road. He gulped a mouthful of pale coffee and went to his car.

NUMBER 110 WANDSWORTH ROAD was not a Brutalist tower but a gabled Victorian house that looked draughty and in need of paint. There was a single brass bell by the door. Belsey rang and heard shuffling down uncarpeted corridors.

"One moment," a woman called.

He got his badge and least threatening smile ready. The woman answered, already trembling. No tremble in the stare, though. Yellow blouse, pleated skirt, thick socks and sandals.

"Miriam Lanzer?"

"Yes."

"I'm sorry to disturb you. I'm a police officer. Does your brother, William, live here?"

"Sometimes. He comes and goes."

Belsey tried to think what that might mean.

"Do you know where I might find him? I'd like to speak to him quite urgently."

"Now? No."

"Can I come in?"

She studied his badge for a minute. When there was nothing more to study she gave it back. They moved in disjointed bursts down the hallway. Miriam Lanzer held a radiator for support. One of her legs didn't work. They entered a front room with a lot of porcelain—circus clowns, nativity scenes, shepherdesses searching for their flocks among the dust. He couldn't see any architectural engineering. There was a copy of the day's *Times* on the table. Belsey folded it over. The woman didn't sit down. She gripped the back of a sofa and stared at Belsey.

"What do you want William for?"

"I'd just like to speak to him. About his work."

"His work? Why?"

"I'm very interested in the work he did for the government. Some time ago now. It sounds like he was incredibly important."

"He is."

"When did you last see him?"

"It's been months. He gets so busy."

"Busy with what?"

"Events. He gives talks, attends ceremonies. People want to ask him about his ideas." Miriam Lanzer took a well used, red address book from the coffee table. She was shaking again. Belsey couldn't tell how much his presence played a part in that.

"This is the number he said to call." She gave him a number and Belsey dialled. He wondered if he could have this conversation in front of her, and he turned away, ready to step into the hall if necessary.

"St. Matthew's," a man answered.

It took Belsey a second to process this. Then he found he couldn't speak.

"Hello?" the manager said. "St. Matthew's Hostel. Can I help?"

Belsey hung up.

"Was he there?" Miriam asked.

Belsey looked at her. He took the address book. W: William—a list of seven addresses in increasingly shaky handwriting, crossed out one by one to form a ladder down to St. Matthew's.

William Lanzer. Bill Lanzer. Bill. What journey came to an end on the second floor of a doss house in Shacklewell?

"No, he wasn't there," Belsey said.

"Is it the right number?" she asked.

"I think so."

He gave her the book. She placed it on a dresser to the side. Then he saw, beside it, propped against a ballerina, a letter headed *Victim Support*. Belsey picked it up. It was a standard letter: the police are doing all they can, call us if you want a shoulder to cry on, etc.

"Were you the victim of a crime recently, Ms. Lanzer?"

"Yes."

"What happened?"

"I had an intruder. Young man, said he was with the electricity board."

"When?"

"I'm not sure. A few days ago."

"What did he take?"

"I can't tell. There's no money here. I don't own anything valuable."

"Did he look at this?" Belsey gestured at the address book.

"I don't know. Why would he?"

"What did he do?"

"He went upstairs. I can't manage the stairs any more. William will check when he comes round."

Belsey climbed the stairs to the first floor. A study had exploded. Papers and files carpeted the floor; wooden furniture was smashed. A roll-top desk and lacquered cabinet lay on their sides, locks broken, one chest of drawers face down

on the floor with its back smashed in. A trunk in the corner
had a mess of loose papers inside two foot deep: school reports, photographs, dissertations, academic journals. Belsey
rifled through the papers. William Lanzer had been a
hoarder. There were plans of shop-fronts, houses, schools.
He found a floor plan of the Red Lion in Westminster, di-
mensions pencilled in. Then less homely structures: reser-
voirs, power stations, seed banks. There were folders of
intricate, hand-drawn sketches and diagrams.

But no Site 3.

Hence Easton's next stop had been St. Matthew's. Belsey
tried to remember the blood map on the hostel wall. Then a
sound came from downstairs, a slow, mechanical rattle he
had not heard for a long time. The unwinding of a dial telephone.

He walked back down. *The Times* had been unfolded.
Miriam Lanzer spun, terrified, clutching the receiver. In her
other hand was a piece of paper. Belsey prised it out of her
arthritic hand. A one-line note, black copperplate script
from a pen that oozed expensively.

If any more problems—Flat 89, 1 Belgrave Square,
0207 245 1193—Edward Strathmore. Do not contact
police.

Belsey put his hand on the phone and ended the call.

"Why don't you sit on the sofa," he said.

Miriam Lanzer sat on the sofa. Belsey took the receiver
from her and dialled 999.

"I've got an elderly lady here who's just had an intruder at her home. She's in shock. Yes, come over please, someone should check she's OK."

He took a knife from the kitchen and cut the phone cord. Then he pocketed the knife and drove to Belgrave Square.

TWENTY MINUTES PAST MIDDAY. LESS THAN SIX HOURS
to find Jemma. Time to take it to the top.

Belsey was learning a lot about his past on the
radio, his relationship with Jemma and his various reasons for having killed her: a plot involving the recycling of seized cocaine, the ménage à

46

trois, possible blackmail. She'd
expressed fears about something
recently. They'd dug out someone who remembered Belsey at
Borough CID and had a nice an-
ecdote about him setting fire to
his desk.

Celebrity had come: a blanket of misunderstanding on a
vast scale. He was that thread of
disgust and secret envy woven into strangers'
days. Disgust, envy and fear: "public warned not
to approach. This is a highly trained police officer." His employer had never been more compli-
mentary. The detective fronting Belsey's manhunt
was DCS David Sandler, a jowly Welshman. The
only thing Belsey knew about Sandler was that
he'd cheated on his wife with a traffic warden.
He was now solidly reassuring the public that all
resources were being drawn upon in shutting
this menace down. Belsey didn't doubt it.

He cruised into west London. Of course, he thought: Belgravia, where spies go to die; grand nineteenth-century squares of stiff, white houses, each pretty as a wedding cake and ice-cold as a vault. He cruised past the gleaming porticos imagining a whole secret service retired here, old wounds playing up. Belsey wondered if he was losing control, wondered about amphetamine-induced psychosis.

He drove a circuit of the square. Number 1 was a mansion block. He parked, went to the front and checked the entrance hall. No concierge inside. No desk. Just red carpet and an arrangement of dried flowers. Twenty golden buttons gleamed beside the intercom. Belsey rang number 89.

"Yes?" The voice didn't sound like it belonged to a man in his nineties.

"I've got a Miriam Lanzer here. She wants to speak to Lord Strathmore. Can someone come down and help her?"

Belsey went back to his car and reversed out of sight. He waited, watching the front of the block. After a moment a guard came out, broad in a dark suit and mirrored shades. He checked the street then went back in. Belsey took his cosh, skipped up the steps to the door, rang every other bell.

"I'm fixing the roof," he said. "There's a leak. Someone called about water leaking down through the flats."

The door buzzed. Belsey waded across the lobby's thick carpet to a lift. The numbers above it were lit at floor five. He took the stairs, running.

The stairs were steep. Stained-glass windows let in something that wasn't light. Belsey got to the fifth floor in time to see the guard unlocking a door. He stepped silently over the carpet and brought the cosh down at the back of the man's head. It was crisp. He got the sweet spot. The guard collapsed.

No weapons on him. The key was still in the lock. Belsey opened the door, slipped inside and closed it behind him.

The flat was dark. A parquet floor led between oil paintings towards the only lit room. Belsey could see a bank of cigarette smoke around the chandeliers. He waited for any other guards to appear, maybe concerned about their friend. No one appeared.

Belsey stepped towards the smoke. He entered the main room. An old man sat in an armchair to the side. Two transparent tubes ran over his ears, into his nostrils. He watched Belsey with watery eyes. Oxygen came from a portable blue case on the card table beside him, next to a pack of Rothmans and an insulin syringe. His hands rested on a tartan blanket that covered his lap.

The room was grand and bare. Light stole in between curtains and was immediately frozen, forming solid columns of smoke and dust. Glass-fronted cabinets stood empty. There was a discoloured mirror framed like a masterpiece. Several artefacts made out of dark wood kept themselves to the shadows. Only one antique that wasn't holding up well. He looked towards the empty corridor, then at his guest.

"Michael?" he asked.

Strathmore's chest rose and fell with effort. Belsey glanced into adjacent rooms, just in case. They were all empty. Off the corridor, to the right, stairs rose elegantly into a darkness of polished wood, an upper floor with no lights on. Belsey returned to the main room. The lord's eyes followed him as he searched.

"Are you here to kill me, Michael?" His voice was hoarse but still officer class: he wanted to know the order of play. He was very thin. Belsey looked into Strathmore's weak eyes and saw synapses shutting down, passageways of memory closing one by one. Don't die on me, Belsey thought. Not yet. The man felt for his cigarettes and knocked them to the floor. Belsey picked them up. He slid one out.

"Why would I want to kill you?"

"I said to keep you alive, you know. I protected you. There were others . . . People with more drastic ideas. Convenience, inconvenience." He said the words carefully, as if they described two great principles of existence. He dragged himself forward in his chair, weight on his right arm. "Do you want to know what happened? Did William tell you?"

"I want to know where Site 3 is."

Strathmore considered this over a couple of wheezing breaths.

"Site 3 is abandoned."

"I'm not looking to rent the place. I need to go there." Belsey checked an ornate bronze clock on the corner table. Two cherubs guarded ticking hands. Almost quarter to one, although he wasn't sure he'd trust any timekeeping device in this particular flat. Belsey lit a Rothmans and took a drag. He handed it to the lord. He was curious to see how it worked with the tubes. It worked fairly normally. Smoke rose into Strathmore's face.

"Do you want an apology?"

"I've told you what I want."

"I knew, when I heard about Douglas, and then William . . . It was a stupid idea having you there. The exercise was ill-judged from the start. But the problem was loved ones, you see." He flicked the cigarette. Ash fell over the blanket. "Loved ones. Those we supposedly won't leave behind. We used to call it the family problem. Could we put families down there? How would it work? Simple things. What would it do to a child?"

"Down where exactly?"

"You hated it. We wanted to know what young boys would do. You showed us." He coughed. "They would not stay still. They would explore. Run away. Maybe you knew more than we did. Wisest of us all."

He's stalling me, Belsey thought. It's an act. He brought the knife out and felt stupid. The clock chimed. Strathmore looked at the knife. "But you have to understand, I am telling you what you need to know."

"Site 3."

"What happened at Site 3 was . . . We thought it was an accident. For years. A tragic accident. I had no idea we'd been infiltrated. I know that you care about this." He uncoiled fingers either side of the cigarette and pointed them at Belsey. "Ferryman. You know it was Ferryman."

"I was starting to have my suspicions."

"We hadn't realised the panic on the Russian side. How could we have known? Instructions from on high, from the Politburo itself, for God's sake—do whatever feels necessary. Strike at the heart. We didn't know until it was far too late."

"Was it you? Were you Ferryman?"

"Me?" The man laughed and then wheezed until he changed colour. He sucked breath in. "But you know . . . I thought you knew. You must know who it was."

Belsey was pondering this when his mobile rang. The screen said *Jemma*. He stepped out of the room, answering quietly.

"Michael? Speak to me. You're not going to believe where I am. I'm with Lord Strathmore." He heard breathing, someone trying to form words.

"Nick?"

"Jemma?"

She gave a small cry.

"Are you OK? Where are you?"

"Nick?"

"It's me. Where are you?"

"It's Jemma."

"I can hear you."

"Help me."

"Is he there?"

"No."

"Where are you?" He couldn't hear her reply if there was one. It sounded like either his phone or hers kept cutting out. He climbed the stairs to the landing on the floor above.

"Jemma? Hello?"

"Nick." She was sobbing now.

"Where are you?"

"I don't know."

"What can you see?"

"I can't . . . He's coming back."

She cut out. Belsey swore. He called Vodafone and got put through to the liaison department.

"This is absolutely urgent. I need a ping location on the following number." He gave them the number. Something in his tone must have communicated necessity. They said they'd run the check. He was pacing the corridor now. He got to a room at the end, a bedroom with sheets folded on the bed.

"We'll call you back," they said.

"No, I'll stay on. I need it now. Immediately."

Belsey checked his watch. He looked at the room, as cold and varnished as the ones downstairs. No family photos. No traces of service to the nation. He opened a mahogany wardrobe. Five white shirts hung down, all neatly pressed, all different sizes. He opened the drawers beside the bed. Empty. He felt the first inklings of dread.

"OK, call me back," he said.

He tried other doors on the corridor and they were locked. Belsey went downstairs and stepped into a bathroom of old, white porcelain. No toothbrush, a cabinet above the sink with one wrapped bar of soap. He turned a tap and it coughed, then ran brown.

The window had been sealed shut. It looked like all the windows were sealed.

Belsey returned to the corridor and studied the bar of light on the threshold strip. It flickered. There were people outside. Flypaper, he thought. Lured to a fucking safe-house. They were good, he had to give them that. They were professionals.

Through the doorway to the living room he saw Strathmore move the blanket on his lap to check a gun.

The balcony was his best option. Belsey was wondering about getting onto it when the front door opened.

"Get your hands off me."

Kirsty Craik was shoved inside.

"This is only temporary," Finch said.

"What exactly is only temporary?"

She seemed in reasonable condition. She wasn't cuffed, bore no visible injuries. They both saw Belsey.

"Nick," Kirsty said.

Finch walked past him to speak to Strathmore. He didn't look happy.

"Are you OK?" Belsey asked Craik, when Finch was out of earshot.

"Yes. What is this?"

"It's like a well appointed prison. I need to get out of here quickly."

"Are you the reason there's a guy on the floor outside?"

"Partly. I've got a lead on Jemma. She just called, but it sounds like she's still being held somewhere. I need to move fast, but it could get messy. I don't know how you want to play it. I can try to get help."

"Oh, you're getting out of here. That's a good idea. Shall we call a cab? There are two more guys waiting at the front, Nick. No one's getting out of here."

"Are they armed?"

"I don't know."

"Strathmore has a gun under the blanket. Keep an eye on that. Know if Finch is armed?"

"Who's Finch?"

"Your escort."

"I don't know. He's not wearing a holster."

"We need to do this before they get back-up."

Belsey picked up the bronze clock.

"Hey, Gary." He threw it hard at Finch's head. The officer ducked. Belsey piled into him, hard—a rugby tackle that drove him to the ground. Strathmore found the gun beneath the blanket and lifted it unsteadily. Craik grabbed his arm, knocking him and the seat over. The front door opened.

"Stop! Don't move!'

Finch scrambled to his feet and bolted for a side room. Belsey went for Strathmore's gun. It was a Webley Revolver, ancient-looking, like something out of a kid's Wild West kit. Belsey fired at the balcony doors and the kickback almost dislocated his shoulder. Glass rained down. Craik ran for the fresh air and Belsey followed. He had a foot outside when he felt a sharp blow to his right arm. Another shot whistled past: the fizz of a pistol with silencer. He climbed over railings to the adjacent balcony. I've been shot, he thought. His phone started ringing. Vodafone. He kicked the balcony doors to the neighbouring flat, then decided to answer the phone.

"Hello?"

"Maybe leave the fucking phone," Craik said. "Get to the roof."

"We have that location for you," the caller said.

"Hang on." The doors wouldn't budge. Craik dragged a glazed garden pot over. They stepped up and pulled themselves to the roof, confronted by a landscape of trellis and satellite dishes.

"Where is it?" Belsey said into the phone.

"Can you hear me?"

"Yeah, go on. What's the location?"

"EC4."

"She's in EC4?"

"The tower she's receiving signal from is in EC4. So she must be somewhere near."

THEY JUMPED DOWN TO A BALCONY ON THE SOUTH SIDE of the building. This time Craik found doors that were already open. They walked through a startled lunch party with fine china and staff in aprons, out to the corridor. Craik pointed to the back stairs. They led down to a tradesman's entrance and out past delivery boxes to an alley.

Belsey's car was where he'd left it. Any security detail had been drawn up to the flat.

47

"I've been shot," he said. "Get in the driver's seat."

She turned and saw the dark patch spreading through his suit.

"Oh shit, Nick."

"I think it just clipped my arm. I could do with something on it."

In truth, pain was becoming like a cloud around him. They climbed in. He gave her the keys and she drove.

"Head east. Jemma's in EC4."

"You've found her?"

"It's a ping location. She called me. She's just about in signal. She didn't sound in a great way. I should possibly go via a chemist."

"I'm on it."

"Where've you been? Apart from Cromwell Hospital?"

"I don't know." Craik turned onto Knightsbridge, checked the mirrors. "I was moved around. Several hours in a hotel room. A lot of time in cars."

"Did Gary Finch have anything interesting to say? About tunnels? Somewhere called Site 3?"

"He said he was protecting me. From you."

"What a hero."

She continued onto Piccadilly, cut left into Mayfair and jumped out at a boutique chemist's. It had gone 1 p.m. Belsey pulled the kitbag onto his lap. *One hundred times more potent than morphine.* Where were the bastards? He rummaged, found a fentanyl stick and split the foil. He clamped it between his teeth. It tasted of plastic and synthetic fruit but the rush was almost instant. He tried to focus. EC4 was the Merrill Lynch building, the old General Post Office headquarters. City of London. Paternoster Square. St. Paul's. It would be police-heavy, private-security-heavy. They'd all have photographs of him, all be briefed and on high alert. He didn't really have a choice, though.

Craik came back with the shopping and told him to strip. He took his jacket and shirt off. She poured water down his arm and pronounced the wound superficial.

"It really doesn't feel particularly superficial."

"If you're conscious enough to feel it, it's superficial. It might just be a bit of glass."

"I was shot, Kirsty. I'm pretty sure."

He held gauze in place while she wrapped bandage and then tape. He put the shirt back on, then the jacket. The shirt had a lot of blood on it. The jacket had a hole above the right elbow that looked like he'd caught it on a nail. He did it up, drank some water. Craik started the car again.

They followed the Strand to Fleet Street, into the City. The lunch surge had begun, buildings disgorging their contents, queues building for sushi and burritos. All was bright and peaceful. Belsey directed her up past the Old Bailey to Newgate

"Keep going, slowly, towards St. Paul's."

He looked out at the surface of the world with a familiar sense of frustration. Jemma had called from somewhere near here. Under Merrill Lynch itself? Down wherever Kyle Townsend had turned up? He could see at least five security guards anxiously guarding the front of the building.

"Stop here," Belsey said, when they were a few metres away.

"What do you want to do?" Craik asked.

"Ahead—by the ruined church—that's the old Post Office headquarters. It has tunnels underneath it. I need to get in. I know she's around here. I don't have any other leads."

"I can distract the guards."

"Give it a shot. If we get separated try to get in touch with Tom Monroe on the *Express*. He knows what's going on. He knows lawyers."

They both got out. Belsey took Strathmore's Webley Revolver and the torch. Kirsty ran over to the guards, badge raised. She led them away from the door, pointing at something supposedly going on a hundred metres from the entrance and very urgent.

Belsey didn't get close. He was halfway across the square when he was spotted by police standing next to the Stock

Exchange across the road. They consulted with a man in a suit with a two-way radio clipped to his belt then began moving towards Belsey.

He tried Jemma's phone as he ran. No answer. Belsey jumped down the stairs into St. Paul's underground station. It was open, trains running, so no one had been in the tube tunnels recently. There was nothing suspicious going on apart from himself. He got attention from some Transport Police officers. They pressed their radios to their ears, then began to follow him through the ticket hall. Belsey exited on the south side. They were thirty seconds behind. Keep moving. He slipped in among the tourists by the cathedral just as two squad cars parked across the top of Ludgate Hill.

He was going to have to take sanctuary. Belsey stepped up the cathedral stairs, moving through the revolving doors into the cool shade, paid an extortionate entrance fee, helped himself to an audio guide. The hush inside the cathedral was startling. Belsey searched for alternative exits. He saw what looked like suited silhouettes in the north transept doorway. Play it safe. He fell in line with a guided tour as they headed downstairs into the crypt, past dark slabs of stone and motheaten flags. Where were hiding places? There was a gift shop, a cafe area, then, at the end, hidden away from the masses, a restaurant. Belsey smiled at the waitress.

"Table for one. At the back, please."

She led him through to the back. Belsey lifted a large menu in front of his face. The menu said *Connoisseur*.

"Any drinks?" the girl asked. Her apron also said *Connoisseur*. Belsey lowered the menu. He thought back to Easton's bank statements, the payments in. The waitress's voice dipped as she saw his expression. "Are you OK, sir?"

"Did a Michael Easton ever work here?"

"Michael? Yes, but not for a few weeks now. Are you a friend?"

"Yes."

"Do you know what happened to him?" she asked.

"What happened to him? No. Why?"

"He just walked off mid-shift. Never saw him again."

"Did you see him walk off?"

"What do you mean?"

"Did you see him walk *out* of the restaurant?"

She looked puzzled. "No."

"I'll get a Bloody Mary. Not too much Tabasco. Do you have horseradish?"

"Yes."

"Plenty of that, and a slice of lemon."

She went over to the bar. Belsey went to the kitchen. The chefs were busy over their pans. He saw an arched, wooden door in the corner. *Staff Only.* He moved for it before anyone could stop him, through to a very tight spiral of stone stairs worn to undulations. He ran down them, past a storeroom with boxes of vegetables, past a passageway crowded with mops. The stairs continued, unlit, scratched with antique graffiti. They descended another twenty feet to a dented steel door speckled with rust.

Easton wasn't working here for the money. He wanted access to what lay below.

"Hello?" Belsey's voice was dulled by the stone. A sign on the door had been painted over at least once, but through the layers he could make out the words: *No Unauthorised Personnel.* He got his fingers around the edge and scraped it open.

A dank corridor, walls brick, floor dirt. Jemma's phone lay on the ground. He picked it up: dead. The narrow passageway led beyond it for ten metres or so. He shone the torch. A white arrow painted onto the bricks pointed deeper in, to where the passage turned a corner.

Belsey walked to the end and looked around it—another stretch. Only, now, the cathedral stone became breeze block. A sign on the wall said *Cathedral: Congregation Zone C.* Then, in smaller letters: *Red Passholders—One Item of Luggage Per Person.*

It all ended at a single door. Belsey's foot buckled as he approached it. He was on a grille of some kind. He shone the torch through the grille and felt dizzy. It was a steep drop, over fifty feet. He couldn't understand what he was seeing.

A long, ghostly white form, like a train. A train formed from strands of cotton wool.

He got down onto the grille and shone the torch along the length of whatever it was down there. The white was mould. Beneath the mould was an old British Rail passenger train, flat-fronted, six coaches stretching towards a tunnel at the far end. It stood beside a platform with a row of shuttered bays, their concertina doors open to expose stacks of cardboard boxes. There were more boxes across the platform, some open: first aid boxes, ration packs, glass bottles.

Rail track, Belsey thought: the FOIs Easton had rattled off: he'd asked about MOD purchase of rail track . . . Something was starting to occur to Belsey but he didn't have time to pursue the thought. *One item of luggage per person . . .*

Then the door back to the cathedral stairs slammed shut. He ran to it. It wouldn't open. He could feel a padlock rattle on the other side of the door. Belsey shouted through but there was a lot of noise starting in the restaurant, drowning him out. People screaming.

He ran back, over the grille, to the single door, and it opened—stairs went down to the platform, but there was a floor between, a red-brick passage into what must have been the embryonic St. Paul's deep shelter, with the familiar ribs and rivets. Belsey searched through. Not unlike the one beneath Belsize. But at the end of the main dorm there was a low entrance into a maintenance tunnel of some kind. The metal panel that had once sealed it bore blowtorch scars.

Belsey squeezed in. Bricks scraped his shoulders and knocked the bullet wound. For a disorientating moment he was between paler stone, an old crypt or Roman foundations. Then he emerged at another tunnel, crossing the first, this one with narrow-gauge rails. He could tell from its height it was the Mail Rail. He followed the tracks left and arrived at a platform with ornate, glazed tiles reflecting his torchlight. They spelt *King Edward Street*. He knew his way around a Mail Rail station now. Belsey climbed up to the platform, through the loading bays and up the concrete stairs.

After two floors he found himself in a low, dark space crammed with sealed boxes marked *For Shredding*. Metal bins overflowed with rubbish bags. There was a small door in the corner. Belsey opened it. It was a cupboard. The cupboard contained a man sleeping. He was old, in a cleaner's uniform. The walls of the cupboard were decorated like an improvised shrine, beads and plastic flowers and a hologram of the Virgin Mary. Belsey shook him gently by the shoulder.

"I was looking for the way out," he said. "I'm lost."

The man barely opened his eyes. He pointed Belsey towards the end of the corridor, past the bins, then settled back again.

Belsey found a shabby service lift. It took him up one floor and then he was in a brighter corridor with humming servers behind frosted glass walls. He caught his reflection and saw he was still wearing the cathedral audio guide. Belsey hung it around a fire extinguisher. He turned a corner, passed a gym, then numbered doors. He tried doors until one opened. It was a boardroom, empty, with platters of sandwiches under cling film, a pack of papers in front of each seat. Belsey took a pack and marched a little more confidently.

A smarter lift took him two more floors up to ground level. Now there were open-plan offices with Bloomberg screens and a lot of employees in headsets. Belsey gave a nod to a woman, winked at a man, ran towards the barriers at the front and jumped them. He dropped the file and circled back towards the cathedral in time to see a crowd gathering with the hesitant air people have after witnessing drama, unsettled and wanting a bit more. They were all staring at the front of the cathedral as if waiting for a headline act. Belsey joined the crowd.

"What happened?" he asked as police pulled up with a lot of noise and lights.

"Guy with a gun," a man in pinstripes said.

"Which way did he go?"

"I don't know."

An American woman with a tourist map turned. "He had

a hostage with him. A girl." She didn't know where he went either.

Belsey walked back to his car. No sign of Kirsty. He found the news on the radio. Nothing on what had just happened in EC4. He checked the news websites on his phone to see if things had got worse for himself. They'd got a lot worse.

Recent photographs of him now, everywhere. The *Express* led the charge: *Sick Cop and Seven Lovers*. There was the picture of Jemma taped to HANDEL, which only Monroe had received. *Nick Belsey came close to prosecution in his time at Borough police station. Express reporter Thomas Monroe was there.* With a picture of the two of them ten years ago, down in the Ship, Belsey holding a wooden crutch like it was a rifle.

He called Monroe's mobile. Monroe wasn't answering. Belsey tried his office line and got a recording. "This is Tom Monroe's desk. Please leave a message."

"Hi Tom, it's Nick Belsey. Here's a message for you, you prick—"

The phone was lifted. A woman said: "Hi there. You want the Advertising Department. Please call this number—"

"I don't want the fucking Advertising Department. I want Tom Monroe. Put him on."

"I can't help you from this desk." Her voice was unnaturally cheerful. "The offer is for jigsaw puzzles. If you have any complaints regarding the promotion please call this number." She gave the number. Belsey wrote it down. It was a mobile number. She hung up. He waited for a moment then dialled.

Someone answered but didn't speak—heels clipped fast down a corridor, then a door opened, a tap ran, a second door was bolted.

"Nick Belsey?" she said. Same woman.

"What's going on?"

"They're going through the office. We're not allowed to leave."

"Who is this?"

"Jill Banner. I work with Tom. They've taken his computer. But he wasn't researching you, I'm sure. He said he'd found something to do with a thing called JIGSAW."

"What did he have?"

"I don't know. This is just from a note he left. There's an arrest warrant out for him now."

"For what?"

"Conspiracy to breach the Official Secrets Act."

"You know the stuff about me is crap."

"I don't know anything. Just that Tom said you were working on something big. This JIGSAW thing. He was researching something for you. That's all I know. Someone from the Cabinet Office just visited the editor. I don't know what's going on. All this attention on Tom, it's not coming from within the paper."

"What do you know about JIGSAW?"

"Just that he left a note—that's what he was working on. Honestly, that's all."

"Where is Tom now?"

"I think Kew."

"Kew?" The name startled him. Those lines, towards the end of Easton's sessions with Green. *New interest in nature . . . Has been spending time at the Botanic Gardens in Kew. Says they are teaching him patience . . . Everything breaks through eventually.* An attraction to Kew was one of the remaining mysteries of Easton's last months. "Why Kew?"

"I don't know."

Belsey was already finding the case notes and bank statements, searching through the torn pages.

"The gardens?"

"I really don't know. When I last spoke to him he was driving to Kew. Please, that's all I can tell you. Someone's coming." The call ended.

BELSEY DROVE TOWARDS KEW, tuning his radio to the channel for Kew Constabulary. Sure enough, by the time he was on Chiswick High Road he picked up arresting officers. It seemed if you threatened to break the Official Secrets Act, you got the executive service—custody in minutes, and nowhere to hide.

"Yes, a Mr. Thomas Monroe. A journalist. What exactly are we meant to do with him, sir?"

"There are instructions to hold him. Just keep him detained while we clarify the situation."

"He'll be at Kew police station, sir. By the gardens."

"OK. Apparently a Gabriel Bennington is on his way."

Belsey sped over Kew Bridge, swinging left towards the police station. He was there in two minutes. He felt some relief seeing the place: it looked halfway between a cottage and a large shed; a keep-warm area for the handful of constables assigned to the Botanic Gardens. Its own front garden was in full bloom.

But it was outside of its comfort zone. Belsey could tell as he approached. A sergeant stood in the car park. They'd put a plastic cone down for their special visitor. A couple of officers glanced out of the windows. Belsey aimed for the cone and crushed it. He lifted his mobile as he got out of the car.

"Yes, of course," he said loudly into it. "It's a police station not an embassy, sir. We'll be with you shortly." He walked past the Sergeant into reception. There were framed photographs of plants on the wall, no officers under fifty. "Sir, the Attorney General can speak to him when we've got him. I'm at the station now." Belsey moved the phone an inch from his ear.

"Where is he?"

A nervous, moustached officer put his cap on and led Belsey through to the secure holding area. Monroe's name was up on an old blackboard. Belsey wiped it off.

"His possessions?"

They were in a bag waiting on the desk. Belsey grabbed the bag. Someone slid the custody book towards him for signing and Belsey tore the page out. He started towards the cell.

"No one in or out, no matter who they say they are. Open it."

The custody officer unlocked Monroe's cell and backed away. The journalist was standing, red-eyed and unshaven. He'd eschewed the rubber mattress and placed himself as far as possible from an iron bucket in the corner.

"Let's go," Belsey said.

"What's happening?"

"Follow me and don't say anything."

They left the cell. Belsey steered Monroe through front reception, past the open-mouthed Sergeant to his car. Monroe blinked at the daylight.

"I need a lawyer," he said.

"You need Amnesty International, Tom. The intelligence services are on their way. Get in."

They climbed into Belsey's Skoda as a fleet of more lustrous cars appeared. Belsey tore past. He was halfway down Mortlake Road before Monroe had the passenger door closed.

TRAFFIC WAS SOLID UP AHEAD, THE ROAD NARROWED TO one channel by Transport Police. Belsey tried to see if they were pulling vehicles over. It didn't look promising. Belsey turned the car around.

"You're covered in blood," Monroe said.

"Someone shot me."

Kew Bridge now had an Armed Response Vehicle parked at one end, a police Transit van at the other. Belsey braked, turned again. It seemed they were trapped in a peninsula of south-west London. He saw signs pointing to Kew Retail Park. It seemed as good an option as any. Crowd cover, at least. Maybe pick up a bargain. He swerved towards it.

"You know you're all over the news," Monroe said.

"I know. I'm shot and I'm all over the news and now I'm trapped in Kew. Why the fuck is that?"

Belsey swung into the retail park: T.K. Maxx, M&S, Next; each occupied its own monumental grey box. T.K. Maxx had the crowds. Belsey parked up close enough to be hidden, but not too far from the exit back to the main road. He kept the engine running.

"The article, about you—they took the photos off my computer," Monroe said.

"I figured that."

"Well you didn't figure this: the IT department had someone visit them two months ago, warning them that they might receive classified intelligence, and to pass on anything that looked remotely suspicious. Sure enough, someone began sending emails a week later, saying they had information about an event in 1983. The sender used the name Michael Forrester. The same thing happened at other papers apparently. Mr. Forrester was firing emails to anyone he could get an address for, only they were all diverted straight to MI6."

"What were these emails saying?"

"I don't know. But apparently a man using the name Michael Forrester went into Wood Street police station ten days ago saying he needed police protection. Did you hear about this?"

"No."

"I spoke to the DI there. This individual thought his life was under threat. Some jobsworth at Wood Street notified the intelligence services and the police were told to place him under arrest. So he fled. Around that time he sends another batch of emails. Only now he's Ferryman. He's been gagged from the start, Nick. You see? Duncan found something. He passed it on. Now our Ferryman has put all press on standby. He wants them to watch you, where you go. He says something is about to happen."

"Great. And why are we in Kew?"

Monroe pointed through the back windscreen. Rising above the retail outlets was a long modern building.

"To see what's been declassified."

"What is that?"

"The National Archives. The date, you see. Now. It's 2013."

"I remember."

"The exercise was 1983, thirty years ago. Duncan Powell tracked declassification dates. Government material is kept out of the public domain for thirty years. Then, unless someone raises objections, it's released. Duncan would track dates, ascertain what made it into the light of day and what had been held back. He called it gap hunting. At the beginning of the year a tranche of new files was released. That was around the time he got in touch with his publisher. So I thought maybe he'd found something in the archives."

"And was there anything there?"

"I never got the chance to find out. Your colleagues picked me up as soon as I crossed the river."

Belsey handed him the last page from the case notes.

"Read this. It's the final session Michael Easton had with his therapist."

Monroe read it out loud: "Even government secrets have their own seasons—they will surface when it is time. In his dreams or someone else's. In slips of the tongue."

The journalist gave a dazed smile. "He's talking about the release of files. Where did you get this?"

"I borrowed it."

Monroe read the entry again.

"He's gone to the National Archives."

"It certainly sounds like it."

"No, he has. Look, this number at the bottom: DEFE then something like 1139."

"What is it?"

"That's a file reference. DEFE means defence-related material."

Belsey started the car.

"Where are we going?"

"Where do you think?"

Monroe pulled the handbrake on.

"I'm not getting arrested again."

"OK. I'm going there. I need to see what it was Duncan Powell found. I need to know where Easton is heading. Kirsty Craik might get in touch with you. Keep an eye on your phone."

Monroe opened the passenger door and jumped out. Then he leaned back in.

"You'll need a pass," he said. "For the archives."

"I've got police badge and a handgun," Belsey said. "I think I'll manage."

BELSEY CUT THROUGH NEAT RESIDENTIAL STREETS. THE National Archives appeared again, rising from stagnant ponds, the size of an airport. He drove right up to the glass doors. He unpacked another fentanyl lollipop and stuck it between his teeth and his gum. His mouth was dry. Belsey tested his pulse. It was there. He could afford up to three pints of blood. He checked the Webley, transferred it to his jacket and angled the rear-view mirror down: blood through his clothes, eyes pinned, jacket bulky with antique weaponry. This wasn't a surreptitious look.

49

He got out of the car and stumbled. Sharpen up. He headed through the revolving glass doors into a reception. The young woman on the desk took one look at him and picked up the phone.

"I'm police," he said. He followed signs for the reading room away from the anxious receptionist through a canteen. There were screens everywhere, it seemed: all showing BBC News—in reception, up on the canteen wall—all with his face on. Why did an archive need so many fucking TV screens? *Nationwide Hunt . . .*

Past lockers, up stairs, breathing, calm.

The first floor had a public area with PC terminals and an enquiry desk before you got to security barriers into the reading room. The reading room was filled with men and women browsing yellowing tomes of officialdom. It shimmered on the other side of the barriers. Belsey blinked. His vision had known sharper days, splintering now into hallucinatory fragments. Posters advised on family research and local history. "Enquiries": he headed for the sign. A small woman in a grey suit and a bald man with a brown beard took one look at him and pressed the alarm button.

"Wait," Belsey said, pointlessly.

He reached for his badge, pulled the gun. Someone screamed. People turned, then a lot of amateur historians hit the floor.

An amber alarm light flashed. The National Archives—that would connect to more than just the garden-centre constabulary. He leaned over the enquiries counter.

"I've got an enquiry. I'm looking for this file." He produced the case notes, tried a wave of the gun. The bearded man was holding up best. He checked the code and entered it into the computer.

"It was recently in use. Should be up here. You don't need to hurt anyone."

"I don't intend to hurt anyone."

The man led him through, past the security barrier. Guards watched the gun, hands raised; they looked as old as the files they were meant to be protecting. To one side were stacks of clear-fronted cabinets, like doors at a morgue. The bearded man checked their numbers, opened one and produced a small box.

"Where do you want it?"

"On the table."

He put it down. It was a plain brown cardboard box the size of a telephone directory. Belsey picked it up with his free hand. It was light. He flipped the lid off. Inside was one tattered manila folder. *MINISTRY OF DEFENCE—TOP SECRET—ACID.* Official stamps overlaid one another. Then, diagonally across them: "Declassified 2013." The next page was the front of the file itself.

MACHINERY OF GOVERNMENT IN THE EVENT OF NUCLEAR WAR
SITE 3 RESEARCH PROGRAMME
COMMAND CHAIN AND INITIATED PERSONNEL

Belsey opened it. He stared at the yellow cardboard back of the folder. Nothing remained inside the sleeves apart from a piece of string and a corner of white paper. Someone had torn the whole thing out.

He closed the box and sat down. He placed the gun on the table, listened to the sirens approaching.

Sorry, Jemma. He would spend his life watching the torchlight disappear. Rewinding that evening and starting again. Almost 3:30 p.m., according to the clock on the reading room wall. She had another two and a half hours to live. And he could do nothing about it.

He tried to light a cigarette and his arm felt like it was encased in metal. Belsey gave up. Through the windows around the side of the room he could see the day over halfway done, mid-afternoon ready to become late afternoon. It was Friday. Out in the world there would be that sweet, quiet relief that, no matter how awful it had been, things were over. The week was over.

He considered self-medicating. He knew what he'd get in custody: some disinterested duty medic with a couple of milligrams of morphine. If he was lucky. He watched the strange scene he'd created, people under desks praying, curled up like it was rest time, their work left open above them. Abandoned pencils scattered. Then he stopped. Every pencil was missing its eraser.

Belsey got unsteadily to his feet. He picked up a pencil, ran his thumb over the metal sleeve where the rubber should have been. He looked around. He wasn't imagining it. There, in a neat pile on the guard's desk, were the missing pink nodules. Alongside other confiscated items: bottles of water, a packet of mints, Tippex. Belsey walked over. The guard was nowhere to be seen. He lifted a sheet of regulations.

Restricted items: food and drink, blades, glue, any kind of eraser.

The bearded man was watching him.

"Do you need something?" he asked.

"I need to know who had that file most recently. Who was the last person to request it?"

The man went back to his enquiries desk and tapped a key.

"A Dr. Joseph Green," he said. "Had it out two days ago."

BELSEY KEPT TO BACK ROADS, HEADING NORTH, TO-
wards Highgate. Towards Windmill Drive. Fragments from the past four days coalesced in his
damaged mind.

*Michael came to London for him. Because he
thought Joseph would help. That's what he said.*

Hugh Hamilton saw Michael
Easton on 17 April. That was
four days after Easton's return
from travelling. But it was Joseph he was after. *Michael had
read all of his work. He quoted
from it. I'm sure Joseph loved
that.* Belsey thought back to his
own first meeting with the doctor. He saw Joseph studying
Military Heritage through the plastic of the evidence bag. That would have been minutes after
Easton had announced that he was done with
therapy, that state secrets will find their own way
out. That he had been spending time at Kew.

No one answered at the doctor's house. The
front door was open. Belsey walked through to the
study. Joseph Green lay face down on the rug, one
arm outstretched. He looked like he was trying to
swim through his own blood. A very old hunting
knife lay a foot from his outstretched hand.

He asks whether I believe in hell, whether killing can ever be justified, whether there is a limit to forgiveness.

Asks if I'd forgive my own killer if I met them, before or after death.

Belsey turned slowly. The doctor had armed himself. He'd come to their final meeting prepared. But the hunting knife was clean. He'd been moving around the desk when he was stabbed by something more effective. The desk was knocked crooked. There had been a struggle in which papers and books had fallen, a handprint where he had tried to support himself against the wall.

Belsey crouched and felt his neck. No pulse. But Belsey could hear breathing. He wasn't the only living person in the room.

He eased himself up. There was someone behind the door. Belsey took the Webley out, then kicked the door hard into the body of the individual. It sprang back towards him.

"No!" Hamilton crouched. He held a leather briefcase in front of him as a shield. Belsey lowered the gun. "I just got here," the disciple spluttered. "I don't have anything to do with this. I just . . . I was told to come here."

A voice in Hamilton's hand said: "Could you repeat which service you require: police, fire or ambulance?"

"Hang up," Belsey said. Hamilton killed the call. He glanced at the gun then Belsey's blood-soaked sleeve. The call had connected. So they would be tracing it. Six-minute average response to a high-priority call in a dense urban area.

"You were told to come here?" Belsey said.

"My wife took a message—Joseph was ready to start participating again, to talk. I should come here immediately. But

I think it was a . . . It wasn't true. It was Michael. Michael who told me to come here." His voice trailed off.

Belsey studied the body again. No blotches of lividity. Less than twenty minutes dead. Hamilton moved for the door.

"Stay there," Belsey said. He turned the body just enough to see multiple stab wounds across the front of the torso then eased the corpse back. "Where was Joseph in November 1983?" he asked.

"Why?"

"I need to know." Belsey glanced around the study as if something might tell him—the old books on anthropology, ritual, nature; *Mankind and Community, The Psychology of Survival.* "The argument you were having with him when I was last here—you were asking him about his training. Was it about that period? The eighties?"

"No. Not at all. It was about Otto Brodsky. His Prague seminars. Just that. I don't—"

"Prague?"

"Yes."

"What about it?"

"This isn't to do with me."

"Tell me about Prague."

"Joseph always said he was in Paris in the late sixties. But everything he wrote in that period echoes the early work of Otto Brodsky. And then I received evidence that Joseph studied with him, in Prague. He's never spoken about it."

"You've got that evidence with you?"

"Yes, I thought . . ." Hamilton looked for somewhere to rest his briefcase that wasn't a corpse. He crouched down again, opened it on his knee and handed Belsey a smudged photocopy. *Akademie Psychoanalýzy.* It was an article written in Czech. Joseph Green's name sheltered amid cramped columns of thick type, exposed by yellow highlighter.

"It's a list of speakers from the 1967 Prague Congress," Hamilton explained, still shaking. He glanced at Green's corpse, too busy bleeding to contest its biography. "Joseph's on the list. Guest of the Prague Psychoanalytic Study Group. That's Joseph delivering a paper, see, followed by Otto Brodsky and Claudio Laks, of the Czechoslovak Institute of Psychiatry."

"Where did you get this?"

"It was posted to me anonymously."

"When?"

"About seven weeks ago." Belsey did the maths. As he expected, seven weeks ago was just after Easton's return from the Czech Republic. "Evidently someone recognised its value," Hamilton said.

"What's its value?"

"The encounter is clearly where he got everything—his whole approach to analysis. And, of course, conveniently for Joseph, very few analysts had the opportunity to study with Brodsky."

"Because Czechoslovakia was communist."

"Exactly. He went there and learnt to imitate a new approach. And when he returned, he passed the theory off as his own. Why else would Joseph be so quiet about his visit?"

"Because he was a spy."

Hamilton adopted an odd smile.

"A spy?"

"He was recruited by the KGB. What did he say exactly when you presented him with this evidence?"

"He was furious," Hamilton said, quietly.

Belsey looked around. Back from Prague, evidence in hand, Michael starts his sessions. And he knows—he knows from the start he is sitting opposite the man who killed his family. He bides his time, toying with his prey. But still wanting more. He needs to find out exactly what happened. He wants to know what Ferryman did, and how to get back there.

"Do you have any idea where Joseph was working in 1983?"

"Some provincial backwater. Working for the government." The strange smile returned, like someone discovering they are the object of a joke.

"Working for the government?"

"A survey of welfare. He didn't talk about it much. He thought it was unglamorous. It was where he met Rebecca."

Again, lines from the case notes were returning to Belsey. *He begins asking questions about my family, my relationship with my wife, how we met.* Belsey imagined Michael here, session after session, getting closer. *He has been turning up for sessions either early or late. Today I arrive and he is sitting behind my desk.*

Belsey stepped over the corpse and sat in the doctor's chair. There were the pencils, the files. There was the defensive wall of framed photographs. A girl on a bike, a sepia couple in their wedding clothes. Finally, in faded colour, a very young Rebecca Green. Belsey wiped the blood off the frame with his cuff. Rebecca stood by a gate with fields behind her. Young and beautiful. Stuck in a provincial back-water. The fields behind her were striped with shadows. The sun was low. The shadows stretched from standing stones.

The main stone was tall and thin. The other six were smaller stumps forming a crescent, like teeth in a jawbone. Belsey turned the desk lamp on. He followed the slope of the fields, past the stones, to the slate of the human habitation in the distance. Roofs clustered around a blunt church spire. Woods ran halfway up a hill above the village.

"What is it?" Hamilton asked.

"Piltbury."

Belsey turned Green's PC on. Here came the sirens, from the west, from Hampstead. He ignored them. He pulled up a map of Piltbury. There was the church, the high street, the hill with the holiday cottage. There were those blank, white spaces all around it. Belsey clicked to satellite view. From the air they weren't so blank; you could see large sections of land fenced off, long, thin buildings at right angles to one an-other. You could also see that something wasn't right with several houses on the edge of the village. Instead of roofs they had ventilation slats.

He found similar structures to the north, about a mile away. Then he spotted a third group, more than two miles south.

Belsey sat back. He stared at the screen, then the photo-graph. Michael gets behind the desk, sees the photo. A new theory emerges: his deep memories aren't subterranean Lon-don after all. He locates the standing stones. Decides it's time for a country break. In Piltbury he must have begun to realise the size of Site 3. That's when he knows he has to find

William Lanzer. He's going in; he needs to know his way around.

Then it's just a question of saying goodbye to the man who killed him and he's off.

4:49 p.m. The front door opened.

"Joseph?"

Rebecca Green. Hamilton looked to the door, then to Belsey. Sirens turned onto the road.

"Joseph? Sweetheart?"

Belsey stepped over the body to the couch. He opened the window and sat on the sill. Hamilton stared at him. The poor bastard was going to have some explaining to do.

"Want to come through the window?" Belsey asked. The disciple shook his head. "Do Rebecca a favour and stop her getting in here. She doesn't need to see this."

Hamilton nodded. He didn't move. Belsey jumped out.

THE POLICE ENTERED 12 WINDMILL DRIVE A FEW SEC-
onds after Rebecca. Belsey held back until they
were inside then ran to his car. The screaming
from the house started as he began to drive.

Warm corpse. Easton had been there less
than half an hour before Belsey arrived. There
was only one quick route to Pilt-
bury. Belsey kept a look-out for
white vans, driving one-handed,
ignoring the pain in his immo-
bile right arm. He put his phone
on speaker and called Wiltshire
police as he swerved onto the
M4, giving a description of
Easton.

51

"Consider him armed and
dangerous. He'll be heading for Piltbury if he's
not already there. He has a hostage with him, a
young woman. She's called Jemma Stevens."

"Piltbury?" They sounded incredulous.
"We're not getting any command-level instructions to that effect."

"Well, all hell's about to break loose. Someone should have told you."

"Who is this?"

There was another call coming in. Belsey
switched.

"Nick? It's me, Kirsty."

"Don't tell me where you are."

"I think I'm safe. Where are you?"

"On the M4. Can you get online?"

"Nick, you need to stop while you're still alive. It's a miracle we made it this far. I can get us help."

"I need you to get a map of Piltbury up. It's got Site 3 under it."

"Piltbury?"

"There's an underground railway from London to Piltbury. Easton had made Freedom of Information requests about the government purchase of rail track—track used for this connection. That's how they would have got the government out of London. That's the last resort—the move."

He managed to open the road map on the passenger seat with one hand.

"I've got Piltbury," Craik said.

"Can you see those fenced-off areas?" Belsey said. "With the long, narrow buildings?"

"The military bases."

"Bases?"

"If that's what you're talking about. There's a few of them. The closest is called Rudloe Manor. Hang on . . . It's an RAF Communications and Command headquarters."

"Where?"

"In Hawthorn. Then there's Basil Hill Barracks half a mile to the east of that. Something called Piltbury MOD Computer Centre just north of the village. The place has more military business than civilian going on."

Belsey balanced the map on his knees. He tried to navigate the village in his mind. He reached the pub. The Quarry House. It struck him now as a curious choice of name.

"In the village there's a pub called the Quarry House. Where's the quarry?"

"Wait. OK, I've got a history of the area. Yeah, it used to be all mining around there. Bath stone, first real rock as you head west from London. The mines are disused now."

"Where were they?"

"Everywhere, by the looks of it. The core was in Spring Quarry to the south-west of Chippenham."

"Where else? How far does it extend?"

"Well, there was a mine at Hudswell, one at Monkton Farleigh."

Belsey pulled up on the hard shoulder, searched the map and found Hudswell and Monkton Farleigh. He got the area on satellite view on his phone. You could trace the mines by the vents. They extended west to Bath, east to Chippenham, down to Melksham in the south. If the bunker occupied the old mines, it was the size of a town. He thought of the blood map and began to adjust his sense of scale.

"How would you get down there, Kirsty?"

"I wouldn't."

"If you really felt you had to."

"A vent."

There appeared to be only one vent that wasn't sheltered amid barracks. It was in a field just beyond a house on the outskirts of Piltbury itself. Hill View House.

"I think I know where he's heading."

He started the car, cut back onto the motorway.

"And you're going to do this on your own?"

"No, I'm taking a lot of supportive friends with me. What do you think?"

"I think you'll be in a great place for people to kill you."

Belsey was trying to decide if there was anything else he needed to say—something honest, maybe a farewell. He lost reception before he thought of the words. It cut as he passed the sign for Piltbury.

THERE WAS SOMETHING WRONG WITH THE SKY. BELSEY
saw as he approached the village. The portion
capping Piltbury was streaked with elaborate
cloud formations. He thought, at first glance,
that there was a fire somewhere, but the smoke
wasn't black, it was bright orange.

He took the turn-off and Piltbury was gone, lost in spreading
orange clouds. Easton must have
covered the area fast, setting off
those Combat Effect flares. The
smoke seemed to have at least five
sources. It was expanding, rolling
out across fields and narrow
country roads, joining other
clouds. It hung in trees, confused
cattle.

52

Belsey wound his window down and heard a
helicopter. It appeared a few seconds later, grazing the top of the smoke, too streamlined for police. As it got closer he saw it was an army Lynx,
low enough for the machine guns to be visible.
Welcome to Wiltshire. Michael had been right to
take precautions.

A second helicopter joined it from the west,
stirring up the smoke trails. Fumes started creeping into the car and Belsey wound the window

back up. The orange pall was now swallowing cottages as it drifted southwest.

He drove on. Smoke congealed, smothering the world. Visibility reduced to a foot or so. There was a bellow of horn, then a green Bedford military truck filled his windscreen. Belsey skidded up the grass verge. Ten seconds later he passed a motorbike on the ground, a camper van in a ditch. Then a convoy of armoured personnel carriers tore past. The countryside was releasing its military.

He checked the mirrors. Someone was on his tail. A flatbed truck appeared from the haze. Its khaki-clad driver waved for him to pull over. Troops appeared at the entrance to the village cradling submachine guns. The soldiers started waving too. Someone had a megaphone:

"Stop now. Do not proceed. This village is closed."

Belsey proceeded. How can you close a village? Objects loomed and vanished: civilian cars, a bus shelter. The police-band radio relayed orders for Wiltshire Police to stay away. Then it cut altogether. They'd jammed the signal. A third helicopter joined the first two, trying to slice through the expanding tangerine fog with a beam of light.

Belsey navigated blind. He aimed for Hill View House. Dogs barked from trees on either side. Red lights flashed on a temporary sign by the roundabout: *ROAD CLOSED*.

He drove past. Two armed men in overalls and respirators tried to block him, then dived out of the way. A bullet ricocheted off the undercarriage of the Skoda and took out his front right wheel. He slid down in his seat as a second smashed a wing mirror. Belsey careered past the church, narrowly missed the phone box and crashed into the woods by Easton's old holiday home. He scraped to a stop with a branch bent against his windscreen. Ahead of him, wedged deeper into the trees, was a white Vauxhall Vivaro. Belsey grabbed the Webley and his torch.

The Vivaro's engine was still warm to the touch, back doors open, packaging for detonation cord and explosives on the floor of the hold. Belsey stumbled on towards the cottage, following a trail of broken branches and scuffed ground. He ran past the cottage to the hillside, over the crest of the hill to what Belsey hadn't seen last time he was here and could barely see through the orange smoke: high chain-link topped with barbed wire. Beyond it, built into the side of the rocky incline, was a small door into the grass.

The fence had been cut. Belsey ran for the gap.

The explosion threw him backwards. He found himself on the ground with soil and stone raining into his face. He covered his head. His ears were ringing. A black dot occupied the centre of his field of vision. Then it faded. As he got to his feet again he realised that some of the ringing was from alarms.

He crawled through the cut fence. Patches of grass smouldered, puddles of flame dotting the field. The hill itself had been torn open to expose concrete and metal. He could feel the heat coming off the fallen bricks. The air was even thicker now, dust mingling with the orange smoke. Broken lengths of wire hung across the newly ripped entrance.

Belsey climbed over the warm rubble. He pushed through the wires and found himself in a narrow aluminium duct. It ended abruptly at a sheer drop with an emergency ladder nailed into the rough stone of the air shaft. Belsey couldn't see the bottom as he started to climb down.

FIVE MINUTES' DESCENT AND HE WAS IN WHAT LOOKED like a cramped corner of the old mine, chipped limestone walls interrupted on one side by flat twentieth-century brickwork. The bricks surrounded a black, blast-proof door. Belsey pulled it open and walked through into neon light.

53

He stood beside a ventilation fan the size of a jet engine. Its twin stood motionless at the distant end of a train platform. Strip lights ran the length of the ceiling. A row of wooden guards' booths faced the tracks: *Consent to Searches. Decontamination Mandatory.* Shrill, metallic alarms echoed from the depths of the bunker.

Belsey walked down the platform to the checkpoint and past the booths into a reception hall with steep escalators on either side like frozen waterfalls. Two boards hung down on chains, giving a choice of sectors: *Cabinet, Air Ministry, Communications, Hospital* . . . Beyond the hall was a crossroads. The passageways leading out from here were wide enough to drive two cars side by side.

Belsey saw movement ahead and ran. Emergency lights striped the darkness. Doorways led into small rooms. Soon he found himself in a zone of offices: chairs wrapped in brown paper, one room with twenty or thirty black telephones tangled on the floor. The air was damp. There was a crushing loneliness in the place. It entered through the nostrils and stuck in the chest, tightening to claustrophobia. After five minutes the offices became bedrooms, with narrow iron bed-frames. Then he reached another crossroads: square concrete corridors, no sign of life. The alarms were fainter now. He ran again, trying to note landmarks: tendrils of seaweed-like growth across the bricks, a pair of sewing machines on a wooden box. He found a guard's booth with a signpost beside it: *BBC Studio ½ mile, Telephone Exchange 1 mile* . . . It had a map of more local facilities pasted to the wall: a dentist, a police station, two workshops, a laundry. Belsey was making his choice when doors began to slam: someone less than a minute away, searching, lost as he was.

"Jemma!" he called, and her voice came back so faint he thought he might have imagined it.

"Nick!'

Then a scream. He headed for the scream. Into the Government Sector, according to the checkpoints. The Government Sector had whitewashed walls. Signs pointed down dark corridors: *Intelligence Staff, Treasury, Home Office*. It was unlit: no alarms, no lights. Belsey switched his torch on. Another scream. The corridor ended at a set of double doors and he pushed through into what looked like a long laboratory with extractor hoods, tea urns on the floor, a row of bread ovens. A few seconds later he was in a canteen with long benches. He tried calling Jemma's name again. Silence.

He headed onto the main thoroughfare. Rooms looked familiar. He knew he hadn't doubled back. Don't lose it, he thought, not now. He arrived at an intersection with a dead rat by the wall and made a mental note of it. There was a different smell now, of places more forgotten, more fungal. He ran past IV-drip stands and crates of cutlery into a long storeroom, its stacks of cardboard boxes rotted into a landscape of half-subsided formations. He aimed his torch.

"Nick, he's got a gun." Jemma's voice was clear. He couldn't see her. A shot whistled past. He moved into the cover of a cardboard stack. Next time he looked they were in the open, two hundred metres beyond him: Jemma with her shorn scalp, Easton with head torch and fume mask. He had equipment strapped to him: rucksack, tool belt, a gun in one hand, a map in the other. Jemma was cuffed to the tool belt. The gun was a semi-automatic of some kind. He fired it again. Belsey waited. In the silence that followed he heard another sound, this one from the maze he'd just passed through. Flapping wings, he thought. Was that possible? Birds. Or maybe the rumble of thunder. It took him a moment to realise it was a lot of heavy military boots.

"Nick!"

A stack of boxes tumbled towards him. Doors slammed on the far side of what was now a more jagged landscape. Belsey pushed his way through, choking on clouds of powdered milk. The sound of boots had become a constant drum roll. He stepped through rotten cardboard, over mounds of ashtrays and nail brushes. He could hear military commands. The sign on the door out of the room wasn't inviting: *NO ENTRY. DANGER.*

Belsey opened it and stared.

A lake stretched away from him, black water rippling beneath a low brick sky. He followed the ripples with his torch and saw Jemma splashing, falling. Easton had one hand around her neck, the other holding his rucksack out of the water as he plunged forward.

Belsey jumped in. The water was freezing. It lapped at his thighs. He held the Webley and torch at chest height and chased as best as he could. The bottom of the lake sloped downwards until the cold clenched around his stomach. Difficult striding. He didn't fancy a confrontation in the water. Jemma's cries echoed off the vaulted brickwork.

Easton was cutting across diagonally. He knew where he was going. Belsey kept in their wake. The far shore appeared, and Belsey saw them haul themselves out of the water before disappearing further into the tunnels beyond.

He dragged himself out thirty seconds later and lay dripping onto a grated walkway. There was a notice on the wall.

WEST CENTRAL SECTOR
SEVERE STRUCTURAL DAMAGE
ENTRY STRICTLY FORBIDDEN.

Belsey got to his feet. A ramp sunk away from the water's edge. Belsey followed the drip trail under low pipes, down a long, tight corridor. He could smell something awful lingering. They were approaching the scene of whatever had occurred. He turned the corner and saw Easton and Jemma sixty metres ahead. Easton had the rucksack off, mask up, working away at the final barrier: a small, dented black door. He had pliers in one hand, gun in the other, det cord and plastic explosives at his feet. Belsey kept close to the wall. Jemma was uncuffed but anytime she moved Easton raised the gun.

"Michael," Belsey said. Easton fired towards him. Belsey pressed himself back against the bricks. He inched closer, watching explosives being moulded, watching the gun hand. He heard the sudden roar of churning water behind him, shouted commands.

"Give her to me. I'm not going to stop you." Easton looked at Belsey. Belsey snapped the Webley and let the bullets spill to the ground. Easton waved Jemma away and she ran. She collapsed into Belsey's arms, then slid from his arms to the ground.

"Are you OK?" Belsey asked, not taking his eyes off Easton. He couldn't hear her answer. It was a stupid question. Easton was alone with the door now. He needed his hands free to sort the detonation cord, but that meant putting his own gun down. Belsey could see him trying to decide. He glanced around, met Belsey's eyes. Then he put his gun down and picked up the pliers.

"There's nothing there. Michael. What do you expect to find?"

No response. Belsey picked up one of the bullets. He looked at the black door, at Easton sweating, almost home. The cord was rigged around the door handles. Get it open, Belsey thought.

Too late.

The corridor was tangled in red and green lines, a cat's cradle of laser sights.

"Step away!"

Easton took a lighter from his pocket. He clicked it as floodlight drowned the corridor. Belsey squinted in the sudden glare.

"Step away with your hands raised or we will fire."

The cord's safety fuse sparked. Easton moved aside. Everything happened at once. Someone shot. The cord blew. There was intense heat, and now everyone was firing, a barrage of metal against metal. The passage filled with acrid smoke. Then silence.

Belsey put his hands up. It seemed prudent. He expected they might do away with him now, under the cover of this moment. They'd shown they could do it efficiently enough. Someone said: "Hold fire."

Easton lay on his back. He'd lost an arm and the left side of his face. Belsey walked over, hands still raised. No one shot him. It seemed this was the actual army rather than some faction of the intelligence services bent on his destruction. He checked there was nothing among the entrails that was still live, ticking or burning, rigged to make a final statement. He paid his last respects. Blood soaked his shoes.

"Step away."

Belsey straightened. He could hear someone tending to Jemma. Beyond Easton's body, the metal door lay off its hinges. Belsey tried to see through the gap. He stepped closer. Then he found himself stepping through.

It took his eyes a moment to adjust. The space was vast, with a domed ceiling high above structures that were themselves two or three floors tall. Supporting pillars rose several hundred feet to the roof. The buildings sheltering beneath the dome formed what appeared to be a street carved from charcoal.

The smell uncoiled in his chest. He had only experienced something like it once before, after a fire at a hospital. You felt it in the bones, sad and sinister. He stepped between the buildings, climbing over debris and fallen beams. Walls had collapsed, revealing shelves, charred desks, piles of books and deep drifts of singed paper. Somewhere in the police part of his brain he was reading the damage, looking for evidence of arson, accelerants, for whatever kept them trapped. He was imagining being eight here. How terrifying. How odd. You would try to escape. Maybe get lost in the maze beyond. And then, to find you could never return . . . He passed stumps of what looked like cinema seats, a small room with the remains of the alphabet around its walls. Then the path opened out and he arrived at a central square bordered by individual stone buildings.

He was turning, wondering where you'd retreat to, what you'd do in the final moments, when he saw it, across the square. Its roof was gone but the bar survived. Belsey stepped over what remained of the Red Lion's front wall. It had seen better days. Glassware lay in sooty shards. He picked up a pewter tankard. A single stool waited by the bar. He swept the ash off and sat down.

Soldiers passed on the other side of the crumbled wall, following the beams of their headlamps, guns lowered. They were silent now. Their lights reached the outer shell of the domed chamber revealing murals painted onto concrete, smoke-blackened depictions of the seasons, fields of corn, phases of the moon. Belsey watched paratroopers, bulky with armour, lowering themselves from hatches in the dome itself, abseiling down and stopping mid-descent, twisting on their ropes.

He was barely aware of the rest. Someone grabbed him. There were stairs, dogs, an electric buggy. He emerged through a narrow doorway into the grounds of a military base with whitewashed barracks and the largest sky he'd ever seen. Jemma lay on the grass, wrapped in a foil blanket, receiving oxygen. Belsey lay down a few feet away from her.

"Sorry," he said.

He declined the oxygen. He breathed Wiltshire air. Scraps of orange smoke unravelled, marbling the sky like drops of blood in water. The air smelt of grass and boot polish. He watched a flag of the Royal Air Force stroke the breeze, then closed his eyes.

Epilogue

FAMILIES CROWDED THE TRAIN TO WILTSHIRE, STAND-
ing in aisles, gazing out as the city became suburbs and then brown fields. Belsey changed at
Chippenham, accompanying the throng onto the
antiquated branch line that would take them towards Piltbury. He could smell bonfires.

Men and women had gathered at Piltbury station, wrapped in waterproofs. It took him a moment to realise that they were all here for the
ceremony as well. The event had brought mini-
cabs out from the adjacent villages. There was a
tentative sense of festivity.

All were heading for the new memorial. It
had been sited at the top of the hill, above the
village, not so far from the vent Michael Easton
had blown. People moved towards it like a
matchday crowd, clogging the village's narrow
high street.

The national papers ran Piltbury and its secrets for several days. There was outrage and
some penitence. It had been, the politicians

agreed, a different world, with the threat of nuclear war, two superpowers, and undoubtedly different people in government. Soon other stories hit the news and interest began to move on. Belsey was suspended on full pay. Senior people scratched their heads. Two days of debriefing had left him and his anonymous interviewers drained. They weren't a great deal older than he was. Besides, all he could reveal was a succession of poor decisions. He may have caused someone somewhere a degree of embarrassment but he felt sure the intelligence services would reform themselves around the wound.

Belsey's tribunal was set for November. He helped Jemma sell her story, which brought in more than a crate of dusty champagne would have done. He couldn't sell his own due to the ongoing investigation into his conduct, but he ensured Monroe had everything, as some form of insurance for himself as well as favours returned. Monroe spun it out and coined in heavily. He got the scoop on the sabotage and mentioned everything apart from the true identity of Ferryman. Belsey asked him about this, over drinks in the Jamaica, and got a vague answer about family privacy, which made him laugh into his pint. But Belsey thought he understood. A secret's nothing once it's shared. Sometimes you want to keep a little back. Or maybe someone had had words with Tom Monroe. Polite ones, anonymously, about where to draw the line. Maybe they gave him money too. Monroe's book on the subject was due out around Christmas.

Kirsty Craik disappeared. A few weeks later, Belsey heard she'd been moved to the Midlands Specialist Crime

Unit. He got a call from a mutual acquaintance on the team, DC Jason Stock.

"She single?"

"I don't know, Jason. Ask her. Is she OK?"

"She asked me if I'd heard from you. Asking after you, like."

"Did she?"

"What's that about? Did you do her, mate?"

Belsey returned to Hotel President. At one point he started packing. Eventually the removal boxes settled in. Sometimes he'd sit at night, listening to the pipes, looking at the picture of the crowd on Walbrook and remember what it felt like, walking beneath London. He had moments, stumbling back along Chancery Lane from the Blue Anchor, turning onto New Oxford Street and glimpsing Centre Point, when it felt like a curtain hadn't been fully drawn. He was back in that other London. And it felt bittersweet, like passing places associated with a love affair. No one else could see it, or no one else cared, so what kind of knowledge was that? He let the city revert to its cover story. Then, as summer released its grip, he read about the opening of a memorial at Site 3.

PILTBURY WAS QUITE PLEASANT without the threat of death stalking its lanes. Early October felt crisp. He walked, enjoying being out of the city. He had not really noticed autumn until now. Past the Quarry House, past Hill View and a *For Sale* sign by the road. He peered inside but the cottage was no longer occupied.

A new path led up from the village, through a small gate to the field that had been chosen for purposes of commemoration. Belsey climbed the hill but didn't join the crowd, choosing to watch from the high ground. A cold, bright wind ruffled proceedings. The memorial stone wasn't so different from the one in Ebsey Cemetery, except this one was currently adorned with poppy wreaths and wooden crosses. Belsey recognised Malcolm and John among the inner circle of attendees, with forty or so other relatives of the dead. Belsey wondered what they'd been brought by all this, whether they felt different. He scanned the crowd. No blonde Sergeant. No Craik. It had been a long shot.

The Home Secretary gave a speech, surrounded by senior members of the civil service. There were a lot of military uniforms, a few police. Finally there were the men in Barbour jackets and brogues, watching from a polite distance, hands joined in front of them like umpires. It wasn't clear if they needed their own closure or if they were still spying, and Belsey wondered if they knew.

It was 1 p.m. This wasn't for him. There was the whole afternoon ahead. He could walk back to Chippenham, over Box Hill. Get a train from there. Time for a rural drink before London. He turned to leave and saw a figure watching him from the gate. She wore jeans and boots, hands thrust into the pockets of a red raincoat.

"I wondered if you'd be here," she said.

"It's a nice day for it."

Craik considered this. The wind blew her hair. Belsey walked over.

"I heard about the suspension," Craik said. "I'm sorry. I tried to put in a word."

"It would have taken a lot of words, words not yet invented. It's good to see you."

"Good."

"Let's get a drink."

"A drink?"

"We deserve one. And dinner."

Craik checked her watch. "My train's in a couple of hours, Nick."

"I know a cottage, an old farmhouse. It's for sale."

"You want us to buy a cottage?"

"I'm saying it's one option, if you miss the train back." He savoured her distrustful eyes.

"It's been quiet not having you around," she said. "Policing has seemed straightforward again."

"Have dinner with me, Kirsty. Keep me company."

She glanced away, towards the ceremony. Ashes from Site 3 were being carried from three military vans, thirty-seven individual boxes each draped in a Union Jack. Beyond this procession, the Avon Valley looked cold and unconcerned: farms, muddy streams, the pale right-angles of military buildings. But robbed of its secret. One fewer of those in the world, Belsey thought. Or maybe there was a constant number and they evaporated only to rain down somewhere else. Craik took his arm. A man in billowing white robes read out the names of the dead. Belsey listened until he got to Michael Forrester.

Acknowledgments

THANKS TO:

Subterranea Britannica for invaluable resources. Any acts of imagination or elaboration are my own.

Also: Silent UK, 28 Days Later, Secret Bases, Cryptome, Nettleden.

OTHER WORKS CONSULTED:

Richard Trench and Ellis Hillman, *London Under London*; Andrew Emmerson and Tony Beard, *London's Secret Tubes*; Antony Clayton, *Subterranean City*; Duncan Campbell, *War Plan UK*; Peter Laurie, *Beneath the City Streets*; Stephen Smith, *Underground London*; Peter Hennessy, *The Secret State*.

ARTICLES:

Richard Moore, "A JIGSAW Puzzle for Operational Researchers: British Global War Studies, 1954–62," *Journal of Strategic Studies*, vol. 20, issue 2 (1997)

Benjamin B. Fischer, "A Cold War Conundrum: The 1983 Soviet War Scare," Central Intelligence Agency Archive (2009)

Vojtech Mastny, "How Able was 'Able Archer'? Nuclear Trigger and Intelligence in Perspective." *Journal of Cold War Studies*, Vol. 11, No. 1 (2009)

THANKS ALSO TO:

Transport For London, The British Postal Museum and Archive, Camden Council, British Telecom, WhatDoThey Know.com; staff at The National Archives, Kelvedon Hatch and Hack Green.

Special thanks to Judith Murray for unfailing support; Alex Bowler for great patience and perspicacity; Ignes Sodres, Carol Andrews, Steven Connor, Briony Everroad. Biggest thanks, once again, to Emily Kenway, without whom I may never have resurfaced.

Waking up on Hampstead Heath not far from a crashed squad car, Detective Nick Belsey wants out—out of London and out of the endless complications of his life. When Alexei Devereux, a wealthy hermit, vanishes, leaving behind a suicide note and his Porsche, Belsey discovers an opportunity—a new identity and a fortune—waiting for the taking.

Unfortunately, there are others who share the detective's interest in Devereux, including Scotland Yard. A dead rich man with suspicious financial holdings is bound to have some dangerous ties and a few ruthless enemies. Now, Belsey and his clever plan are about to be overshadowed by far more ambitious players with their own brilliant—and deadly—scheme.

Combining dark humor, dazzling twists, and a sharp narrative style, *The Hollow Man* is a tour de force of suspense.

HAMPSTEAD'S WEALTH LAY UNCONSCIOUS ALONG
the edge of the Heath, Mercedes and SUVs frosted
beneath plane trees, Victorian terraces unlit. A
Starbucks glowed, but otherwise the streets were
dark. The first solitary commuter cars whispered
down East Heath Road to South End Green. Detective Constable Nick Belsey listened to them, faint in the
distance. He could still hear individual cars, which meant it was
before 7 a.m. The earth was cold
beneath his body. His mouth had
soil in it and there was a smell of
blood and rotten bark.

1

   Belsey lay on a small mound
within Hampstead Heath. The
mound was crowded with pine trees, surrounded
by gorse and partitioned from the rest of the
world by a low iron fence. So it wasn't such an
absurd place to seek shelter, Belsey thought, if
that had been his intention. His coat covered the
ground where he had slept. A throbbing pain
travelled his upper torso, too general to locate
one source. His neck was involved; his right
shoulder. The detective stood up slowly. His
breath steamed. He shook his coat, put it on and
climbed over the fence into wet grass.

From the hilltop he could see London, stretched towards the hills of Kent and Surrey. The sky was beginning to pale at the edges. The city itself looked numb as a rough sleeper; Camden and then the West End, the Square Mile. His watch was missing. He searched his pockets, found a bloodstained napkin and a promotional leaflet for a spiritual retreat, but no keys or phone or police badge.

Belsey stumbled down a wooded slope to the sports ground, crossed the playing field and continued along the path to the ponds. His shoes were flooded and cold liquid seeped between his toes. On the bridge beside the mixed bathing pond he stopped and looked for early swimmers. None yet. He knelt on the concrete of the bridge, bent to the water and splashed his face. Blood dripped from his shaking hands. He leaned over to see his reflection but could make out only an oily confusion of light and darkness. Two swans watched him. "Good morning," Belsey said. He waited for them to turn and glide a distance away, then plunged his head beneath the surface.

A SQUAD CAR REMAINED IN THE EAST HEATH parking lot with the windscreen smashed, driver's door open. Blood led across the gravel towards the Heath itself: smear rather than spatter, maybe three hours old. Faint footprints ran in parallel to the blood. Belsey measured his foot against them. The metal barrier of the parking lot lay twisted on the ground. The only impact had been with the barrier, it seemed. There was no evidence of collision with another car, no paint flecks or side dents. The windscreen had spilled outwards across the hood. He stepped along the edge of the broken glass to a wheel lock lying on the ground and picked it up. It must have come straight through the front when he stopped. He was lucky it hadn't brained him. He put the lock down, collected a handful of wet leaves and wiped the steering wheel, gearstick and door handles.

He left the parking lot, onto the hushed curve of road leading from Downshire Hill to South End Green. He walked slowly, keeping the Heath to his left and the multimillion-pound houses to his right. Everything was perfectly still. There is

2

a golden hour to every day, Belsey thought, just as there is in a murder investigation: a window of opportunity before the city got its story straight. He tried the handles of a few vehicles until the door of a Vauxhall Astra creaked towards him. He checked the street, climbed in, flicked the glove compartment and found three pounds in small change. He took the money and stepped out of the car, shutting the door gently.

He bought a toothbrush, a bottle of water and some cotton balls from an all-night store near the hospital. It was run by two Somali brothers.

"Morning, Inspector. What happened?"

"I've just been swimming. It feels wonderful."

"OK, Inspector." They gave shy grins and rang up his purchases.

"Still haven't made inspector, though."

"That's right, boss." The owners didn't look him in the eye. If the damage to his face worried them, they didn't seem inclined to inquire further. Belsey collected his change, took a deep breath and walked up Pond Street to the police station.

Most London police operated out of modernist concrete blocks. Not Hampstead. The red, Victorian bricks of the station glowed with civic pride on Rosslyn Hill. Above the station lay the heritage plumpness of the village and, down the hill, the dirty sprawl of Camden Town began. Belsey sat at a bus stop across the road watching the late turn trickling out of the station, nocturnal and subdued. At 8 a.m. the earlies filed in for morning start of shift meeting. He gave them five minutes, then crossed the road.

The corridors were empty. Belsey went to the lockers. He

found the first-aid box and took aspirin, a roll of bandage and antiseptic. He removed a broken umbrella from the bin and prised his locker open: one spare tie, a torn copy of *The Golden Bough*, but no spare shoes or shirt. Belsey returned to the corridor and froze. His boss, Detective Inspector Tim Gower, stepped into the canteen a few yards ahead of him. Belsey counted to five, then padded past, up the stairs to the empty Criminal Investigation Department office, and sat down.

He kept the lights off, blinds closed, grabbed the night's crime sheet and checked he wasn't on it. A fight in a kebab shop, two break-ins, a missing person. No Belsey. He searched the desk drawers for his badge and ID card and they were there. So this was what was left of him.

He ran a check on the totalled squad car and it came up as belonging to Kentish Town police station. Belsey called.

"This is Nick Belsey, Hampstead CID. One of your cars is in the East Heath parking lot . . . No, it's still there . . . I don't know . . . Thanks."

Belsey locked himself in the toilet and stripped to the waist. He studied his face. A line of dried blood ran from his left nostril across his lips to his chin. He ran a finger along the blood and judged it superficial, apart from a torn lip, which he could live with. His right ear was badly grazed and his right cheekbone hurt to touch but wasn't broken. Dark, complex bruises had begun to bloom across his chest and right shoulder. He cleaned the wounds and spat the remaining fragments of broken tooth out of his mouth. He looked wired, both older and younger than his thirty-eight years. His flat detective eyes were regaining light. Belsey removed his trousers, dampened the bottoms and rinsed his suit jacket so the worst of the Heath was off. He hung his coat up to dry, put his trousers back on, then returned to the office. He looked under his colleagues' desks for a pair of dry shoes but couldn't see any.

The call room had sent up a list of messages for him—calls received over the past few hours. They had come from several individuals he had not spoken to for years, and some distant relatives and an old colleague. *You tried to get hold of me last night* . . . He didn't remember calling anyone. A vague dread pressed at the edges of his consciousness.

He opened the blind in front of the small window beside his desk. The night had evaporated, the air turned hard, with thin clouds like scum on water. It was an extraordinary day, Belsey sensed. A midwinter sun hung pale in the sky and there was a clarity to it all. A man in shirtsleeves opened up a drugstore; a street cleaner shuffled, sweeping, towards Belsize Park tube station. City workers hurried past. Out of habit Belsey wondered if he should cancel his credit cards, but the cards had cancelled themselves a few days ago. His old life was beyond rescue. It felt as if without the cards he had no debt, and without the debt he was free to run.

The important thing was to stay calm.

Belsey smoothed the sheet of jobs on his desk: one fight, two break-ins, a missing person. His plan formed. The control room had put an alert note by the missing person half an hour ago. It meant they thought someone should take a look, although adult disappearances weren't police business, and it was probably just the address that caught their eye: The Bishops Avenue. The Bishops Avenue was the most expensive street in the division, and therefore one of the most expensive in the world. No one pretended the rich going missing was the same as the poor.

He stuck a message on the sergeant's desk—*On MisPer*—and signed out keys for an unmarked CID car. Then he went downstairs, checked there was enough gas in the tank and reversed onto Downshire Hill.

About the Author

Oliver Harris has an MA in creative writing from the University of East Anglia, in addition to degrees in English and Shakespeare studies, and recently received his PhD. His first novel *The Hollow Man* launched the Detective Nick Belsey series. He also reviews for the *Times Literary Supplement*. He lives in London.

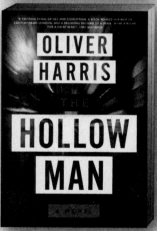